WHISPERS OF THE WIND

Whispers of the Wind

A TORCORVION TALE

Seth Himebaugh

Seth Himebaugh

Copyright © 2023 by Seth Himebaugh

All rights reserved. No part of this book may be reproduced in any manner whatsoever without written permission except in the case of brief quotations embodied in critical articles and reviews.

First Printing, 2023

To my Grandma Stone,

For the countless tales you spun and the adventures we embarked on in the realm of imagination. Your spirit nurtured my inquisitiveness and stoked the fires of my passion for the fantastical. As you now traverse the boundless heavens, may you explore with no limits.

And to my dear son, Benjamin,

May you always have the courage to venture into the unknown, to chase the horizons of your dreams. Let not fear tether your spirit, for the world is vast and filled with wonders waiting to be discovered. Remember that every great story begins with a single step into the unknown, and no great quest is complete without hardship. Explore, dream, and let your heart guide you.

With all my love and gratitude,

Seth Himebaugh

Contents

Dedication		v
Prologue		2
I	Promise	4
II	Wind's Embrace	19
III	Elandari	25
IV	Dwarrin	37
V	Zephyran	144
VI	Centarion	151
VII	Goblikar	168
VIII	Faelari	179
IX	Hook-Stick	199
X	Řazzbłûd	210
XI	Lünthårä	218
XII	Orukuthûndar	230
XIII	Snaga'Mok	243
XIV	Blâdur'Grōldūn	251
XV	Xolesh	261
XVI	Gnomarik	274

XVII	Spellweaver	286
XVIII	Training	297
XIX	House of Gnardok	309
XX	The Gnardoks of Time	325
XXI	Speculation	334
XXII	Master Inventor	341
XXIII	Grivzant	348
XXIV	Confrontation	355
XXV	Chrono-Core	366
XXVI	Descent	377
XXVII	Halindelar	387
XXVIII	The Sundering	400
XXIX	The Pantheon	410

Epilogue — 424

Appendix — 427

Map

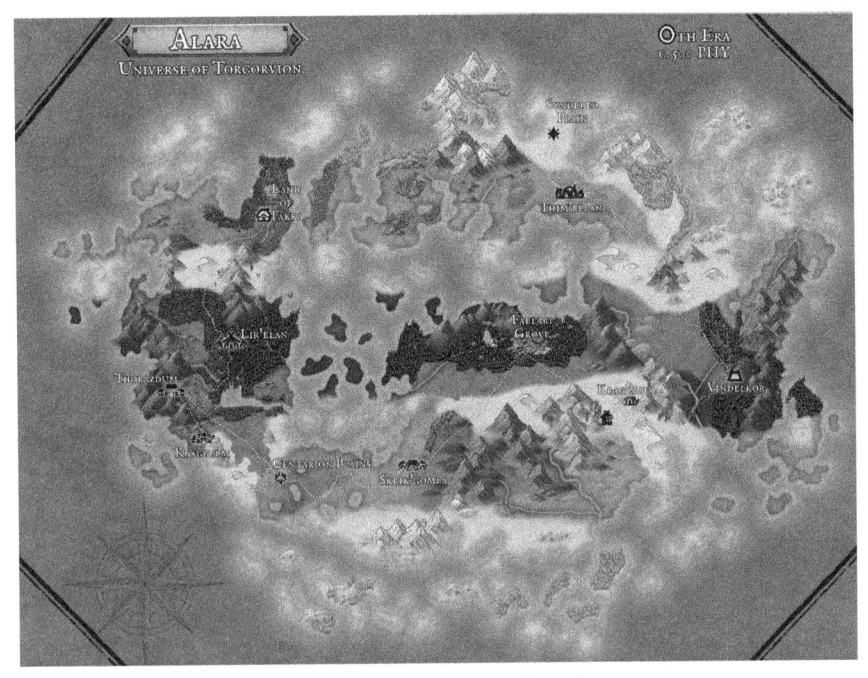

Map of Alara circa 500 PHY
Seth Himebaugh | Inkarnate

Prologue

"In the ancient days, when dawn first kissed the land of Alara, I awoke. I was as raw as the earth beneath my feet, my heart beating with the rhythm of the young world. I was the First-Born, the Witness. My name was Takka.

I watched as the golden rays of the Bringer of Dawn caressed the world. The whispers in the winds spoke, and as they fluttered through the trees, I saw the leaves shimmer and glow. From the wind's embrace, slender, graceful men emerged, their songs as pure as the starlight. Their ears stood tall, taking in every last note of harmonic dissonance provided by Alara's breathing surface.

Then the earth rumbled, and I beheld the Bringer of Dawn, with its chisel, as it carved the mountains and caverns. From the heart of the stone, small, sturdy men of the earth emerged, their resolve as unyielding as the stones they were born from.

I wandered through boundless plains, following the Bringer of Dawn wherever he stepped, where the sky was alight with thunder and storms. A clash of lightning, and the beast men were born. They roared with the strength of tempests, fierce and untamed.

In the shadows of the moonlit night, trickster spirits played among the trees. They laughed and whispered secrets, and from the shadows, nimble, impish creatures took form, their mischief as unpredictable as the night's wind. Mirthful and elusive, they danced through the night.

Beneath the ancient groves, the sands of the earth mingled and tinkered. Each grain a vessel of potential, and from them, little sprightly folk emerged, their ingenuity as boundless as the forest's depths.

In the cozy hollows and meadows, a warm flame danced. Its embers took form as the gentle-hearted kin, their spirits as nourishing as the earth's bounty; kind and gentle, spreading warmth and cheer.

The auroras danced in the heavens, their grace unmatched. They wove dreams and inspirations through the skies, and from their light, ethereal winged beings arose, their light as enchanting as the first dawn.

The winds roamed the vast lands, free and boundless. It entwined with the earth, and from their union, proud horse-men galloped forth, their wisdom as vast as the open fields. Strong and wise, they galloped with the spirit of the wind.

As I stood upon a hill, watching these new beings exploring the gift of life, I felt the embrace of the Bringer of Dawn once more. I was no longer alone; the world was alive with kin, each unique yet born of the same essence.

In the echoes of the winds, the stories are told, and though we are different, we are kin under the same dawn. We are the Children of Alara, born of wind, stone, flame, and starlight."

- Takka, The First-Born, The Witness (c. 10000 PHY

I

Promise

I took a seat on the dewy grass in a glade near my ancestral tribal lands, underneath a large gnarled oak tree. The fresh grass was cool and moist underneath my bare feet, and I mindlessly tore several small clumps of green blades from the ground as I allowed myself to drift away with the sound of the wind brushing its cooling fingers against my skin. The ancient oak's leaves fluttered in the soft breeze, each one whispering its own quiet song. Somewhere high above, a cardinal's cheerful chirps punctuated the gentle chorus. A squirrel chattered as it scampered up the weathered trunk, scrambling from one gnarled branch to the next. I rested against the sturdy oak and let its rough bark support me. With eyes closed, I drank in the sounds of the woodland symphony all around. The world serenaded me with its own special music. Tornu's voice floated on the wind as naturally as the pollen. The heat of the day pressed upon us, a stark reminder that we were at the threshold of Loriven, the final chapter before the embrace of the Solara season.

"Yoran, my boy, every whispering leaf, every grain of sand beneath our feet on Alara, it's all alive, all pulsing with life. Treat them, every single one, with the same reverence and care you would give to our own clan."

Dropping the blades of grass back to the ground, I soaked in Tornu's words, heeding his admonition. Tornu's eyes met mine, a wise and gentle gaze that has seen more sunrises than any other in our tribe. His voice took on a soft, melodic cadence, as calming as the rustle of leaves in the wind. "Behold this vast world, brimming with life's dance. Just as the mighty oak shelters us, and the gentle wind graces our skin, you too are woven into this tapestry of existence. That burning spark of curiosity within you, it's a melody, yearning to blend with the symphony of the unknown. Few in our clan hear that call, but it's a song you and I, we dance to it together."

He paused, his gaze falling to the grass beneath us. His fingers idly toyed with the blades, their rugged texture a clear distinction to his aged, soft skin. His eyes held a gleam, not just of wisdom but also of a long past memory. "Yet, with every step into the unknown, shadows loom. Beyond our embrace, other tribes, creatures, and forces of Alara might not greet you with open arms. Treading new paths is not mere whimsy; let caution be the lantern that guides your steps." His eyes met mine again, and he reached out, placing a warm, comforting hand on my shoulder. His tone, while still gentle, held an element of determination.

"Still, never let fear anchor your soul. It's but a guardian, there to shield us. Never a cage. Heed its whispers, but never let it shackle your steps. Dance to your heart's rhythm, my boy. It's the echo longing to harmonize with the grand song of Alara." Tornu's voice seemed to blend with the surrounding sounds of the forest, echoing the wisdom of ages. "Drink in the world, Yoran. Absorb its lessons. Honor its essence. We are all threads in Alara's grand tapestry. Journeying its vastness will tune you into its heartbeat, and therein, discover your own pulse. They might seem distinct, but every note we play resonates with, and is embraced by, the grand chorus of Alara. And in return, it echoes with ours."

His words settled into me, their meaning sinking deep. I met his kind eyes and weathered face. In them I now saw the years of walking his own path, forging his own song. I nodded slowly, heartbeat steady.

The fear of finding my voice amidst the symphony no longer clutched so tight. I breathed out, gaze clear. The music awaited, its notes still unsure, but my song was in there too, waiting to be sung. Much of my time as a youth was spent with Tornu. Though he did not bear the title of chief or the accolades of a grand hunter, my uncle, Tornu, held an esteemed position within our tribe, revered not only for his age but for the wisdom that came with it. He became my guardian when tragedy befell my family. When I was but a child, my parents began to show unmistakable signs of an affliction that our tribe had come to dread, one that had lurked in the shadows for almost four hundred cycles. Their vitality waned, their spirits dimmed, and they became shadows of their once vibrant selves. Though not many had been taken by this mysterious ailment over the centuries, its touch was always the same – relentless and devastating. Tornu took me under his wing after the untimely demise of my parents, providing the care and guidance I desperately needed. Our tribe, resilient and enduring, had called this valley home since the days of Takka, the Witness, from the dawn of creation. Through all our trials, the memory of those lost to the disease, including my parents, became a poignant reminder of our shared history and the challenges we've overcome. We held Takka in great esteem, and followed his principles closely. The main code of living we adhered to was Takka's rooted nature.

Though he was witness to a great many creations, he had not much desire to explore the vast world around him. Our tribe may have held firmly to that sentiment - but my uncle and I felt much differently. Although Tornu, for as long as I had been alive, and probably even longer, had not ventured more than a few hundred paces outside of tribal borders, when he spoke of the lands of Alara, he spoke with a tone of yearning, nostalgia - and a twinge of regret - regaling me with tales of great scaled and roaring beasts whose steps shook the earth, mountains that stretched up above the clouds, and scale-covered, leathery-winged giant birds whose breath could melt the hardest stone, and landscapes so beautiful they would leave one breathless.

We paced the lands outside our tribal grounds on an almost daily basis, resulting in a worn footpath surrounding our village, just outside where most of our kin were willing to roam. Tornu instilled in me a desire to explore, see the vast world, and learn all there was to learn. He spoke of a song that Alara sang, that the children of Alara could sing along with, if they would listen closely enough to learn. If only our kin would cease their daily commotion long enough to hear. Though Tornu lamented that he knew not the words or the rhythm of the song enough to play along, he had heard it sung by other creatures a few rare occasions throughout his life.

As we approached the village entrance after our day's trek, the comforting familiarity of home began to greet our senses. The gentle hum of the brook that skirted the outlands of our village was the first sign of home. Its constant, soothing babble was a familiar melody that had lulled generations of our kin to sleep. The cool, damp smell of the water mingled with the rich, earthy aroma of fertile soil - a scent signature that was unique to our nurtured and cherished land. The small footpath worn in the ground by Tornu's and my treks shifted from untamed wilds to a well-trodden trail - its soil compact and familiar beneath our feet.

We passed by our sacred totem pole, its wooden countenance weathered by time yet vibrant with the spirit of our ancestors. It was a living chronicle, bearing the tales of The Unseen - ethereal beings from realms beyond our comprehension, their stories etched deep into the grain of the totem. At the top, the Bringer of Dawn was depicted, the creator of Alara and all its children. Its form was an intricate swirl of patterns, a radiant aura that seemed to shimmer in the dappled sunlight. It was a symbol of the genesis of our world, the dawn of all existence. Below it, the Eternal Sentinel stood guard, a stalwart protector of harmony. Its figure was steady and unyielding, an embodiment of its ceaseless vigil over the Bringer of Dawn's creations. Next, the Verdant Sage was carved into the wood. His form shifted from that of an ancient tree to a mighty bear-like beast with antlers of an elk, a tribute to his kinship with nature. His presence on the totem pole was a reminder of the cycles of life and the wisdom found in the rhythms of nature. Further down, the Luminous Muse was depicted. Her figure seemed to glow with an ethereal light, a reflection of her radiant beauty and grace. Her presence on the totem pole was a symbol of the joy and splendor of creation. Finally, at the base, the Sifter was carved, an entity of preservation and balance that had twisted into an obsession with control. Its form was fluid and chaotic, a marked difference to the other figures on the totem pole. The totem pole stood tall, a stalwart guardian at the entrance of our village. It was a herald of our return home, a silent storyteller whispering the tales of the Unseen to all who passed by.

The distant echo of laughter, voices, and endless toil became gradually louder as we drew closer. Our tribe's dialect, a rhythmic cadence as natural to us as our own heartbeats, was a symphony that evoked warmth and community. There were sounds of children at play, their innocent laughter resonating like a joyful melody amidst the ambient sounds of tribal life.

From the heart of the territory wafted the comforting scents of food being prepared. The aroma of roasting meat over the communal fire, the earthy scent of freshly harvested roots and herbs, and the sweet fragrance of berries being mashed for desserts. The smoky scent of the hearth fire underscored it all. A homely smell that I had always associated with safety and togetherness.

As we crossed the threshold into our tribal heartland, we were met by the sight of our kinfolk going about their daily tasks. The communal huts, made of timber and daub, stood in a harmonious cluster. The smiling faces of our tribe, the verdant hues of our cultivated fields, the children chasing each other around the central fire - those sights spoke of life, survival, and harmony. Returning from the wilderness, those sounds, smells, and sights wove a tapestry of familiarity and comfort around us, a warm welcome that silently spoke the words, 'You're home', with every crossing of the threshold.

At the heart of the camp, our leader's abode stood a little more grand, adorned with symbols of our history and heritage. His name was

Ansel. A robust figure who bore the mantle of leadership like a second skin. Ansel wasn't related by blood to Tornu, yet their connection ran deep, tethered by the shared respect for our people and land. Ansel and I, on the other hand, often butted heads. More than once he had called me a "wandering dreamer", a teasing jab, hinting that I would rather be frolicking, wandering, and wasting time than doing anything productive. Despite our disagreements, there was a deep love and kinship between us. Ansel was a man of imposing stature, with broad shoulders that held the weight of the tribe's responsibility. His face was a tableau of wisdom, etched with lines of age and experience. His hair was long, graying at the temples, and often tied back in a traditional manner, revealing sharp, observant eyes. Those eyes had seen many Isendurs and Aravells, held the knowledge of countless stories and bore the gentle authority of a well-respected leader. Ansel was known to possess a voice as resonant as a rolling thunder, yet his laughter was as infectious as a child's. A natural-born leader, he led not with fear but with respect, and his calm demeanor reassured our people, promising safety in his guidance.

The tribe, under Ansel's leadership, was steeped in tradition. A deeply rooted respect for the land coursed through the veins of each member. We saw ourselves as the caretakers of Alara, believing that our very existence was intertwined with the health and prosperity of the land we lived on. Our reverence for Takka was palpable in our every ritual. We lived on the same land where Takka, the First-Born, had settled, considering it an honor and a sacred duty to preserve and protect this birthplace of humanity. Despite the vastness of Alara and the opportunities it offered for exploration, the tribe chose to remain settled. This decision wasn't borne out of fear or lack of curiosity but out of a deep-seated sense of responsibility. Our folklore was filled with tales of Takka's adventures, of his connection to Alara, of his respect for every creature, and of his wisdom. Each story passed down through generations, reminding us of our roots. Our legacy. We had cultivated a rich and vibrant culture around our land. The earth beneath our feet wasn't just soil - it was a cherished kin, teeming with life, holding stories from the time of Takka. We had mastered the art of living in harmony with the land over the last five centuries, our practices reflecting a beautiful symbiosis.

Our dwellings were a blend of natural resources and ingenious craftsmanship, causing minimal disruption to the environment. Our attire was woven from plant fibers and dyed with natural colors, signifying our resourcefulness and respect for Alara. As a community, we gathered around bonfires, sharing stories, wisdom, and laughter. Music was our language of joy, each rhythm echoing the heartbeat of the land. Food was not just sustenance; it was a celebration of the earth's bounty. Every meal was a ritual of gratitude, a feast honoring Alara's generosity. Living amidst these beliefs and values, I was not just a member of the tribe, but a proud inheritor of a tradition that bound me intrinsically to the land. To Alara. Our lives were a tribute to our ancestors, especially to Takka, whose spirit was believed to live on in the sacred land we called home. My desire to explore, and my lack of a tether to these lands, were all that separated me from the rest of my tribe, save for my uncle Tornu.

"In from another day's aimless journey on the winds of curiosity, I see?" Ansel's voice broke through the symphony of village life as Tornu and I entered the heart of the tribe's territory. His deep, resonant voice held a teasing lilt, and his eyes twinkled with amusement as he stepped forward to greet us. Tornu chuckled, his eyes reflecting the shared camaraderie between him and Ansel.

"Aye, Ansel," he replied, his voice filled with mirth. "But in your wise words, isn't every step upon Alara's soil a lesson learned, my old friend?"

Ansel looked at me, his sharp eyes softening as he ruffled my hair with his massive hand. "This one carries too much of your spirit, Tornu," he said, his gaze flickering between me and my uncle. He said it with jest, but there was a tone of affection underlying his words. He then patted my shoulder, his touch firm yet comforting. "Remember, Yoran," Ansel said, his tone serious now, "Our very essence is woven with this soil and our kin. The breath of Takka courses through our veins, our rituals, and the earth we steward. You and Tornu might let your minds soar to distant horizons, but never forget the ground that nurtured you." The familiar banter, the gentle ribbing, the shared laughter - it was all part of the comforting routine that greeted us every time we returned from our treks. And even as Ansel teased us, his eyes held an understanding. He understood our shared spirit of exploration, even as he gently reminded us of our roots.

The heart of the tribe was buzzing with life. The children played, the women prepared meals, the men toiled, and the elderly shared their wisdom. The sight was like a well-practiced dance, each member of the tribe playing their part in harmony. Our leader, Ansel, stood like a beacon, guiding us, leading us, holding the tribe together. His jests, his deep understanding of our nature, and his unyielding dedication to our tribe's traditions were constant reminders of the wisdom and depth of our tribe's culture. Our roots were deep in the lands where Takka, the First-Born, had settled. The sacred essence of our tribe was palpable in our everyday life. Our strong adherence to our roots was a source of pride and identity for each member of the tribe. Despite Tornu's and my yearning to explore the vastness of Alara, our hearts were deeply connected to the heritage we were born into. We respected and valued the strong foundation our tribe offered us - a culture that revered the land and practiced a lifestyle that upheld the principles of our ancestors.

Ansel's jest was a gentle reminder that while our spirit yearned to explore and understand the rhythm of Alara's song, we must not forget the rich culture that binds us together. We were a part of a tribe that believed in the sanctity of the land and the sacred duty to protect and nurture it. The familiar sights, sounds, and smells of the tribe's bustling life felt like a warm embrace, welcoming us home. And even as we were jestingly reprimanded by Ansel, we were reminded of our shared bond, our shared heritage, and our shared love for the land that had nurtured us for generations. Our tribe may not have shared Tornu's and my desire to explore, but they understood it, even if not to the same degree. They respected it. And they welcomed us, wandering dreamers, back into the fold with warmth and acceptance, reminding us that no matter how far we wandered, our roots would always be here, in the land of Takka.

On like that we continued for cycles, drawn forth by the song of the unknown. With every venture, our bond deepened, the rhythm of our hearts echoing the rhythm of the world we yearned to understand. During one exploration, a venture just like any other, our shared laughter echoed against the ancient trees, our footprints marking the ever-changing canvas of the forest floor. The sun dappled through the emerald canopy above, casting playful patterns on Tornu's seasoned face, every line a reminder of his wisdom and our shared journeys. As we moved further into the wild unknown, the familiar thrill of discovery coursed through our veins, a silent promise of another unforgettable adventure.

It was never uncommon for us to find marvelous creatures just outside our tribal borders. We'd seen a great many things over the cycles. Everything from fyndors - much akin to the great, leather-winged creatures with flaming breath that we call zephyrans, however fyndors are much smaller. They are not nearly as formidable or intelligent as the zephyrans (which are entirely uncommon anywhere near our tribal lands) but are still a wonderful sight to behold. The fyndors are strongly connected to Alara, each displaying a trait of a specific elemental type: fire, water, earth, or air. This can manifest in their breath and coloration. Fyndors have eyes that resemble precious gemstones, their color depending on their elemental affinity. Instead of wings, fyndors have protective, scale-covered shields on their sides. These shields are so strong that they can deflect even the sharpest of arrows; to elerans - majestic creatures, part lion and part eagle, who typically live in the mountainous regions surrounding our lands. Elerans have the ability to generate and manipulate electricity. Their roars are accompanied by sparks, and they can channel electricity through their claws. Along with the body of a lion and wings of an eagle, elerans possess feathered antlers similar to those of a stag, giving them an even more majestic appearance. Elerans also have an intricate and beautiful flight dance that they perform during courtship or before a storm; to astriels - winged equine creatures whose manes and tails look and feel like soft, fluffy clouds, giving them an ethereal appearance. Astriels can manipulate wind currents around them, allowing them to travel at extraordinary speeds and change direction almost instantaneously. Their wings sparkle with a brilliance akin to a starlit night, an enchanting sight to behold.. Flocks of these winged horses grazing in the wild were a common yet awe-inspiring sight; to ignins - fire-resistant lizards known to inhabit volcanic regions. Ignins can envelop their bodies in flames, making them nearly untouchable. When doing so, the flames don't consume them but rather add to their radiant and fiery appearance.Unlike most creatures, Ignins can swim in lava and often make their homes near active volcanoes. Ignins can absorb heat from their surroundings, either to store for later use or to manipulate the temperature of their immediate environment.

In that respect, this venture was no different than any other; except this time, we encountered a creature unlike anything I had ever seen before. With the dawn's warmth on our skin and the thrill of discovery in our hearts, Tornu and I ventured into the unexplored depths of the wilderness. We had seen many creatures: a playful flutterswarm soaring in synchronized flight, a herd of majestic placidon grazing on the vast plains, and even a rare, solitary aerospark napping in a sunlit clearing. Our world was brimming with enchanting life. We had come across a dark, dense forest that day, its branches intertwined like an unbroken chain of hands holding the sky. We ventured into the green abyss, the sunlight struggling to penetrate the canopied labyrinth above. Suddenly, the leaves rustled above us, an eerie chill wrapping around us like a cold shroud. I looked at Tornu, seeing his eyes focused upward, and followed his gaze. Through the dappled sunlight filtering down from the canopy above, a huge shadow descended, and the silhouette of an immense birdlike creature spread across the forest floor. A moment of dreadful recognition passed over Tornu's face.

"A celestriker!" he hissed, pushing me behind him. The celestriker swooped down, its talons extended, aiming straight for me. But Tornu, the seasoned explorer, threw himself in front of me, taking the brunt of the celestriker's deadly attack. A deep, painful cry erupted from Tornu as the creature's talons found their mark. I stood there, frozen in fear, as the beast lifted itself back into the sky. But Tornu was relentless. Despite the agonizing pain, he shouted, urging me to move, to run. His strength, his will, shocked me out of my terrified paralysis. We ran, darting between the dense trees, the celestriker's angry cries echoing from above. Tornu, weakened from his wounds, faltered, but I held him, guiding us deeper into the forest until the cries of the celestriker faded into the distance. We were safe, for now.

That day, we returned to the camp, Tornu's body laden with wounds, my heart filled with terror. The unforgiving reminder of the dangerous world beyond our haven was carried back into our tribe, etched onto Tornu's wounded form. Our world was just as dangerous as it was beautiful. And my fear of what lay beyond our haven, beyond the known, had found its root.

As we emerged from the dense forest, our figures drenched in the dying light of the day, a silence fell over the tribe. The usually bustling life in the village seemed to hold its breath. It was not an empty silence - but filled with a gasp of shock and fear. Children stopped in their tracks, woven toys falling from their hands. Women with baskets full of fruits and grains froze, their eyes widening. The men working on their tools paused, the thuds of their hammers fading into the silence. Ansel was the first to break free from the shock, his eyes wide but his actions decisive.

The teasing lilt that was so familiar in his voice was absent as he shouted, "Get Aida! *Now!*" His command brought the villagers out of their stupor, and a young boy sprinted towards the healer's hut. The leader of our tribe rushed towards us, his eyes filled with worry, yet his demeanor controlled and focused. He knelt next to Tornu, his weathered hands carefully assessing the extent of the wounds. His stern, usually teasing gaze softened as he looked at Tornu, replaced by a worried frown.

"These wounds speak of a formidable creature's touch. Tell me, Yoran, what did you encounter in the wilds?" Ansel asked me, urgency threatening to overtake his voice.

"We... we were exploring, as we always do... It came out of nowhere - Tornu called it a... a '*celestriker*'?" Came my shuddering reply.

"No celestriker should've come this close to the village," Ansel muttered more to himself than us, a deep furrow marking his forehead as he took in Tornu's condition. He looked at me, his eyes probing, looking for signs of injury. Upon finding none, his tense shoulders relaxed ever so slightly, but the worry in his eyes did not diminish. "And are you unharmed?" he asked, his tone a rare mix of relief and concern.

After I assuaged his concerns for my own safety, Ansel helped me support Tornu, and we slowly made our way towards the healer's hut. The tribe members followed, their faces etched with concern, a pronounced divergence from the usual warmth and cheerfulness that greeted us on our returns. That day, the tribe didn't act as though they were welcoming back wanderers; they welcomed back warriors, who had faced the deadly, uncertain side of the wilderness. The night did not bring the usual laughter and camaraderie but a heavy silence filled with fear and concern. The ties that bound us as a tribe tightened, as if collectively holding its breath, praying for the safety of one of its own. The spirit of Takka was palpable that night, stronger than ever, reminding us that we were a tribe, a family, bound together in joy and in hardship.

The following weeks were a time of change and uncertainty for the tribe, and particularly for me. Our usually vibrant village fell into a muted rhythm, the laughter and cheer replaced by hushed conversations and worried glances. The land that had always felt familiar and comforting seemed transformed. It was as though the attack on Tornu had left a mark on not just him but the tribe as a whole. Our adventures into the wild were always fraught with a certain amount of danger, but this close encounter with mortality cast a long shadow over our collective psyche. In the midst of it all, Ansel was a pillar of strength. He, who had known Tornu since childhood, wore his concern well.

But his worry did not cripple him; instead, it seemed to drive him. He was a constant presence by Tornu's side, keeping vigil as Aida worked her best to heal him. When he wasn't with Tornu, he was leading the tribe, his actions reinforcing the bonds of our community, his words reminding us all that even in the face of adversity, we were one, stronger together. As for me, the weeks were a battle of my own. My days were spent by Tornu's side, the cool touch of his hand a reminder of the adventure that had nearly cost him his life. The tribe knew me as the young explorer, always eager to venture into the wilderness, but now, the very thought filled me with fear. I longed for the thrill of discovery, the beauty of unknown lands, but the image of Tornu's blood-soaked figure haunted me.

It was as if the wilderness had two faces: the one that promised adventure and discovery and the other that held potential threats and dangers. My heart yearned to follow the first, but my mind was plagued with thoughts of the second. I couldn't imagine stepping into the wilderness without Tornu by my side. His experience, his guidance had always been my compass. Without him, I felt lost, unanchored. Nights were the hardest. The darkness seemed to echo my fears, amplifying them. Sleep was elusive, the quiet punctuated by Tornu's pained moans. Each morning, I woke up with the hope that Tornu's condition would improve, that his strong figure would be sitting up, ready to share another tale of his past explorations. Aida and her assistants assured me he would make a recovery. But each day, he seemed to drift further away, his grip on my hand weakening.

The passing weeks became a blurred amalgamation of the same routine - hopeful mornings followed by tense afternoons and sleepless nights, the days marked by a measured rhythm of fear and hope. Yet, there was one day that refused to blur into the fog of memories, one day that stood stark and clear, the details etched into my mind like a scar that would never fade. It was the day the first rays of dawn seemed to hold a new promise, a strange peace that made me hope that maybe, just maybe, Tornu would recover. As the light crept into our huts, the village was rousing from its slumber, the air punctuated by the usual chorus of bird songs and murmured greetings. Yet, there was an undercurrent of anticipation, a subtle change in the rhythm of the tribe. As the morning unfolded, Tornu seemed more awake, his eyes clearer than they had been for weeks. His voice was weak, but his spirit was as strong as ever, his hand firm as he held mine. Ansel, who had spent the night by Tornu's side, was visibly relieved to see the glimmer of vitality in his old friend.

The day passed in a hopeful haze, the tribe slowly returning to its normal rhythm, driven by the optimism that seemed to be painted in the morning sky. Ansel went back to managing the tribe, his figure once again a beacon of strength and leadership. The sounds of hammers and laughter slowly filled the air, children once again running free without the shadow of worry over them. It was as if the tribe was finally breathing easy after weeks of tense silence. As the afternoon stretched into evening, Tornu beckoned me closer. His eyes, tired yet resolute, held mine. "Yoran," he said, his voice a mere whisper, "sit with me." As I settled beside him, he started speaking. His voice was soft, each word seeming to cost him effort. He spoke of the wild, of the thrill of discovery, of the beauty and terror that lay beyond our village. He reminded me of the excitement that exploration had always sparked in us, the shared bond that connected us in our love for the unknown.

"But, Tornu," I started, my voice shaky, "You make it sound as though you'you're not going to pull through. I can't...I can't do it without you. The fear..."

Tornu held my gaze, his expression stern, yet his eyes shimmering with compassion. "Fear is a part of the journey, Yoran. But do not let it become the journey itself," he said, his voice carrying an intensity that cut through my apprehensions. "Promise me, Yoran. Promise me you'll not stop exploring. Promise me you'll not let the fear hold you back."

"I..." I began.

"Promise me!" He demanded.

The urgency in his voice was unsettling. I nodded, promising him what he wanted to hear, the weight of his words sinking into my heart. As the night descended, Tornu's breaths became shallow, his grip on my hand growing weaker. But as he lay there, his eyes fixed on mine, a strange peace seemed to settle over him. His lips moved one final time, his voice barely a whisper, "Remember your promise, Yoran. The song of Alara awaits your harmony."

And with that, he exhaled a slow breath, his hand going limp in mine. As the realization of his departure settled in, the night echoed with my silent cries, my heart heavy with loss. The wilderness had taken away my guide, my mentor, leaving behind an unfulfilled promise and a journey yet to be completed. After Tornu's passing, the tribe was engulfed in a profound silence. His absence was a void that could not be filled. I found myself wandering, truly aimlessly, my heart heavy with the weight of his last words. The promise I had made to him echoed in my mind, a constant reminder of the journey I had yet to complete.

Weeks turned into months, and months to a cycle, and the tribe slowly began to find its rhythm again. But I was still lost, caught between the safety of our lands and the call of the unknown. Tornu's words, 'The song of Alara awaits your harmony,' haunted me. I knew I had to honor my promise to him, but the fear of the unknown held me back.

II

Wind's Embrace

One morning, well before the sun began its daily pilgrimage across the sky, I found myself climbing a familiar tree. It was the same tree under which Tornu and I had spent countless mornings, lost in the beauty of the world around us. As I sat on the thick branch, my fingers gripping the rough bark, I felt a strange sense of calm wash over me. It was as if the tree, the wind, the very air around me was whispering words of encouragement, urging me to keep my promise to Tornu. Perched high in the familiar tree, I watched as the world below began to stir with the first light of dawn. The forest was coming alive, the air filled with the chorus of birds greeting the new day. The leaves rustled softly as the wind danced through the branches, their whispers carrying stories of the night just passed. This tree held a special place in my heart. It was here that Tornu and I would often sit, nestled in the comforting embrace of the roots, as he shared tales of the vast world beyond our tribe. His voice would rise and fall with the rhythm of the wind, weaving stories of towering mountains, roaring beasts, and landscapes so breathtaking they seemed to belong to another world.

As I sat there, high above the ground, I could almost hear his voice in the rustling leaves, see his face in the dappled sunlight filtering through the branches. I remembered his laughter, the twinkle in his eyes as he spoke of his adventures, the passion in his voice as he spoke of the unknown. His tales were not just stories; they were lessons about life, about our world, about the spirit of exploration that he so deeply cherished. I closed my eyes, letting the sounds of the forest wash over me. The rustle of the leaves, the chirping of the birds, the soft sigh of the wind - they were all part of the symphony of nature, a melody that Tornu had taught me to appreciate. In the quiet solitude of the morning, I could feel his presence, his spirit intertwined with the very essence of the world around me. Opening my eyes, I let my gaze wander over the landscape below. The world was awakening, the first rays of the sun casting long shadows over the forest floor. And then, something caught my eye. In the distance, amidst the familiar canvas of the forest, was an anomaly - a formation of stones standing in a clearing. They seemed out of place, their presence a mystery that disrupted the familiar landscape.

A sense of intrigue washed over me. The stones were calling to me, their silent voices echoing in the depths of my being. It was a call that stirred the spirit of exploration within me, a call that I knew I had to answer. As I descended from the tree, I felt a strange sense of anticipation. I was about to step into the unknown, to embark on a journey that was as much a tribute to Tornu as it was a promise to myself.

The stones were not just unusual; they were out of place, alien, and yet they seemed to resonate with an energy that was eerily familiar. It was as if they were calling out to me, their silent voices echoing in the deepest recesses of my soul. A call that was impossible to ignore. With every step towards the stones, the air around me seemed to grow denser, the whispers of the wind growing quieter as if the world itself was holding its breath. The forest, usually a symphony of life, fell into an unnatural silence. The only sound was the thudding of my heart, a steady drum echoing the rhythm of my growing apprehension. As I neared the stones, their details became clearer. They were old, weathered by time and elements, yet they stood strong, their presence commanding respect. They were etched with markings, symbols that seemed to dance in the dappled sunlight, their meanings as elusive as the stones themselves.

The stones were like a mystery, a puzzle waiting to be solved. And as I stood there, at the edge of the clearing, I knew that this was the beginning of a journey, a path that was laid out by fate. A path that I was destined to follow, no matter where it led I reached out, my fingers tracing the grooves of the etchings. The stone was cool to the touch, its surface rough and worn. As my fingers moved over the symbols, a strange sensation washed over me. It was as if the stones were alive, their energy pulsating beneath my fingertips. And then, as my fingers traced the final symbol, a word rose up within me. It was not a word I spoke, but one that seemed to emanate from the very core of my being.

'Su-Tha...' I whispered, the words carried away by the wind.

The moment the words left my lips, the world around me shifted. The wind picked up, its whispers growing louder, more insistent. It swirled around me, its touch gentle yet powerful, its voice carrying a message that seemed to resonate with the very essence of my being. Leaves and grass swirled around me in a dance of nature. Then, without warning, everything changed. The world around me was transformed in an instant. The lush greenery of the forest was replaced by a landscape of devastation. Trees, once towering and majestic, were now charred skeletons, their blackened branches reaching out to the sky like desperate pleas for mercy. The ground was scorched, the once vibrant carpet of grass and flowers reduced to ashes. The air was thick with smoke, the acrid scent of burning wood and foliage filling my nostrils. The clear blue sky was now a canvas of despair, painted with thick, heavy smoke that blotted out the sun. The light that managed to filter through was a sickly orange, casting an eerie glow on the ruined landscape. The once peaceful chirping of birds was replaced by a deafening silence, the forest's symphony of life extinguished. In the distance, I could see what remained of a large village, much larger than my own. Buildings that once were home to hundreds, if not thousands, were now crumbling ruins, their structures gutted by fire. The streets were littered with debris, the remnants of a civilization brought to its knees. I could see figures moving among the ruins, their bodies hunched, their movements slow and heavy with despair. The river that once flowed with clear, sparkling water was now a murky stream, its surface reflecting the flames that consumed the land. The water was tainted crimson with blood. My sight was filled with scenes of destruction and despair. People were running, their faces etched with fear and confusion. Their cries echoed in the wind, a chilling cacophony of despair that sent shivers down my spine. I could see the fear in their eyes, the hopelessness that had taken hold of their hearts.

As quickly as it had come, the world returned to its normal state. I was left standing in the clearing, the stones silent once more. But the echo of the word '*Su-Tha*' lingered in the air. I stood there, my mind racing, trying to make sense of what had just happened. Was it the words that triggered the vision? Or was it something else entirely? I had never seen a village so large, so advanced. Could it have been a glimpse into the future, an age of iron and steel? Or was it a vision of the past, a time long forgotten? The possibility of it being a prophecy sent a chill down my spine. The destruction, the despair, the fear - was that what awaited us? Or was it just a figment of my imagination? A sign of a deteriorating mind, brought on by the loss of my mentor? I shook my head, trying to clear my thoughts. The questions were overwhelming, each one leading to another, creating a web of uncertainty that threatened to consume me. I needed answers, but all I had were more questions.

With a deep breath, I whispered the words again.

'*Su-Tha.*'

I said them cautiously, hesitantly, not wanting to trigger another vision. I braced myself, waiting for the world to shift, for the vision to return. But all that came was the gentle embrace of the wind, its touch soothing, its whispers comforting. I let out a sigh of relief, my heart still pounding in my chest. The wind's embrace was a welcome respite from the chaos of my thoughts, a moment of calm in the storm of uncertainty. But as I stood there, the vision still fresh in my mind, I knew that my journey was just beginning. My promise to Tornu would be kept.

Returning to the village, I sought out Ansel. His imposing figure was easy to spot, standing tall amidst the hustle and bustle of our tribe. His eyes met mine, and I saw a flicker of concern pass over his features. He knew something was amiss.

"Yoran," he greeted, his voice deep and resonant. "You look troubled. What weighs on your heart?"

I hesitated, then decided to confide in him. I told him about the strange vision, the words that had come unbidden to my lips, and the wind's embrace. As I spoke, Ansel's eyes never left mine, his expression thoughtful. When I finished, he was silent for a long moment.

Then he said, "Alara doesn't weave visions lightly, especially ones of such intensity. And you, Yoran, with that insatiable thirst for discovery and wisdom... I see your story becoming a pivotal note in Alara's timeless melody. Tornu once whispered tales of magical utterances, of words he witnessed beings wield on rare occasions during his young wanderings. It sounds like '*Su-Tha*' may be such words." He paused, looking at me with a seriousness that made my heart pound. "Tornu perceived a fire within you, Yoran. A flame fueled by wanderlust and a hunger for knowledge. He wouldn't have entrusted you with the taking up his mantle of traversing Alara if he doubted your strength. I sense that Alara's fate rests upon you walking the path you're destined for, wherever it may lead."

"But what is my destiny?" I asked, my voice barely more than a whisper. "How do I know what path to take?"

Ansel smiled, his eyes softening. "You have a spirit that yearns to roam. It's a song in your heart that seeks the harmony of the unknown. A song that Tornu recognized and nurtured. Follow that song, Yoran. Let it guide you." His words, though comforting, left me with more questions than answers. But they also ignited a spark of hope within me. Perhaps, with time, I would understand the meaning of my vision and find my place in Alara's grand song. Ansel's words lingered in the air, a reminder of my roots and the promise I had made to Tornu. His gaze held a mix of sternness and understanding, a silent encouragement to keep my promise. I nodded, a silent vow passing between us. I would honor Tornu's memory. I would explore, and I would not stop until my destiny had been made clear.

The following morning, met by the crisp Loriven air, I found myself standing at the edge of our village, the familiar sights and sounds now tinged with a sense of finality. I took a deep breath, the cool morning air filling my lungs, and with a last look at the place I called home, I stepped into the wilderness. The forest was alive with the sounds of nature, a symphony of rustling leaves, chirping birds, and the distant murmur of a river. It was a world teeming with life, a world that was waiting to be explored. As I ventured deeper into the forest, I felt a strange sense of familiarity. It was as if the forest was welcoming me, its whispers guiding me.

III

Elandari

I found myself standing in a clearing. The same clearing where I had discovered the stone formation. The same clearing where I had first spoken the words "*Su-Tha*". The memory of that day washed over me, a reminder of the promise I had made to Tornu. I felt a strange sense of peace. I was on the right path. Days turned into nights and nights into days as I journeyed through the forest. I encountered various creatures, some friendly, others not so much. Each encounter, each observation was a lesson. However, a particular encounter offered more than just a lesson. While exploring, I was confronted by a small but aggressive creature, known by my tribe as a Venombiter. Known for its razor-sharp teeth and agility, the Venombiter lunged at me. Relying on my instincts and survival skills, I defended myself with a large stone and swift kicks. In the struggle, the creature succumbed to its injuries, leaving behind its venom-laced carcass as a grim trophy of our encounter. The confrontation served as a stark reminder of the inherent dangers of the forest. I realized I needed more than stones and quick reflexes for protection.

Drawing from the knowledge ingrained in me over seventeen cycles of life in my tribe, I decided to create a spear. Selecting a sturdy yet flexible branch, I painstakingly carved it into a smooth rod, honing one end to a point. For the spearhead, I looked to the remains of my fallen adversary. The Venombiter's bones, renowned for their strength, seemed ideal. Carefully, I chiseled a bone into a sharp point. Using strong vines and tree sap for adhesive, I fastened the bone head onto my spear. Holding the completed weapon, its weight and balance in my hands, a profound sense of triumph surged within me. The bone-headed spear, gleaming ominously under the dappled sunlight filtering through the canopy, was a reflection of my survival skills and the wisdom of my tribe.

With determination, I continued my journey, following the whispers of the wind. Each day brought new discoveries, new lessons, and with each step, I felt closer to fulfilling my promise to Tornu. Before I knew it, I found myself rooted in the heart of an expansive, dense forest. My legs had stilled, no longer guided by an unseen force. I simply existed, a solitary figure amidst the verdant expanse. The forest's pulse seemed to echo my own, a rhythmic thrumming that whispered of life in its rawest form. Alara's heartbeat, I realized, was in sync with mine, a harmonious symphony that resonated in the very marrow of my bones.

I stood there, a silent observer, drinking in the forest's grandeur after a month of travel, now at the onset of the Solara season, the beginning of the month of Sylthal. Every sight was a painting, every smell a memory, every sound a melody. A profound sense of admiration swelled within me, filling my chest till it felt near to bursting. Just as I was losing myself in the forest's embrace, a flicker of movement caught my eye. Nestled between two towering trees, a figure emerged, ethereal and regal. She was slender, her form exuding an elegance I had never witnessed before. Her ears were a fascinating sight, small at the lobe and gradually widening, extending into a soft point just above the crown of her head. It was an enchanting deviation from the human form, an exemplification of her otherworldly beauty.

Her hair, a cascade of liquid gold, flowed down her shoulders, kissing her waist. It moved with a life of its own, dancing in the gentle breeze. Her hands moved through the air, a graceful ballet that seemed to mimic the flow of water. Trails of magic followed her gestures, glimmering in the air before being swept away by the breeze. It was a sight to behold, a dance of magic and nature. She spoke no words, yet her silence was a language of its own. With every gesture, she wove a tapestry of vibrant colors and prisms, a spectacle that held me captive. The culmination of her silent incantation was a small, wisp-like creature, a beacon of light that seemed to guide her path. It was a moment of pure magic, a glimpse into a world that was as breathtaking as it was mysterious.

Tearing my gaze away from the enchanting woman was a task that seemed near impossible, such was the allure she held. But the impossible became reality as I realized she was not alone. Several figures, each as captivating as the next, surrounded her. They were unique in their appearances, yet there was an undeniable similarity that bound them together, a shared lineage that was as clear as day. One of the men, standing at the forefront of the group, caught sight of me before I could announce my presence. His eyes met mine, a silent acknowledgment passing between us. He called out to me, his voice a soft melody that reminded me of a delicate woodchime swaying in the breeze. His words were foreign, a language I had never heard before, yet the invitation in his tone was unmistakable. I found myself drawn towards them, curiosity pulling me in like a moth to a flame. As I approached, I realized that the curiosity was mutual. His gaze held a spark of interest, a silent question that mirrored my own. We were different, from different worlds perhaps, yet in that moment, we were united by the shared curiosity that danced in our eyes.

The following weeks found me journeying through the verdant expanse of the forest alongside the group of twelve elandari. As we traversed the labyrinth of trees and streams, I remained vigilant, ever watchful for signs of the ominous threat I had glimpsed. Eventually, we found a common ground - language. We began to teach each other our tongues, using the objects we found along our path as visual aids. Twigs, leaves, rocks - they became our tools of communication, each one representing a word in our respective languages. Over time, the foreign sounds began to take on meaning. I learned that they called themselves "*Elandari*", a term I found difficult to mimic. I settled for "Elves", a word that seemed to capture their ethereal grace. They taught me their majestic names - Illadrathil, daughter of the eldest elandar, Tilithor. Her brothers, Hilithir and Rivellos, stood by her side. The remaining nine, Thalindra, Arandir, Lirael, Caladrel, Elendiir, Findril, Ithilwen, Talathion, and Sariel, were the elected protectors of their sÿlvarị. I introduced myself as Yoran. They spoke of their sÿlvarị, or tribe, a term that roughly translated to "enclave". These twelve were part of a larger sÿlvarị, a community of 86 others. Their connection to Alara and its primal forces was profound, particularly with the forests. Their sÿlvarị were nestled within large groves, an illustration of their deep bond with nature.

The elandari began to teach me about "spell words", a concept that was as fascinating as it was complex. "*Su*" and "*Tha*" seemed to be two such words - however, Illadrathil explained that the elandari have no need of knowing them, as Alara simply causes their will to transpire. While they knew of these spell words and, upon seeing my use of "*Su-Tha*", confirmed Ansel's theory that they are indeed such words, they were unable to teach me more. While my tribe revered Alara, or "Anorë" as the elandari called it, our connection was nothing compared to the elandari's affinity for the world - this "sun-realm". Weaving spell words was as natural to them as breathing, an innate ability that left me in awe. They could manipulate the world around them in complete silence, a spectacle that was truly magnificent to behold. I found myself yearning to learn more, to understand their connection to the world, and perhaps, in doing so, understand my own.

In the days of my sojourn with the elandari, as we traversed the verdant expanse of the forest on their prolonged patrol, a rhythm, as steady as the heartbeat of the earth itself, began to shape our existence. The inaugural month, I found myself in the enchanting company of Illadrathil, a mentor as gentle as the morning dew on a leaf's edge.

"Illadrathil," I'd begin, each word a thoughtful step, still feeling the weight of her name's beauty upon my tongue. "Your language, it's like an age-old song that's been sung by the forest itself. The melody seems to flow with the breeze and carry tales whispered by the rustling leaves. I've yearned to understand, to hear those tales clearer. Might you teach me? Guide me through the dance of your words so that I might join in the song?" With a soft smile, eyes shining with the wisdom of the forest, Illadrathil replied,

"Yoran, the language of my people is not merely spoken; it is felt with the heart and sung with the spirit. But I see the genuine desire in your eyes. I will guide you through our ancient melodies, so you too may embrace the whispers of the woods. Be patient, and let the forest speak to you." Each word was a note, each sentence a melody, each conversation a symphony. The elvish language was not just a means of communication, but a living, breathing entity, a mirror reflecting the soul of the elandari. As the days turned into weeks, I began to grasp the subtle nuances of their language, the way '*Aelin*' was not just the moon, but a symbol of wisdom and serenity, or how '*Ciriel*' was more than a lady of the lake, but a guardian of water sources. Each word was a story, each phrase a poem, each dialogue a saga.

But the language was not the only gift Illadrathil bestowed upon me. She opened my eyes to Anorë, the world that cradled us in its green arms. I saw how the elandari did not merely live in Anorë, but were a part of it, their lives intertwined with every leaf, every stone, every creature.

"Melion," she began, her gaze piercing as if she could see beyond the horizon, her eyes deep pools mirroring the vibrant emerald canopy overhead, "Anorë is more than just land and trees. It is the very essence of our being, our life force. We don't merely inhabit this place; we are interwoven with its spirit. When the trees sway, they echo our heartbeats. The birds' songs are harmonies of our shared stories. And the wind? It carries our hopes, our dreams, our dances. We are not merely inhabitants of Anorë; we are its heart and soul, inseparable and eternal." In the dappled sunlight that filtered through the leaves, in the hushed whispers of the wind, in the gentle murmur of the brook, I began to understand. I was not just learning the language of the elandari, but their way of life, their connection with Anorë, their harmony with the world. And in that understanding, I found a rhythm, a melody, a song that would forever echo in the chambers of my heart.

Yet as we ventured further into the heart of the forest, where the trees stood like ancient sentinels and the shadows held whispered secrets, an unforeseen event shattered our rhythmic existence. Talathion, the offspring of Arandir, had vanished, as if swallowed by the forest itself. A shroud of worry descended upon us, as tangible as the mist that clung to the forest floor. The faces of the elandari, usually as serene as a moonlit lake, were etched with lines of concern. Their eyes, mirrors of the forest, reflected a storm of unease. The melody of our journey, once a harmonious symphony, was now a discordant tune. Our purpose shifted, as sudden and swift as a falcon changing its course. The forest, once a realm of exploration, transformed into a vast, daunting labyrinth. Every tree became a potential hiding place, every shadow a cloak of invisibility, every rustle a whisper of hope.

"Mel'aran," Illadrathil spoke, her voice slicing through the stillness, the normally lilting and melodic cadence now edged with a fierce urgency. "Our priority is to locate Talathion. The expanse of Anorë may be vast, challenging our every step, but the strength of our determination, our unity, will see us through." And so, our exploration became a search, our curiosity replaced with determination. The rhythm of our days changed, the melody altered, but the song continued. For in the heart of the forest, amidst the towering trees and whispering shadows, we became not just a group of travelers or patrolling guards, but a family.

Arandir, typically a beacon of mirth amongst us, was now a portrait of anxiety. His laughter, once as infectious as the joyous trill of a songbird, was silenced, replaced by a grimace that seemed etched into his features. His eyes, usually sparkling with the light of a thousand stars, were clouded with worry, a storm brewing in their depths. The other elandari, mirrors of Arandir's concern, shared in his silent torment.

Their faces, usually as tranquil as a still lake, were marred by creases of worry. Their eyes, reflecting the emerald canopy above, held a flicker of fear, a spark of uncertainty. The forest was now a hushed whisper, a silent prayer for Talathion's safe return. And so, we committed ourselves to the search, our hearts echoing with a single purpose. The rhythm of our days was now a drumbeat of determination, the melody a chant of hope, the song a hymn of unity.

In the ensuing weeks, we fragmented into smaller factions, spreading ourselves thin across the vast expanse of the forest. The towering trees stood as silent witnesses to our desperate search, their leaves whispering prayers to the wind. The severity of our plight, rather than driving us apart, served as an unexpected adhesive, binding us together in a tapestry of shared concern. The worry for Talathion, like a thread, wove itself into the fabric of our group, creating a bond as strong as the roots of the ancient trees surrounding us. It was an unspoken pact, a silent agreement that transcended words, a connection that pulsed with every beat of our hearts.

"Mel'aran," Illadrathil would say, her voice a soft murmur amidst the rustling leaves, "we may come from different paths, but our destination is the same. We are united in our search, bound by our concern for Talathion." The cloak of nightfall proved to be our greatest challenge. The campfire, once a stage for tales of mirth and laughter, was now a forum for fretful deliberations. The flickering flames danced to the rhythm of our anxious discussions, casting long, wavering shadows that mirrored our fears. We spoke of potential sanctuaries, of lurking perils that Talathion might encounter, our voices a low hum against the symphony of the nocturnal forest. Yet, with each new dawn, hope was reborn. The first rays of sunlight, filtering through the emerald canopy, painted the forest in hues of gold and green, a visual symphony that breathed fresh life into our weary spirits. The morning dew on the leaves, the chirping of the birds, the gentle rustle of the wind - they all whispered promises of a new day, a new beginning.

"Mel'aran," Illadrathil would say, her eyes reflecting the golden dawn, "each sunrise brings fresh hope, a renewed strength. We must harness this energy, channel it into our search."

And so, with the break of each day, our resolve was fortified. As our search unfolded, I found myself frequently in the company of Arandir. Our shared worry for his son, like an invisible thread, wove us together in an intricate dance of concern and hope. Through this shared experience, I was granted a window into the profound depths of the elandari's bonds, their unshakeable faith, their unwavering hope. Arandir, a pillar of strength amidst the storm of worry, was a beacon of inspiration. His face, etched with lines of concern, held a steadfast determination that was as immovable as the ancient trees surrounding us. His eyes, clouded with worry, sparkled with an unyielding hope that was as luminous as the stars above.

Arandir's gaze settled on mine, a storm of emotion beneath the steady surface of his eyes. "Mel'aran," he began, the weight of a father's fear palpable in his voice, "my son, my boy, he's out there in the vastness of this wilderness. The elandari, we've faced adversity time and again, but we've always held firm. We don't let despair consume us; we don't let fear guide our steps. Hope, unwavering and pure, is our guiding star. It's what keeps us moving forward."

I swallowed hard, trying to comprehend the depth of his anguish. Taking a deep breath, I replied, "Arandir, I might never truly grasp the weight of your heart's burden, the sheer magnitude of a father's fear for his child. But know this, my friend — I stand beside you, resolute and committed. We'll traverse every inch of this land until we find Talathion. No forest, no danger, no shadow will deter us. We're bound by this shared quest." Through Arandir, I saw the strength of the elandari, their unwavering resolve, their unyielding hope. His strength, even in the face of his own worry, was a clear indicator of the spirit of the elandari.

After what seemed like an eternity of relentless searching, spanning countless sunrises and sunsets, we found Talathion. He was ensnared in the grasp of a deep ravine, a prisoner unable to escape its rocky confines. A collective sigh of relief, as palpable as the wind rustling through the leaves, echoed through the forest, a symphony of joy reverberating off the sturdy trunks. With careful hands and gentle words, we extricated him from his rocky prison, each movement a symbol of our shared relief. We carried him, a precious cargo, back to our camp, the forest seeming to breathe with us, sharing in our joy.

Arandir's face lit up, eyes shimmering with unshed tears of relief, as his voice, usually so composed, broke into an elated chorus, "Mel'aran!" He exclaimed, joy bubbling forth, "Against all odds, amidst this vast and unpredictable forest, we've found him! My son, my Talathion, he's safe!" The rescue of Talathion was a moment of pure elation, a beacon of joy piercing the shroud of worry that had enveloped us. It was a moment that wove us even closer together, our shared relief strengthening the bonds that held us.

The final month of my sojourn with the elandari was dedicated to the restoration of Talathion's health. Each day, we watched as the strength returned to his body, as the light sparked back into his eyes. Arandir's face, a canvas of relief, mirrored the gradual healing of his son, each day a brushstroke of recovery painting a picture of hope. Yet, amidst the relief, a bittersweet anticipation began to stir within me. The wind, like a distant call, began its gentle beckoning, whispering of the inevitable parting that loomed on the horizon. The forest, once a realm of exploration, was now a home, the elandari not just companions, but friends.

Though I spent three months with them, time seemed to lose its meaning in the company of the elandari. Yet, one day, in the month of Orendar, the middle of the Solara season, I felt a familiar push, a gentle nudge from the wind that had guided me to this point. It was time to move on. I bid farewell to the elandari, their majestic presence forever etched in my memory. Our farewells were not goodbyes, but wishes for a bright path. "Mel'aran alu thero," they said, their voices a soft melody that echoed in the forest. As I set off on my journey, they gifted me several elandari moonstones. They were said to possess a powerful connection to Anorë's primal forces, a tangible reminder of the time I had spent with the elandari. In their dormant state, the moonstones appeared as small, oblong orbs, the size of my thumb. Their surfaces were smooth and cool to the touch, reminiscent of the crisp, night air in the depths of the elandari forest. They were made of a seemingly translucent material, like ghostly teardrops suspended in time, an ephemeral marriage of glass and polished river stones. When they caught the light, the moonstones shimmered with an internal luminescence, projecting a cascade of soft silvers and muted grays, as if each one held a slice of the moon itself. The celestial bodies seemed to change under my gaze, flickering between opaqueness and clarity like some sort of arcane riddle. I could feel an odd sensation as I held them - a tingling that seeped into my skin, the sensation not unlike a faint, harmonious hum. This was a sensation that spoke of latent magic, a promise of protection, guidance, and the mysteries that these stones were yet to reveal. The weight of them was comforting in my hand - like a woven toy one might have carried with them since childhood - giving me a sense of grounding, reminding me of the solidity and surety of my elven companions, even when they were not physically present. Even in their quietude, I could sense the life within the stones, a deep pulsing undercurrent, mirroring the heartbeat of the elandari forest. They seemed to be whispering ancient secrets in a language older than time, offering me both a farewell gift and a bond that would endure the tests of time and the trials of my journey.

With the moonstones in my possession and the wind at my back, I ventured forth, ready to follow wherever the winds would take me. I meandered through the heart of the elandari forest for several more hours that day. The sun traced its path across the sky, reaching its zenith as I lost myself in the labyrinth of trees and streams. The forest was alive with the sounds of nature, a symphony that was as captivating as it was soothing. Suddenly, a melody unlike any other filled the air, stopping me in my tracks. It was a symphony, a harmonious blend of notes that seemed to dance on the wind. Beautiful birds, their feathers a striking contrast of black and white, soared through the canopy. They danced along the branches, their movements as graceful as a ballet.

Their song was a melody of joy and freedom, a tune that seemed to resonate with the very heartbeat of the forest. Their partners joined them, their voices blending in perfect harmony, enriching the melody with their own notes. It was a song and dance of unity, a demonstration of the harmony that existed in nature. Never in the lands of my tribe had I encountered such a spectacle. The melody was a marvel, a symphony that seemed to capture the very essence of the forest. I stood there, a silent observer, lost in the beauty of the moment. The forest, the birds, the melody - it was a moment of pure magic.

As the sun continued its ascent, I stumbled upon a running stream. Its waters were a brilliant silver, shimmering under the sunlight in a dazzling display. The sight was almost blinding, a spectacle of nature that held me captive. I knelt by the water's edge, the cool earth beneath me a comforting presence. As I dipped my hands into the stream, a wave of emotions washed over me. Memories, fragmented and fleeting, surged through my mind. They were echoes of countless lives, generations that had come before me, their stories etched in the waters of the stream. I brought the water to my lips, its coolness a balm to my parched throat. As I drank, I felt a cleansing sensation, a purging of fatigue and weariness. A comforting warmth enveloped me, a gentle embrace that seemed to seep into my very core. The stream was more than just water. It was the lifeblood of Alara, a conduit of life that nurtured countless beings within its embrace. As I sat there, the cool water lapping at my hands, I felt a profound connection to the world around me. The stream, the forest, the melody of the birds - they were all part of a larger symphony, a symphony of life that I was now a part of.

As the sun began its descent, painting the sky with hues of orange and purple, I stumbled upon a small woodland village. Another sÿlvarị. I approached with a sense of reverence, a respect for the sanctity of their home. I waited patiently at the village gates, the cool evening breeze a comforting presence. The elandari elders emerged from the village, their faces etched with wisdom and kindness. They greeted me warmly, their surprise evident as they discovered my rudimentary understanding of their language and culture. They informed me that the village was in the midst of a festival, a celebration of the changing seasons. With a warm smile, they invited me to join them for the night. I accepted their invitation with a sense of gratitude, eager to partake in their celebration. The festival was a spectacle of colors and sounds. The villagers donned vibrant masks and outfits, their colors reflecting the changing leaves. The air was filled with laughter and music, a melody that seemed to echo the joy of the villagers. We danced under the moonlight, our movements a celebration of life and change. We shared food, stories, and laughter, the night alive with the spirit of the festival. As the night wore on, the villagers offered me a bed for the night, a gesture of hospitality that warmed my heart. I fell asleep to the sound of the wind rustling through the trees, a lullaby that seemed to echo the rhythm of the forest.

IV

Dwarrin

The following morning, the wind nudged me awake, its gentle push a reminder of my journey. I bid farewell to the villagers that cool Orendar evening, three months having passed since I began my journey, their smiles a warm memory as I ventured forth, ready to follow wherever the wind would take me. In the muted embrace of twilight, I heard a soft whimper, a desperate cry for aid borne on the evening wind. It was a sound that tugged at the strings of my heart, a melody of distress that seemed to echo within my very soul. I found myself drawn towards it, my heart drumming a frantic rhythm against the cage of my ribs, each beat a signal of the urgency of the moment. I wove my way through the underbrush, the scent of damp earth and decaying leaves filling my nostrils. The forest, usually a symphony of life, had fallen eerily silent, as if holding its breath in anticipation. The only sound was the rustle of leaves underfoot, the crunch of twigs, and the faint, persistent whimper that guided me.

The sight that met my eyes was one that would haunt my dreams for many nights to come. A young Ryathane, its majestic wing ensnared in the metal jaws of a hunter's trap. The trap, a cruel device of cold metal and sharper-than-death teeth, was a noticeable disparity to the natural beauty of the creature it held captive. The Ryathane's eyes, usually twin lighthouses of wisdom and tranquility, now flickered with the raw, primal light of pain and fear. The vibrant hues of its irises were dulled, the spark of its spirit dimmed by the agony it was enduring. Its breath came in ragged gasps, each one a proof of its struggle, and its scales, usually shimmering like a thousand tiny sunsets, were dull and lackluster. I could feel the heat of its fear, taste the bitter tang of its pain in the air. The sight of such a majestic creature brought low by such a cruel device filled me with a burning rage, a fierce determination. I knew then, in that hushed twilight, that I would do whatever it took to free this creature from its torment.

My mind whirled, spinning back to the recent lessons with Illadrathil, the elven princess. Her voice, soft as a Solara breeze yet firm as the roots of an ancient tree, echoed in my mind. She had taught me the Elandari art of "Amn Vilya" or "Soothing Touch," a healing practice that harnessed the radiant energy of Anorë through the ethereal glow of moonstones. I remembered the way the moonstones had pulsed a soft, silver light in my hand, their cool, smooth surface humming with a power that seemed to resonate with the very beat of my heart. I remembered how Illadrathil had guided my hands, her touch as light as a feather, as she showed me how to channel the energy, how to weave it into a soothing balm for wounds both seen and unseen, explaining that the glow of the stones would glow a different hue depending on the situation their bearer found themselves in, and the intent of their will. And then there was the Súrion tree. Illadrathil had spoken of it with a reverence that had made me understand the true value of this unassuming plant. Its bark, she had said, was known for its curative properties. I remembered the way she had carefully peeled a piece from the tree, her hands moving with a grace and respect that spoke volumes about her connection with the natural world.

Now, as I stood before the trapped Ryathane, her lessons took on a new urgency. I reached into my pouch, my fingers closing around the cool surface of a moonstone. I could feel its energy pulsing, a comforting rhythm in the palm of my hand. I looked around, my eyes scanning the forest until they landed on the familiar silhouette of a Súrion tree. Taking a deep breath, I reached out, my hands hovering over the Ryathane's injured wing. The moonstone in my palm pulsed with a cool energy, a soothing rhythm that seemed to echo the heartbeat of the forest itself. I could feel the energy, like a river of tranquility, flowing from the stone, through my veins, and into my fingertips. As I channeled this energy into the Ryathane, I felt a connection form, a bond that transcended the physical. I could feel its pain, its fear, but also its will to survive, its determination to fly again. It was a raw, primal emotion that resonated within me, filling me with a sense of purpose.

With my other hand, I applied a paste made from the Súrion bark to the wound. The bark, ground into a fine powder and mixed with the dew of the forest, formed a salve that was known for its curative properties. As I gently spread the paste over the wound, I could see the Ryathane's eyes soften, the flicker of pain dimming as the healing properties of the Súrion bark began to take effect. The forest around us seemed to hold its breath, the usual symphony of sounds muted as if in respect for the healing ritual taking place. The only sound was the soft rustle of leaves in the wind, a gentle lullaby that seemed to soothe the Ryathane's fears. As I continued to channel the energy of the moonstone, I could feel the Ryathane's wing begin to relax, the tension easing as the healing energy worked its magic. The trap, once a symbol of pain and fear, now lay forgotten, its cruel purpose overshadowed by the healing power of Amn Vilya and the curative properties of the Súrion bark. In that moment, under the watchful gaze of the twilight sky, I felt a sense of peace. I was not just Yoran, a simple wanderer. I was a healer, a friend, a beacon of hope in the hushed twilight of the forest. And as I looked into the Ryathane's eyes, I saw not just a creature of the forest, but a fellow being, a survivor, a mirror of the indomitable spirit of life itself.

The initial days of our journey together were a crucible of patience and trust. The Ryathane, though it seemed to comprehend my intentions, maintained a cautious distance. Its eyes, while no longer flickering with fear, held a guarded wariness that spoke volumes about its past encounters. I shared my food, tearing my meager rations into pieces small enough for the Ryathane to consume. I watched as it ate, its eyes never leaving mine, a silent conversation passing between us. I was not its captor, but its companion, and with each shared meal, I could see the barriers between us slowly crumbling.

The forest was not without its dangers, and more than once, I found myself standing between the Ryathane and a predator, wielding my simple bone-tipped wooden spear. Each time, I could see the surprise in its eyes, a silent question - why would this biped risk his life for a creature of the forest? And each time, I answered not with words, but with actions, my determination to protect it speaking louder than any words could. As the days turned into nights and the nights into days, a bond began to form between us. It was a connection that transcended species, a mutual understanding born of shared experiences and shared hardships. The Ryathane, in its own unique way, expressed its gratitude. Its eyes, once filled with fear and wariness, began to regain their tranquil glow. It was a subtle change, a softening around the edges, a warmth that hadn't been there before.

Over the course of the next two months, from Maruvial through Thalindor, the season shifted from Solara into Verindal, and the bond between us deepened, growing stronger with each passing day. The Ryathane, once a wary companion, now led me through the hidden parts of the forest, its paths winding through a world that seemed untouched by time. We ventured into glades aglow with luminescent flowers, their soft light painting the forest in hues of ethereal blues and purples. The air here was thick with the scent of blossoms, a sweet perfume that seemed to seep into my very soul. We drank from brooks of crystal clear water, their gentle babble a soothing melody that echoed through the silence of the forest. I learned to interpret the Ryathane's sounds and body language, each chirp and flutter of its wings a word in the language of nature. It was a language without words, a symphony of sounds and movements that spoke volumes about the world around us. I learned to listen, not just with my ears, but with my heart, my soul, my very being.

The Ryathane taught me to see the forest not just as a collection of trees and plants, but as a living, breathing entity. I learned to feel its heartbeat, to sense its moods, to understand its silent whispers. It was a profound understanding, a connection that went beyond the physical and touched the very essence of my being. As the days passed and the Ryathane's wing healed, its strength returning with each passing sunrise, I knew our time together was drawing to a close. The realization hung over me like a shadow, a bittersweet reminder of the transient nature of life.

The day of parting arrived, as inevitable as the setting sun. I watched as the Ryathane, now fully healed, spread its wings, their span an exhibit of its resilience, its will to survive. With a final glance in my direction, a silent farewell in its tranquil eyes, it took to the skies, disappearing into the embrace of the forest. A sense of loss washed over me, a void left by the departure of my companion. But within that void, there was also a newfound understanding, a deeper appreciation of the natural order. Life was a cycle, a series of meetings and partings, of connections made and lost. The Ryathane had been a part of my journey, a chapter in my story, but it had its own path to follow, its own story to write. If I was honest with myself, I had been struggling to move on from my time with the elandari. The memories of my mentor, of the lessons learned and the bonds formed, had been a constant companion, a comforting presence in the solitude of the forest. I had made a promise to my mentor, a vow to carry on his legacy, but the thought of leaving behind the companions I had made along the way filled me with a sense of dread. But the Ryathane, in its own unique way, had taught me a valuable lesson. It had shown me the ephemeral beauty of connections, the fleeting nature of relationships. It had taught me that it was okay to form bonds, to make friends, but it was also okay to let go, to move on when the wind beckoned.

As I neared the edge of the forest, it gave way to a large open field, surrounded by towering mountains on every side. The dense canopy of trees started to thin, revealing glimpses of the sky above. And there, piercing the horizon, was the silhouette of a great mountain, taller and wider than all the others. Its peak rose majestically above the treetops, a sentinel standing guard over the forest. The mountain was a sight to behold. Its slopes were a tapestry of colors, a blend of earthy browns and greens, interspersed with patches of white where snow clung to the higher altitudes. The peak was shrouded in a veil of clouds, a crown of white that added to its regal appearance. The sight of the mountain filled me with a sense of awe. Its sheer size was humbling, a reminder of nature's grandeur. I could see the rugged terrain, the jagged rocks that lined its slopes, the thin trails that snaked their way up towards the peak. The mountain range stretched out for miles each way, forming a half-circle at the edge of the vast field.

The wind, my constant companion, urged me forward. It whispered in my ear, its voice a gentle caress against my skin. It was leading me towards the mountain, towards a new chapter of my journey. I felt a sense of anticipation, a thrill of excitement at the prospect of what lay ahead. With the wind at my back and the mountain in my sights, I pressed on. Emerging from the forest's embrace, I found myself standing at the precipice of a vast canyon. The world opened up before me, a sprawling plain that stretched as far as the eye could see. Across the plain, the mountain stood tall and proud, its peak a beacon amidst the vast expanse. Nestled at its base, barely visible from my vantage point, was what appeared to be a small village. With the wind guiding me, I began my journey across the plain. The landscape was a glaring discrepancy to the dense forest I had left behind. The plain was a sea of grass, its waves rippling under the gentle caress of the wind. The mountain loomed in the distance, a constant presence that seemed to grow larger with each step I took.

By midday, I had reached the outskirts of the village. As I drew closer, I realized that it was indeed small, a quaint settlement nestled in the shadow of the mountain. The houses were modest, their architecture a blend of simplicity and functionality. The villagers, much like their homes, were small in stature. The tallest among them barely reached my chest. Yet, their height did not reflect their build. They were hardy and sturdy, their bodies a manifestation of a life of labor and resilience. Their wide frames were an evident contrast to their height, a balance of strength and compactness. As I stood at the edge of the village, I took a moment to appreciate the sight. The small houses, the hardy villagers, the towering mountain - it was a scene that spoke of a life lived in harmony with nature. With a sense of anticipation, I stepped into the village.

Their voices were a bold juxtaposition to their stature, loud and booming, echoing across the plain. The gruffness of their tone was startling, a sound that seemed to reverberate in the air. As I approached, their eyes met mine, their gazes filled with suspicion. We were strangers to each other, our appearances as foreign as our languages. The heartiest among them stepped forward, his steps firm and confident. He looked me up and down, his gaze assessing, evaluating. His eyes held a spark of curiosity, a silent question that mirrored my own. I held out my hands, palms upwards in a universal gesture of peace. I hoped my intentions were clear, that my gesture would bridge the gap between us. With a grunt, he turned away, his gaze lingering on me for a moment longer. He spoke in their gruff language, his words a series of terse sounds that I could not understand. Yet, his tone held no hostility, a sign that perhaps my gesture had been understood.

An elder of theirs then approached me, his steps slow and measured. He began to communicate through a series of grunts and gestures, a language that was as foreign as it was fascinating. He tapped his chest with a closed fist, a rhythmic thud that echoed in the silence. "Thrumir," he said, his voice a deep rumble. "Thru-" Thud. "-mir". Thud. I echoed his words, my voice a soft contrast to his gruff tone.

"Thru...mir. Thrumir?" I pointed towards him, my question hanging in the air. A warm smile spread across his face, his eyes twinkling with amusement. He chuckled, a deep sound that seemed to resonate in the air. His nod was vigorous, a confirmation of my understanding. I returned his smile, the warmth of his amusement infectious. Mimicking his gesture, I tapped my chest and said, "Yoran." His smile widened as he repeated my name, his voice filled with excitement. The sound of my name in his gruff tone was a bit jarring, but it served as a reminder of the connection we were building, a bridge between two strangers in a land foreign to my eyes.

Thrumir extended his arms, his gesture encompassing our surroundings. "Dwarrin!" he declared, his voice filled with pride. His eyes sparkled with a sense of belonging, a love for his home that was as clear as day. My confusion must have been evident, for his smile faded as he read my expression. He tapped his chest again, repeating, "Thrumir. Dwarrin." He pointed towards the sturdy figure who had initially greeted me. "Balgruff. Dwarrin." His gaze scanned the area before landing on a stout lady, her chin adorned with a fair amount of stubble. "Bruna. Dwarrin." The pieces of the puzzle began to fall into place. These creatures referred to themselves as "Dwarrin". I tried to mimic the pronunciation, but my tongue stumbled over the unfamiliar sounds. My best attempts resulted in a word that sounded like "Dwarven". It seemed fitting, a term that captured their sturdy build and hardy nature. And so, I began to refer to them as "Dwarves", a name that would forever remind me of my first encounter with these fascinating beings.

In the weeks that followed, we embarked on a journey of mutual learning. The language barrier that stood between us began to crumble, replaced by a shared understanding. We communicated through hand gestures and guttural sounds, each one a word in our respective languages. It was a slow process, filled with moments of confusion and laughter, but with each passing day, we grew more fluent in each other's tongues. As our understanding grew, so did our friendship. Thrumir and I found a common ground in our shared curiosity, our desire to learn from each other. Our conversations, once filled with gestures and sounds, began to take on meaning. We shared stories of our homes, our cultures, our lives.

Thrumir became more than just a friend. He was my guide in this new world, a beacon of familiarity in a sea of unknowns. Thrumir shared tales of the dwarrin, painting a picture of a proud and sturdy race. They were beings carved from stone, their bodies evident of their resilience. They took pride in their physical prowess, their strength a symbol of their enduring spirit. Tournaments were a common occurrence, a chance for the dwarrin to showcase their strength and compete in a display of visceral power. But their strength was not their only pride. The dwarrin were renowned for their craftsmanship, their hands capable of creating works of art from the raw materials of the earth. Their creations were a reflection of their connection to Alara.

The dwarrin referred to Alara as "Krüma", a term from their language that translated to 'Stone-Heart'. It was a fitting name, a model of their affinity for the earth and its depths. They were creatures of stone and earth, their hearts as steadfast as the mountains they called home. As Thrumir shared these tales, I found myself captivated by the culture of the dwarrin. Their pride, their strength, their connection to Krüma - it was a world that was as fascinating as it was foreign. And I was eager to learn more, to delve deeper into the world of the dwarrin.

In the early days of my time with the dwarrin, Thrumir would take me through daily life. The mountain, with its imposing stature and intricate network of tunnels, was the heart of the dwarrin community. As Thrumir led me through its winding passages, the rhythmic sound of pickaxes striking stone echoed around us. The miners, their faces smeared with dirt and sweat, worked tirelessly, extracting precious ores and minerals. Their dedication was palpable, each swing of their tool an emblem of their connection with the earth. Patrolling the borders was a different experience altogether. We would walk the perimeter of the village, ensuring its safety from potential threats. The dwarrin warriors, with their keen eyes and sharp senses, were always on alert. They moved with a quiet confidence, their steps measured, their gaze unwavering. Thrumir would often point out strategic points, explaining the importance of each location in the defense of their home. The crafting area was a hub of activity. The sound of hammers striking anvils, the glow of molten "vorgrund", and the skilled hands of the dwarrin smiths were a sight to behold. Thrumir introduced me to the art of crafting with vorgrund. This metal, with its unique properties, was malleable yet incredibly strong. I watched in awe as the smiths transformed raw ore into intricate weapons, armor, and tools. Each piece, with its intricate designs and impeccable craftsmanship, was a tribute to the dwarrin's skill and dedication.

During our time together, Thrumir shared stories of the dwarrin's past, tales of bravery, sacrifice, and unity. He spoke of their beliefs, their connection to the earth, and their unwavering loyalty to the "thârûm". He taught me their language, each word a window into their culture and way of life. The phrases, the idioms, the nuances – all gave me a deeper understanding of the dwarrin mindset. One evening, after a hearty meal of roast gurduffut - a gamey, tusked creature that resembled a rat the size of a dog - and potatoes, Thrumir and I sat by the warm glow of the campfire, its flickering light casting dancing shadows on the walls of the town. The atmosphere was serene, the soft hum of the village in the distance a comforting backdrop to our conversation. Thrumir, with a thoughtful expression, reached into his satchel and pulled out an ancient-looking stone tablet, its rough edges broken and worn from cycles of use.

Thrumir's eyes held a deep reverence as he took the tablet into his hands, his fingers tracing its symbols tenderly. "Yoran," he rumbled with a voice filled with pride, "before you lies the 'Dwarrin Varkûn', the very heartbeat of our people's past." As he carefully ran his fingers along the roughly hewn dwarrin lettering, revealing the meticulously crafted runes and vivid sketches, he continued, "These stories, this knowledge, it's been handed down from elder to youngling, ensuring that every dwarrin understands the weight and honor of our lineage."

As the night deepened, Thrumir narrated stories from the stone, his voice filled with passion and reverence. Each tale was a lesson, a moral compass guiding the dwarrin through the challenges of life. I listened intently, captivated by the rich tapestry of their history, the tales of valor, the sagas of unity, and the chronicles of sacrifice. One particular story spoke of a sacred tunnel, rich in gold, a place where the first dwarrin had discovered vorgrund. This tunnel, Thrumir explained, was a symbol of their bond with the earth, a monument to their heritage and craftsmanship. It was this very tunnel that we were scheduled to inspect the next day, a routine check to ensure its sanctity remained undisturbed.

The next morning, as we ventured into the depths of the mountain, the weight of the previous night's tales fresh in my mind, we were met with a sight that neither of us had expected. The sacred tunnel, which should have been a pristine reflection of dwarrin craftsmanship, now bore the unmistakable signs of intrusion. The walls, which should have been smooth and meticulously carved, were now marred by unfamiliar tool marks. The sanctity of the place had been violated, and the weight of this desecration hung heavily in the air. The tunnel, which had always been a symbol of the dwarrin's dedication and precision, now felt violated. The walls, which once showcased the meticulous handiwork of Thrumir's clan, were now defaced with crude and hasty gouges. These unfamiliar tool marks stood out starkly against the otherwise smooth and expertly carved stone. Thrumir's face tightened as he ran his fingers over the fresh scars on the tunnel walls. The dim light from the lanterns cast shadows that danced eerily, highlighting the gravity of the situation. The air grew tense, the usual ambient sounds of the mountain's heartbeats replaced by a heavy silence.

"This isn't the work of my kin," Thrumir murmured, his voice echoing slightly in the confined space. His eyes now bore a steely glint of anger and concern. The sanctity of their domain had been breached, and the implications of this were not lost on either of us. We proceeded with caution, our steps measured and deliberate. Every so often, Thrumir would stop to inspect the walls, trying to decipher the intentions of the intruders. The unfamiliar tool marks suggested a hurried job, possibly indicating that whoever was responsible knew they were trespassing on forbidden ground. As we delved deeper into the tunnel, the signs of intrusion became more evident. Discarded tools not of Thrumir's clan's craftsmanship, remnants of makeshift camps, and even some discarded ore bags littered the pathway. It was clear that this wasn't a one-time occurrence; someone had been exploiting this tunnel for a while.

Thrumir's concern grew with each discovery. This wasn't just about the unauthorized mining; it was a breach of trust, a violation of the sacred boundaries that the dwarrin held dear. The sanctity of their home, their very livelihood, was under threat, and the weight of this realization hung heavily between us as we continued our investigation. The alien tools lay strewn about, their unfamiliar shapes and materials contrasting sharply with the traditional dwarrin implements. Each tool bore the mark of a different craftsmanship, one that was not honed within the walls of Thrumir's village.

But it was the symbols that drew our attention the most. Carved with deliberate intent, they stood out against the naturally rugged texture of the tunnel walls. Thrumir knelt, tracing the symbols with his fingers, his touch gentle despite the anger evident in his posture. Thrumir's voice dropped to a growl, heavy with an edge of distaste I hadn't witnessed before. "The Kraggelm," he rumbled with scorn, "their ambitions have always been a thorn in our side, but this... this is a direct provocation." Each symbol was intricate, a combination of geometric patterns and runes that unmistakably identified the Kraggelm clan. Their presence here was a bold statement, a challenge, and a declaration of intent. The implications were clear. The Kraggelm clan were not just mining; they were marking their territory, staking their claim in a place they had no right to be. This was more than just a violation of boundaries; it was a blatant act of aggression, a challenge to Thrumir's clan's authority and dominance in this region.

I could see Thrumir's mind hard at work, the weight of the situation pressing down on him. The usually vibrant and lively dwarrin leader now seemed burdened, the weight of leadership and the responsibility to his clan evident in every line on his face.

Thrumir's brow furrowed deeply, his eyes holding a steely glint. "This cannot stand," he declared with conviction. "The Kraggelm have overstepped their bounds, and we're bound to make them regret it." The gravity of the situation was palpable, and as we made our way back to the village, the looming conflict with the Kraggelm clan cast a shadow over our journey. As we stood there, in the heart of the tunnel, the gravity of the situation began to sink in. This was not just a violation of territory; it was a challenge, a provocation that could ignite a conflict among the clans. The peace that had prevailed for generations was at risk, and we found ourselves at the heart of it. In that moment, under the weight of the earth and the burden of impending conflict, Thrumir and I knew that we had a responsibility. We had to alert his clan, to prepare for what might come.

As we navigated our way back through the labyrinthine tunnels, Thrumir began to unravel the history of the feud between the two clans. His voice echoed off the stone walls, a somber melody that told a tale of rivalry and resentment.

Thrumir's footsteps reverberated, setting a rhythm as he spoke, voice echoing throughout the expansive tunnels. "Many moons ago," he began, his tone reverent, "we unearthed an 'urkhas' vein," pausing momentarily, he stooped to pick up a glinting gold flake from the ground, emphasizing its significance. "This urkhas, it wasn't just any. It shone like the rays of the morning sun, reflecting Krüma's very heart. A treasure both we, the Thorazdum, and Kraggelm hungered for." He sighed, eyes glazing with recollections of times past. "This river of golden wonder, snaking beneath our feet, became a beacon of aspiration, a mark of Krüma's favor."

His voice deepened, echoing the weight of history, "Both clans staked their claim, brandishing ancient rights and traditions, arguments as old as our first forefathers. The disagreement, it ran as deep and winding as our mines, mirroring the rich strands of urkhas stretching through the belly of Krüma." There was a pause, the gravity palpable, "The air grew thick, like awaiting a storm's first roar. Each day, every shadow held a potential skirmish, each echo a potential battle cry. But fate, in its capriciousness, made the river of urkhas vanish, fading till it was but a mirage of its former self. A full-blown war was averted, but the embers of resentment? Those never quite went out. They lie there, smoldering, a drakkar awaiting its moment to erupt."

Thrumir's voice, usually filled with the hearty laughter of a dwarrin content with his lot, was somber as he recounted the history. The weight of the past was evident in his eyes, the burden of a feud that had spanned the last five generations. "Our clans, they've lived in a peace as thin as the blade's edge," Thrumir began, the weight of history pressing upon his every word. "Every step we take in these tunnels," he paused, letting the echoes of their footfalls fill the void, "is a reminder of the fragile accord that binds us. Lately, however, the Kraggelm grow restless. Their audacity knows no bounds." His fingers brushed against the tunnel walls, caressing the scars left by foreign tools. "These markings, they're not ours. The Kraggelm, they tread where they shouldn't, daring to disturb soil that's borne our ancestors' footprints for countless moons. Every corner of this mine, every stone, tells the tales of our people, the hard work, the sacrifices. These tunnels, they aren't just pathways; they're the lifeblood of our thârûm, a testament to our dwarrornak."

His gaze hardened, a spark of anger igniting in his eyes. "The Kraggelm, their audacity knows no end," Thrumir's voice rumbled, echoing the deep-seated anger within him. "They now dare to delve into our sacred tunnels, openly flouting the age-old customs that have kept the balance between clans. It's more than a mere violation; it's a mockery, a direct affront to our very honor and the legacy of our ancestors!"

"Could they be after the urkhas again?" I pondered aloud. Thrumir, a hint of fire in his eyes, responded with a forceful thud of his fist against the tunnel's rock.

"This isn't merely about chasing urkhas, lad. It's deeper than that. It's a matter of pride, of recognizing the borders and traditions that have shielded us from bloodshed for ages. It's about safeguarding the legacy of our thârûm, the spirit and essence passed down from our forebears." His voice tempered, carrying a weight of sorrow. "I dread the path this could pave, the looming storm of strife. Dwarrin, we're built tough, but even the mightiest mornal can fracture under duress." Meeting my eyes, he continued with resolute conviction, "Yet, we shan't simply watch as they dishonor us. We're of the Thorazdum bloodline, birthed from Krüma's depths. We shall guard our heritage, our dwarrornak. For our strength mirrors that of the vorgrund in our blades, and we shall remain unyielding."

Thrumir's voice was heavy with worry as he voiced his fears. He believed that the Kraggelm were preparing to reignite the old conflict, their actions a spark that could set ablaze the dormant feud. The peace that had prevailed for decades was hanging by a thread, the balance disrupted by the audacious actions of the Kraggelm. As I listened to Thrumir, I could feel the tension in the air, a palpable unease that seemed to seep into the very stones around us. The peace and camaraderie that I had come to associate with the dwarrin clans were at risk, overshadowed by the looming threat of conflict.

Upon our return to the thârûm, Thrumir wasted no time in informing the leader, Balgruff, of our discovery. Balgruff's face, usually a stoic mask of authority, tightened with concern as he listened to Thrumir's account. Without hesitation, he called for a council meeting of the elders in the thârûm, a gathering of wisdom and experience to discuss the evidence and the potential threat posed by the Kraggelm. The meeting was conducted with a solemnity that spoke of the gravity of the situation. The evidence was presented, the tools and symbols examined, the implications discussed. The voices of the elders, usually filled with tales and laughter, were somber, their words measured and thoughtful.

As the council gathered, the air was thick with anticipation. Thrumir, Balgruff, and I were joined by three other elders of the Thorazdum thârûm: Haldorr, the grand blacksmith, Bruna, the historian, and Fargrim, the Elder and master craftsman. Balgruff, his voice echoing in the council chamber, initiated the discussion.

"Here we gather, in the heart of our thârûm, to deliberate on the brazen moves of the Kraggelm thârûm. Their trespasses into our realm, their audacity to dig within our very tunnels. But before we dive deep into this matter, I call upon each member of this council to share their immediate sentiments and apprehensions." Haldorr, his voice as sturdy as the metal he worked with, chimed in. His eyes, usually twinkling with mirth, were hardened with resolve.

"It's not merely land they tread upon," he started, his voice booming in the council's vast chamber. "It's our very dwarrornak they trample with their heedless steps. A peace sculpted through countless seasons, painstakingly preserved, is now in jeopardy." He paused, allowing his gaze to touch upon every council member. "As dwarrin, as Thorazdum, these hallowed tunnels are our life's work. Krüma has yielded her treasures to our hands, our lineage has toiled and triumphed beneath this very mountain, imbuing the stone underfoot with their legacy."

His tone escalated, echoing the collective sentiment in the chamber. "But the Kraggelm, in their arrogance, do not merely trespass our lands. Their actions mock our dwarrornak, our storied lineage. They dig within our realms, showing sheer disdain for the accord that has long kept a fragile peace." His clenched fist pounded the stone council table, its thunderous sound punctuating his fervor. "Passivity is no longer an option. Our honor, our legacy demands swift, resolute action. The very essence of Thorazdum compels us to rise."

Bruna rose, her eyes reflecting the gravitas of the moment, her voice infused with the wisdom accrued through countless cycles. "This trespass cannot be overlooked," she began, allowing her words to resonate within the chamber. "I find myself in agreement that the Kraggelm's deeds are a gross violation of the mutual respect that has long united our clans. This runs deeper than mere urkhas or land; this is the very fabric of our peace, our coexistence, being rent asunder." She paused, her eyes momentarily closing as if weighing the gravity of the situation. "Their actions teeter on the brink of shattering our delicate accord, igniting a fire that could engulf us all. We must ponder what legacy we are shaping for the children of Thorazdum, the future that will unfold in the wake of our choices." Opening her eyes, a steely resolve took hold. "Our response must embody both wisdom and the unwavering strength that marks us as dwarrin. We must make it known, to the Kraggelm and to all thârûms, that the disruption of our peace will not be tolerated. If our legacy, our very essence, calls us to war to preserve what we hold dear, then we must be prepared to answer that call."

Fargrim, his eyes alight with a discerning intensity rarely diverted from his meticulous craftwork, interjected with a voice honed to a fine edge. "We must deliberate our course with the same care we would apply to forging a blade," he began, his voice resonating through the chamber. "To react in haste might spark a battle we are ill-prepared to wage. While the Kraggelm's brazen acts undoubtedly strike at our honor and disrupt our peace, we must not allow our ire to steer us into folly." His voice, so often echoing the rhythmic song of his smithing, now took on a more contemplative cadence. "We are Thorazdum, offspring of the Krüma, renowned not only for our might but our wisdom." He paused, his expression thoughtful, as if shaping the words with the precision he would apply to his metalwork. "Each potential course must be weighed, the ramifications assessed. For war may exact a toll far steeper than mere urkhas. It may fracture the peace we have cultivated, the unity that binds us as one. We must tread with caution, guided by the wisdom that has long defined us."

Balgruff, exuding an air of command with eyes that held the room with unwavering authority, shifted his focus towards Thrumir. "Thrumir," he began, his voice deep and resolute, embodying the gravity of their council, "you have ventured through the tunnels, you've witnessed firsthand the brazen encroachments of the Kraggelm. Your feet have trodden the paths where they dared to tread, your eyes have seen the signs of their contempt for our traditions." He paused, allowing the weight of his words to settle in the room, before his voice grew more intent. "Tell us your thoughts, your insights. What say you on this matter?" Thrumir, his voice filled with the weight of his concern, took a deep breath before he began.

"I've felt the uneasy silence in the tunnels, seen the marks left by the Kraggelm," he started, the depth of his experience evident in his tone. "There's no doubt, their deeds are an assault on the peace we've upheld, a slap to our face, a scorn towards the legacy we revere." He stopped, allowing a moment of reflection before his eyes ignited with an intense but controlled fire. "However, we must remember, we are not the Kraggelm. We are Thorazdum. We don't act from mere spite or unbridled greed. Our actions are guided by respect for our traditions, our thârûm, our lineage." His voice then softened, adding a note of wisdom. "We shouldn't respond to violation with violation, to scorn with more scorn. Instead, we must demonstrate the integrity of our character, the profoundness of our wisdom. Yes, we shall protect our land, our honor, our serenity, and with force if required. But we must do so in a manner that embodies the core principles of Thorazdum, the values that distinguish us. We cannot, and we will not, resort to reckless and needless bloodshed."

Balgruff, his gaze steady and authoritative, nodded at each member of the council in turn. "I extend my gratitude to each one of you for sharing your insights, your wisdom," he began, the tone of his voice resonating with a blend of humility and authority. "The words spoken here are not merely words; they carry the heft of our lineage, our heritage. They're imbued with the soul of Thorazdum, and they will illuminate our path in the turbulent days ahead." His eyes swept across the faces before him, a look of resolve hardening in his eyes. "We are Thorazdum. We have been tested by time, challenged by circumstances, yet we have always emerged with solutions. We have never failed to safeguard our honor, our tranquility, and our unity. We shall prevail once more, guided by the enduring principles that make us who we are, and armed with the collective wisdom that has been shared here today."

Balgruff's voice, imbued with a solemn resolve, continued to command the attention of the council chamber. "Now, we must turn our eyes to the annals of our past, to the conflicts and tribulations we have weathered and conquered. We must delve into the wellspring of our history, extracting the wisdom and insights that lie within." His gaze, unflinching and resolute, fixed on the council members. "We shall recount the struggles of the last four hundred cycles - from the era of division when dwarrin separated into our distinct thârûms, through the myriad challenges we've surmounted. It's from these tales of resilience and triumph that we will draw the wisdom, the strategy, to navigate this confrontation with the Kraggelm. We will forge a path that honors our legacy, guided by the lessons of our forebears." His words were more than a directive; they were a beacon, illuminating a course rooted in tradition and tempered by experience.

Bruna's voice, filled with the wisdom of her cycles and the gravity of memory, resonated in the council chamber, each word weaving the fabric of a tale from Thorazdum's history. "Three hundred and seventy-two cycles ago, we were forced to confront a challenge that bears striking resemblance to what we face today with the Kraggelm. The clan of Gromthak, emboldened by arrogance, trespassed upon our lands and breached our peace. Though we extended the hand of reason, sought dialogue and understanding, they turned a deaf ear, a blind eye. They persisted in their violations, heedless of our honor and traditions."

Her eyes, reflecting the council chamber's flickering light, held a depth of sorrow and determination. "We were driven to a painful decision. We met their disdain with force, their infringement with just retribution. The ensuing conflict was savage and costly, a dark chapter in our history. But it was a conflict we could not shy away from. It was the crucible in which our honor was tested, our peace restored." Her voice, though somber, carried a firm resolve. "Should the Kraggelm persist in their transgressions, we must stand ready to defend our lands and our legacy. We must be prepared to wield the sword of justice with the same fortitude that guided us in times past." Her words, a blend of caution and conviction, served as both a warning and a guidepost for the path that lay ahead.

Fargrim's voice, seasoned with experience and softened by wisdom, resonated in the chamber as he recounted a tale that stood in contrast to the previous stories of conflict. "Three and a half hundred cycles past, our ancestors faced an intrusion by the clan of Dwarrūnda, much akin to the challenge presented by the Kraggelm today. The echoes of the conflict with Gromthak still resonated in our halls, but this time, our leaders chose a different path, guided by foresight rather than force."

He paused, his eyes reflecting a thoughtful intensity as he continued. "We sought a resolution not through blades and battle, but through a symbol of peace and understanding. We offered the Dwarrūnda an artifact of great value, a masterfully crafted amulet imbued with the very essence of the Krüma. This token was more than a mere gift;

it was a tangible embodiment of our desire for harmony, a bridge of goodwill."

His voice, usually marked by the rhythmic cadence of his craft, was imbued with a measured gravity. "They saw our sincerity. They understood our desire to find a path of mutual respect. They reciprocated our gesture, and from that day forth, an alliance was forged, a bond that has endured to this very cycle."

Fargrim's gaze swept across the council, his words a plea for reflection. "We must remember that we are not only a people of strength but also a people of wisdom. We are the children of the Krüma, and our legacy is not merely one of war but of diplomacy and discernment. As we face the transgressions of the Kraggelm, let us consider all paths, all options. Let us remember the lessons of our history and choose our course with care." His words lingered in the chamber, a reminder that the power to shape the future lay not only in the strength of their arms but in the wisdom of their choices.

Haldorr's voice, filled with the gravity of experience and the pain of memory, echoed in the council chamber as he shared a tale of a dark and painful chapter in Thorazdum's history. "One hundred and fifty cycles past," he began, his deep, resonant voice carrying the weight of the story, "our people faced the relentless ambition of the Skarnvoldûn thârûm. Their numbers were vast, their hunger for our lands unquenchable."

The room seemed to darken as he continued, his words painting a vivid picture of a time of conflict and loss. "We tried to find a peaceful resolution, but it was to no avail. The Skarnvoldûn were deaf to reason, blind to our pleas for peace. The battles were brutal, the losses unbearable. Two thirds of our thârûm, our kin, were lost. Our lands were taken, our honor tarnished, the very heart of Thorazdum shattered."

His voice, as steadfast as the metal he worked with, trembled with the emotion of the tale. "But we made a choice, a choice born of wisdom and foresight. We chose to retreat, to rebuild, to look to the future rather than linger in the past. It was a time of darkness, a time of mourning. But we endured. We rose from the ashes, our strength renewed, our resolve unbroken."

His gaze, shadowed with the memory, met the eyes of each council member as he concluded, "We must never forget the lessons of our past. We must learn from our mistakes, our losses, our victories. As we face the challenge of the Kraggelm, we must be guided by the wisdom of our ancestors, the strength of our convictions, and the courage to choose our path with care. We are Thorazdum, and our legacy is not merely one of battle, but of resilience, of wisdom, and of hope." His words lingered, a solemn reminder of the stakes at hand and the importance of choosing their course with thoughtfulness and care.

Thrumir, his eyes distant as memories of the past resurfaced, slowly began to speak, his voice echoing in the council chamber. "Two hundred cycles ago," he recalled, "we found ourselves challenged by the clan of Grûldûk, who lusted after a mine we had just discovered, filled with the precious vorgrund."

He paused, his gaze thoughtful, reflecting the weight of the historical decision he was about to recount. "The Grûldûk's greed, much like the Kraggelm's now, drove them to encroach on our claim. The path of conflict was clear, a road we could have easily traveled." His voice carried a note of wisdom, a remembrance of a path not taken. "But we saw another way. Unlike the urkhas, the vorgrund claim was not tied to our very identity, our thârûm. We chose to give the Grûldûk the mine, to quench their thirst for the ore."

His voice deepened, a blend of contemplation and conviction. "It was a decision met with resistance, even anger. Some saw it as weakness, as a betrayal of our very essence. But it was a choice that preserved peace, a decision that turned a potential enemy into an ally." His gaze hardened, his voice filled with a question that dared to challenge the council's preconceived notions. "Could we not find a similar path with the Kraggelm? Could we not avert war, protect our legacy, by offering them a claim rather than a blade?"

A heavy silence settled over the chamber, the shock of his suggestion palpable. Faces turned to Thrumir, their expressions a mixture of disbelief and indignation. The idea of relinquishing a claim, especially to the Kraggelm, was an affront to their honor, their tradition. Thrumir's words, though laden with the wisdom of the past, hung heavily in the air, a challenge to their very way of thinking, a question that demanded careful consideration.

Balgruff broke the heavy silence that had settled over the council chamber, his voice, usually a commanding presence, now imbued with a certain grace and understanding. "Thrumir, your words bring to mind the wisdom of our ancestors, the strategies that have seen us through many a conflict," he began, his eyes meeting Thrumir's, acknowledging his courage. "But we must remember that this vein, this precious ore, is more than a mere possession. It dwells within the heart of our mountain, in the very essence of our being."

He paused, his voice softening as he delved into memories long past. "When I was but a young dwarrin of twelve cycles, my beard no longer than my throat's length, I witnessed our thârûm's leader engaged in tireless negotiations with the thârûm of Barrgrin." His eyes took on a distant look, lost in the reflections of history. "Those negotiations stretched on for more than three months. The details were kept from me, but I observed, I learned. In the end, not only was peace maintained, but we had forged an alliance, a bond that lasts to this very day."

His gaze returned to the present, meeting the eyes of each council member with a resolute determination. "We must tread with caution, with wisdom. We must consider the paths that lie before us, explore the potential for negotiation, as we did with the Barrgrin. And if negotiations falter, we must remember the allies we have gained, the bonds we have forged. Our history guides us, our legacy strengthens us. Let us choose our path with care, with the wisdom of the Thorazdum."

Thrumir, feeling the weight of the council's eyes on him, their disapproval like a physical presence in the chamber, cleared his throat and began to speak, his voice filled with a sincerity that resonated in the silence. "I beg your forgiveness for any confusion my words may have caused," he said, his eyes meeting each council member's, one by one.

"I never intended to imply that we should surrender the mountain, our very heart and soul. That would be unthinkable."

He paused, choosing his words with care, his voice tinged with a thoughtful determination. "What I meant to propose was the possibility of finding a middle ground with the Kraggelm, a specific claim of urkhas within our mountain that could be shared. A place they could mine without encroaching on our core lands, our very essence." His gaze was steady, his words filled with conviction. "Perhaps this could be a path to a resolution, a way to forge a compromise that upholds our honor, our legacy, while avoiding the devastation of war. It is a thought, a consideration, one I believe we should at least explore." His voice trailed off, leaving the council to ponder his proposal, a suggestion that challenged tradition but offered a path to peace. The council chamber was filled with a heavy silence as the members pondered Thrumir's words. The weight of the decision, the implications of such a compromise, hung in the air. The council members exchanged glances, their expressions thoughtful, as they considered the possibility of a peaceful resolution that would benefit both clans. The silence stretched on, each member lost in their thoughts, weighing the potential outcomes of such a decision. Bruna, her eyes reflecting the wisdom of her cycles, broke the silence.

Bruna's voice cut through the contemplative silence of the council chamber, her tone firm yet thoughtful. "While the idea of a compromise is noble," she began, her eyes flicking between Thrumir and Balgruff, "we must not lose sight of the reality of our past dealings with the Kraggelm. Ours is a history fraught with tension, mistrust, and betrayal. Can we truly trust them to honor a resolution? Or will they perceive our willingness to compromise as a sign of weakness, a chance to seize more than we offer?" She paused, her gaze sweeping the room, making sure her words reached every ear. "Before we rush to judgment, we must delve into the very core of our relationship with the Kraggelm. We must dissect their motivations, their desires, their very essence. Only by understanding them completely can we hope to craft a decision that will truly serve the interests of both clans and preserve the delicate peace we have nurtured."Her words hung in the air, heavy with the weight of history and responsibility. Balgruff, his eyes reflecting the wisdom of many cycles, nodded in agreement, acknowledging the depth of her insight.

"Bruna speaks wisely," he began, his voice reverberating in the chamber. "The history of our dealings with the Kraggelm is not just a tale of the past; it's a map that guides our present decisions. It's a tapestry woven with the threads of trust, ambition, betrayal, and power. Understanding our past is more than crucial; it is essential to making an informed decision." He paused, his gaze turning to Bruna, his eyes reflecting both respect and expectation. "Bruna, you possess a profound understanding of our history, the depth of our connection and conflicts with the Kraggelm. I ask you to recount the tale of our rivalry, to breathe life into the memories of our ancestors, to help us see the path that has led us to this crossroads. Your voice, echoing with the wisdom of the ages, can illuminate the way forward for all of us."

Bruna, her eyes reflecting the flickering light of the council chamber, began her tale with a gravity that commanded attention. "The rivalry between Thorazdum and the Kraggelm is not a recent wound; it is a scar that dates back many cycles," she started, her voice deep and resonant. "Once, there was harmony between our ancestors and the Kraggelm. We traded goods, we broke bread together, we shared tales by the fireside. Our clans were united in purpose, bound by mutual respect and understanding." She paused, her gaze distant as she delved into the annals of history. "But as the cycles passed, our clans grew in size and ambition. Tensions began to surface, like cracks in a finely wrought blade. Disputes over territory, resources, even over the very essence of the Krüma, began to pull us apart." Her voice, a vessel carrying the weight of history, continued with a sorrowful cadence. "What began as small skirmishes grew into larger conflicts. Trust was shattered, replaced by suspicion, resentment, animosity. The Kraggelm, driven by a hunger for power, a thirst for wealth, repeatedly encroached upon our lands, igniting confrontation after confrontation." Her words slowed, each one carefully chosen, as she reached the heart of the matter. "Though there were moments when peace seemed within reach, when treaties were signed and alliances momentarily forged, the core of the rivalry remained, festering and unyielding. The Kraggelm's relentless ambitions, their insatiable desire for dominance, stood in stark contrast to our values, our longing for peace and harmony. They have always been at odds with who we are, with what we stand for." The room fell silent, the heavy words settling over the council like a shroud. Haldorr, his eyes reflecting the pride of his craft and the wisdom of his years, nodded in somber agreement, acknowledging the truth in Bruna's words.

"Bruna's recounting is accurate," he began, his words resonating in the chamber. "Our very identity was forged in the fires of those early conflicts with the Kraggelm. They saw us not as miners, stone masons, and traders, but as a barrier to their ambitions, a rival to be subdued. We were forced to adapt, to evolve, not out of a lust for power but out of a fundamental need to protect what was ours." His voice, deep and filled with authority, continued. "We, the Thorazdum, became renowned crafters of weapon and armor, not out of desire for conflict, but out of necessity. The relentless aggression of the Kraggelm required us to hone our skills, to stand firm, to defend our lands, our honor, and our legacy. Our craftsmanship became not just a trade but a symbol, a statement of our strength, our resilience, our refusal to bow." He paused, letting his words sink in. "The weapons and armor we crafted were not simply tools; they were a part of our very soul, our response to the Kraggelm's insatiable ambition. They became sought after by clans far and wide, a testament to our skill, our resolve. But more importantly, they became a symbol of our identity, our survival, our prosperity in the face of relentless challenges." Fargrim, his eyes filled with a blend of contemplation and understanding, nodded slowly, recognizing the truth in Haldorr's words.

Fargrim, his voice filled with both urgency and a poignant understanding, addressed the council. "I had hoped for a peaceful resolution," he began, the sharpness in his voice tempered by a clear desire for reason. "But hearing the tales of our past, the history of our rivalry with the Kraggelm, I am forced to acknowledge the complexity of the situation." His gaze swept the room, eyes resting briefly on each member. "The Kraggelm's actions, their aggressive encroachments, their disregard for our boundaries—these are not mere isolated incidents. They echo a pattern, a reflection of their relentless ambition, their willingness to challenge our very way of life." He paused, letting his words hang in the air, the weight of his concern palpable. "While my heart still clings to the hope of diplomacy, of finding a path towards common understanding, we cannot ignore the potential threat they pose. Not just to our claim on the urkhas vein, but to our traditions, our peace, our prosperity." His voice, firm yet filled with the complexity of the situation, continued. "We must be prepared to stand our ground, to defend our lands, our honor, and our dwarrornak if it comes to that. The Kraggelm have shown time and again their willingness to test our resolve. We must show them our strength, our unity, but also our wisdom in how we respond."

The council chamber, carved deep within the heart of the mountain, was dimly lit by the soft glow of luminescent crystals embedded in the walls. Their pale blue light cast eerie shadows that danced and flickered, mirroring the unease that permeated the room. The stone walls, etched with ancient runes and symbols of the Thorazdum lineage, seemed to pulse with the weight of history, bearing silent witness to the gravity of the council's deliberations. The air was thick with tension, the weight of the past and the uncertainty of the future pressing down on the room. It was almost palpable, like a heavy fog that clung to every surface, muffling the sounds and making each breath feel laborious. The scent of burning incense, meant to invoke clarity and wisdom, wafted through the chamber, its smoky tendrils intertwining with the underlying metallic tang of cold stone. The council members sat in a semi-circle, their faces illuminated by the soft glow of the crystals. Their expressions were a tapestry of concern, determination, and contemplation. The deep lines on their faces, etched by cycles of hard work and responsibility, seemed even more pronounced in the dim light. Their eyes, windows to their souls, reflected the depth of their thoughts, the weight of their decisions. In the center of the room stood a large, circular stone table. Its surface was worn smooth by countless meetings, countless decisions. Atop it lay various artifacts – tools, maps, and symbols – each telling a story, each holding a piece of Thorazdum's history.

The silence in the room was profound, broken only by the occasional shuffle of a foot or the soft rustle of a robe. It was a silence filled with anticipation, with respect for the gravity of the moment, and with the collective hope of finding a path forward for the Thorazdum. Thrumir, having listened intently to each member of the council, took a deep breath, the weight of the moment evident in his posture.

Thrumir, his eyes fixed on the council members, spoke with a softness that gradually gave way to determination. "I see now," he began, his voice a gentle echo in the chamber, "the depth of our history with the Kraggelm, the challenges we've faced, the complexities and sacrifices that have shaped our past. While my heart sought a peaceful resolution, a way to heal the rift between our clans, I cannot ignore the wisdom shared here." His voice grew firmer, filled with resolve. "I propose we increase our patrols, both along our borders and within the very tunnels that define our home. We must be vigilant, attentive to every movement, every sign of possible aggression from the Kraggelm." His words, a blend of caution and hope, continued. "We are Thorazdum, the children of Krüma. We have weathered storms, endured trials, and always emerged strong. We must now prepare, with wisdom and vigilance, to ensure the safety and prosperity of our thârûm. Not only for ourselves but for the generations to follow. Our dwarrornak and our honor depend on it."

Bruna, her eyes reflecting the wisdom of her cycles, nodded slowly. "Thrumir speaks truly. Vigilance is our best defense. We must be prepared for any eventuality."

Haldorr, his gaze steady and resolute, chimed in, "The safety of our thârûm is paramount. Increasing our patrols is a wise course of action."

Fargrim, his eyes sharp and focused, added, "We must be proactive, not reactive. I stand with Thrumir's suggestion. We must safeguard our lands and our legacy."

One by one, the members of the council voiced their agreement, their voices echoing in the chamber, a chorus of unity and determination.

Balgruff, having listened to each member of the council, rose from his seat, his presence commanding the attention of the room. "The council has spoken," he began, his voice echoing with authority. "We will increase our patrols, maintain vigilance, and ensure the safety of our thârûm. Additionally, I will send a patrol to our allies in the Barrgrin, Grûldûk, and Dwarründa thârûms requesting their aid."

He paused, letting his words resonate in the chamber. "This meeting is adjourned. Let us move forward with purpose, with unity, and with the strength of the Thorazdum." With a final nod, Balgruff signaled the end of the meeting, and the council members began to rise from their seats, their resolve strengthened by the collective decision.

As I stepped out of the council chamber, the heavy stone door closing behind me with a resonant thud, the voices of the elders still echoed in my mind. Their words, filled with the weight of history and the gravity of the decisions to be made, hung in the air, a reminder of the path we were about to tread. The chamber, with its dimly lit crystals and ancient runes, had felt like a different world, a world steeped in tradition and history, a world far removed from my own. As a human in the midst of the dwarrin, I was an outsider, a spectator to their deliberations. Yet, under Thrumir's wing, I had been granted a glimpse into their world, their struggles, their resilience. The council's decision marked a turning point. The days of peace, of camaraderie, were behind us. Ahead lay a path fraught with challenges and uncertainty. The Thorazdum were preparing for a potential conflict, their peaceful existence threatened by the ambitions of the Kraggelm. As I walked down the dimly lit tunnel, the cool stone beneath my feet, I felt a mix of apprehension and determination. The Thorazdum were not just my hosts, they had become my friends, my family. Their fight was now my fight.

Over the next few days, the thârûm was a hive of activity. The usually calm and peaceful rhythm of life had been replaced by a sense of urgency, a collective drive to prepare for the potential conflict. The sound of hammers striking metal echoed through the tunnels as the blacksmiths worked tirelessly, crafting weapons and reinforcing armor. The miners, too, were hard at work, fortifying the tunnels and securing the borders. Bruna, the wise yet ferocious elder, volunteered for patrol duty. She joined the thârûm's standard warriors, her presence a validation of the gravity of the situation. The daily patrols had been increased to four groups of six warriors, a significant increase from the typical two groups of two. The sight of Bruna, clad in armor and wielding a weapon with a determination that belied her age, was both inspiring and sobering. As I watched the preparations unfold, a mix of emotions washed over me. There was fear, of course, a natural response to the looming threat. But there was also a sense of admiration, of respect for the Thorazdum. Their unity, their resolve, their willingness to stand up for their home and their honor, was a sight to behold.

One day, as the sun cast its golden glow over the village and the villagers were immersed in their daily tasks, a sudden interruption shattered the tranquility. A group of Kraggelm warriors, their armor glinting in the sunlight, marched into the village, their footsteps a drumbeat of impending confrontation. They were led by their clan leader, a formidable dwarrin named Grommok, his presence a towering declaration of his authority and strength. Their sudden appearance sent a ripple of alarm through the thârûm. The once bustling village seemed to freeze in time, the rhythm of daily life abruptly disrupted by the sudden intrusion. The sound of hammers striking metal, of chisels shaping stone, the usual symphony of industriousness, was replaced by a hushed silence, broken only by urgent whispers. Villagers exchanged anxious glances, their hands pausing in their tasks, their expressions a mirror of the concern that gripped the thârûm. The children, usually running around in playful abandon, clung to their parents, their innocent faces clouded with confusion and fear.

As I watched the Kraggelm warriors march into the village, a question nagged at the back of my mind: Where were the patrols? The Thorazdum had been vigilant, their warriors constantly monitoring the borders and the tunnels. Why hadn't they stopped the Kraggelm from entering? I knew the areas they were patrolling stretched out in each direction quite some distance. The labyrinthine network of tunnels and the vast expanse of the borderlands were not easy to monitor, even with the increased patrols. But the Kraggelm were not known for their subtlety. Their sturdy build and heavy armor were not suited for stealthy maneuvers. Could they have slipped past the patrols? It seemed unlikely, but not impossible. It would have taken a level of cunning and stealth that belied their usual approach. The thought sent a shiver down my spine. If the Kraggelm were capable of such deception, what else were they capable of? Despite the unsettling thoughts, I knew that speculation wouldn't help. We had to deal with the situation at hand. The Kraggelm were here, and we had to face them, with all the courage and unity the Thorazdum were known for.

The Kraggelm's march through the village felt like a slow-motion scene from a nightmare. Their armored figures, bathed in the harsh sunlight, cast long, ominous shadows that seemed to stretch across the entire thârûm. Despite the fear, despite the disruption, there was a palpable sense of defiance in the air. The Thorazdum were not a clan to be easily intimidated. As the Kraggelm warriors continued their march, the villagers began to gather in the village square. They emerged from their homes and workshops, leaving their tasks behind, drawn by the urgent whispers and the growing sense of alarm. Their faces were now etched with concern and curiosity. Their eyes, a mix of different shades of blue, grey, brown, and green, were all fixed on the approaching warriors. The square, usually a place of camaraderie and laughter, was now a stage for an impending confrontation.

Despite the tension, there was a sense of unity among the villagers. They stood together, their shoulders touching, their hands clasped.

Their whispers, filled with worry and speculation, created a low hum that echoed through the square. As the Kraggelm warriors drew closer, the hum of whispers fell silent. The villagers watched in apprehensive silence, their breaths held, their hearts pounding. Thrumir, his face a mask of determination, stood at the forefront of the gathered villagers. His broad shoulders were squared, his stance firm, his gaze steady and unwavering. His usual jovial demeanor was replaced by a silent resolve that radiated from him like a blazing inferno, a clear signal of his readiness to protect his thârûm. His hands rested lightly on the hilt of his weapon, a silent promise of defense. His posture was a silent challenge to the intruders, a clear message that they were not welcome here.

Balgruff, the thârûm leader, stepped forward to join Thrumir at the forefront. His presence was a symbol of authority and unity, a beacon of leadership for the gathered villagers. His tall figure, though shorter than a human's, was imposing, his posture radiating a quiet strength that seemed to fill the square. His face was etched with determination. His eyes, a deep shade of blue that mirrored the luminescent crystals of the thârûm, were fixed on the approaching Kraggelm warriors. His hands, calloused from cycles of leadership and responsibility, rested at his sides, ready to defend the Thorazdum. The sight of Balgruff, standing alongside Thrumir, was a powerful image. It was a clear message to the Kraggelm, an affirmation of the unity and resolve of the Thorazdum.

The air in the village square was thick with tension, a palpable force that seemed to press down on us, muffling the usual sounds of life. The usual hum of conversation, the rhythmic clanging of metal on stone, the laughter of children playing, all had been replaced by a heavy silence. It was as if the village itself was holding its breath, waiting for the confrontation that seemed inevitable. The silence was a vivid differentiation to the usual vibrant energy of the square. The stone structures, usually bathed in the warm glow of the sun, now cast long, ominous shadows. The villagers, usually bustling with activity, now stood still, their eyes fixed on the approaching Kraggelm warriors. Grommok, his eyes fixed on Balgruff and Thrumir, marched into the square with a purposeful stride. His warriors followed in precise formation, their steps echoing ominously against the stone. Their faces were stern, their expressions unreadable behind the cold metal of their helmets. Their eyes, visible through the slits in their armor, were unyielding, a clear reflection of their resolve. Their presence was a deliberate provocation, a challenge thrown at the feet of the Thorazdum. The Kraggelm warriors stood tall and imposing, their armor glinting menacingly in the sunlight. Their weapons, held in a relaxed but ready grip, were a silent promise of conflict, a stark reminder of the threat they posed.

The square was now a stage for this tense standoff. The villagers watched in apprehensive silence, their eyes moving between the Thorazdum leaders and the Kraggelm intruders. As Grommok and his warriors came to a halt in the center of the square, the silence deepened, becoming almost tangible. It was as if the very air was holding its breath, the weight of history and animosity pressing down on the gathered crowd. The usual sounds of the village - the laughter of children, the rhythmic clanging of the blacksmith's hammer, the soft murmur of conversation - were all but forgotten, replaced by a heavy stillness that echoed with the tension of the moment. The eyes of the two clans met across the square, a silent battle of wills playing out in the space between them. It was a dance as old as the clans themselves - a dance of challenge and defiance, of pride and honor. The Kraggelm, with their stern faces and unyielding eyes, were a picture of aggression and provocation. The Thorazdum, standing firm and united, were a mark of resilience and determination. In that moment, the square was more than just a gathering place. It was a battlefield, a stage for the silent struggle between two of the earliest thârûms. The tension was a palpable force, a thread of electricity that connected each individual, binding us all in a shared anticipation of what was to come. As the sun cast long shadows over the village square, painting the scene in a stark contrast of light and dark, I knew that we were standing on the brink of a significant confrontation. The tension in the air was like a drawn bowstring, taut and ready to snap. The actions of the Kraggelm, their intrusion into the village, were more than just a show of force. They were a deliberate challenge, a spark that could ignite the smoldering feud into a full-blown conflict.

The Kraggelm, with their stern faces and unyielding eyes, stood in the center of the square, their presence a dark stain on the tranquility of the village. Their intrusion was a clear violation of the unwritten rules that governed the clans, a blatant disrespect of the Thorazdum's territory. Grommok, standing tall and imposing at the head of his warriors, took a step forward. His armored boots echoed against the stone of the square, the sound cutting through the heavy silence like a knife. His eyes, a piercing gray that seemed to glow in the harsh sunlight, were fixed on Balgruff and Thrumir. His face, a rugged landscape of scars and weathered lines, was set in a stern expression, a clear reflection of his resolve.

The silence of the square seemed to deepen as he moved, the very air holding its breath in anticipation of his words. The villagers watched in apprehensive silence, their eyes moving between the Kraggelm leader and their own. Grommok, his figure as imposing as the the mountain range that encircled the village, drew in a breath that seemed to pull the very air from the surroundings. His voice, when it came, was a rumble, a thunderous echo that reverberated off the stone walls of the mountains.

"Ah, Thorazdum," Grommok purred, his voice a venomous charm that resonated in the very core of the village. "So steadfast, so resolute in your barornak. But allow me to enlighten you with the truth of the Kraggelm, the truth that we are the rightful heirs to what lies beneath your feet." His words, oozing with insidious grace, were as alluring as they were unsettling. "Our barornak is rooted in the ancient traditions, in the very essence of our kin. What's the matter? Feeling... cornered?" His gaze swept over the crowd, a predator eyeing its prey. "We are dwarrin, born of grandeur and destined for more. We are the children of something far greater, my dear friends. All thordums bow to Kraggelm." His voice, honeyed yet with a sharper edge, continued to weave its dark spell. "Comfortable with your barornak? Good... for now. But know this: we will not be denied our gabdurak. We will not be denied what flows through the veins of Krüma, as it flows through ours." His words rose, a crescendo dripping with dark promise. "The urkhas calls to us, as it has always done. Let's see if your thrumgar breaks as easily as your bones, dear Thorazdum. For we will not be denied. Every whisper, every doubt about our barornak, I place it there. And it shall haunt you until you yield." His laugh, a chilling sound, lingered long after he had spoken.

Grommok's words, a dark melody that caressed the very stones of the village, drew the dwellers into his twisted game. "Ah, dear Thorazdum," he cooed, his voice dripping with venomous charm, "the Kraggelm will have what is rightfully ours. The disputed gabdurak? The urkhas? Our dwarrornak? All thordums bow to Kraggelm, and we will not be denied." His gaze, a predatory glint, settled upon Balgruff. The silence thickened, a tangible fog of unease. "Balgruff," he whispered, the name a serpent's hiss that reverberated off the walls of the village, "You, the so-called kazadornak of this village. You, who claim to hold sway with the Thorazdum." His voice was a low rumble, filled with dark insinuations. "Hear my words and heed them well. The Kraggelm will not be denied our gabdurak. Our ambition will not be thwarted by mere durthakornums or words." His voice soared, a cruel elegance in every syllable. "A promise carved in the very bones of this thordum, a promise that echoes in the hollow chambers of your meager durnorn. A promise that we will have what is ours. Think of it as a dance, Balgruff, one that spirals ever closer to inevitability." His words, a deliberate challenge, a warning laced with malice, hung in the air. The silence that followed was a haunting void, the villagers' eyes darting, the weight of Grommok's words a suffocating presence. His voice then dropped to a low growl, a sound that seemed to claw its way from the depths of the village, sending a chill through the crowd.

Grommok's eyes, unyielding and sharp as the edge of a blade, were fixed on Balgruff. "Balgruff," he purred, his voice a mix of dark amusement and veiled menace, "the time for games is over. The Kraggelm do not merely watch from the shadows; we claim what's ours." His words were a slow, honeyed poison that seemed to seep into the hearts of those who listened. "You think the Thorazdum can deny us our barornak? You think walls and dwarrornak can keep us at bay when we kragdurnum?" His gaze swept the crowd, a gleam in his eyes, his voice carrying the weight of doom. "Ah, the traditions, the ancestral rites you cling to—they're like delicate threads, easily snipped." His words painted a vivid tapestry of conflict and retribution. "The urkhas that flows through the veins of this gabil, it calls to us, and that cannot be hidden behind feeble barornaks and false bravado." He leaned forward, his voice dropping to a whisper that was somehow more terrifying than a shout. "Should you continue to deny us, dear Thorazdum, know this: Our rage will be a fire that consumes, our vengeance a storm that shatters. We will carve our dwarrornak into the very stones of your durthakornum, our dammaz a testament to your folly." His voice rose, a crescendo that echoed through the square, "Your harnazes will crumble, your defenses will fall. You will seek harnornak in distant kazakars, only to find the shadows have teeth. Your thrumgar will wane, your resolve will falter, and you'll discover too late that 'mercy' is a word unknown to the Kraggelm." His words, a chilling prophecy, a promise of a battle that would be waged with neither mercy nor restraint, hung heavy in the air. "Remember this moment, Thorazdum, the moment you were offered a choice and chose defiance. The storm kragdurnums, and you will know the wrath of the Kraggelm. You will taste the bitter fruit of your denial, and you will understand that our people's thrumgar, once kindled, is a blaze that cannot be quenched." His voice trailed off, leaving a silence filled with dread, the very air seeming to tremble with the weight of his words.

Grommok's final words echoed through the square, a grim promise that hung in the air like the ominous rumble of a distant bonfire, yet to be ignited. As his voice faded, the silence was shattered by the uneasy murmur of the villagers. The Thorazdum, usually a jovial and hearty folk, if somewhat reserved and stern towards outsiders, were now etched with concern and fear.

Whispers spread like a breeze through the crowd, the words 'Kraggelm', 'Urkaz', and 'Krâgzar' repeated in hushed tones. The villagers exchanged uneasy glances. The weight of Grommok's words, his promise of conflict and retribution, hung heavy in the air, a palpable tension that seemed to seep into the very stones of the village. The square, usually filled with the rhythmic cadence of the smiths at work and the cheerful banter of the villagers, was now filled with a tense silence. The Thorazdum, their faces reflecting the flickering light of the fire, looked to Balgruff, their leader, for guidance.

As an outsider, I could only watch, my understanding of the dwarven language and culture still in its infancy. But even I could feel the tension in the air, the palpable unease that Grommok's words had stirred. Balgruff stood tall amidst the sea of uneasy faces. His countenance, usually as steady and unyielding as the mountain that encased their village, now bore the mark of a leader facing a grave challenge. His eyes met Grommok's in a silent battle of wills. The square fell silent, the villagers holding their breath as they watched the two leaders. The tension was as palpable as the heat from a fire, the air thick with anticipation. The only sound that could be heard was the distant echo of the hammers in the forge, a grim reminder of the looming conflict. Balgruff's gaze did not waver, his resolve as unyielding as the walls that protected their village. His silence was an unambiguous split from Grommok's fiery monologue, his calm demeanor a beacon of hope amidst the sea of unease. Balgruff stood firm. His gaze met Grommok's, a silent refusal to be intimidated by the Kraggelm's imposing presence.

"Grommok," Balgruff's voice emerged, deep and resonant, a sound as solid as the stone beneath their feet. "You come here speaking of dwarrornak and barornaks, brandishing threats as if they were urkaz. You forget that we, the Thorazdum, are children of the same thordum, dwarrin of the same gabîl." His tone was as unyielding as vorgrund, the weight of leadership in every word. "Our barornak to the urkhas is as rooted in tradition as yours, a dwarrornak carved in stone." His eyes narrowed, and his voice lowered, every word a declaration, every syllable a vow. "You speak of krâgzar, but know this: Our vorgrund stands united, our resolve is a durthakornum. By Thorazdum's halls, we will not waver. As the thordum stands, so do we." A pause, a silence filled with gravity and purpose, then he continued, his words razor-sharp, his tone unwavering. "Our anvil does not yield, Grommok. Every dwarrin under my watch is a durthakornum unto themselves. We will not surrender our gabdurak. We will not relinquish the urkhas that flows through this thordum." His voice rang out once more, a clear, resonant sound that echoed through the square. "Tread carefully, Grommok. The line is drawn here. We will defend what is ours with the might of the barazdum behind us. Your threats fall on stone, and stone does not bend." His words, a solid and immutable challenge, hung in the air, a testament to the strength and resolve of the Thorazdum.

Balgruff's voice resonated, strong and unbreakable, a wall of conviction. "Kraggelm," he pronounced, his tone a stern warning, "heed these words and heed them well. Strike at the thordum with aggression, and you strike at the very heart of Thorazdum. We are the keepers of these lands, the guardians of our dwarrornak." His eyes locked with Grommok's, a challenge in his stare, his words a solid vow to all who would hear. "We are Thorazdum, steadfast as the unyielding peaks. No threats will shatter our thrumgar. No shadow will cast doubt upon our dwarrornak." His tone deepened, a low rumble that echoed through the assembly. "Think not that we will stand idle, Kraggelm. The flame that guides us is not easily extinguished. Your desire to claim what is not yours will meet a wall that does not falter, a defense that knows no retreat." His words settled, a solemn promise, a line drawn in stone and steel. "We will hold our gabdurak, as firm as the thordum's embrace. Your kragdurnum will find no foothold here. Mark these words, Grommok, for they are as unchangeable as the path of the stars. We will not yield."

With a voice as enduring as the stone halls of their ancestors, Balgruff spoke, the sound echoing through the square. "Here we stand, a thârûm of unwavering resolve, a thârûm bound by dwarrornak and thrumgar. Together, we are a durthakornum that no storm can breach, a flame that no wind can extinguish." His eyes met Grommok's, and in them was a defiance that would not bend. "We are guardians of our dwarrornak, defenders of our barornak. We will not falter before threats, nor bow to intimidation." Grommok's face tensed, his eyes sharpening, a storm brewing behind them. But Balgruff's posture remained firm, the might of his conviction evident in every word. "Our path is clear, our thrumgar unshaken. We are Thorazdum, Grommok. We will face your challenge with the resilience of the deep gabil, with the steadfastness that has defined us for generations." His voice held the weight of history, the legacy of a people who had endured and thrived. "Know this, Kraggelm: We will not be swayed. We will harnorn what is ours with a thrumgar that does not yield, with a courage that knows no bounds. Our unity is our harnaz, our resolve our sword. We will not be broken."

The square was silent, the villagers holding their breath as they watched the two leaders. The tension was a palpable force, a storm cloud that hung over the village, threatening to break at any moment. The situation had not escalated into violence, but the threat of it lingered in the air. Grommok's gaze swept over the crowd, his eyes reflecting the flickering light of the fire. His gaze returned to Balgruff, a silent acknowledgment of the challenge met. The gauntlet had been thrown back at his feet, the Thorazdum's determination to stand firm a clear message to the Kraggelm. The standoff between Balgruff and Grommok lingered in the air, a haunting melody that echoed through the square long after their words had faded. Led by Grommok, storming away and not so much as glancing back, the Kraggelm began to leave the village. Their departure was marked by a deliberate slowness, each step a lingering challenge, each glance a silent promise to return.

The villagers watched in silence as Grommok and his warriors retreated, their figures slowly disappearing into the shadows of the mountain that encased their village. The air was thick with unspoken threats and unresolved tension, a storm cloud that refused to dissipate. The square was now silent. The villagers, their faces reflecting the flickering light of the fire, watched in silence as the Kraggelm departed, their eyes filled with a mix of relief and apprehension. As Grommok and his warriors disappeared into the shadows of the mountain, the villagers remained, their faces a complex tapestry of concern and determination. The young and old alike watched the retreating figures, a silent vow in their gaze.

As the last of the Kraggelm disappeared past the village walls, I made my way over to Thrumir. Despite the tension that hung in the air, his face was a mask of calm, his eyes reflecting the steady glow of the fire. He placed his hand firmly upon my middle back, reaching up above his head due to his dwarven stature, a silent invitation to follow him. We moved away from the square, and Thrumir led me to a place away from all the commotion, a quiet corner of the village where the looming threat of conflict seemed a world away. The peace and camaraderie that had bound the Thorazdum together were still present here, a clear distinction from the tension that hung over the square.

"Did you understand what just transpired, Yoran?" Thrumir asked, his voice a low rumble that echoed the seriousness of the situation.

"I understood some of it," I admitted, "but a lot of the words were foreign to me." Thrumir nodded slowly in understanding, his hand moving to scratch his long bushy beard in contemplation, his eyes holding a thoughtful look.

"Come with me, Yoran," Thrumir said, his voice echoing slightly in the vastness of the mountain tunnel. He led me towards the entrance, his steps steady and sure, the glow from the village fires casting long shadows on the stone walls.

As we walked, Thrumir began to explain the meaning of the words that Balgruff and Grommok had used. "Dwarrin," he said, "refers to us, the Forgeborn. It's a term of unity, of shared heritage. Urkhas is the gold that flows through the veins of Krüma, the world. It's more than just a mineral to us; it's a symbol of our birthright."

"Gabdurak," he said, "means 'territory.' It signifies a specific area or land that a group or individual considers their own, a place they have a right to by tradition or law."

"Barornak," Thrumir clarified, "refers to 'a claim,' a declaration of one's right to something. It's a term that carries weight, signifying a deep connection or entitlement to what is being claimed."

"Gabîl," he said, "is earth, the very ground we stand on, the foundation of our lives. It's a symbol of stability and endurance."

"Thrumgar," he explained, "is fire, a symbol of our spirit, our determination. It's what fuels us, what keeps us going in the face of adversity."

"Dwarrornak," he said, "means 'legacy'. It is the story, the traditions, the meaning that we pass down throughout the generations going forward."

"Kazadornak," he said, "is the leader, the one who guides and protects. Balgruff is our Kazadornak, our guiding light in these dark times."

"Barazdum," he continued, "is a forge, a place of creation and transformation. It's where raw materials are turned into something useful, something beautiful."

"Urkaz," he said, "is wealth, but not just in the material sense. It's the wealth of our culture, our traditions, our shared history."

"Durnorn," he explained, "is a bastion, a stronghold. It's a symbol of our resilience, our determination to stand firm in the face of adversity."

"Thordum," he said, "is a mountain, a symbol of our strength and endurance. It's a reminder of our connection to the earth, our respect for its power and majesty."

"Durthakornum," he said, "is a fortress, a place of safety and security. It's a symbol of our determination to protect what is ours."

"Kragdurnum," Thrumir explained, "means 'Advance,' often used in the context of battle strategy. It signifies a forward movement, a push towards a goal, particularly in the face of opposition."

"Dammaz," he said, "is a hammer, a tool of creation and transformation. It's a symbol of our ability to shape our own destiny."

"Harnaz," he said, "is a shield, a symbol of our commitment to protect and defend. It's a reminder of our unity, our shared purpose."

"Kazakar," he explained, "is a cave, a place of shelter and safety. It's a symbol of our connection to the earth, our respect for its power and majesty."

"Harnornak," he continued, "refers to 'Protection.' It's something one might seek in times of hardship or danger. It's a symbol of safety, a shield against adversity."

As he finished, we stood before a large stone door, the echoes of his words still lingering in the air. The meanings of the dwarrin words had added a new depth to the confrontation I had witnessed, a complexity that I was only beginning to understand. The large stone door before us seemed ancient, its surface etched with intricate patterns that hinted at tales of old. Thrumir placed his hand on a particular rune, pressing it gently. With a low rumble, the door began to move, revealing a dimly lit room beyond.

As we stepped inside, the soft glow of a desk torch illuminated the space, casting flickering shadows on the walls. The room, though small, was filled with stone tablets of various sizes, their edges showing signs of age and frequent use. Dust particles danced in the torchlight, and the scent of old stone filled the air. Thrumir moved with purpose, his eyes scanning the shelves until they settled on one particular tablet. He reached out, carefully extracting the heavy block of stone and placing it on the desk.

"This," he said, pointing to reveal dwarven script accompanied by detailed illustrations, "is a lexicon of our language. It pairs our words with correlating images, making it easier for those unfamiliar with our tongue to understand." I leaned in, examining the runes. The illustrations were detailed, each image paired with its corresponding dwarrin word. A mountain paired with "Thordum," a shield with "Harnaz," and so on. "This should help you, Yoran," Thrumir continued, his voice gentle. "It's important for you to become more familiar with our language, especially given the challenges we face." I nodded in gratitude, realizing the weight of the gift he was offering.

The days that followed were a blur of stone carvings. Each morning, as the sun's rays began to pierce the deep caverns of the Thorazdum village mountain, I found myself seated at that old wooden desk, the lexicon of tablets spread before me. The weight of the stones were not just in their physical heft, but in the depth of their contents. On the first day, my fingers traced the detailed illustration of an axe, its blade sharp and gleaming even in the etched form. "Belgarn," I whispered, the word feeling foreign on my tongue. The image next to it was of a smaller tool, used for cutting wood. "Belkar," I read aloud. The intricacies of the dwarrin language began to unfold before me, each word a key to a deeper understanding of their world. By the third day, I had moved on to the elements. A beautiful drawing of a crystal caught my attention. "Gravaz," I murmured, appreciating the artistry that went into both the word and the image. Beside it was a depiction of a jewel, shimmering even on stone. "Gravgar,", a jewel, I noted, the similarities in the words hinting at their interconnected meanings. On the fifth day, I delved into the words of nature. The image of a mountain, majestic and towering, was labeled "Thordum." I could almost feel the cold wind blowing at its peak, the sense of solitude it represented. The word for seed, "Thrygar," was paired with a delicate drawing of a sprout, "Thryorn." The cycle of life, from the smallest seed to the mightiest mountain, was captured in the dwarrin tongue. As the days passed, Thrumir would occasionally join me, offering insights into the nuances of certain words or sharing anecdotes related to them. "The word 'Kazadûm'," he once told me, pointing to the depiction of a grand hall, "is not just a place. It's a symbol of our unity, our shared history."

By the end of the week, I had not only expanded my vocabulary but had also gained a profound appreciation for the Thorazdum and their rich heritage. The tablets were not just a collection of words; they were a tapestry of stories, beliefs, and values. And as I reshelved the stones one evening, I realized that I was no longer an outsider looking in. I was becoming a part of their world, one word at a time.

In the days that followed the confrontation with Grommok and the Kraggelm, the council convened once more. The chamber, carved deep within the heart of the mountain's tunnels, was dimly lit by the soft glow of runic lanterns. Their light cast a gentle blue hue upon the ancient stone walls, revealing intricate carvings that told tales of the Thorazdum's storied past. The long, oval table at the center was made of a single piece of "Durorn" - stone, its surface polished to a smooth finish.

Balgruff, with his thick white beard and piercing blue eyes, sat at the head of the table. His presence, as always, commanded respect. "We face a challenge not quite like any in our dwarkarnak," he began, his voice deep and resonant. "The very foundation of our stendornak is at stake."

Fargrim, the eldest among them, nodded in agreement. His skin was a map of wrinkles, each one a signature of the centuries he had witnessed. "The enemy is not just at our gates," he said, his voice quivering slightly, "but they came within our midst. We must act swiftly."

Bruna, the dwarkarnorn, or "historian", adjusted her position in her stone chair and placed a large tablet before her. "The dwarrornak of our ancestors is filled with tales of valor and conquest," she said, her fingers skimming the runes. "While we must learn from their wisdom, we should also remember their might."

She paused, looking up at the council with a fierce determination in her eyes. "Our history is not just about preserving the past, but also about carving our future. We have faced adversaries before and emerged victorious, not just through diplomacy but through the sheer force of our will and strength."

Slamming her hand on the table, rattling the stone tablet before her, she continued, "We must rally our warriors, arm them with the finest thorgarnaks and prepare for a decisive strike. It's time the enemy learns that the Thorazdum are not just keepers of tales but also fierce defenders of their stendornak."

Haldorr, the grand brazadur, or "blacksmith", clenched his fist, the muscles in his arm tensing. "Our barazdur are ready," he declared. "We can fortify our defenses, craft thorgarnaks of unmatched quality. But we need guidance on where to focus our efforts."

Thrumir, the dûrkûrharn, or runekeeper, carefully laid out a set of intricately carved stones before him. Each stone bore a rune, symbols of power and enchantment. "These dûrnor are not just for inscriptions," he began, his voice filled with reverence. "These are dûrkûn - runes - they are the culmination of our crafting, the final touch that imbues our weapons and armor with unmatched strength. We must ensure that every piece we forge is enchanted with the right rune, for they will be crucial in the battles to come."

He picked up a dûrkûn, its surface shimmering in the dim light. "This one," he continued, "is the dûrkûn of '*Wid*' - harnornak. We must prioritize its use for our front-line warriors. And this," he said, holding up another, "is the rune of breaking - '*Mor*', perfect for our belgarns and blades to break through the enemy harnazs."

The council members exchanged glances, understanding the gravity of their task. The decisions they made in the coming days would shape the fate of the Thorazdum for generations to come. With a collective nod, they began their deliberations, each contributing their unique expertise and perspective to the challenges that lay ahead.

With a voice as solid as the walls of the council chamber, Balgruff began, the weight of leadership evident in his tone. "This affront by the Kraggelm, their bold intrusion into our thordum, strikes at the very heart of our honor," he declared, each word a carefully chosen stone in the fortress of his argument. "They mine our lands, challenge our authority, and in doing so, they test our resolve."

Fargrim's gnarled hand slammed down upon the table, his eyes narrowing at the map before him, aged wisdom turning to frustration. "By the ancient barazdums, look at their diggings, right near our sacred springs!" he growled, his voice gravelly with years of experience and newfound bitterness. "These young miners, with their reckless picks and shovels, they risk poisoning our very lifeblood. In my day, we respected the bones of the gabîl, knew where to cut and where to leave be. But this... this is a fool's gamble. It's our whole thârûm they're putting on the line, and for what? A handful of shiny stones? Bah! Let's put an end to this durorn-headed nonsense before it's our doom they dig."

Bruna's eyes blazed with the fire of her conviction as she spoke, her voice resonant with the history she so cherished. "The Kraggelm dare to encroach upon lands that hold the echoes of our forefathers' triumphs? In cycles past, our people bled and battled to secure this thordum. And now they think to defile it with their greed?" Her voice rose, sharp with anger. "By the valor of the First Hammer's strike, I won't see their legacy tarnished. Let us not forget what this ground means to us, what it has cost us. We will stand as they did, as firm as the mountains themselves, and teach these trespassers that the Thorazdum are not a lineage to be trifled with!"

Haldorr's voice, steady and grounded like the anvil he worked upon, cut through the tension. "I feel the heat of Bruna's words, and the flame of our ancestors' legacy burns in us all. But let's not forge ahead without the proper preparation," he cautioned, his eyes reflecting the wisdom of his craft. "Our barazdur, they're bending their backs at the forge, and the thorgarnaks they create need a master's touch to be imbued with the right enchantments. We need to fan the embers of our readiness, not rush into a blaze uncontrolled. If we attack without the tempered strength of our thorgornaks, we risk breaking like poorly wrought vorgrund. Let's shape our response with the patience of a seasoned smith, and when the time's right, we'll strike with a force that resonates like the ring of a perfect hammer blow!"

Thrumir's voice rang through the chamber, resonant and deep, like the very core of the mountain he revered. "Aye, the forging of the dûrkûn is a task as patient and steady as the shaping of the land itself," he began, his words bearing the weight of tradition and wisdom. "I've prepared a method to imbue our thorgarnaks with these dûrkûn, but it's a path that winds through time and precision, not a mere hack and slash." His eyes twinkled with the understanding of the craft, meeting those around the council table. "The Kraggelm might rush with all the folly of a cave-in, but we'll stand, not merely as durorns but as the very foundation of the thordum. Our thorgornaks will bear the might of the dûrkûn, forged with a care that's as ancient and enduring as the roots that cradle our home. And when we meet the challenge, we'll be as unbreakable as the peaks that tower above us."

Balgruff's voice filled the room, heavy with the awareness of the task at hand. "Grommok of the Kraggelm stands before us, not just as a name but as a trial to be faced," he began, his tone steady and unwavering. "Ruthless, indeed. Cunning, without question. Yet, he leads an army, not a united front. We stand as the heart of the thordum, unbroken and resolute. We'll not be swayed by numbers or trickery." His gaze swept across those gathered, a firm and reassuring presence. "We've faced storms and quakes, and still, our stronghold endures. So shall we face this challenge, with the strength of our heritage and the unity that binds us. Grommok may have his army, but we have our resolve. We are Thorazdum."

Bruna's voice rose, echoing through the chamber with the force of conviction. "Grommok, that crafty fiend, thinks he can stand against the Thorazdum? Let him come! Our heritage pulses with the courage of our ancestors. Our strength is unbreakable, our will unshaken!" She slammed her fist on the table, her eyes ablaze. "We've weathered storms fiercer than this, and we've emerged sturdier, our resolve forged in battles and tempered by victories. Grommok's might may be known far and wide, but he has not faced the might of the Thorazdum. Let him taste the vorgrund of our stendornak and feel the weight of our stendûr. We shall remind him of a history he seems to have forgotten, a history where we've triumphed, time and time again!"

The council members continued to deliberate, weighing their options and formulating a plan. There was a marked distinction between the first deliberation and the last; the first had been qyite gormal, each word and thought spoken in a calm, measured manner. This meeting, however, the fires of each of the dwarrins' spirits burned straight through the shield of formality that had previously restrained their impassioned words. Their verdict was unanimous: they would ready themselves for an impending assault from the Kraggelm. This decision was not born out of fear but from a steadfast commitment to safeguard their thârûm and uphold the honor of their ancestors. Thrumir, with his vast knowledge and seasoned leadership, was chosen to spearhead the village's defensive measures. As the council turned to him, Thrumir's jovial demeanor, often lit up with tales of mining adventures and camaraderie, was replaced by a solemn gravity. Accepting the mantle, his gaze held a steely resolve, a silent promise to his kin that he would do everything in his power to fortify their home against the looming threat. The council, in their wisdom, recognized the importance of knowledge in times of uncertainty. They resolved to dispatch scouts, the silent sentinels of the Thorazdum, to keep a vigilant watch on the Kraggelm's activities. These scouts, adept at moving stealthily through the rugged terrains of the thordum, would be their unseen eyes in the dense forests and shadowed valleys, their ears attuned to the faintest whispers of the wind carrying secrets. The chosen scouts were draped in cloaks of deep green and brown, blending seamlessly with the wilderness. Their boots, crafted from the hide of the Gaborn (soil) beasts, left nary a trace on the forest floor. Each carried a "Kragornak" (scout's) horn, a tool to signal any immediate danger or significant findings. This decision was not just a precautionary measure but a reflection of the council's depth of understanding. They grasped the intricate dance of war and peace, knowing that in the delicate balance of power, information was as vital as vorgrund. The scouts' mission was clear: to observe, to listen, and to return with knowledge that could tip the scales in favor of the Thorazdum.

With the meeting adjourned, Thrumir, a fire of purpose burning in his eyes, wasted no time in mobilizing the villagers. The heart of the village, the serene square that once echoed with laughter and the melodies of daily life, now resonated with a different kind of energy. The cobblestones, which had witnessed countless festivals and celebrations, became witness to rigorous training sessions. The rhythmic clang of metal meeting metal filled the air, punctuated by Thrumir's commanding voice guiding the villagers through drills. Makeshift wooden dummies were erected, serving as practice targets for strikes and parries. The village's young and old, from seasoned miners to eager children, stood shoulder to shoulder, their faces a canvas of determination and grit. Mothers, fathers, and even grandparents took up arms, each driven by a shared purpose to defend their home.

One day, as the sun cast long shadows across the square, Thrumir approached me. In his hand, he held a dagger, its blade gleaming in the waning light. "This is a dwarrin dagger he said, handing it to me. The hilt was adorned with intricate dûrkûn (runes), and the balance felt perfect in my hand. "It's time you learned to wield it," Thrumir added, a hint of pride in his eyes. Under his watchful gaze, I began my training, the weight of the dwarrin dagger a constant reminder of the responsibility we all shared in the face of the impending threat.

In the heart of the village square, Thrumir stood tall, a beacon of strength and knowledge. His voice, deep and resonant, echoed across the gathered crowd, instilling in them the principles of dwarrin warfare. This ancient art was not just about brute force; it was a symphony of mind and muscle, a delicate balance between raw power and refined strategy. With every word he spoke, Thrumir painted a vivid picture of battles past, of Thorazdum thorgornaks (warriors) who had mastered this dance of thorgarnaks (weapons). He emphasized the importance of 'Stendornak' (honor) and 'Stendûr' (loyalty) in every strike, every parry. As he began his demonstration, the villagers watched in rapt attention. Thrumir's movements were fluid, each step and swing seamlessly flowing into the next. The blade of his weapon glinted in the sunlight, tracing arcs of silver as he showcased various techniques. It was as if he was performing a dance, a dance where every motion was honed to perfection, every turn a presentation marking cycles of training. His words served as a rhythmic backdrop to his actions, guiding the villagers through the intricate choreography of combat. "Anticipate your opponent's move," he would say, demonstrating a swift parry, "and strike when they least expect it." The villagers, inspired by Thrumir's prowess and wisdom, hung on to every word, every demonstration, eager to imbibe the essence of dwarrin warfare and ready themselves for the challenges ahead.

Amidst the bustling square, I found myself not just as an observer but an active participant, my very being absorbed in the intricate dance of warfare and defense. The smooth texture of my new dagger, the weight of the dwarrin shields, the rhythm of the drills - every sensation was a lesson, every moment an education. The dwarrin's approach to battle was not just about the clash of steel; it was a philosophy, a way of life. I began to grasp their innate understanding of the land, how they used the rolling hills, dense forests, and jagged cliffs to their advantage. Every rock, every tree was a potential ally in their defense. But beyond the tactics and techniques, it was the spirit of the dwarrin that truly resonated with me. Thrumir's teachings illuminated their deep reverence for the balance between raw power and calculated strategy. They believed that true strength was not just in the might of one's arm but in the unity of the clan, in the collective will to protect and persevere.

As the days turned into weeks, Thrumir's words painted a vivid tapestry of the dwarrin's legacy. Tales of valor, of battles won not just by the blade but by the heart. Stories of honor, where every warrior stood firm, bound by an unbreakable bond of loyalty and determination. Through Thrumir's guidance, I was not just learning the art of combat; I was being initiated into a world that celebrated the enduring spirit of the dwarrin, a world where honor was the truest measure of strength. The once tranquil village underwent a transformation, its very landscape echoing our collective determination to shield the Thorazdum's home from impending danger. Every hand, young and old, joined in the monumental task of fortification, each nail driven, each stone laid, a symbol of their unwavering resolve. Barricades rose from the ground, their robust wooden frames intertwined with thick ropes and reinforced with vorgrund. These weren't just barriers; they stood as silent sentinels, their imposing presence a clear message to any who dared approach with ill intent. Lookout posts, strategically placed at vantage points, dotted the village's perimeter. These wooden towers, standing tall against the backdrop of the thordum, were manned by vigilant kragornaks - scouts. Their keen eyes scanned the horizon, ever watchful, ever ready. The soft flicker of torches from these posts became a beacon in the night.

The following day, as the sun traced its arc across the sky, the village pulsed with a newfound energy, a fervor that spoke of unity and purpose. The once leisurely cadence of daily life, marked by the melodic chinks of mining and the hum of crafting, had transformed into a symphony of urgency and readiness. The open fields, where children once played and elders basked in the sun, now echoed with the rhythmic thud of boots and the clang of weapons. Makeshift training arenas sprang up, their grounds etched with the footprints of countless drills and exercises. The villagers, who had once found solace in the depths of the earth, extracting its treasures and molding them into artifacts of beauty, now stood tall, their spines straightened by a shared purpose. Their hands, once stained with ore and clay, now gripped the hilts of swords, axes, and shields, their movements guided by the teachings of Thrumir. Under his watchful eye, the villagers evolved, their spirits forged in the crucible of impending conflict, their resolve unyielding. Amid the fervor of training drills and the rising structures of defense, a hushed stillness descended upon the village square one evening. A scout, his cloak muddied and face etched with fatigue, approached Balgruff with a heavy heart. The setting sun cast long shadows, adding to the somber atmosphere.

"Balgruff," he began, his voice carrying the weight of his message, "it's been nearly a moon's turn since the Kraggelm's unexpected arrival. One of our patrols from that fateful day - the patrol that was to request aid from our allies... they haven't returned." The news hung in the air, a palpable tension gripping the gathered villagers. The square, which moments ago had been alive with the sounds of preparation, now stood in a hushed silence, the gravity of the scout's words sinking in.

Balgruff's face, usually a mask of stoic leadership, betrayed a flicker of concern. The missing scouting party wasn't just a group of warriors; they were kin, friends, and family to many in the village. The village leader took a deep breath, steadying himself. "We must organize a search party," he declared, determination evident in his voice. "Every moment counts. We owe it to our brethren to find them and bring them home." As the villagers rallied around Balgruff's call, the unity and resolve of the Thorazdum shone through. In the face of uncertainty and potential loss, their spirit remained unbroken, their bond unyielding. The vast expanse of the mountain echoed with the determined calls of the search parties. From the labyrinthine tunnels that snaked deep beneath the earth to the dense canopies of the surrounding forests, every nook and cranny was scoured with fervent hope. The vast plains, with their tall grasses swaying in the wind, were combed meticulously, each step taken with the hope of uncovering a clue, a sign, any trace of the missing patrol. Days turned into nights and nights into days, with the relentless sun and the silvery moon bearing witness to the Thorazdum's unwavering determination. Campfires dotted the landscape, their flickering flames a beacon of hope in the enveloping darkness, as the search parties regrouped, shared information, and pressed on.

Yet, despite their tireless efforts and the vast terrain covered, the mountains remained silent, offering no answers. The tunnels, usually filled with the familiar sounds of mining and the soft glow of gemstones, stood eerily quiet. The forests, with their ancient trees and hidden secrets, gave no hint of the patrol's whereabouts. The plains, vast and unending, held onto their mysteries. A heavy pall of uncertainty hung over the village. The absence of any trace, any clue, was haunting. In the heart of the village, beneath the shadow of the towering mountains, Balgruff stood, his posture weighed down by the heavy decision he was about to make. The village square, usually a hub of activity, was filled with an anticipatory silence, the air thick with tension.

With a deep sigh, Balgruff raised his hand, signaling for attention. "My kin," he began, his voice carrying the weight of his responsibility, "we have searched every crevice of the mountains, every corner of the forests, and every inch of the plains. Our hearts yearn for answers, for a sign of our missing brethren." He paused, taking a moment to gather his thoughts, the weight of his next words evident in his eyes. "But the looming threat of the Kraggelm draws near. Our thârûm, our very way of life, is at stake. We must focus our energies on preparing for the battle that awaits." The murmurs of agreement and understanding rippled through the gathered crowd, but the undercurrent of sorrow was palpable. Balgruff continued, "It breaks my heart to call off the search, but we must prioritize the safety of our entire thârûm. We will honor the missing patrol in our fight, ensuring their sacrifice is not in vain."

The rhythmic cadence of the clan's preparations echoed throughout the village, a symphony of determination and unity. Amidst the clang of metal and the shouts of instruction, my attention was irresistibly drawn to the intricate designs and masterful craftsmanship of the dwarrin's weaponry. Each blade, each hilt, seemed to tell a story, their artistry an echo of the legacy and pride of the Thorazdum. As I marveled at the weapons, tracing the intricate dûrkûns etched onto a finely crafted axe, Thrumir approached, a knowing smile playing on his lips. "The weapons of the dwarrin are not just tools of war," he began, his voice filled with reverence. "They are a reflection of our history, our values, and our very soul." Guiding me through the armory, Thrumir shared tales of legendary smiths, "skaldorns", who had forged weapons of unmatched power, of battles won by the sheer might of a dwarrin blade, and of the sacred rituals involved in their creation. He spoke of the balance between form and function, how every curve and edge was meticulously crafted for both efficiency and beauty. Holding up a shield adorned with a detailed depiction of the Thorazdum, he explained, "This is not just a protective barrier; it's a symbol of our unyielding spirit, our connection to the land."

In the heart of the armory, amidst rows of gleaming weapons, Thrumir gently lifted a particularly striking axe, its presence commanding immediate attention. "This," he began with a hint of pride in his voice, "is a 'belgarn'." The belgarn was a masterpiece of dwarrin craftsmanship. Its blade, forged from the finest ores of the mountain, gleamed with a sharpness that was both menacing and mesmerizing. The edge, a stamp of countless hours of honing, promised both precision and power. But beyond its formidable appearance, the belgarn held deeper significance. "To the dwarrin," Thrumir explained, "the belgarn is not just a tool of war. It embodies our profound bond with the earth, a symbol of our ability to harness and shape the very elements that birthed our civilization." I traced my fingers over the handle, feeling the intricate carvings that adorned it. Each symbol, meticulously etched into the vorgrund, told a story of the dwarrin's rich heritage. Tales of valor, of unity, of respect for the land and its bounties. "These symbols," Thrumir continued, "are a reminder of our vows, our stendornak, and our commitment to preserving the dwarrornak of our ancestors." Holding the belgarn, I felt a surge of respect, not just for its craftsmanship but for the culture and values it represented.

Thrumir, with a gleam of reverence in his eyes, moved to a grand pedestal where a majestic hammer rested. "Aye," he whispered with a sense of awe, "the 'dammaz'." Lifting the dammaz was no small feat, its heft immediately evident, a manifestation of the dwarrin's indomitable spirit and tenacity. This was not just a tool; it was a badge of their enduring strength, their capacity to weather storms and emerge stronger, to mold and shape the very fabric of their world. "The dammaz," Thrumir began, his voice echoing the weight of the hammer's significance, "represents our unyielding spirit. In its strikes, you can feel the pulse of our determination, our resolve to stand tall, no matter the adversities we face." My eyes were drawn to the hammer's head, a canvas of intricate engravings that seemed to dance in the torchlight. Each engraving, meticulously etched with precision, told tales of the thârûm's glorious past. Battles won, challenges overcome, legacies built. "These," Thrumir pointed, his fingers tracing the patterns, "are not just designs. They are chronicles of our journey, reminders of our stendornak and the unity that binds us." Holding the dammaz, one could feel the weight of history, the pride of generations past, and the unwavering commitment of the dwarrin to forge ahead, united in purpose and spirit.

Thrumir, with a twinkle in his eye reminiscent of the night sky, unveiled a beautifully crafted set of knives, their arrangement immediately evoking images of celestial patterns. "These," he said with a touch of reverence, "are the 'stjernhalds'." The term "stjernhald" directly translated to "constellation," but in the hands of the dwarrin, it took on a dual meaning. These were not just throwing knives; they were a celestial symphony in vorgrund, each blade representing a star, their collective form a testimony to the dwarrin's connection to the cosmos.

"These knives," Thrumir began, his fingers delicately lifting one, "embody our bond with the night sky, our understanding of the rhythms and mysteries of the universe." The blade caught the ambient light, reflecting it in a dance of shimmering patterns. Its edge was honed to perfection, promising precision, while its form whispered of grace and elegance. The craftsmanship of the stjernhalds was unparalleled, each knife a masterpiece of balance and beauty. "In the hands of a skilled dwarrin," Thrumir explained, "these knives dance, their trajectories as predictable as the paths of the stjernazs - the stars - yet as mesmerizing as a meteor's trail." Holding one of the stjernhalds, I felt a deeper connection to the world of the dwarrin, their reverence for the cosmos, and their ability to blend artistry with purpose, creating tools that were both functional and breathtakingly beautiful.

As Thrumir guided me through the lore and craftsmanship of these weapons, I came to understand their importance in dwarrin culture. I also came to understand the symbolic meanings of these weapons, their connection to the earth, the stars, and the unyielding strength of the dwarrin. They were a reflection of their worldview, their understanding of the complex dance of life and conflict, their respect for the balance that governed their world.Under the gentle guidance of Thrumir, the armory transformed from a mere collection of weapons to a living museum, each artifact echoing tales of the dwarrin's rich heritage. As I delved deeper into the lore and artistry behind each weapon, the very fabric of dwarrin culture unraveled before me.

The "belgarn," with its earthy connection, spoke of the dwarrin's symbiotic relationship with the land, their reverence for its bounties, and their role as its stewards. The "dammaz," mighty and unyielding, mirrored their resilience, their ability to shape their destiny, much like the hammer shapes the metal. The "stjernhalds," with their celestial inspiration, were a pointer to their cosmic consciousness, their understanding of the vast universe and their place within it. But beyond the tangible, these weapons held deeper symbolic meanings. They were not just tools of combat; they were philosophical compasses, guiding the dwarrin through the intricate dance of existence. The balance of the blades, the precision of the throws, the strength of the strikes, all mirrored the dwarrin's understanding of life's delicate equilibrium. Thrumir's teachings illuminated this worldview, revealing a culture that revered the balance between might and mind, between the tangible and the ethereal. "Our weapons," he often said, "are but an extension of our beliefs, our respect for the forces that shape our world." Through this journey, I came to see the dwarrin not just as skilled warriors and artisans, but as philosophers, their weapons a reflection of their profound understanding of the intricate tapestry of life, conflict, and the eternal balance that governs all. With every tale Thrumir spun, the world of the dwarrin unfolded before me, each narrative thread weaving a tapestry rich in tradition, honor, and reverence for Krüma. Their tales were not just of battles and bravery but of a deep-rooted connection to the land, the stars, and the very essence of existence. The more I listened, the more I was drawn into this mesmerizing world, a realm where strength met wisdom, where pride was tempered with humility.

Thrumir, sensing the spark of curiosity in my eyes, gestured towards a magnificent door at the far end of the armory. The door itself was a work of art, adorned with intricate carvings that seemed to dance and shimmer in the torchlight. Scenes of valor, of unity, of the dwarrin's bond with Krüma were etched into its surface, each detail meticulously crafted. With a gentle push, the door swung open, revealing a chamber that took my breath away. The room was a masterful blend of architecture and artistry, its walls and ceiling polished to a mirror-like sheen. The reflections created a mesmerizing kaleidoscope, showcasing the legendary weapons and armor that adorned the room. Each piece, from the mightiest axe to the most delicate circlet, was displayed with reverence, their histories and significance palpable in the air.

"This," Thrumir whispered, his voice filled with pride, "is the heart of our heritage, the essence of the Thorazdum." As I stepped further into the chamber, I felt an overwhelming sense of awe, a realization that I was not just exploring a culture but stepping into a living legacy, a world where the past and present converged in a dance of honor, strength, and profound respect. Amidst the myriad of weapons and artifacts, Thrumir guided me to a pedestal at the center of the chamber. Resting upon it was a hammer of unparalleled grandeur, its very presence commanding reverence. "This dammaz," Thrumir began, his voice tinged with a mix of pride and humility, "is my life's work." The hammer, carved from the heart of the mountain, bore the weight and resilience of the ages. Its stone surface, though rugged, gleamed with a polish that spoke of countless hours of dedication. It was not just a tool; it was a vindication of Thrumir's mastery, a symbol of the dwarrin's unparalleled craftsmanship. But what truly captivated me were the intricate dûrkûns that adorned the hammer. These runes, etched with precision along the shaft and the flat ends, shimmered with an ethereal glow. Each dûrkûn was more than just a design; it was a word of power, a conduit of magic. "Every dûrkûn," Thrumir explained, his fingers tracing the symbols, "imbues this dammaz with a distinct enchantment, a gift from the cosmos, a reflection of our bond with Krüma." Holding the hammer, I could feel the energy pulsating through it, the weight of the enchantments, the legacy of the dwarrin. It was a bridge between the tangible and the mystical, a proclamation of the dwarrin's understanding of the delicate balance between craft and Alara. In the hallowed silence of the chamber, Thrumir's voice resonated, each word imbued with reverence as he began to unveil the mysteries of the hammer's enchantments. With every rune he named, the history and essence of the dwarrin seemed to come alive, echoing tales of valor, wisdom, and the intricate dance of battle.

"*Fin*," he murmured, his fingertip gently caressing the rune, its glow intensifying momentarily. "Enduring," he translated, a reminder of the dwarrin's resilience, their ability to withstand the tests of time and adversity.

"*Bel*," his voice deepened, moving to the next rune. "War," he explained, a symbol of their warrior spirit, their readiness to defend their honor and homeland.

"*Gareth*," he whispered, the shadows in the room seeming to deepen. "Shadow," a nod to their ability to move stealthily, to strike from the unseen.

"*Fuga*," he continued, the rune shimmering with a fleeting light. "Flee," not a sign of cowardice, but of strategic retreat, of knowing when to fight and when to regroup.

"*Mor*," he intoned, the weight of the word palpable. "Break," a promise of the hammer's might, its ability to shatter barriers and defenses.

"*Kan*," he said with a protective undertone. "Shield," a symbol of defense, of the dwarrin's commitment to safeguard their kin and legacy.

"*Brog*," he concluded, the rune pulsating with intensity. "Fury," a reflection of their passion, their unwavering spirit in the face of challenges.

Drawing back, Thrumir gazed at the hammer with a mix of pride and reverence. "Kronthar," he declared, "the Shieldbreaker." The name was not just a title; it was a proclamation of the hammer's formidable power and the genius of its creator. As I beheld Kronthar, a profound respect welled within me.

After the reverent unveiling of Kronthar, Thrumir's demeanor shifted slightly, from pride in personal creation to a broader appreciation for the collective mastery of his people. With a gesture, he beckoned me to follow him deeper into the chamber, where other magnificent creations stood in assertion of the skill of the dwarrin. "As you've seen with Kronthar," he began, his voice filled with a warmth that spoke of community and kinship, "each weapon here is not just a tool, but a story, a legacy of its creator and our thârûm." As we meandered through the armory, Thrumir paused before each artifact, sharing tales of the artisans behind them, their inspirations, and how they represented thârûm as a whole. Each story was a window into the rich tapestry of the Thorazdum culture, their values, and their deep-rooted sense of community.

"You've heard the term 'thârûm' often," Thrumir mused, catching my inquisitive gaze. "In your tongue, it might closely resemble 'clan'.

But for us, it's more profound." He paused, searching for the right words. "Imagine an extended family, bound not just by blood but by a shared passion, a craft that defines them, that courses through their veins." He gestured around the room, "Every masterpiece here is a proclamation of our thârûm's dedication, our collective spirit channeled into their craft. It's more than just a clan; it's a living legacy, a continuum of shared knowledge and purpose. When the fires of battle with the Kraggelm first began to roar, these weapons and armor became the foundation of our thârûm. For the first hundred or so cycles, we had begun to establish ourselves as a thârûm of enchantments. My grandest great father was the first Thorazdum runekeeper - a skill that has been passed down through the generations of my blood, but was given up as a thârûm in favor of arms crafting for defense against the Kraggelm." As Thrumir spoke, I began to grasp the depth of the dwarrin's communal bond. The term 'thârûm' was not just a label; it was an embodiment of their ethos, a reflection of their intertwined destinies, and their unwavering commitment to their craft and kin.

Thrumir's steps led me to a magnificent battleaxe, its presence dominating the space around it. "Behold," he whispered with a sense of reverence, "Mornath, the Earth Cleaver." The battleaxe was a masterpiece of design and function. Crafted by Haldorr, the renowned grand blacksmith of the thârûm, its reputation was legendary. The blade, forged from the heart of the Thorazdum mountains, gleamed with a sharpness that seemed almost otherworldly. Thrumir recounted tales of its edge, so finely honed that it could effortlessly split the delicate beard hair of a dwarrin maiden. But Mornath was more than just its blade. The head of the axe bore intricate geometric patterns, each one meticulously etched to resemble the rugged mountains and steadfast rocks. It was a tribute, an homage to the very earth from which its metal was birthed. Drawing my attention to the handle, Thrumir spoke of its origin. Wrapped in a rich, dark leather, it bore the mark of a formidable beast, one that Haldorr had faced and defeated in a legendary duel of strength and wit. The beast's demise had not been in vain; its hide now adorned Mornath's shaft, while its meat had nourished the thârûm, sustaining them for three bountiful weeks. As Thrumir described Mornath's prowess, his voice was tinged with awe. "This belgarn," he declared, "is not just a weapon. In the hands of a skilled dwarrin, it can cleave through solid stone as if parting the very air."

Holding Mornath, one could feel the weight of its legacy, the pride of its creator, and the indomitable spirit of the dwarrin. It was a display of their craftsmanship, their connection to the earth, and their tales of valor and triumph.

Guiding me further into the armory, Thrumir paused before a warhammer that exuded an aura of both reverence and power. "This," he began, his voice filled with a mix of awe and pride, "is Thuldrum, known as the Forge's Breath." Thuldrum was not just a weapon; it was a marvel of dwarrin innovation. Crafted from the finest steel, one aspect of uniqueness lay in its core, which was infused with melted gemstones, giving it a lustrous sheen and unmatched strength. Thrumir recounted its history, explaining that Thuldrum was the first weapon in the thârûm to be forged from steel, marking a pivotal moment in their metallurgical journey. And such was its unparalleled craftsmanship and rarity of metal that it would remain the last weapon forged with steel for centuries. The warhammer's design was both functional and imposing. Its massive head bore two distinct sides: one flat, designed for delivering crushing blows, and the other, a menacing spike, promising deadly precision. But Thuldrum's true marvel was its ability to glow with a fierce red-hot intensity when swung, a feature imbued by Balgruff, the esteemed leader of the thârûm. This ethereal glow was not just for show; it was a symbol, a manifestation of the forge's fury and passion, burning hot enough to melt a vorgrund wall when the enchantment was called upon.

Drawing me towards the end of the chamber, Thrumir gestured to a beautifully crafted shortsword, its elegance and design immediately captivating. "This," he began, his voice imbued with a deep respect, "is Galaron, known to many as the Echo Blade." Galaron was a witness to the artistry and innovation of the dwarrin. Forged by Borgrim, the talented eldest son of Bruna, it was crafted from a unique blend of metals: the warm hue of copper intertwined with the lustrous sheen of silver. The result was a blade that was as mesmerizing to behold as it was formidable in combat. Despite its slender and almost ethereal appearance, Galaron was no mere ornament. It was a weapon of precision and power. Its name, Galaron, or the "Echo Blade", was derived from the distinctive resonating sound it produced upon striking. This wasn't just a clang of metal; it was a hum, a vibration that seemed to echo the very power and essence of the blade. Thrumir, holding the blade up to the light, spoke of its prowess. "In the hands of its master," he explained, "Galaron's strikes are as swift and relentless as sound itself. Its resonance is not just an auditory marvel but a benchmark of its perfect balance and design."

As the tales of the legendary weapons came to a close, Thrumir paused, taking a moment to absorb the grandeur of the chamber around us. The weight of history, the pride of craftsmanship, and the essence of the dwarrin seemed to envelop the room. With a deep, contented sigh, he looked around, a hint of satisfaction gleaming in his eyes, as if he was silently paying homage to the legacy of his people.

Turning his gaze to me, he inquired, "How fares your training with the dwarrin dagger I lent you?" His voice held a genuine curiosity, a mentor's concern for a pupil's progress. I hesitated for a moment, searching for the right words.

"It's a marvel," I began, "far superior to the rudimentary spear I crafted from the bones of a venombiter at the outset of my journey." Thrumir considered my words, his brow furrowing in thought. The silence stretched for a moment, filled with the echoes of our earlier conversation. Finally, he spoke,

"Training and adaptation are crucial, especially in these times. But rest is equally important." With a gentle nod, he advised, "You should retire for the evening, gather your strength for the days ahead." He paused, glancing towards the chamber's exit. "I'll be heading home shortly myself. But first, I have a matter to discuss with Haldorr." As Thrumir's words settled, I felt a mix of gratitude and admiration. Here was a leader of sorts, a mentor, who not only understood the weight of our situation but also the importance of balance, of rest and preparation, of duty and care.

As dawn broke the next day, and in the days that followed, the village was a hive of activity. The rhythmic cadence of hammers striking anvils, the determined shouts of warriors in training, and the hum of preparations for the impending confrontation with the Kraggelm thârûm filled the air. Yet, amidst this cacophony of preparation, I found myself drawn into a quieter, yet equally profound journey - a deep dive into the very soul of the dwarrin culture. Thrumir, with the wisdom of a sage and the patience of a seasoned mentor, became my guide through this intricate tapestry of values and beliefs. He began with "Stendûr," a term that resonated with depth and significance. It wasn't just about loyalty; it was the very essence of the bond that each dwarrin shared with their thârûm. More profound than mere allegiance, Stendûr encapsulated a trust so deep, a unity so profound, that it bound them together, especially in times of adversity. It was the invisible thread that stitched the fabric of their society, ensuring that no dwarrin ever stood alone. But the lessons didn't stop there. Thrumir delved into "Thorâk," a term that evoked the fierce spirit of the dwarrin in battle. It wasn't just about martial prowess or physical might. Thorâk was the embodiment of valor, of an unwavering spirit that refused to yield, even in the face of overwhelming odds. It was about defending not just their homes, but the very values and principles that defined them, with a resolve that was as steadfast as the mountains they called home. As Thrumir imparted these teachings, I began to realize that, for the dwarrin, these weren't mere words or abstract concepts. They were the very bedrock of their existence, the pillars that upheld their society. They were the compass that guided their every action, the ethos that shaped their identity.

With each passing day, as I stood shoulder to shoulder with the villagers, immersed in the rhythm of their preparations and the cadence of their training, a profound realization began to dawn upon me. The tales and teachings of Thrumir were not mere stories; they were alive, palpable in every gesture, every glance, every strike of the dwarrin. The essence of Stendûr was evident in the way the villagers came together, their collective efforts seamlessly intertwining. It was in the way they supported one another, the way a seasoned warrior would guide a novice, the way a blacksmith would lend a hand to a builder. It was in their shared laughter, their mutual respect, their unwavering commitment to the well-being of their thârûm. Every gesture, every word, every shared moment was an acknowledgement of the deep bond of trust and unity that Stendûr represented. Thorâk, on the other hand, was a fire that burned brightly in their eyes. It was in the fierce determination that marked their faces as they trained, the unyielding spirit that refused to waver, even in the face of daunting challenges. It was in the way they stood tall, as tall as their short frames would allow, ready to defend their homes, their families, their very way of life. The very ground seemed to resonate with their resolve, their unwavering spirit echoing the tales of valor and courage that Thrumir had shared.

With each sunrise that painted the horizon, my role within the village continued evolving. The knowledge and skills I had garnered from my own tribal upbringing began to find their place amidst the dwarrin's preparations, blending seamlessly into their tapestry of defense. As I worked alongside the dwarrin, there was a harmonious melding of hands and hearts. The barricades, once mere constructs of wood and stone, began to embody our collective spirit. My hands, guided by the wisdom of my tribe, moved in tandem with the skilled hands of the dwarrin, each nail driven, each stone positioned, becoming a touchstone of our shared purpose and unity. Beyond the physical labor, I found opportunities to share the strategic insights of my people. As I spoke, the dwarrin gathered around, their attentive eyes and nodding heads a clear indication of the respect they held for the knowledge I brought. My words, once foreign, now wove into their plans, bridging the gap between our cultures and strengthening the bond that had grown between us. The days were a dance of collaboration, where the lines between the dwarrin and me began to blur. In this shared endeavor, our differences became our strength, and the bonds that blossomed were a chronicle of the power of uniting, of learning from one another, and of standing united in the face of adversity.

As the days melded into one another, a subtle shift began to manifest within the village. The initial wariness that had marked the villagers' interactions with me began to wane, replaced by a growing sense of camaraderie and respect. It was evident in the minutiae of their gestures, in the warmth that now tinged their glances. The nods that once held a hint of skepticism now conveyed approval. Shared smiles, once reserved, now blossomed freely, echoing the mutual respect that had grown between us. Conversations flowed more easily, with villagers pausing in their tasks to exchange words, eager to listen, to learn, and to share in the knowledge I brought. The boundaries that had once defined me as an outsider began to dissolve, replaced by an unspoken understanding that I was now an integral part of their community. My efforts, my contributions, had woven me into the very fabric of their society. I was no longer a mere observer, standing on the periphery. I had become a part of their collective heartbeat, a fellow defender of the home and values they held dear.

Amidst the fervor of battle preparations, I found myself drawn into the intricate tapestry of the dwarrin language. The words, each carrying the weight of tradition and meaning, became a daily pursuit for me. I practiced their pronunciations, rolling the sounds off my tongue, savoring the rhythm and cadence unique to their dialect. I delved deep into terms related to warfare and defense. "Thorâk," which encapsulated the essence of battle, became a word I would often murmur under my breath, feeling its power. After some time, I learned the difference between the names of their weapons, "Thorgarnak," and the titles bestowed upon their warriors, "Thorgornak." The principles of honor and bravery were encapsulated in words like "Stendornak" for honor and "Stendûr" for loyalty. The language, with its complexities, was a dance of tradition and meaning. Words like "Krüma," referring to Alara. I was determined to not just learn but to understand, to immerse myself in the nuances and intricacies of their speech. With each word I practiced, with each phrase I uttered, I felt a deeper connection to the dwarrin. Their language was a bridge, linking me to their world, their values, their essence. It was a journey of discovery, of understanding, of communication, and I was wholeheartedly committed to it.

The sun cast long shadows across the fortified village, its golden hue reflecting off the newly erected barricades. The air was thick with anticipation, the Thorazdum dwarrin moving with purpose, their every action a paragon of their unwavering resolve. Amidst this hive of activity, Thrumir and I stood on a vantage point, our eyes scanning the landscape, taking in the fruits of our collective labor. The unity of the Thorazdum was palpable. Their shared determination, their collective spirit, their unwavering commitment to their principles of honor and bravery – it was all evident in their every gesture, their every word. I stood beside Thrumir, the weight of the impending conflict pressed heavily on my heart.

Breaking the silence, I turned to him, my voice carrying the weight of my thoughts. "Thrumir, have we considered every path? Every possibility?" I began, choosing my words carefully. "While we prepare for war, might there be another way? A way that could spare both the Thorazdum and the Kraggelm the devastation of conflict?" Thrumir's gaze met mine, his eyes searching, weighing my words. I continued, "What if we were to send a peace delegation to the Kraggelm? A group that could represent your thârûm, that could communicate our desire for a peaceful resolution, our willingness to find common ground?" The suggestion hung in the air, creating a tension that thickened with each passing moment. The weight of my suggestion seemed to settle heavily upon Thrumir. For a moment, he stood silent, his gaze distant, lost in thought. The lines on his face deepened, and a shadow of sorrow passed over his eyes. The gentle breeze rustled his beard as he took a deep, contemplative breath.

"Agh, I wish it were so simple," he began, his voice carrying a depth of emotion, a mix of hope and resignation, his fatigue evident in the shortened, less formal words he used. "Believe me, lad, I'd give anything t'avoid th'impending bloodshed, to spare our people the 'orrors o' war." His eyes, usually so full of fire and determination, now held a hint of sadness. "The thought o' losing even one o'our Thorazdum kin t' the Kraggelm's ruthlessness weighs heavy on me." He paused, collecting his thoughts before continuing, "But the Kraggelm... they're a diff'rent breed. Their hist'ry, their actions, have shown us they're not ones to heed reason 'r diplomacy. Their thirst f'r power, f'r dominance, often blinds 'em to the path o' peace." Thrumir's gaze met mine, his eyes searching for understanding. "The council 'n' I've deliberated on this, weighed every option, every possible course o' action. And while the path o' diplomacy's noble, we fear it may fall on deaf ears. The risk, the potential cost, is too great."

As he spoke, the gravity of our situation became even clearer. The choices before us were not easy, and the road ahead was fraught with uncertainty. But in Thrumir's words, in his resolve, I saw the heart of a leader, one who bore the weight of his people's fate with courage and determination. As I stood beside Thrumir, listening to the weight of his words, observing the depth of his emotions, a realization began to dawn upon me. While Balgruff was undeniably the leader of the Thorazdum thârûm, a position he held with grace and wisdom, there was something about Thrumir that exuded a quiet, unassuming leadership. It was in the way he spoke, the way he carried himself, the way he interacted with the villagers. There was a magnetism, a natural authority that drew people to him, that made them listen, that inspired trust. Yet, what struck me most was the humility that underpinned Thrumir's strength. He never sought the spotlight, never desired the mantle of leadership. He was content in his role as the Dûrkûrharn, the Runekeeper. His passion lay in the intricate art of enchanting, in imbuing the thârûm's weapons with dûrkûns that harnessed Alara's primal powers. His dedication to this craft, to ensuring the safety and strength of his people, was evident in every rune he etched, every enchantment he invoked. But beyond his craft, Thrumir's heart was that of a true servant leader. He was always there, ready to step in, to offer guidance, to take on whatever task Balgruff, their revered Kazardornak, deemed essential for the thârûm. His commitment was unwavering, his loyalty unquestionable. In the quiet moments, as I observed Thrumir, I couldn't help but wonder what the Thorazdum thârûm would look like under his leadership. Not that I doubted Balgruff's capabilities, but there was something about Thrumir, a depth of understanding, a compassion, a strength that was both gentle and firm. Yet, I also sensed that Thrumir would never desire such power or responsibility. He was content in his role, in his service, in his dedication to the thârûm. And that, in itself, I thought, was a standard of the true heart of a leader.

Taking a deep breath, I mustered the courage to press on, feeling the weight of the situation and the importance of exploring every avenue for peace. "What if," I began, choosing my words carefully, "we approached this differently? Instead of a full delegation, perhaps a smaller party could be sent to the Kraggelm. A party that wouldn't risk the loss of a valuable member of the thârûm." I paused, gauging Thrumir's reaction, before continuing, "I could lead - or even be the sole constituent of this party. My outsider status might be an advantage, a neutral presence that could bridge the gap between our two peoples." The idea hung in the air for a moment, and I pressed on, "Instead of territorial claims, we could offer the Kraggelm a compromise - some of the urkhas they seek. You have a surplus, and it could be a gesture of goodwill, a way to broker peace. Furthermore, we could propose a consistent supply of the urkhas from the mountain each cycle, forging not just a truce but a lasting alliance." I could see the gears turning in Thrumir's mind, the weight of the decision evident in his eyes. The silence that followed my proposal was palpable, the tension in the air thick enough to cut with a knife. Thrumir's gaze, usually so sharp and decisive, now bore a contemplative look, his eyes searching the horizon as if seeking answers from the mountains themselves. Slowly, the stern lines of his face began to soften, giving way to a thoughtful expression. It was clear that my words had resonated, that they had sparked something within him. The traditional dwarrin way was to stand firm, to defend their honor and their home with unwavering resolve. But here was a different approach, a path less traveled, a possibility of forging a new future.

He turned to face me, his eyes meeting mine with an intensity that spoke volumes. Thrumir leaned back, his voice resonating like the deep vibrations of a mountain's heart. "Your suggestion, young one, is like a vein of urkhas hidden in solid duron. Not the traditional dwarrin path, I'll grant you that, but it sparkles with potential." His eyes, wise and reflective, considered the prospect, feeling the shift in the atmosphere. "A chance to sidestep the dark clouds of war, to find a path less traveled by our ancestors but urkazen in promise." He let the words settle, letting their echoes fill the chamber, and his gaze settled on the distant walls as if seeing far beyond them. When he turned back, his eyes were filled with the spark of possibility, and his voice carried the weight of his experience. "There's wisdom in these durorns, deeper than the roots of our ancient thordum, but sometimes, it takes fresh eyes to see new paths. Your idea, though unorthodox, holds the glimmer of hope." A slow smile spread across his face, and he nodded, his tone resolute. "We shall carry this to the council, for even the sturdiest of traditions must sometimes bend to embrace the future."

As dawn's first light painted the sky, Thrumir and I made our way to the council chamber. The weight of the proposal pressed heavily on my shoulders, but Thrumir's reassuring presence beside me bolstered my confidence. As we approached the grand entrance, the intricate carvings on the door seemed to tell tales of past deliberations, of decisions that had shaped the fate of the Thorazdum thârûm. Balgruff, with his imposing stature, sat at the head of the table, awaiting our arrival, his eyes reflecting the wisdom of countless seasons. To his right was Bruna, her historian's mind a repository of the thârûm's past, her insights invaluable in guiding its future. Fargrim, with his age-worn face, represented the voice of tradition, his cycles lending a depth of understanding to the proceedings. And Haldorr, the grand blacksmith, whose hands had shaped many a dwarrin weapon, brought a practical perspective to the table. Thrumir cleared his throat, drawing the council's attention. With a nod from Balgruff, he began to relay our proposal. The idea of sending a peace delegation, of offering the Kraggelm a consistent supply of urkhas, was laid out in detail. The room was thick with anticipation as each word was weighed, each possibility considered. The ensuing discussion was a dance of intellect and emotion. Bruna, with her historian's perspective, drew parallels from past conflicts, highlighting instances where diplomacy had borne fruit. Fargrim, ever the traditionalist, voiced concerns about deviating from the dwarrin way, but also acknowledged the potential benefits of forging a new path. Haldorr, practical as ever, pondered the logistics, the feasibility of the proposed urkhas supply. As the debate ebbed and flowed, the council's collective wisdom shone through. Each voice, each perspective, added layers to the discussion, painting a nuanced picture of the challenges and opportunities that lay ahead. The looming threat of the Kraggelm hung over the proceedings like a shadow, a constant reminder of the stakes at hand. The weight of the decision was palpable, the air thick with tension and hope. But amidst the uncertainty, one thing was clear: the Thorazdum thârûm was united in its quest for a peaceful resolution, its heart and soul committed to finding a path that would ensure the safety and prosperity of its people. Standing amidst the council, the weight of the moment pressed heavily upon me. The chamber, usually filled with the steady hum of deliberation, was now thick with anticipation. Each decision made within these walls had the power to shape the destiny of the Thorazdum, and I felt the gravity of that responsibility.

Balgruff, with his imposing presence, leaned forward, his fingers steepled in contemplation. His eyes, which had seen countless seasons and faced innumerable challenges, bore into me, assessing the merit of the proposal. Those eyes had witnessed the Kraggelm's transgressions firsthand, had seen their hunger for territory and dominance. They held a wariness, a caution born from experience. Yet, as I spoke, weaving a vision of a peaceful resolution, I saw a subtle shift in Balgruff's demeanor. The hard lines of skepticism began to soften, replaced by a thoughtful consideration. He was a leader who knew the price of war, who had seen the pain and loss it brought. The idea of a diplomatic solution, of a chance to avoid that pain, resonated with him. Drawing a deep breath, Balgruff finally broke the silence. "While I have reservations," he began, his voice resonating with authority, "I cannot ignore the potential of this path. We must explore every avenue, every possibility, to protect our thârûm." His words, filled with both caution and hope, echoed in the chamber, met with a chorus of nods and murmurs. The silence that followed Balgruff's agreement was almost tangible, the air in the chamber thick with the weight of the decision. His voice, a bastion of authority, had set the course, and the ripples of his words spread through the room. Faces that had been etched with worry now showed traces of hope, though the undercurrent of apprehension remained, an omen of the gravity of the situation.

With the decision made, the focus shifted to the composition of the delegation. Thrumir, with his vast knowledge of dwarrin traditions and his steadfast dedication to the thârûm, was an obvious choice. His presence would lend credibility and weight to our mission. My inclusion was a nod to the fresh perspective I brought, my proposal having paved the way for this diplomatic endeavor. Joining us were several esteemed members of the thârûm, each chosen for their unique strengths and insights. Their inclusion spoke volumes about their stature within the community, their cycles of service and wisdom making them invaluable representatives. As the delegation was finalized, the enormity of our task became clear. We were not just individuals; we were the voice of the Thorazdum, the bearers of their hopes and fears. Our mission was to bridge the chasm of mistrust, to find common ground in a landscape marred by conflict. The weight of this responsibility pressed down on us, but it was also a guiding light that spoke of the trust the thârûm had placed in us. We were united in purpose, determined to seek a path of peace in the shadow of war.

In the days leading up to our departure, the village was a hive of activity. Supplies were gathered, provisions packed, and strategies discussed. Thrumir and I, along with the other members of the delegation, pored over maps, familiarizing ourselves with the terrain and plotting our course. Every detail was considered, every eventuality planned for. The cart we were to take was a robust, wooden structure, its wheels carved from the heartwood of ancient trees, and its frame reinforced with vorgrund bands. The barrels, each meticulously crafted by Haldorr, were filled to the brim with the shimmering urkhas ore. The golden gleam of the ore caught the sunlight, casting a warm glow that contrasted starkly with the gravity of our mission. The promise of seven barrels per cycle was a significant offering, a recognition of the Thorazdum's commitment to peace. As the day of our departure dawned, a somber mood enveloped the village. The usual sounds of laughter and the clinking of tools were replaced by hushed conversations and whispered prayers. The villagers, in a show of solidarity, gathered in the village square, forming a sea of faces, each one telling a story of hope, fear, and unwavering support. Children clung to their parents, their innocent eyes wide with a mix of curiosity and apprehension. Elders, their faces lined with the wisdom of cycles, offered silent blessings, their hands raised in a gesture of protection. Friends and families came forward, embracing members of the delegation, their hugs tight with emotion, their words a mix of encouragement and caution.

As we climbed onto the cart, the weight of our responsibility pressing down on us, the villagers' gaze followed. Their eyes, usually sparkling with mirth and mischief, were now pools of hope and trust. In their silent watch, we felt the collective heartbeat of the Thorazdum, a rhythm of unity and determination, urging us forward on our mission of peace. The path to the Kraggelm's territory wound through dense forests, over craggy hills, and across whispering meadows. The wilderness around us was a tapestry of nature's beauty, but its splendor was overshadowed by the gravity of our mission. Each step we took was deliberate, the rhythmic clopping of the cart's wheels and the soft thud of our boots the only sounds breaking the stillness. Birds occasionally flitted overhead, their songs muted, as if they too sensed the importance of our journey.

The trees gradually gave way to a more open landscape as we neared Kraggelm territory. The change in scenery was mirrored by a shift in the atmosphere. The air grew colder, the wind carrying with it whispers of uncertainty. The once vibrant hues of the forest were replaced by the stark, rugged beauty of the Kraggelm lands. As we entered their domain, we were immediately met with a reception that was as cold as the wind that swept through the plains. Kraggelm warriors, their faces painted with fierce patterns and their bodies adorned with armor, stood in formation, their eyes scrutinizing our every move. Their expressions were a mix of suspicion and curiosity, their postures rigid with readiness.

Behind the frontline of warriors, we could see clusters of Kraggelm villagers, their gazes equally wary. Children peeked out from behind their elders, their innocence juxtaposed against the tense atmosphere. The silence was almost deafening, broken only by the occasional rustle of armor or the distant cry of a bird. Our delegation halted, the weight of countless eyes upon us. The tension in the air was a tangible force, pressing down on us, reminding us of the delicate nature of our mission and the fine line we tread between peace and conflict. The grand hall of the Kraggelm was a vast expanse, its walls adorned with intricate carvings that told tales of their history and conquests. Towering pillars, hewn from the very mountains that surrounded their territory, held up the cavernous ceiling. Torches lined the walls, their flames casting flickering shadows that danced in tandem with the stories etched into the stone. The atmosphere was thick with anticipation, every echo, every footstep magnified in the silence that preceded our proposal. Standing before Grommok, the Kraggelm's imposing Kazadornak, we began to lay out our proposal. His throne was a monolithic structure, carved from a single block of obsidian, its dark surface contrasting sharply with the golden sheen of the urkhas barrels we had brought. As we spoke, our voices resonated through the hall, the words carrying the weight of our hopes and the gravity of the situation.

We spoke of a future where Thorazdum and Kraggelm could coexist, where mutual respect and shared interests could pave the way for cooperation and peace. The cart laden with urkhas ore stood as a tribute to our sincerity, its gleaming contents a symbol of our commitment to finding a peaceful resolution. Yet, as we presented our case, it was clear that Grommok's attention was divided. His large frame shifted restlessly upon his throne, his fingers drumming an impatient rhythm on its armrests. Every so often, he would beckon a Kraggelm maiden, whispering instructions that sent her scurrying off, only to return moments later with an assortment of delicacies. He would take a bite, his gaze wandering, seemingly more interested in the flavors of his meal than the words we spoke.

The contrast between the gravity of our proposal and Grommok's apparent disinterest was insulting. Each gesture, each distracted glance, added to the tension in the room, making the already challenging task of diplomacy even more daunting. Yet, we pressed on, our determination unwavering, our hope undiminished. In the grand hall of the Kraggelm, a vast chamber adorned with banners depicting their conquests and intricate carvings of their history, we stood before Grommok, the Kraggelm's Kazadornak, awaiting his answer. As we finished presenting our proposal, Grommok, with a wave of his hand, signaled one of his guards. "Fetch them," he commanded in a voice that resonated through the hall. We exchanged glances, uncertain of who "them" referred to.

Grommok reclined, his grand throne cradling his form as his eyes, sharp and assessing, wandered over each visitor. A smile, as cold as the wind through the mountain's peaks, played on his lips. "Ah, my unexpected guests, you come into the heart of Kraggelm, bearing the frail olive branch of peace?" His voice, smooth and insidious, wrapped around the room. "You must understand, we Kraggelm are like the molten lava beneath the earth's crust, ceaseless, relentless, and forged by pressure and heat."

He leaned forward, eyes gleaming with a dark fire. "You speak of respect? Respect is the clash of swords, the taste of victory, the cry of the vanquished. It's a treasure hard-earned through blood and vorgrund, not mere words." His gaze locked onto the cart of urkhas, and his smile widened, turning into a predatory grin. "Urkhas, now that's a symbol, isn't it? Shiny, alluring... but without edge or bite. Much like your proposition."

His voice dropped, becoming a velvet whisper, laden with menace. "Our dwarrornak is carved with the thorgarnaks of conquerors, written in the ink of our enemies' blood. We do not bend; we break. We do not follow; we lead. We do not plead; we demand." He paused, letting the silence deepen, his words a suffocating blanket of dread. "Your offer is... interesting. A trinket, a bauble. But know this, peace with the Kraggelm is not bought; it's won. And winning," his eyes narrowed, voice dripping with cruel amusement, "requires more than shiny trinkets. It demands the courage to dance with the flames, to embrace the chaos, to face the terror of the Kraggelm and survive." His laugh, soft and cold, lingered in the air, a haunting echo of his dark promise.

Grommok's eyes glinted, a cold fire burning within them, as he regarded the assembled group. "Ah, the veins of urkhas, pulsing deep within your thordum's bosom," he began, his voice as smooth as sharpened steel, laced with dark promise. "We did not approach your village on a mere fancy. It was a proclamation of our barornak, a testament to the Kraggelm's indomitable will." His voice grew more intense, the words tumbling out like stones in an avalanche. "Idle threats are for the weak, the indecisive. When I declared our intent, it was a vow - a sacred oath carved in the very durorns of our conviction." He leaned in, his presence filling the room, his eyes piercing. "To you, urkhas may be a symbol of prosperity, a glinting treasure to hoard. To us, it is the heartbeat of the thordum, a manifestation of our strength, our dominion, our destiny." His voice dropped to a chilling whisper, a velvet caress hiding a lethal edge. "Your thordum sings a song of power, and we will not be deaf to its call. We will not be swayed by mere words or feeble offers. The urkhas calls to us, and we will answer, with force." He sat back, the cold smile returning to his lips, a promise and a warning intertwined. "We will take what is ours, and woe to those who stand in our path. The Kraggelm's hunger is never sated, and our reach," he paused, his eyes narrowing, "is as endless as the thordum's depths."

The heavy doors of the hall creaked open, drawing our attention. The dwarrin guard returned, and behind him, a sight that sent a chill down our spines. Several prisoners, their faces battered and bruised, were dragged into the hall. They wore heavy chains made of vordgrund, which clinked with every step they took. Their eyes, once filled with the fire of the Thorazdum spirit, now held a mix of pain and defiance. Recognition dawned on us as we took note of their tattered green and brown cloaks, and the worn gray boots the prisoners wore. They were members of the Thorazdum thârûm, the very patrol that had gone missing weeks ago, after being sent out to request aid from the Thorazdum's allied thârûms. Their appearance confirmed our worst fears and added a new layer of complexity to our negotiations. Grommok smirked, clearly enjoying the shock on our faces. "You understand," Grommok purred, his eyes flicking towards the captives with a glimmer of dark delight, "the Kraggelm's way is to seize what pleases us." His gaze then shifted to his audience, ensnaring them with a stare that seemed to penetrate their very souls. A grand sweep of his hand, a motion both graceful and menacing, directed his guardsmen forward. Their axes gleamed, drinking in the dim illumination of the chamber, an ominous echo of their master's intent. The air thickened, laden with a dread that seemed to suffocate the room. Everyone's breath caught, a shared anticipation of the violence that loomed. Grommok's hand rose again, slower this time, a conductor orchestrating a symphony of fear. The guardsmen's axes lifted in unison, a tribute to the relentless force that was the Kraggelm. Grommok's smile was a thing of malice, a razor-edged promise, as he declared, "We do not bargain. We do not plead. We simply take. And woe be to those who dare oppose our desires." His eyes lingered on the terrified prisoners, his satisfaction a palpable, malevolent force. "This is our strength, our dominion. And in the shadow of the Kraggelm, mercy withers and dies." A moment after he finished speaking, Grommok flung his upstretched hand downwards.

Time seemed to slow as the blades descended. The sharp, chilling sound of metal meeting flesh echoed through the hall, followed by the haunting thud of the Thorazdum citizens' heads landing on the cold, unforgiving stone. The room was filled with a deafening silence, broken only by Grommok's sinister laughter. It reverberated through the hall, a chilling reminder of the brutality and ruthlessness of the

Kraggelm's leader. The horror of the moment, the sheer finality of the act, was overwhelming, casting a shadow of despair over all Thorazdum who bore witness. Grommok's laughter subsided, and he leaned forward, his eyes piercing through the dim light, locking onto each member of our delegation. The weight of his gaze was oppressive, a tangible force that seemed to push down on us.

Grommok's voice, cool and deliberate, slithered through the room. "These prisoners," he began, his tone rich with scorn, "were not merely captured, but chosen. They stood as symbols of your defiance, your insolence in the face of the Kraggelm might. They were a testament to your arrogance, a challenge to my rule, my dominion." His words were punctuated by a silence that was thick with dread, his enjoyment of our terror evident in his predatory gaze.

"But the satisfaction I derived from their demise," he continued, his lips curling into a twisted smile, "has quenched my thirst, for now. Their suffering was a melody to my ears, a harmony of power and control." His eyes flicked over us, drinking in our horror, our disbelief. "Today, I feel magnanimous - benevolent even. You may scurry back to your holes, your kazakars, your thordum." His voice dripped with disdain, a mocking tribute to the Thorazdum heritage. "Tell your children, your thorgornaks, your people, that the shadow of the Kraggelm is stretching, growing. We will come for all that you value, all that you cherish. The veins of urkhas, the very soul of your land, it will be ours." His gesture to the corpses was casual, dismissive, a brutal reminder of our powerlessness. "Witness what we've wrought today, and know that it is but a prologue. Flee now, back to your doomed durthak, and await the tempest that will surely follow." His laughter, cold and hollow, lingered in the air long after his words had ceased, a haunting echo of the doom he had promised.

The long journey back to the village was a silent one, each step echoing the weight of our failure and the grief of our loss. The once vibrant colors of the wilderness seemed muted, the songs of the birds less cheerful, as if nature itself mourned with us. The rhythmic creaking of the cart wheels and the soft clop of our mounts' hooves were the only sounds that punctuated the oppressive silence. As we approached the village, the familiar sight of the Thorazdum homes, nestled against the backdrop of the towering mountain, brought a fresh wave of sorrow. The villagers, who had gathered in anticipation of our return, could read the outcome in our downcast eyes and slumped shoulders. Whispers spread like wildfire, and the air grew thick with grief and disbelief. Balgruff, his face etched with lines of worry, approached us, seeking confirmation of the rumors that had already begun to circulate. As Thrumir recounted the events, the leader's face grew graver with each word, the weight of leadership pressing heavily upon him. The village square, which had been a hub of activity and preparation, grew still. Children, sensing the gravity of the situation, clung to their parents, their innocent eyes wide with confusion. The elders, their faces a tapestry of wisdom and experience, whispered amongst themselves, their expressions a mix of sadness and determination.

That night, the usual sounds of camaraderie and laughter were replaced by hushed conversations and quiet sobbing. The glow of the torches seemed dimmer, their flickering flames casting long shadows that danced mournfully against the stone walls. As I lay in my makeshift bed, the weight of my failed plan pressed down on me. The hope I had held, the possibility of a peaceful resolution, had been snuffed out, replaced by the grim reality of impending war. The faces of the fallen scouts haunted my dreams, a stark reminder of the cost of conflict and the price of my failure.

The sun rose each day to a village transformed. The once open pathways were now lined with barricades, constructed from sturdy vordgrund and reinforced with thick beams of wood. Every entrance and exit was guarded, with watchtowers erected at strategic points, their silhouettes standing tall against the backdrop of the mountain. Children, who once played freely in the village square, now assisted in gathering supplies, their innocence replaced with a maturity that belied their cycles. Women, their hands once skilled in crafting and weaving, now mended armor and sharpened blades, their fingers moving with a purpose born of necessity. Men, their muscles straining, dug trenches and erected palisades, their sweat and toil an indicator of their resolve. Thrumir, with his deep knowledge of dwarrin warfare, took charge of the training sessions. The village square, which had once echoed with laughter and song, now resounded with the clash of steel and the shouts of instruction. Villagers, young and old, practiced combat techniques, their movements a dance of precision and power. Under Thrumir's watchful eye, they honed their skills, preparing for the battle that loomed on the horizon. In the evenings, the village gathered around roaring bonfires, their flames casting a warm glow against the cold stone of the dwellings. Elders recounted tales of past battles, their stories a mix of heroism and caution, serving both as inspiration and warning. Songs of valor and bravery filled the air, their melodies a balm for weary souls.

Yet, amidst the preparations, there was an undercurrent of anxiety. Hushed conversations took place in shadowed corners, as villagers discussed the impending threat of the Kraggelm. The memory of the fallen scouts was fresh in their minds, a grim reminder of the ruthlessness of their adversaries. Through it all, the spirit of the Thorazdum thârûm remained unbroken. Their unity, their shared purpose, their unwavering determination, shone through in every action, every gesture. They were a people bound by honor and tradition, ready to defend their home and their way of life against any threat. The cobblestones of the square, which had once felt the soft tread of children's feet and the rhythmic dance of festivals, now echoed with the determined steps of dwarrin warriors. Each dawn brought with it a renewed sense of purpose, as villagers gathered, weapons in hand, ready to learn and practice under Thrumir's guidance. His voice, usually reserved for tales and enchantments, now rang out with commands and corrections, shaping the thârûm into a formidable force. Metal clashed against metal, creating a symphony of determination. Villagers paired off, practicing their strikes and parries, their movements fluid and precise. Thrumir moved among them, his eyes sharp, correcting a stance here, praising a well-executed move there. Every so often, he would demonstrate a technique, his body moving with a grace and power that left no doubt about his expertise. Away from the square, atop the village's walls and towers, the lookouts kept their vigil. Their silhouettes, backlit by the setting sun or the pale moonlight, were a constant reminder of the threat that loomed. Their eyes, trained to pick out the slightest movement, scanned the landscape, searching for any sign of the Kraggelm. Every rustle of leaves, every snap of a twig, was cause for alertness. As night descended, the village took on a hushed tone. The comforting chirps of crickets and the distant howl of a wolf were now interspersed with the soft murmurs of the guards communicating with each other. Torches, their flames flickering in the gentle breeze, illuminated the pathways, casting long shadows that danced and swayed.

The first light of dawn was just beginning to pierce the horizon one morning, casting a soft, golden hue over the village. The air was cool and crisp, carrying with it the earthy scent of the mountain and the faint chirping of early birds. The village was still, most of its inhabitants wrapped in the embrace of sleep, the tranquility only occasionally broken by the distant sound of a rooster heralding the new day. Thrumir stood at the entrance of my makeshift dwelling, his silhouette framed by the emerging sunlight. His usually composed face was animated, the corners of his eyes crinkling with barely contained excitement. His beard, which had always been meticulously groomed, seemed slightly disheveled, hinting at the haste with which he had set out this morning. His heavy boots shuffled impatiently on the stone floor as he waited for me to rise. "I've somethin' t' show you," he began, his voice a low rumble, filled with a mix of eagerness and mystery. But before I could even process his words or the questions they invoked, he interrupted himself, his impatience evident. "Never mind what now. Just come." I hurriedly pulled on my boots and grabbed a cloak, my curiosity piqued. What could have the usually stoic Thrumir so animated? As I stepped out, I noticed that he had already started walking, his pace brisk, his steps echoing purposefully against the cobblestones. The village, bathed in the soft glow of dawn, looked ethereal. The stone dwellings, the pathways, the central square - everything seemed to shimmer in the morning light, casting long, stretching shadows. But

Thrumir seemed oblivious to the beauty around him, his focus singular, his destination clear in his mind. As we walked, the anticipation built. Every step, every turn, felt like a prelude to a revelation. And as the village slowly began to stir, with the first signs of life emerging from the dwellings, I couldn't help but wonder what awaited us at the end of our journey.

The path to Haldorr's barazdum, or forge, was lined with cobblestones, worn smooth by countless footsteps over the cycles. As we approached, the rhythmic sound of a hammer striking metal grew louder, a specimen of the relentless work that took place within. The forge itself was an imposing structure, built from dark, weathered stone, with thick wooden beams supporting its roof. Plumes of smoke billowed from its chimney, carrying with it the distinct scent of molten metal and burning coal. Inside, the barazdum was a symphony of controlled chaos. The heart of the forge was a massive furnace, its flames dancing wildly, casting an orange glow that illuminated the entire space. Tools of all shapes and sizes hung meticulously organized on the walls, their polished surfaces gleaming in the firelight. Anvils, tongs, and molds were scattered around, each with a specific purpose in the intricate dance of blacksmithing. Haldorr stood at the center of it all, his massive dwarrin frame dwarfing the anvil before him. His skin was slick with sweat, and his beard, streaked with gray, was tied back to keep it away from the flames. His eyes, sharp and focused, lit up as he saw us, a warm smile breaking through his soot-covered face.

"Aye, Thrumir! And our young friend!" he boomed, his voice echoing in the vastness of the barazdum. "I've been expecting you."

Thrumir, with a hint of pride in his voice, introduced the day's agenda. "Haldorr will guide you in crafting a dagger, a weapon that will be uniquely yours."

Haldorr's eyes twinkled with mischief as he leaned in closer, "So, do you have any special trinkets to make this blade truly your own?" I hesitated for a moment, my fingers brushing against the pouch that held the elandari moonstones. These were gifts from the elandari, their ethereal glow a disclosure of the magic they held within. With a deep breath, I carefully extracted the moonstones and handed them to Haldorr.

His eyes widened in appreciation. "Ah! Those must be rare and powerful gravorns! These will make your blade not just a weapon, but a work of art." The reverence for the "gravorns", gems, in his voice was unmistakable, and I felt a surge of anticipation for the masterpiece that was about to be created.

The barazdum was alive with the sounds of creation. The roar of the furnace, the rhythmic pounding of Haldorr's dammaz in my hand under his guidance, and the hiss of metal being quenched in water at his instruction. The heat was intense, a tangible force that pressed against my skin, making beads of sweat form on my brow. But amidst this cacophony and heat, a masterpiece was taking shape. The metal we used for the blade was standard dwarrin vorgrund, a precious metal that the dwarrin had mined from the very heart of the mountain. Its name, "sky rock", was apt, for the metal had a lustrous sheen that seemed to shimmer and dance, reflecting the colors of the sky at dawn and dusk. As Haldorr guided me in working the metal, folding and refolding it, the blade began to take shape, its surface gleaming with a brilliance that was almost otherworldly.

But the true magic lay in the hilt. The elandari moonstones, gifts from the enigmatic Illadrathil, were set into the hilt with meticulous care. They pulsed with a soft, ethereal light, their blue-green luminescence casting a gentle glow that contrasted beautifully with the cold gleam of the vorgrund blade. These stones were more than just adornments; they were a bridge between two worlds, a tangible reminder of the bond I had forged with the elandari.

The handle of the dagger was a work of art in itself. Carved from heartwood, another rare and durable wood gifted by the elandari - one they had placed inside my pack without my knowing - it felt warm and reassuring in my hand. Its intricate grain patterns told a story of ancient forests and whispered secrets. The crossguard, masterfully shaped to resemble intertwined thorns, added an element of elegance and protection, its design both functional and aesthetically pleasing. Under

Haldorr's watchful eye and with his expert guidance, the dagger was finally complete. It was a harmonious blend of dwarrin craftsmanship and elandari magic, a weapon that was both beautiful and deadly. As I held it, I could feel its balance, its weight perfectly distributed, making it an extension of my own arm.

The ambient glow of the forge dimmed as we stepped away, replaced by the cooler, muted light of the mountain's interior. Thrumir and Haldorr walked beside me, their sturdy frames casting long shadows on the stone floor. The weight of their pride was palpable, not just in the way they looked at me, but in their very posture. Their chests swelled, their steps firm and purposeful. Thrumir's eyes, usually so focused and intense, now sparkled with a warmth that was both paternal and proud. "Look at that hilt," he exclaimed, his voice filled with admiration. "The way those gravorns catch the light, it's as if the very essence of Krüma is captured within." His fingers brushed the hilt of the dagger, the gentle touch of a master craftsman acknowledging a job well done. Haldorr, the grand blacksmith, usually a man of few words, nodded in agreement. His gaze now lingered on the dagger, taking in every detail, every curve, every gleam. There was a hint of a smile on his lips, a rare sight that spoke volumes about his feelings.

Without another word, Thrumir gestured for me to follow him deeper into the mountain. The path led us through winding tunnels, the walls echoing with the whispers of ancient dwarrin tales. We arrived at a heavy wooden door, its surface adorned with intricate carvings of runes and symbols, the mark of the Runekeeper. Pushing the door open, Thrumir revealed his Runekeeping chambers. The room was a sanctum of magic and lore, its walls lined with shelves filled with ancient stone tablets, scrolls of thinly shaped vorgrund plates, and vials of mysterious liquids. In the center stood a large stone table, its surface etched with runes that pulsed with a soft, ethereal glow. This was the heart of the dwarrin's magical tradition, the place where weapons were imbued with power, where the arts of enchantment and runecrafting were practiced. And I was about to witness it firsthand. The chamber, dimly lit by the soft glow of enchanted crystals, was filled with an air of reverence and anticipation. Thrumir, his face illuminated by the ambient light, began to explain the art of dûrkûnsal. His voice, usually so commanding, took on a softer, more melodic tone as he spoke of the traditions and techniques passed down through generations of dwarrin Runekeepers.

He began with the basics, teaching me the significance of each rune, dûrkûn, the way they were drawn, the precise strokes and curves that gave them their power. He demonstrated with practiced ease, his fingers dancing over a piece of parchment, leaving behind intricate symbols that seemed to shimmer with an inner light. As the hours passed, I found myself drawn into the world of dûrkûnsal, captivated by the blend of artistry and magic that it represented. Thrumir's teachings were a window into a world of power and tradition, a world where words could shape reality, where symbols held the key to untapped potential. Finally, it was time to enchant my dagger. We placed it on the stone table, its blade gleaming in the soft light. Thrumir guided my hand as we began to engrave the runes. The first, "*Su*", was drawn with sweeping strokes, capturing the essence of the wind. Next came "*Hael*", its delicate curves a realization of the softness of a whisper. "*Nor*" was more intricate, its design speaking of bonds and connections. And finally, "*El*", a radiant symbol that seemed to capture the very essence of light.

As each rune was engraved, the blade seemed to come alive, pulsating with an inner light, its surface shimmering with the power of the enchantments. The air in the chamber grew thick with magic, the very atmosphere charged with energy. Thrumir, his face a mask of concentration, chanted softly, his voice weaving a spell that bound the enchantments to the blade. The runes glowed brighter with each word, their power resonating with the very core of the dagger. When it was done, we both took a step back, admiring our handiwork. The dagger, once a simple weapon, was now a thing of beauty and power, its blade etched with symbols of magic, its essence forever changed by the art of dûrkûnsal. The chamber's atmosphere was thick with the weight of the moment, the soft glow of the enchanted crystals casting a serene light upon us. Thrumir, his eyes reflecting deep thought, suggested the name "Faelthorn". The name rolled off his tongue, each syllable resonating with significance and history. "*Fael*", meaning whisper, and "*thorn*", reminiscent of the wind's unpredictable nature, combined to form a name that perfectly captured the essence of the dagger.

I repeated the name, feeling its weight, its resonance. "Faelthorn," I whispered, the name echoing softly in the chamber. It felt right, a fitting tribute to the journey that had brought me to this moment, to the friendships forged in the heart of the mountain, to the lessons learned in the heat of the forge and the quiet of the Dûrkûnsal chamber. Holding Faelthorn in my hand, I felt its power, its energy. The blade, with its newly engraved runes, seemed to hum softly, its vibrations a gentle reminder of the magic that now coursed through it. The elandari moonstones set in its hilt glowed softly, their ethereal light a memento of the bonds I had formed with the dwarrin and the elandari.

Throughout my long life, on the rare occasions I have needed to wield Faelthorn, in the stillness of the night or the heat of battle, whenever I unsheathed it, a surreal calm would descend upon me. The world seemed to pause, its relentless rhythm momentarily stilled, replaced by a profound silence that felt both eerie and comforting. The ambient sounds - the chirping of crickets, the distant murmur of voices, the rustling of leaves - would fade, as if nature itself was paying homage to the blade's power. With Faelthorn in my grasp, I felt an intimate connection to the wind. It whispered secrets in my ear, its gentle tendrils wrapping around me, guiding my movements. The dagger's enchantments transformed me. My footsteps became weightless, each stride echoing the soft rustle of leaves carried on the wings of a gentle zephyran. The world around me seemed to blur, its colors and sounds melding into a harmonious dance of light and shadow. There were moments, fleeting yet profound, when I felt myself dissolve into the wind. My physical form would waver, becoming translucent, almost ghostly. In those instances, I was not just a warrior wielding a blade; I was the embodiment of the wind itself - silent, swift, and unseen. My presence was as intangible as a passing breeze, yet as impactful as a gale. Every time I have wielded Faelthorn, it was a transcendent experience, a dance of elements and emotions. The blade was not just a tool; it was a vessel. An advocate for the ethereal beauty of the wind, the silent strength of a whisper, and the unbreakable bonds that had forged it. Each swing, each thrust, was a reminder of the journey I had undertaken, the friendships I had nurtured, and the legacy I was destined to leave behind.

One serene night, as the dwarrin villagers slept, was transformed into a maelstrom of chaos. The soft glow of the moon, which had often bathed the village in a gentle luminescence, now illuminated a scene of fierce combat. The Kraggelm, their dark armors glinting in the moonlight, moved with a predatory grace, their every step echoing their thirst for conquest. The initial moments were ones of disarray for the Thorazdum thârûm. The suddenness of the attack caught many off-guard. But the training and preparations of the past weeks kicked in swiftly. Villagers, roused from their sleep, grabbed their weapons and rushed to defend their homes. The rhythmic beats of the dwarrin war drums began to resonate, rallying the defenders and providing a counterpoint to the cacophony of battle. Thrumir, his belgarn gleaming, led a group of warriors to repel the invaders at the village's main entrance. His voice, strong and unwavering, shouted commands, guiding the defense and bolstering the spirits of the thârûm. Elsewhere, dwarrin took positions on rooftops and towers, their stjernhalds finding targets with deadly precision. The village's pathways and alleys, which had once echoed with laughter and shared tales, now became chokepoints and battlegrounds. Every corner, every shadow, held potential danger. The Kraggelm, using their knowledge of the terrain, tried to exploit any weakness, but the Thorazdum, with their deep connection to their home, defended it fiercely. The clang of vorgrund on vorgrund, stone on stone, the shouts of warriors, the grunts of effort, and the cries of pain melded into a symphony of conflict. Sparks flew as blades met, casting eerie glows in the darkness. The scent of burning torches mixed with the metallic tang of blood, creating a heady and unsettling aroma.

The night was pierced by the sudden cacophony of war cries, the clashing of steel, and the guttural shouts of the Kraggelm. The once tranquil Thorazdum village was thrown into chaos. The moon, hanging high in the sky, cast eerie shadows on the ground, creating a surreal landscape of light and darkness. The torches that lined the village pathways flickered wildly, their flames dancing in the wind, casting an orange glow that painted the scene with an otherworldly hue.

In the midst of this pandemonium, I found myself disoriented, the suddenness of the ambush catching me off guard. My heart raced, adrenaline pumping through my veins. I had faced danger before, had hunted beasts in the wild, but this was different. This was war, a maelstrom of violence and fury. Drawing Faelthorn from its sheath, I felt its weight in my hand, its cool metal a compelling contrast to the heat of the battle. The blade shimmered in the moonlight, its edge gleaming with a deadly promise. As I moved, the elandari moonstones embedded in its hilt began to pulse with a deep crimson light, their luminescence casting a soft glow around me. The stones, once a symbol of friendship and trust, now served as a signal, warning me of the imminent danger that lurked in the shadows. Relying on the dagger's enchantments, I navigated the battlefield with a grace I didn't know I possessed. Each swing, each thrust, was guided by the wind's whisper, the blade moving with a fluidity that belied its deadly intent. The world around me seemed to slow, each moment stretching into eternity, as I danced amidst the chaos, Faelthorn singing its song of war. Yet, for all its magic, I was still unaccustomed to the brutality of battle. The sights and sounds were overwhelming, a sensory assault that threatened to consume me. The cries of the wounded, the metallic tang of blood in the air, the relentless onslaught of the Kraggelm - it was a nightmare brought to life. But with Faelthorn in my hand and the elandari moonstones glowing their warning, I was determined to stand my ground, to defend the thârûm and the mountain I had come to cherish.

The suddenness of an alarm - a horn blowing in the wind - shattered the tranquility of the night, its shrillness echoing through the mountainous terrain, a striking divergence from the gentle lullabies of the nocturnal creatures. The villagers, roused from dreams and the warmth of their beds, sprang into action. The once quiet pathways of the village were now bustling with activity, as men, women, and even the elderly, grabbed weapons and armor, their movements swift and purposeful. The moonlight bathed the village in a silvery glow, casting long shadows that danced and flickered with the movement of torches. The soft glow of lanterns emerged from homes, creating pockets of light in the enveloping darkness. Faces, usually warm and welcoming, were now etched with lines of determination and resolve. Eyes that once sparkled with mirth now burned with the fire of defiance. As the Kraggelm forces descended upon the village, the night was set ablaze with the fury of battle. The rhythmic beat of war drums, the metallic clang of axes, hammers, and swords meeting shields, and the guttural war cries created a soundscape of chaos and valor. The Thorazdum, their bodies adorned with armor crafted of vorgrund and accented with urkhas, both from the very mountains they called home, moved with a synchronicity that spoke of countless hours of training and preparation. Their strikes were precise, their defenses impenetrable, each movement a bar of their unwavering spirit and the love for their homeland. Amidst the swirling maelstrom of combat, individual acts of heroism shone through. A young dwarrin, barely of age, fending off multiple attackers with a fierceness that belied his cycles; an elderly woman, her hands steady, launching stjernhalds that found their mark with deadly accuracy; and groups of warriors, standing back to back, forming impenetrable barriers against the onslaught. The village square was now the epicenter of the conflict, its cobblestones stained with evidence of the fierce battle being waged. The Thorazdum, with their backs against the wall, fought not just for survival, but for the very soul of their village, their dwarrornak, and their future.

The tide of battle ebbed and flowed, the Thorazdum's defensive lines bending under the sheer force of the Kraggelm numbers, but never breaking. The Kraggelm, their dark vorgrund armor adorned with menacing red symbols, likely painted in blood, and their faces painted with crimson and black war colors, moved like a relentless storm, their formations tight and their strikes coordinated. Their war cries, a cacophony of aggression and intent, echoed through the mountainous terrain, a chilling reminder of their thirst for conquest. Yet, the Thorazdum, their armor gleaming under the moon's silvery touch, stood resolute. Their shouts of defiance and calls to arms were a beacon of hope amidst the chaos. The very ground they stood upon seemed to lend them strength, as if the mountain itself was rallying to their cause. Their shields formed impenetrable walls, their weapons moved in harmonious arcs, cutting down foes with precision and determination. Every fallen Thorazdum was avenged tenfold, their memory fueling the fire of resistance. In the midst of this maelstrom, I found myself surrounded by warriors on all sides. The weight of Faelthorn in my hand was both a comfort and a reminder of the stakes. Each swing, each thrust, was guided by the teachings of Thrumir and the hours spent in the training square. The elandari moonstones embedded in the dagger pulsed with a soft crimson glow, their light a beacon in the darkness, guiding my strikes and illuminating my foes.

Around me, the Thorazdum moved with a grace and fluidity that belied the ferocity of the battle. Their movements were a dance of survival, each step, each parry, a herald of their skill and training. Their war cries, a mix of defiance and camaraderie, resonated with my own heartbeat, a shared rhythm of hope and determination. Together, we stood as one, a united front against the overwhelming odds, our spirits unbroken, our resolve unyielding. Amidst the swirling melee, I found myself locked in combat with multiple Kraggelm warriors. Their movements were swift and coordinated, their tactics honed through countless battles. Their eyes, cold and calculating, sought any sign of weakness, any opening to exploit. Yet, with every thrust of their weapons, every menacing advance, I drew upon the strength and teachings of the Thorazdum. Thrumir's lessons, the hours spent in the training square, became my guiding force, coupled with Faelthorn's primal magic, allowed me to anticipate and counter their every move. The weight of Faelthorn in my hand became an extension of my will, its blade dancing through the air, deflecting blows and finding its mark with deadly precision. The ethereal crimson glow of the elandari moonstones seemed to pulse in tandem with the beat of my heart, their light casting an otherworldly sheen on the battlefield.

As the hours wore on, the once-clear night sky began to lighten with the first hints of dawn. The silhouettes of warriors, both friend and foe, moved against the backdrop of the emerging day, their shadows long and distorted. The once-pristine grounds of the village were now marred with the scars of battle - broken weapons, discarded shields, and the bodies of those who had given their all in defense of their home. Everywhere I looked, I saw acts of bravery and sacrifice. The Thorazdum, their armor dented and smeared with the grime of battle, stood their ground with unwavering determination. Their war cries, a mix of defiance and sorrow, echoed through the mountainous terrain, a haunting reminder of the price of war. The very air was thick with tension, the metallic tang of blood mingling with the earthy scent of the mountain. The sounds of battle - the clash of steel, the shouts of command, the cries of pain - created a symphony of chaos and determination. Through it all, I fought on, driven by a singular purpose: to protect the village, the thârûm, and the friendships I had forged. The horizon began to blush with the first hues of dawn, casting a soft, golden light over the battlefield. The retreating figures of the Kraggelm warriors became mere silhouettes against the awakening sky, their movements deliberate and coordinated. Their retreat was not borne out of defeat but strategy, a chilling reminder that this was merely a lull in the storm, a brief respite before the tempest resumed.

As the last of the Kraggelm disappeared into the distance, an eerie silence settled over the village. The once-vibrant square, which had echoed with the sounds of clashing weapons and battle cries, now bore witness to a different scene. The ground, littered with discarded weapons and the remnants of battle, told a tale of fierce combat and unwavering determination. Villagers, their faces lined with exhaustion and streaked with the grime of battle, moved with purpose. Makeshift tents were erected, and the wounded were carefully carried to the training ground, which had been swiftly repurposed into a field hospital.

The rhythmic chants of the dwarrin healers filled the air, their hands moving in practiced motions as they applied poultices and bandages, their voices soft and soothing as they whispered words of comfort. The scent of medicinal herbs wafted through the air, mingling with the more somber undertones of blood and sweat. Families huddled together, their embraces a symbol of the relief of survival and the grief of loss. Children clung to their parents, their eyes wide with a mix of fear and wonder, their innocence a manifest incongruity to the harsh realities of the night. Throughout the village, there was a palpable sense of unity and resilience. The Thorazdum had faced a formidable foe, had stood their ground against overwhelming odds, and had emerged battered but unbroken. The events of the night had forged them into a tighter-knit community, their shared experiences a mirror of their indomitable spirit and unwavering resolve.

The village, once a haven of camaraderie and shared stories, now buzzed with a different kind of energy. The rhythmic clanging of metal on metal echoed through the air as blacksmiths worked diligently, mending broken weapons and forging new ones. The barricades, which had borne the brunt of the Kraggelm's assault, were being fortified with renewed vigor. Sturdy logs and thick planks were hauled and positioned, their placement strategic, designed to withstand another onslaught. Every corner of the village was a hive of activity. Lookout posts, once a symbol of vigilance, were now critical vantage points. Warriors, their eyes sharp and alert, scanned the horizon, their senses attuned to the slightest hint of movement or danger. The weight of responsibility on their shoulders was palpable, their duty clear and unwavering. The aftermath of the battle was evident everywhere. Buildings, once symbols of the village's resilience and craftsmanship, now bore the scars of conflict. Walls were scorched, roofs had gaping holes, and windows were shattered. The ground, which had once echoed with the laughter of children and the chatter of villagers, was now a somber landscape. Broken shields, discarded stjernhalds, and the occasional piece of torn fabric told a silent story of the fierce combat that had taken place. In the makeshift infirmary, the wounded were a stark reminder of the price of the battle. Healers moved with purpose, their hands deftly tending to gashes, bruises, and broken bones. The moans of pain and the whispered words of comfort were a constant undertone, a somber chorus in the aftermath. The atmosphere in the village was thick with a mix of determination and trepidation. The knowledge that the Kraggelm would return weighed heavily on everyone's minds. The villagers, their faces etched with fatigue and concern, moved with a sense of urgency. Conversations were hushed, their tones serious, the topic invariably about the impending attack. The Thorazdum thârûm, having faced the ferocity of the Kraggelm once, were now grappling with the looming threat of another confrontation. The unity and strength of the community had been tested, and the shadow of uncertainty cast a pall over the village. The coming battle, its outcome unknown, loomed large in everyone's thoughts, a storm on the horizon that was drawing ever closer.

The village was a whirlwind of activity, each individual engrossed in their tasks, their focus unwavering despite the weight of the impending threat. The rhythmic sounds of hammers and chisels echoed through the air as structures were mended and reinforced. Healers, their hands stained with herbs and salves, moved with a quiet efficiency among the wounded, their touch gentle yet firm, their expressions a blend of compassion and determination. Amidst this backdrop of urgency, I found myself deep in thought, the gears in my mind turning rapidly. The dwarrin's expertise in mining, their innate connection to the earth, had always fascinated me. Their ability to read the land, to understand its secrets and harness its resources, was unparalleled. As I observed the villagers, a spark of inspiration ignited within me. The terrain around the village, with its intricate network of tunnels and caverns, was an attestation to the Thorazdum's mastery over the earth. Their knowledge of the mountain's veins and pathways could be our secret weapon, a strategic advantage that the Kraggelm might not anticipate.

I envisioned a plan where we could use the tunnels to our benefit, perhaps setting up ambush points or creating diversions. The very earth that the Kraggelm sought to claim could be turned against them, its labyrinthine depths a potential trap. The idea was bold, perhaps even audacious, but it held promise. As the concept took shape in my mind, I felt a surge of hope. The situation was dire, but with the right strategy and the Thorazdum's unique skills, we might just have a fighting chance. The battle was far from over, and with this newfound idea, I felt a renewed sense of purpose and determination.

In the dimly lit council chamber, the weight of the situation hung heavily in the air. The room, usually filled with the steady hum of discussion, was silent as I laid out my proposal. The flickering torchlight cast dancing shadows on the walls, illuminating the faces of Thrumir and the council of elders as they listened intently. The concept was simple yet audacious: to use the very earth beneath our feet as a weapon. The Thorazdum's deep connection to the land, their unparalleled expertise in mining and tunneling, would be our secret weapon. I envisioned a maze of tunnels, a subterranean labyrinth designed to disorient and trap the Kraggelm warriors. As I spoke, I could see Thrumir's mind spinning, his eyes narrowing in thought. The council, their expressions a mix of intrigue and caution, weighed the merits of the plan. The idea of using the earth, a source of life and sustenance for the dwarrin, as a means of defense was both innovative and fitting. A controlled cave-in would be the linchpin of the strategy. It would require precision, a keen understanding of the mountain's geology, and impeccable timing. If executed correctly, the very ground would rise up against our adversaries, sealing them within the mountain's embrace and forcing their retreat. But the risks were evident. One miscalculation, one misstep, and the plan could backfire, endangering our own people. The council's deliberation was palpable, each member weighing the potential rewards against the inherent dangers. Thrumir, ever the voice of reason, voiced his concerns and hopes in equal measure. The council exchanged glances, their collective wisdom a beacon in these uncertain times.

The council chamber, usually a place of decisive action and an air of formality, was thick with tension and fatigue. The room, dimly lit by the soft glow of lanterns, was filled with the low murmur of voices as the elders debated the merits of my proposal. The walls, adorned with dwarrin tapestries, seemed to absorb the weight of the discussion, bearing silent witness to the gravity of the decision at hand. Fargrim, his brow furrowed and his voice deep with concern, was the first to break the silence. He voiced his reservations, reminding the council of the risks involved in trusting another of my plans. His words were not of disdain but of genuine worry for the safety of the thârûm. The memory of the recent failed diplomatic mission was still fresh, and Fargrim's caution was a comment on his protective nature. The other council members listened intently, their faces a canvas of contemplation. Each elder, in turn, weighed in, their words a reflection of their wisdom and experience. The room was filled with a mix of hope, skepticism, and determination.

Thrumir, his gaze steady and his demeanor calm, acknowledged Fargrim's concerns. Yet, he also spoke of the potential rewards, of the chance to turn the tide of the battle, of the innovative nature of the plan. His words were a beacon of reason, a call to consider all possibilities in the face of adversity. The deliberation continued, the council members exchanging glances, their collective wisdom guiding their decision-making. And then, after what felt like an eternity, a consensus was reached. Despite the risks, despite the uncertainties, they agreed to give the plan a chance. The decision was not made lightly, but with a profound understanding of the stakes at hand. The village, which had once echoed with the sounds of daily life and camaraderie, was now alive with a different kind of energy. The dwarrin, despite the fatigue that clung to their bones, moved with a purpose that was palpable. Their eyes, usually filled with warmth and mirth, now held a steely determination, a fire that spoke of their unwavering commitment to their thârûm. Everywhere I looked, there were villagers working in unison. The once-quiet corners of the village were now bustling hubs of activity. The clang of pickaxes striking the earth, the scrape of shovels, and the muffled conversations of strategy filled the air. The very ground beneath our feet seemed to vibrate with the energy of the preparations.

The tunnels, the heart of the plan, were a marvel of dwarrin engineering. Their design was intricate, a maze meant to confound and trap the Kraggelm. As I descended into the depths, the coolness of the earth enveloped me, the dimly lit tunnels a flag for the dwarrin's expertise. Every junction, every twist and turn, was meticulously planned, each one serving a purpose in the grand strategy. Working alongside the Thorazdum, I felt a deep sense of camaraderie. Our hands, stained with the earth, moved in tandem, our efforts synchronized in a dance of creation. Their encouragement, their shared purpose, bolstered my spirits, reminding me that we were all in this together.

The sun had barely risen when the ominous sounds of the Kraggelm war drums echoed through the valley. Their approach was heralded by the dust clouds that rose from their march, the horizon darkened by their vast numbers. The once peaceful dawn was shattered by the war cries of the Kraggelm, their intent clear and deadly. The Thorazdum, their faces set in grim determination, took their positions. The air was thick with tension, each breath a statement of the gravity of the situation. The village was again the epicenter of a fierce battle. The clash of weapons, the shouts of warriors, and the cries of the wounded filled the air, painting a vivid picture of the chaos that had once again descended upon us.

As the battle raged on, our strategy was clear: lead the Kraggelm towards the rigged tunnels. But the intensity of their assault was overwhelming. The group of villagers, brave souls tasked with the crucial role of luring the Kraggelm into the south tunnel, were caught in the ferocity of the Kraggelm's charge. Their valiant efforts were cut short, their sacrifice a stark reminder of the cost of the conflict. In the midst of the chaos, Balgruff's voice rang out, strong and authoritative. His shout, filled with determination and leadership, pierced through the cacophony of battle. "Leave 'em to me!" he declared, signaling to Thrumir. The weight of his decision was evident in his eyes, the responsibility of the task clear in his stance. Balgruff, the seasoned leader of the Thorazdum, was ready to put himself in the line of fire, to ensure the success of the plan and the safety of his thârûm. The battlefield was a whirlwind of movement and strategy, each group executing their part of the plan with precision and determination. The once familiar landscape of the village was transformed into a maze of conflict, each turn and corner a strategic point in the unfolding battle.

Balgruff, his urkhas-lined vorgrund armor glinting in the sporadic sunlight that broke through the dust and smoke, led the charge towards the south tunnels. His presence on the field was like a beacon, drawing the main thrall of Kraggelm intruders towards him. Every step he took was measured, every maneuver calculated. The Kraggelm, their focus fixed on the formidable leader of the Thorazdum, followed him, their numbers a dark tide surging towards the tunnel's entrance. To the west, the "skaldorns", smiths, of the Thorazdum, but skilled warriors in their own right, used their skills and agility to lead another battalion of the Kraggelm. Their movements were a dance of combat, their tactics a demonstration of their training and experience. They weaved through the battlefield, drawing the Kraggelm's attention and leading them towards the western tunnels, their path marked by a clash of weapons and the determined shouts of the skaldorns. Meanwhile, to the east, a diverse troop of villagers and warriors worked in unison. Their unity was a powerful sight, the villagers, once simple inhabitants of the thârûm, now stood shoulder to shoulder with seasoned warriors. Together, they led the remaining Kraggelm forces towards the eastern tunnels, their combined efforts a symbol of the thârûm's resilience and determination.

From a distance, the scene was a choreographed dance of strategy and combat. The three groups, each leading a portion of the Kraggelm forces, moved with purpose, their paths diverging towards the tunnels. The plan, despite the chaos and intensity of the battle, seemed to be unfolding as envisioned. The hope of turning the tide of the conflict rested on the success of this intricate strategy. The tunnels now became the stage for a deadly game of cat and mouse. The Thorazdum, with their intimate knowledge of the labyrinthine network, moved with purpose and precision, leading the Kraggelm deeper into the trap. The echoing footsteps and distant shouts created an eerie orchestra, the darkness of the tunnels amplifying the tension. As the Kraggelm warriors pursued, their focus solely on their prey, they failed to notice the subtle signs of the impending trap. The strategically weakened walls, the faint markings indicating the trigger points, all went unnoticed in their blind aggression. Amidst the chaos, Faelthorn's crimson glow illuminated my path, its magic enhancing my agility and speed whilst simultaneously warning me of the danger all around. The world surrounding me seemed to blur as I sprinted through the tunnels, the wind whispering past me, guiding my steps. The distance between me and the Kraggelm invaders widened, and soon, the familiar figure of Balgruff came into view. His armor, dented and scratched from the battle, gleamed faintly in the dim light, his stance an embodiment of his determination. As we converged deep within the tunnel, a signal, a resonating horn blast, pierced the air. The very ground beneath us trembled, a deep rumble echoing through the tunnels. With a deafening roar, the earth shifted, the walls of the tunnels collapsing in a controlled avalanche of rock and soil. The trap had been sprung. The sounds of battle were momentarily drowned out by the cacophony of the cave-in, the very earth swallowing a significant portion of the Kraggelm forces. But in the midst of the chaos, an unexpected tremor shook a section of the tunnel that wasn't meant to collapse. Dust and debris clouded the air, and when it settled, Balgruff and I found ourselves cut off, our path blocked by fallen rocks. In the dim light, the silhouettes of six Kraggelm warriors emerged, their intent clear. The trap had worked, but not without its complications. We were cornered, outnumbered, but not defeated. The fight was not yet ended.

The dimly lit tunnel became a dance floor of flashing blades and swift movements. Faelthorn, glowing with an ethereal light, became an extension of my arm. Each swing, each thrust was guided by its magic, the blade finding its mark with deadly precision. Two of the Kraggelm attackers, taken aback by the dagger's power and my newfound combat prowess, struggled to defend themselves. Their movements, though swift and aggressive, were no match for the wind-like agility Faelthorn granted me. With a series of swift strikes, they were dispatched, their bodies collapsing to the cold stone floor. Beside me, Balgruff, the seasoned warrior, faced a more daunting challenge. Four Kraggelm warriors, their blades gleaming with malice, surrounded him. But Balgruff's experience and skill shone through. With each parry, each counter strike, he held his ground, his movements a monument to his cycles of training and battle-hardened resolve. But the odds were against him. In a heart-wrenching moment, as i finished off the second of my attackers, a Kraggelm blade found its mark, piercing Balgruff's side, puncturing his lung. A gasp of pain escaped his lips, but even in his weakened state, his warrior spirit did not waver. Coughing with a roar of defiance, he unleashed a powerful swing, channeling all his remaining strength. The blade cut through the air, and in one fell swoop, all four Kraggelm attackers lay defeated.

As Balgruff's strength waned, he collapsed, his body heavy with the weight of his injuries. I rushed to his side, my heart heavy with the realization of his sacrifice as he drew his last breath, unable to utter any final words. From the other side of the collapsed tunnel, the muffled sounds of the remaining Kraggelm could be heard. Their advance, halted by the unexpected turn of events and the loss of their comrades, was filled with confusion and panic. The sounds of their retreat echoed through the tunnel, their footsteps growing fainter. The stillness of the aftermath was suddenly shattered by a deafening blast. The ground trembled beneath our feet once more, and a cloud of dust and debris billowed into the air. The echo of the explosion reverberated through the tunnels, a definitive opposition to the previous silence.

From the direction of the eastern tunnels, a series of bright flashes illuminated the darkness, followed by the unmistakable sound of explosions. The force of the blasts was so intense that it sent shockwaves through the ground, causing small pebbles and rocks to dance in response. As the dust began to settle, the silhouette of a group of Thorazdum dwarrin emerged from the clearing smoke. Their faces, blackened by soot and streaked with sweat, bore expressions of relief and determination. It was evident that they had used their knowledge of the earth and their mining expertise to create makeshift explosives, a last-ditch effort to free themselves from the trap they had inadvertently fallen into. The dimly lit tunnel was filled with a mix of urgency and somberness. One of the dwarrin, his face streaked with dirt and determination, stepped forward. "We foresaw the possibility of such an event," he began, his voice echoing slightly in the confined space. "We've brought components for quick explosives for this very reason." As he and a few others began methodically placing the explosives with practiced hands, ensuring they were positioned for maximum effect, the rest of the group gathered around Balgruff's still form. The air grew thick with emotion as they paid their respects to their fallen leader. Soft murmurs of remembrance and grief intermingled, creating a poignant backdrop to the meticulous work being done nearby. The explosives were set, and with a final nod of readiness, the dwarrin retreated to a safe distance. A muffled boom resonated through the tunnel, followed by the sound of falling rock and debris. As the dust settled, a path to the outside world was revealed, the once-impassable blockade now a mere memory. With a reverence reserved for the most honored among them, several dwarrin gently lifted Balgruff's body, cradling him as if he were still with them. The procession moved slowly, each step heavy with the weight of loss, as they emerged from the tunnel's confines into the open air, carrying their fallen leader back to the heart of the thârûm.

The once embattled village now stood, its structures bearing the scars of conflict, yet its spirit unbroken. The aftermath of the battle was evident in the debris scattered around, the remnants of barricades, and the marks left by the fierce combat. But amidst the signs of warfare, there was a palpable sense of unity and determination. The villagers moved with purpose, their hands working diligently to mend what had been broken, to heal those who had been hurt. The sounds of hammers and chisels intermingled with the soft murmurs of comfort, as the wounded received gentle tending. Everywhere I looked, there were scenes of camaraderie and cooperation, a community coming together in the face of adversity.

As the sun began its descent, casting a golden hue over the village, the dwarrin gathered in the central square. Their faces, marked by the grime and sweat of battle, were alight with pride and relief. They had faced a formidable foe and had emerged victorious. This victory was not just a showcase of their strategic prowess, but also to their indomitable spirit - their "thrumgar". A large bonfire was lit, its flames reaching skyward, mirroring the renewed hope of the thârûm. Around it, the dwarrin danced and sang, their voices rising in harmonious melodies that spoke of bravery, sacrifice, and unity. The night was filled with stories of valor, of narrow escapes, and of the strength of the community. Laughter echoed, and for a moment, the weight of the battle seemed a distant memory, replaced by the warmth of the celebration and the bond of the thârûm. The village square, bathed in the warm glow of torches and the central bonfire, became a stage for recognition and honor. The night, filled with the harmonious melodies of dwarrin songs, took on a reverent tone as the time for accolades approached.

I stood among the dwarrin, the weight of their gaze upon me. Their eyes, once wary of an outsider, now held a gleam of respect and gratitude. Thrumir stepped forward, his voice echoing through the square, recounting my strategic contributions to the village's defense. As he spoke, the crowd nodded in agreement, their voices rising in a chorus of appreciation. The warmth of their gratitude enveloped me, an essence capturing the bond we had forged in the crucible of battle. Bruna, the fierce historian, was next to be honored. Tales of her valor spread through the crowd, her ruthless strength in battle becoming the stuff of legends. With each Kraggelm she had felled, she had etched her name into the annals of dwarrin history. The crowd cheered her name, their voices a proclamation emphasizing her prowess and the respect she commanded. But the loudest cheers were reserved for young Galdrûn. The child I had seen fighting off the invading Kraggelm, who had shown courage beyond his cycles, was hailed as a hero. The tale of his bravery, of how he had stood his ground against the invaders to protect his younger sister, was recounted with awe. The number of Kraggelm he had single-handedly defeated - thirty-two in total - was a symbol of his indomitable spirit. As his name echoed through the square, the Thorazdum raised their weapons in salute, their voices filled with pride and admiration.

The atmosphere in the village square changed, the jubilant cheers and songs giving way to a somber, reflective mood. The torches seemed to flicker more gently, casting a softer glow on the gathered dwarrin. Thrumir stepped forward once more, his voice heavy with emotion.

"In the heart of our mountains, where the roots run deep and strong, we come together, not just in the joy of victories but in the solemn duty to remember those who've stood tall for our thârûm," Thrumir began, his voice resonating like a deep echo through ancient tunnels. His eyes, like torches in a dark mine, met each gaze, binding them in shared remembrance. "Balgruff, our guiding star for eighty-seven cycles, carved his love and devotion into the very stone of our home." Murmurs of assent and gestures of respect rumbled through the assembled dwarves. Every soul bore an engraving of Balgruff's wisdom, a nugget of his guidance, a memory of warmth in the cold stone halls. "He journeyed with us for 140 cycles, and in each one, he was a steadfast pillar, a source of light in our deepest caverns." The oldest among them, with beards long and white, gave knowing nods, the weight of countless days visible in their eyes. The younger kin, who had only known the comforting shade of Balgruff's leadership, drank in the tales, sensing the depth of the legacy before them.

"In the shadows of our deepest mines, where the very durorn remembers, his valiant stand will be whispered for ages to come," Thrumir's voice held the tremor of a quake, laden with grief. "He wasn't merely our beacon atop the thordum, but kin, guide, and steadfast companion. This day, we lift our belgarns, not just in salute to the dwarrornak of a Kazadornak, but in gratitude for the warmth, stendûr, harnornak, and commitment he shared with every soul he met." An enveloping stillness settled upon the gathering, with every dwarrin diving deep into their own troves of memories with Balgruff.

The night, filled with a mix of celebration and mourning, took another significant turn as Bruna, Fargrim, and Haldorr stepped forward, their movements deliberate and synchronized. The three of them, each respected in their own right, carried with them an air of solemnity and purpose. Thrumir, standing tall and proud, looked on with a hint of surprise in his eyes. The trio approached him, their steps echoing softly in the hushed square. Bruna, her historian's wisdom evident in her gaze, held a beautifully crafted crown. Made of solid vorgrund, its poins coated in urkhas, resembling a dark mountain range with golden snow-covered peaks, the crown gleamed under the torchlight, its intricate designs showcasing the craftsmanship of the dwarrin. It wasn't just a decorative piece; its sturdy construction promised protection, a statement reflecting the dual role of a leader - both a figurehead and a protector. Beside her, Fargrim the Elder held a heavy fur cloak, its rich texture and quality evident even from a distance. The cloak, dyed in the deep hues of the Thorazdum colors - a deep, oceanic blue, accented by gray - was lined with the softest furs, symbolizing both the warmth of leadership and the protection it offers to its people. Haldorr, the grand blacksmith, stepped forward, his voice resonating with pride. "Thrumir, much like a blade is tried and tested in the barazdum, so too have you been through the fires of dedication for our thârûm. Your wisdom, like the finest tempered vorgrund, has never wavered." Haldorr pointed to the crown and cloak with a firm hand. "These aren't just adornments, friend. They're the very metal and fabric of our trust, our hope. With them, we choose you to be the anvil upon which the fate of Thorazdum is forged. Rise as our next Kazadornak!"

The square, already thick with emotion, now held its collective breath. The weight of the moment, the transition of leadership in such trying times, was palpable. Thrumir, usually so composed, seemed momentarily overwhelmed. He looked at the crown, the cloak, and then into the eyes of each member of the council, finding affirmation in their gazes. Accepting the gifts, he spoke, his voice filled with gratitude and determination.

"In the shadows of these thordums, where our ancestors laid their first durorns, I stand humbled by your trust. My heart, solid as these ancient durorns, will strive tirelessly for our thârûm. Together, like the interwoven veins of urkhas beneath our feet, we'll face the morrow's trials and ensure that the tales of Thorazdum echo for ages yet unborn." The assembly roared in agreement, their voices resonating far across the mountains like a chorus of hammers on anvils. As the night's canvas painted tales of old and new, the dawn of a renewed Thorazdum thârûm was unmistakable.

The jubilant atmosphere of the celebration was palpable, with the sounds of laughter, singing, and merriment filling the air. The villagers, their spirits lifted by the recent victory and the crowning of a new leader, reveled in the moment, their faces glowing with pride and relief. Amidst the festivities, Thrumir stood tall, his presence a beacon of strength and leadership. However, as the night wore on, a change came over him. His gaze, which had been scanning the crowd, suddenly froze. A spark of realization flashed in his eyes, and his jovial demeanor shifted to one of deep contemplation. With a depth echoing the caverns of old, Thrumir's voice, strong as bedrock, halted the festivities. "Did anyone set eyes upon Grommok during the battle?" The gravity of his question pressed down, like a boulder upon a mine's entrance. Whispers fluttered like bats in the dark, as dwarrin warriors and kinfolk exchanged searching looks. The name of the Kraggelm leader brought a chill to the atmosphere, and as the realization set in, it became clear that no one had seen him during, or after, the conflict. Thrumir's face darkened, the lines of his brow deepening. His eyes, usually warm and inviting, now held a determination wrought of vorgrund. Without another word, he gripped his axe tightly, its handle creaking under the pressure of his grasp. With purpose in his stride, he began to walk away from the village, his silhouette a patent variance against the backdrop of the celebratory fires. I, sensing the gravity of the situation, quickly fell into step behind him. Several other warriors, their faces etched with concern and determination, joined us. Together, we followed Thrumir, our steps echoing in the stillness of the night, the weight of the unknown pressing heavily upon us.

The moonlit path to the Kraggelm hall was eerily silent, the aftermath of the day's battle still palpable in the air. As we approached the imposing gates of the hall, the silhouettes of several guards became visible, their postures relaxed, untouched by the day's conflict. Their unsuspecting stance was a stark delineation to our group, led by Thrumir, whose every step was filled with purpose and determination. Without hesitation, we engaged the guards. The element of surprise was on our side, and the vengeance burning in our hearts made the confrontation swift and brutal. The guards, caught off guard and unprepared, stood no chance against our onslaught. Their cries were quickly silenced, and we pressed on, our path now clear. As we delved deeper into the Kraggelm village, wounded warriors from the earlier battle emerged from the shadows, their injuries evident in their limping gaits and bloodied bandages. Despite their weakened state, they attempted to bar our way, their loyalty to their thârûm driving them to defend the grand hall. But their efforts were futile against the force of our determination. Thrumir, his face a mask of cold fury, led the charge. He moved with a grace and power that belied his size, his every action a witness confirming his skill and strength. He didn't even need to draw his weapon. With his bare hands, he dispatched the Kraggelm warriors, their feeble attempts to defend themselves no match for his might. The path to the grand hall lay open, and we pressed on, the weight of our mission driving us forward.

The grand hall, usually a place of majesty and power, was now the stage for a confrontation of epic proportions. The vast room, adorned with intricate carvings and lit by the soft glow of torches, was dominated by the imposing figure of Grommok. His initial shock at our sudden entrance was palpable, his eyes widening in disbelief. But as the leader of the Kraggelm, he quickly masked his surprise, his posture straightening, his face hardening into a mask of authority. Opening his mouth, Grommok began to speak, his voice deep and resonant, echoing through the hall. "You dare to-" he started, but his words were cut short, silenced by the force of Thrumir's interruption. Thrumir stepped forward, his presence filling the hall, his voice dripping with cold fury.

"Last we were here, you had no thirst for words," Thrumir boomed, each syllable echoing like a hammer striking stone, revealing the fury and resolve within. "Now, my thirst for deliberation has been quenched, Grommok." Holding Grommok's eyes with a gaze as unyielding as vorgrund, he declared, "Craved the tang of blood, did ye?" With the resonance of an ancient war drum, his voice thundered, his emotions breaking through his dwarrin council member formality, "Good. F'r blood'll be th' only brew y' savor t'night." Silence blanketed the hall, the implications of Thrumir's proclamation dense as the rock of their homeland.

The grand hall, with its towering pillars and intricate carvings, became the backdrop for a scene of desperation and retribution. Grommok, the once mighty Kazadornak of the Kraggelm, hesitated for a split second, his eyes locking onto Thrumir's, calculating his chances. It seemed, for a fleeting moment, that he was about to draw his weapon and face Thrumir head-on. But instead, in a move that betrayed his formidable facade, he turned on his heels, attempting to flee from the confrontation.

Thrumir, however, was prepared. With a swift motion, he reached into his belt and drew a stjernhald. With a practiced flick of his wrist, he sent the blade hurtling through the air. The hall echoed with the whistle of refined vorgrund as it found its mark, embedding itself deep into Grommok's muscular thigh. The force of the impact brought the Kraggelm leader crashing to the ground, his escape thwarted. On the chill embrace of the stone beneath, Grommok's veneer of dominance began to fracture. That silky, taunting voice now wavered, dripping with a desperation uncharacteristic of the cruel leader. "Mercy, if you will," he murmured, each word laced with the sting of defeat. "Gifts of vorgrund, urkaz, lands... your every whim satiated!" Thrumir loomed above, casting a shadow that seemed to consume the hall's meager luminescence. He listened to Grommok's pleas, his face an inscrutable mask. His eyes bore into Grommok, cold and unyielding, revealing nothing of his intentions, leaving Grommok, and everyone present, in suspenseful anticipation. The silence in the grand hall was palpable, broken only by Grommok's desperate pleas. Thrumir's towering presence loomed over the fallen Kraggelm leader, his shadow casting an ominous veil over the scene. The tension in the room was thick, every eye fixed on the two figures at the center.

"Where was the mercy f'r my kin?" Thrumir's voice boomed, echoing off the stone walls. His words were filled with a torrent of raw emotion, a mixture of pain, anger, and a thirst for justice. The weight of his question hung in the air, a stark reminder of the atrocities committed by the Kraggelm guards under Grommok's command. Grommok's eyes widened in terror, realizing the gravity of his situation. But before he could muster a response, before he could utter another plea, Thrumir's actions spoke louder than any words could. With a swift, decisive motion, Thrumir's axe arced through the air, its gleaming blade catching the dim light of the hall. There was a sickening thud as the blade found its mark, embedding itself deep into Grommok's skull. The finality of the act resonated throughout the hall. The once mighty Kazadornak of the Kraggelm lay defeated, his reign of terror brought to a swift end by the very people he sought to subjugate. The room was silent, save for the heavy breathing of those present, each processing the gravity of what had just transpired.

The journey back to the Thorazdum village was a somber one. The weight of the day's events pressed heavily on our shoulders, each step a reminder of the sacrifices made and the lives lost. The village, nestled within the protective embrace of the mountain's half-circle outcropping, stood as a beacon in the distance, its familiar silhouette a comforting sight after the day's turmoil. As we entered the village, the weariness of battle and the emotional toll of the day became evident. Faces that once held determination and resolve now bore the marks of exhaustion and grief. The village, which had been a hub of activity and preparation just hours before, was now eerily quiet, the only sounds being the soft murmurs of villagers comforting one another and the distant cries of the wounded. I found a quiet corner in the village and settled down, the weight of my own exhaustion pulling me into a deep, dreamless sleep. The events of the day replayed in my mind, a whirlwind of emotions and memories that would stay with me forever.

The following weeks were a blur of recovery and rebuilding. The Thorazdum, ever resilient, worked tirelessly to repair the damage and tend to the wounded. Their spirit, unbroken by the events of the battle, was an exhibit of their strength and unity. As the days turned into weeks, I found myself growing more attached to the Thorazdum and their way of life. But as much as I cherished the bonds I had formed, I felt the familiar pull of the wind, its gentle caress beckoning me to continue my journey. The promise I had made to my mentor Tornu echoed in my mind, a constant reminder of my vow to never cease exploring. With a heavy heart, I prepared to leave the Thorazdum village, the memories of my time there forever etched in my heart. The evening was drawing to a close, the orange hues of the setting sun casting long shadows across the village. I approached Thrumir, the weight of my impending departure heavy on my heart. As I relayed my decision, his eyes, always so full of wisdom and understanding, met mine with a mixture of sadness and respect.

Before I could say more, Thrumir signaled to Haldorr, who stepped forward, cradling something in his arms. With a nod from Thrumir, Haldorr unfurled a magnificent set of "harndûreng" - chainmail. The armor shirt, meticulously crafted from interlocking rings of the shimmering vorgrund, caught the firelight, casting a radiant glow. Each ring, perfectly shaped and intertwined, was a signature representing the unparalleled craftsmanship of the dwarrin smiths. Thrumir, his voice filled with emotion, spoke of the chainmail's significance. "This harndûreng is not just a piece of armor. It is a symbol of duty, of the responsibility a warrior takes upon themselves to protect those they hold dear." He continued, "You stood with us, fought alongside us, and for that, you are one of us. This is our way of acknowledging your bravery and ensuring you carry a piece of the Thorazdum with you, wherever your journey takes you." I was rendered speechless, the weight of the gesture leaving me overwhelmed.

The four months I had spent amidst the Thorazdum, from the golden changing of leaves of Valandar at the peak of Verindal breeze to the snowy air of Nolariel in the middle of the Isendur season, had been a journey of discovery, a deep dive into the heart of a culture that was both as ancient and vibrant as Alara itself. Every interaction, every shared moment, had been a lesson, a window into the soul of the dwarrin people. Their courage in the face of overwhelming odds, their unwavering unity even in the darkest of times, had left an indelible mark on me. I had seen firsthand the embodiment of stendûr, the fierce loyalty that bound them to their thârûm, a bond that was unbreakable, forged in the fires of adversity. Their battle spirit, thrumgar, that surged through their veins, was not just a concept but a living, breathing force that propelled them forward, driving them to defend their home and their kin with a ferocity that was awe-inspiring.

But it wasn't just their valor in battle that had left an impression. The joyous celebrations, the shared moments of triumph, the songs and dances that echoed through the village, all spoke of a people who knew how to celebrate life, to find joy even in the midst of challenges. My linguistic journey had been equally enriching. The dwarrin language, with its rich tapestry of words and phrases, had opened up new vistas of understanding. Words like "Kazadornak" (leader), "Vorgrund" (sky rock), and "Thârûm" (clan) had become a part of my vocabulary, each term a key to unlocking deeper insights into their culture. The intricacies of their battle strategies, the rituals that marked their celebrations, the traditions that had been passed down through generations, all came alive through the words I had learned.

The village square, where we had shared so many moments, was now filled with the entire thârûm, each member present to bid me farewell. Children, with their innocent eyes wide with curiosity, clung to their parents, sensing the gravity of the moment. The warriors, with whom I had stood shoulder to shoulder in battle, stood tall, their postures a mix of solemnity and respect. Thrumir, the newly appointed Kazadornak, stepped forward, his hand extended in a gesture of friendship. As our hands met, I felt the rough texture of his palm, a mark signifying the hard life of the dwarrin. His grip was firm, and in that simple gesture, I felt the weight of our shared experiences, the bond that had been forged in the crucible of battle. Bruna, the fierce dwarrin maiden - a historian with whom I had shared many a battle strategy, approached next. Her nod, a simple tilt of her head, spoke volumes. It was an acknowledgment, a silent thank you for the role I had played in their defense.

The younger ones, like Galdrûn, approached hesitantly, their eyes shining with unshed tears. They handed me small tokens, trinkets they had made, each one a symbol of their gratitude and affection. The air was thick with emotion, the weight of the impending departure hanging heavily over us. The words "Grundvar s'karr", "Sturdy tunnels", echoed through the square, each voice adding to the chorus, each phrase a blessing, a wish for my safe journey.

As I began my trek away from the village that day in Nolariel, having spent four months among the dwarrin, and having begun my trek nearly nine months prior, the silhouette of the mountain looming large against the snow swept horizon, I took one last look back. The thârûm stood there, a sea of faces, each one a memory, a chapter in the story of my journey. The biting wind carried their voices to me, a gentle reminder of the time I had spent with them, a whisper of the adventures yet to come.

V

Zephyran

With the wind guiding my steps, I continued on my journey, ready to face whatever lay ahead. My journey led me past the Kraggelm territory to a great chasm, a vast scar that marred the surface of Alara. It was a sight to behold, a stark reminder of the raw power of nature. The chasm stretched out before me, its depths shrouded in shadows. Carefully, I made my way around to the other side, my steps cautious and measured. The edge of the chasm was treacherous, the ground unstable, but I navigated it with a steady determination. As I neared the other side, I noticed a strange sight. Luminescent plants were growing through the snow, close to the edge of the chasm, their gentle glow illuminating the surrounding area. The plants were unlike anything I had seen before, their light a soft beacon in the darkness.

Not long after my encounter with the luminescent plants, I stumbled upon a river that seemed frozen - not in ice, but in time. The water was held in place by an unseen barrier, a wall of invisible force that prevented its natural flow. As I approached the river, I could see life teeming within its depths. Fish of all shapes and sizes, their scales a kaleidoscope of bright, natural shades, swam aimlessly within the confined water. Small insects skimmed the surface, their wings beating in a frantic rhythm - all frozen in place, frantically seeking release from the invisible chains that bound them. It was as if their essences were crying out for aid, their lives hanging in the balance, pleading for mercy from an unknown force. I stood at the edge of the river, my mind racing. The lives of these creatures, small as they were, depended on the river's flow. I could feel their desperation, their fear, their hope. It was a palpable force, a cry for help that resonated within me. As I focused my attention on the water, I felt a connection, a communication that transcended words. It was as if the river itself was speaking to me, its voice a whisper in my mind. I responded in kind, a single word slipping from my lips.

"*Flux*," I murmured, the word barely audible.

Instantaneously, the river began to flow again. The unseen barrier shattered, the water rushing forward with a renewed vigor. The fish swam freely, the insects resumed their dance on the water's surface. Life returned to the river. A sense of peace washed over me, a wave of gratitude from the river and its inhabitants. I had learned another spell word, a gift from Alara itself. It was a reminder of the connection between all living things, and of the power of nature and the magic that flowed through it.

As I continued on my journey, a thought began to nag at the back of my mind. Was it possible that all humans shared this mystical connection with Alara, yet most never listened close enough to notice? Or was I alone in my unique bond with our homeland's primal forces? These questions swirled in my mind, a puzzle with no clear solution. I pondered over them, my thoughts a whirlwind of curiosity and wonder. Yet, despite my contemplation, I found no answers. The mystery remained, a riddle wrapped in the enigma of Alara's primal forces. Despite the unanswered questions, I pressed on. The winds at my back were relentless, pushing me forward on my journey.

As I continued my travels, I noticed a change in the skies above. They began to darken, a foreboding canvas of deepening grays and blues. It was an overt distinction to the darkness I had witnessed in my vision, the day I first spoke to Alara's primal forces. This was different, more natural, yet no less ominous. It was the darkening that heralded the arrival of a storm. The air around me grew heavy, the scent of rain hanging in the air. I could feel the electricity, the tension that signaled the coming tempest. It promised to be a fierce storm, its power evident in the rapidly darkening skies. I found myself in a valley, its open expanse offering little in the way of shelter. I scanned the landscape, my eyes searching for any form of refuge from the impending storm. Yet, the valley was barren, its terrain offering no protection from the elements. With the storm fast approaching and no shelter in sight, I steeled myself for the challenge ahead. The winds at my back seemed to push me forward, urging me to press on despite the looming storm. As the storm drew closer, the rumblings of thunder began to echo through the valley. The sound was a low, rolling growl, a primal roar that resonated in the pit of my stomach. It was a clear warning of the storm's impending arrival, a harbinger of the tempest to come.

Within an hour, the storm had descended upon me. The once bright skies were now a dark, roiling mass of clouds, their ominous presence casting a gloomy pall over the icy landscape. I was still without shelter, the valley offering no refuge from the storm's fury. Rain began to fall, a torrential onslaught that drenched me to the bone. The droplets were large and heavy, their impact a sharp reminder of the storm's power. My skin and hair were soaked within moments, the rain relentless in its assault. In a desperate attempt to find shelter, I found myself shivering, hugging the edges of the valley. I moved as close to the valley walls as I could, hoping to find some semblance of protection from the rain. Yet, the valley offered little in the way of shelter, its open expanse leaving me exposed to the elements.

In my desperation, I found myself calling out to Alara, seeking its protection. I yearned for the words, the spell words that could offer me shelter from the storm. Yet, in that moment, the words eluded me. I was left at the mercy of the storm, its power a stark reminder of nature's untamed fury. As the storm raged around me, fear began to creep into my heart. The storm was unpredictable, wild, and uncontrollable - much like the tragic event that had shaken me to my core before I embarked on this journey. The memory of my mentor, Tornu, being taken by the celestriker, flashed before my eyes. His death was sudden, unexpected, a cruel twist of fate that had left me reeling. The storm mirrored the chaos of that fateful day, the unpredictability of it all stirring a sense of dread within me. The rain, the thunder, the flashes of lightning - they were all reminders of the celestriker's attack, of the raw, untamed power of nature. Tornu's death had made me question my desire to explore, to venture into the unknown. It was a harsh reminder of the dangers that lay beyond the safety of our village, of the risks that came with stepping into the wild. Now, as I stood in the midst of the storm, those doubts resurfaced. I felt small, insignificant against the might of the storm. The fear was a cold, gnawing sensation in my gut, a blatant separation from the warmth of my connection to Alara. I was at the mercy of the storm, just as Tornu had been at the mercy of the celestriker. Yet, despite the fear, I knew I had to press on. I had embarked on this journey for a reason, driven by a desire to explore, to learn, to connect with Alara on a deeper level. To keep my promise to my mentor. The storm was a challenge, a test of my resolve. And I was determined to face it head-on, just as I had faced the loss of Tornu.

After what felt like an eternity, I found myself gasping for breath. The storm was relentless, its fury unabated. In my exhaustion, a word slipped from my lips, a whisper carried away by the wind. "*Hav*," I muttered, the word a plea to Alara. And Alara answered. Within minutes, illuminated by the sporadic flashes of lightning, I saw a shadow in the sky. It was a large, winged creature, soaring effortlessly through the storm. It circled above me, its form a dark silhouette against the stormy skies. As I squinted against the rain, I could make out the shape of a large, predatory bird-like creature. Its form was reminiscent of the celestriker, yet distinctly different. Its body was more leather than scale and feather, and its head was elongated, ending in a beak-like face. A zephyran! For a moment, fear gripped me. I feared that the creature had singled me out as its next meal. But my fears were quickly put to rest when the creature landed nearby. It perched above me, its large, scale-covered wing unfurling to provide shelter from the storm. It was an unexpected sanctuary, a refuge offered by a creature of Alara. With a sense of gratitude, I took shelter under the zephyran's wing. I thanked

Alara for its provision, my words a soft murmur against the roar of the storm. For over an hour, I rested under the zephyran's protective wing, the storm raging around us. It was a moment of respite, a brief pause in my journey, until the storm finally passed.

As the storm finally subsided, the air around me began to clear. The rain ceased its relentless assault, the thunder quieted, and the dark clouds began to part, revealing the sky once more. In the newfound calm, the zephyran stirred. With a loud shriek that echoed through the valley, it unfurled its massive wings. The wings were leathery, covered in scales as strong as metal, their impressive span casting a large shadow over the ground below. With a powerful flap of its wings, the zephyran took to the skies. The sound of its ascent was a thunderous clap, a resounding attestation to the creature's strength. I watched as it soared higher and higher, its form growing smaller until it was but a speck in the vast expanse of the sky. The departure of the zephyran marked the end of the storm, and the continuation of my journey. I was once again alone, but with a renewed sense of purpose and determination. The storm had passed, and I was ready to face whatever lay ahead.

As I continued my journey, the ravine I had been navigating began to narrow. The towering walls of the canyon seemed to close in around me, their rocky faces a stark reminder of the rugged terrain I was traversing. Just as I neared the end of the ravine, something caught my eye. There was a glint of polished, dark stone, a fleeting shimmer that stood out against the natural white and gray hues of the snowy canyon. It was just above the crest of the canyon walls, a brief flash that was gone as quickly as it appeared. A chill ran down my spine. Was I being watched? The thought was unsettling. The sheen of the dark stone suggested the presence of others, their intentions unknown. I found myself scanning the canyon walls, my eyes straining to catch another glimpse of the mysterious glint. But there was nothing. The glint was gone, leaving only the rugged landscape of the canyon in its wake. The silence of the ravine seemed to deepen, the sense of isolation growing with each passing moment. I was alone, yet the feeling of being watched lingered, a disquieting reminder of the unknown dangers that lay ahead. With a sense of caution, I continued my journey. The ravine gradually gave way to a different landscape, the narrow confines of the canyon opening up to reveal a vast expanse of open land.

Before me, having traveled for the entirety of Nolariel, lay a snowy plain, a sprawling canvas of nature's artistry. Even through the snow, it was a riot of color, the white ground peppered with a multitude of flowers in every shade of blue, grey, and purple imaginable. The vibrant blossoms swayed gently in the breeze, their sweet fragrance filling the air. Interspersed among the flowers were plants and bushes, their foliage a lush green that contrasted beautifully with the coolish blooms. The plain was a living tapestry, a majestic mural of the diversity and beauty of Alara's flora. Scattered across the plain were clusters of tall trees, their towering dark green and brown forms a sharp disparity to the low-lying flowers and plants. Their branches reached towards the sky, their needles rustling softly in the wind. Running through the heart of the plain were rivers and streams, their waters glistening under the sun. They branched off in different directions, their winding paths carving a network of waterways across the landscape. The sight was breathtaking, a serene panorama that offered a moment of respite from my journey. The vast open plain was a distinct deviation to the ravine I had just traversed, its beauty a welcome sight after the rugged terrain of the canyon.

As I ventured further into the plain, a movement in the distance caught my eye. There were figures, small and impish, their green forms standing out against the white backdrop of the plain. They were not too far off, their presence a curious sight in the serene landscape. Upon closer inspection, I noticed that they were adorned in crude armor. Dark leather coverings adorned with bone protections cradled their heads, shoulders, and chests, the material a clear opposition to their green skin. The armor was rudimentary, yet it gave them an air of ruggedness. In their hands, they carried weapons. Medium-sized clubs and sharpened sticks that they held like spears which, in comparison to their small frames, seemed quite large and unwieldy. Yet they held onto them with a firm grip, their determination evident in their stance.

They were moving towards the north-western edge of the plain, their progress marked by a series of stumbles and falls. Every so often, they would cast glances back in my direction, their eyes wide with a mix of curiosity and wariness. Their attention was easily diverted, and they would often stumble over each other in their distraction. The sight was both amusing and intriguing.

As I continued to observe, the small creatures soon reached their destination. They disappeared into an outcropping of trees near the edge of the plain, their green forms blending seamlessly with the foliage. Their departure left the plain seemingly empty, the bright landscape returning to its peaceful state. Intrigued, I decided to follow them, albeit from a safe distance. I made my way across the plain, my eyes fixed on the outcropping of trees where the creatures had disappeared. Their presence had piqued my curiosity, their hurried departure suggesting a sense of urgency that I couldn't ignore. However, my pursuit was abruptly interrupted. Just as I was nearing the outcropping of trees, I was met with an unexpected encounter. An encounter that would once again change the course of my journey, reminding me of the unpredictability of my quest and the diverse inhabitants of Alara.

VI

Centarion

The Great Takka's tales were filled with stories of the creation of each race, and among them, the tales of the horse-men were the ones I found most difficult to believe. That is, until the day I encountered them on the plains at the beginning of Duravorn, the final month of the Isendur season. As I was tracking the small green bipeds, my path was suddenly blocked by the towering figures of the horse-men. The sight of them was awe-inspiring, their majestic forms a living archetype embodying the truth of Takka's tales. They were half-horse, half-man, a blend of species that was both fascinating and intimidating. Their lower bodies were equine, their muscular legs ending in sturdy hooves that stamped the ground with a resonating thud. Their upper bodies, however, were distinctly human. Their coats were a mix of assorted browns, grays, tans, and blacks, the colors blending seamlessly to create a stunning display. They stood tall and regal, their presence commanding respect. Seeing them for myself, I could attest to the truth of Takka's claim regarding their majesty.

From the group of horse-men, a leader emerged. He was a mighty figure, his dark chestnut coat glistening under the sun, his mane flowing like a cascade of shadows. His presence was commanding, his stature a clear indication of his authority among the group. In his hand, he held a spear. The weapon was as impressive as its wielder, its shaft polished to a shine, ending in a tip that held a gleaming emerald stone. The stone caught the light, its green hue a salient contrast to the dark chestnut of the horse-man's coat. With a swift movement, the leader stepped forward, his hooves thudding against the ground. He raised his spear, the emerald stone gleaming menacingly as he pointed it at my throat. The gesture was clear, a warning and a challenge rolled into one. I was an intruder in their land, and the leader was ready to defend his group if necessary.

Despite my awe at the grace and nobility that these horse-men exuded, I couldn't ignore the unease that crept up on me. Their silent approach had caught me off guard, and their readiness to resort to threats of violence was unsettling. Instinctively, I raised my arms, my hands open in a universal gesture of peace. I held no weapon, bore no ill will, and I hoped they would understand my intentions. Remembering customs I had been taught by the elandari, I decided to bow. It was a sign of respect among the elandari, and I hoped that the horse-men would interpret it in a similar manner. I bent at the waist, my head lowered in a show of deference.

The silence stretched on for a few moments, the tension in the air palpable. Then, I felt a shift. The atmosphere seemed to ease slightly, the oppressive tension lessening. I dared to look up, and found the spear no longer pointed at my throat. The leader had withdrawn his weapon, his stance less threatening. It was a small victory, a sign that they were willing to hear me out. The encounter was far from over, but I had made the first step towards a peaceful resolution. The leader of the horse-men continued to hold my gaze, his eyes piercing through me as if he could see into my very core. His head tilted slightly, a gesture that I interpreted as curiosity. He then spoke, his voice deep and sonorous, echoing across the vast plains. The words were unfamiliar to me, a mix of clicks and equine-like brays that I couldn't comprehend. Recognizing my confusion, the leader made a move. He reached out with one hand while the other moved to secure his spear in a sling on his back. Now with both hands free, he began to make a series of subtle hand gestures. His fingers moved in a complex dance, each movement seemingly deliberate and meaningful.

I watched, trying to decipher his silent language. His gestures were intricate, involving both hands and all his fingers. It was a language of its own, a way of communication that was as foreign to me as their spoken words. Despite my best efforts, I struggled to understand his meaning. In that moment of confusion, a young horse-woman stepped forward. She held in her hands two bunches of strange purple leaves. With a grace that was almost mesmerizing, she brought the leaves close to her mouth. She began to make a series of soft sounds - a mix of whinnies, brays, and whispers that seemed to be directed at the leaves themselves. As she spoke, something extraordinary happened. The leaves began to glow, emanating a soft, luminescent blue light. It was a sight that was both beautiful and otherworldly, an affirmation illuminating the magic that was woven into the very fabric of Alara. The glow faded as quickly as it had appeared, leaving behind only the strange purple leaves in her hands. Once she finished her incantation, she extended one of the bunches of leaves towards me. Her gestures were clear, instructing me to take the leaves and place them against my ear. I was unsure of what to expect, but the curiosity that had led me on this journey urged me to comply. I reached out, taking the offered leaves and bringing them close to my ear.

As I continued to interact with these fascinating creatures, a profound connection began to form. Their language, once alien and indecipherable, started to weave itself into my understanding. The sounds they made, which had initially seemed like mere animalistic noises, began to take on distinct shapes and forms in my mind. I found myself comprehending their words, their expressions, their intentions. And to my surprise, they seemed to grasp my words with equal ease. It was as if a veil had been lifted, revealing a shared language that transcended our different origins. The leader of the group, a figure of authority and wisdom, stepped forward once more. His eyes, full of intelligence and curiosity, met mine as he began to speak. His voice was deep and resonant, each syllable carefully pronounced, echoing in the quiet forest around us. "I am Kallistos," he said, his words clear and distinct in my mind. He gestured towards the female who had bestowed upon me the gift of understanding. Her eyes, very much like her father's, sparkled with a kind of joy that was infectious. "This is my daughter, Eudora," Kallistos introduced her, his voice filled with paternal pride. They went on to explain the nature of the leaves that had granted me this newfound comprehension. In their language, these were known as "*Saela-Hathir*". The words rolled off their tongues in a melodious rhythm, the syllables harmonizing with the rustling of the leaves around us. "*Saela*", they explained, meant "soft-speaking", a word that perfectly captured the gentle rustle of the leaves as the wind caressed them. "*Hathir*" translated to "Grass" or "Vegetation", a testimony underlining the life-giving power of the earth that nurtured these plants.

The *Whispering Leaves*, as I came to call them, were more than just a means of communication. They were a bridge between our worlds, a symbol of the shared understanding that was blossoming between us. As I stood there, amidst these creatures, with the soft whispering of the leaves in my ears, I felt a sense of excitement. Kallistos continued his explanation, his voice a soothing rhythm in the quiet plain. He shared that their noble race was known as the centarion. I attempted to mimic the pronunciation, my tongue stumbling over the unfamiliar syllables. "*Centreon*," I said, the word feeling foreign in my mouth. Kallistos quickly corrected me with a patient smile, his own pronunciation smooth and practiced, navigating the brays and whinnies with ease. He suggested that if the full pronunciation proved too difficult, I could simply refer to them as "*Centaurs*". The term "*Centarion*", he explained, held a deeper meaning in their language. It was akin to our phrase "Starborn Wanderer", a title that seemed to encapsulate their essence perfectly. These were beings born of the cosmos, their spirits as boundless as the star-studded sky, forever wandering and exploring the vast expanses of the world.

The centarion lived in communities that bore a striking resemblance to herds. They referred to their groups as "Astalder", a term that translated to "Star Herds". The name painted a vivid picture in my mind: a group of centarion moving as one under the vast, starlit sky, their bodies casting long shadows on the earth beneath them. They were a nomadic race, their hearts as free as the wind, their spirits untamed and wild. Their lives were a ceaseless journey under the celestial canopy, a chronicle recounting their love for exploration and freedom. As Kallistos shared these details, I found myself captivated by the centarion's way of life. Their connection to the cosmos, their nomadic lifestyle, and their sense of community were all deeply fascinating. I felt a profound respect for these Starborn Wanderers, these centaurs, who lived their lives in harmony with the world and the stars above. I also found myself reminded of Tornu, and our shared love of exploration.

Kallistos continued his narrative, his voice a steady rhythm in the stillness of the plain. He shared that the centarion had sensed a new presence in the plains bordering their forest, a presence that had piqued their interest; it seemed to be a neighboring "Thazrik" clan. At the mention of this unfamiliar term, I found myself compelled to inquire further.

"Who, or what, are the Thazrik?" I asked, my curiosity piqued. Kallistos responded with a description that painted a vivid image in my mind. The thazrik, he explained, were small, green bipeds. The centarion regarded them with a mix of annoyance and caution, a sentiment that seemed to stem from the thazrik's mischievous nature. This characteristic was reflected in the centarion's linguistic nuance of the word "thazrik", hinting at a deeper understanding of these creatures' behavior. As Kallistos spoke, a realization dawned on me. The creatures I had noticed observing me as I journeyed through the ravine might have been members of a thazrik clan. The thought sent a shiver of excitement through me. My journey had already introduced me to the elandari, the dwarrin, the centarion, and now, it seemed, I was on the brink of encountering another fascinating species. The world around me was teeming with life and mystery, and I found myself eager to learn more about these unique inhabitants of the land.

During the five months I spent with the astalder of centarion, beginning in Duravorn - the final month of the cycle - and ending in the sun-sun-kissed month of Sylthal, I was immersed in a world of knowledge and wisdom that was as vast as the plains they roamed. Each day was a new lesson, a new story, a new insight into their way of life.

The centarion were generous teachers, sharing their skills with a patience that was as steady as the rhythm of the earth beneath our feet. They taught me how to navigate by the stars, their fingers tracing the constellations in the night sky as they explained their movements and meanings. They showed me how to listen to the wind, to understand its whispers and interpret its messages. They guided me in the art of survival in the wild, demonstrating how to find water, identify edible plants, and track animals. But their teachings went beyond mere survival skills. They shared their wisdom through centarion tales, stories that were as old as the stars themselves. These tales were woven with lessons of courage, wisdom, and respect for the land. They spoke of centarion heroes, of epic journeys under the starlit sky, of battles with mythical beasts, and of the eternal quest for knowledge and understanding. As I listened to their stories, huddled around the fire under the vast, open sky, I felt a profound connection with the centarion. Their tales were more than just stories; they were a reflection of their values, their beliefs, and their deep respect for the world around them.

The time I spent with the astalder was a journey of discovery and learning. I was not just a visitor in their world; I was a student, a part of their community, a fellow wanderer under the starlit sky. And as I learned from them, I found myself growing, not just in knowledge and skills, but in understanding and respect for the world around me. The centarion shared with me tales of the first of their kind to tread upon the fields of Alara - a figure of legend named Ka'len. They spoke of a time shrouded in the mists of creation, when the grasslands were still fresh and unspoiled, and the hooves of the centarion had yet to leave their mark on the surface of Alara. In their language, this pristine world was known as "Atharal". To the centarion, deeply intertwined with the rhythms of nature and the cosmos, the term "Atharal" held a profound significance. It translated roughly to "Harmony's Breath", a phrase that beautifully encapsulated their belief in the interconnectedness and balance of all things. The centarion philosophy was deeply rooted in this concept of harmony, balance, or unity, represented by the term "Athar". It was a concept that spanned the entirety of existence - the cyclical dance of the seasons, the celestial ballet of the stars and planets, the silent growth of flora, the ceaseless ebb and flow of life itself. "Ral", on the other hand, was a symbol of breath, spirit, or life-force. It was a presentation unveiling the centarion's belief in the animate nature of the world, their view of all existence as being imbued with a spiritual essence or breath. It was a belief that breathed life into every rock, every leaf, every gust of wind, transforming the world into a living, breathing entity. Thus, "Atharal" was a word that conveyed the centarion's belief in the vital unity and harmony of all life and existence. It painted a picture of the world not merely as a physical reality, but as a breathing, spiritual entity engaged in a cosmic dance of harmony and balance. It was a symbol of their deep reverence for the natural world, and their role as stewards of this delicate balance and harmony. As I listened to their tales, I found myself captivated by the depth and beauty of their worldview, a perspective that saw the world not just as a stage, but as a partner in the dance of existence.

The centarion told me of the moment when the wind and the earth collided, a moment of cosmic significance that gave birth to Ka'len. They described it as a streak of silver light that danced across the plains, a beacon of life and energy that marked the birth of their kind. The imagery was breathtaking, a model epitomizing the centarion's deep connection with the natural world and the cosmos. The wind and the earth, in their narrative, were not just elements of nature, but guiding forces that shaped the lives of all astalders. The wind, with its ceaseless movement and boundless freedom, was a symbol of the centarion's free-spirited nature, their desire to explore and experience the world. The earth, with its stability and nurturing qualities, represented their deep respect for life and their role as stewards of the land. The tale of Ka'len's birth was a powerful reminder of the importance the centarion placed on freedom. It was a vessel carrying the essence of their belief in living life on their own terms, guided by the forces of nature and the cosmos. As I listened to their tale, I felt a deep admiration for the centarion, for their reverence for freedom, and for their respect for the guiding forces of the wind and the earth. It was a story that resonated with me, a story that spoke of a way of life that was as beautiful as it was profound.

The centarion spun tales of the Saela-Hathir, the Whispering Leaves, that were as enchanting as the rustling of the leaves themselves. They spoke of a time when the plains were silent, devoid of the gentle whispers that now filled the air. In this quiet world, there lived a wise, old centarion named Thirar, who spent his days in communion with the earth, his ears attuned to its silent language. One day, amidst the silence, Thirar heard a whisper. It was not just any whisper, but the voice of the earth itself, Atharal, speaking to him. It was a moment of profound connection, a moment when the boundary between the centarion and the earth blurred, giving way to a deep understanding. Thirar shared this wisdom with the centarion, teaching them to listen to the whispers of the earth. Since then, the centarion have believed that the Saela-Hathir whispers secrets to those who listen closely, that the earth shares its wisdom with those who are willing to hear.

The centarion were not just storytellers and philosophers; they were also skilled hunters. They took me under their wing, teaching me the art of the bow. At first, I joined them in their hunts on foot, my human pace a notable incongruity to their swift, graceful movements. I was a novice in their world, my steps clumsy and slow, my presence a hindrance rather than a help. But the centarion were patient teachers. Eudora, with her strength and gentleness, came to my aid. She swept me up with her strong arm, placing me gently on her back. From this new vantage point, I was introduced to the thrill of hunting on horseback. The centarion guided me through the process, their instructions clear and patient. They taught me to balance on the back of a moving centarion, to aim with precision, to release the arrow with a steady hand. It was a challenging task, one that tested my balance, my focus, and my patience. Months passed before I began to see progress. My arrows, which had once missed their mark by a wide margin, started to find their target. I was nowhere near the centarion's level of skill and marksmanship, but I was improving. Each successful shot boosted my confidence, each miss, a lesson in patience and perseverance.

Over the months I spent with her astalder, Eudora and I forged a bond that was as strong as the ancient trees that surrounded us. She was my guide, my teacher, my friend. It was Eudora who introduced me to the centarion art of listening to the whispers of the earth, a practice that was as profound as it was beautiful. She showed me how to place my ear against the ground, to feel the subtle vibrations that pulsed through the earth. She taught me to tune into the ebb and flow of the land, to sense the rhythm of Alara beneath my fingertips. It was a skill that required patience and sensitivity, a deep connection with the world around me. It took me a few days to begin sensing Alara's rhythm in this way. At first, all I could feel was the hard ground beneath me, the silence of the earth. But with Eudora's guidance and my continued practice, I began to perceive the subtle movements of the earth. I could feel the distant rumble of a large beast moving through the forest, the gentle pulse of the earth as it breathed. Occasionally, Alara would reveal a new spell word to me through this method. It was a moment of profound connection, a moment when the boundary between me and the earth blurred, giving way to a deep understanding. I was not just a visitor in Alara; I was a part of it, connected to its rhythm, its pulse, its whispers.

The centarion ensured that the enchantment on the Saela-Hathir, the Whispering Leaves that Eudora had given me, remained continually refreshed. This allowed our conversations to continue, bridging the gap between our different languages. They explained that the enchantment Eudora had whispered into the leaves would fade after a brief period, necessitating its renewal. However, they could not teach me the spell words to restore the enchantment myself. This was not due to any unwillingness on their part, but rather a fundamental difference in the way they interacted with Alara's forces. Much like the elandari, the centarion did not need to use spell words to harness the power of Alara. Their native tongue was so closely connected to Alara's balance that they could use their own language as an alternate "spell language". This revelation fascinated me. The centarion's language was not just a means of communication, but a tool to interact with the world around them. It was an attestation corroborating their deep connection with "Atharal", a connection that was so profound that it transcended the need for spell words. Their language was a part of the world, a part of the balance of Alara, allowing them to tap into its forces with a word, a whisper, a breath.

It was Kallistos who introduced me to the art of celestial navigation, a skill that was as fascinating as it was useful. At first, the centarion's system of seasons and months was difficult to decipher due to the linguistic differences. However, with time and patience, I began to understand how each month and season of the centarion cycle correlated with the months and seasons of human cycles. In my own language, the seasons were known as Aravell, Solara, Verindal, and Isendur. Aravell was a time of new life, when animals birthed their offspring and plants bloomed in a riot of colors. Solara was a time of intense heat, when the sun blazed in the sky. Verindal was a time of change, when the vibrant hues of the landscape shifted into warm shades of oranges, reds, and yellows. Isendur was a time of intense cold, when many creatures sought shelter or fell into a deep slumber.

Each season was comprised of three months, each named after Takka's teachings and principles passed down through the generations. In Aravell, there were Elaris, Tavarin, and Loriven, representing the principles of sowing hope, nurturing growth, and living in harmony with life. In Solara, there were Sylthal, Orendar, and Maruvial, symbolizing the embrace of knowledge, perseverance through adversity, and the celebration of abundance. Verindal consisted of Thalindor, Valandar, and Esriven, representing the embracing of change, reflection on past seasons, and preparation for the coming cold. Finally, Isendur contained Ithendar, Nolariel, and Duravorn, symbolizing the protection of home and community, learning from stillness, and the rekindling of spirits in anticipation of the coming Aravell.

While I found myself in agreement with the principles passed down from the First-Born, I struggled to reconcile with his decision to settle after only exploring a small part of Alara. Similarly, I questioned the choice of my ancestors to follow suit. This vast world was teeming with mysteries and wonders yet to be discovered, and the thought of confining oneself to a single corner of it was something I found difficult to comprehend. My own fears had nearly led me down a similar path. The loss of Tornu had shaken me to my core, filling me with a trepidation that threatened to anchor me to the familiarity and safety of my tribe. It was a temptation that was hard to resist, a call to comfort that was difficult to ignore.

But I am glad now that I chose to honor my promise to my mentor. I chose to step out of my comfort zone, to embrace the unknown, to continue my journey. It was a decision that was not easy to make, but one that I am grateful for now. It has led me to experiences and discoveries that I would have missed had I chosen to stay, to moments of wonder and awe that have enriched my journey. While Kallistos did not delve into the origins of the names of their cycles and seasons in great detail, he shared with me a wealth of knowledge about the constellations and their correlation with each season. Over the remaining three months I spent with them, he wove tales of the centarion beliefs regarding the constellations and their cultural significance.

One night, as Duravorn's chill deepened and the last of Isendur's embrace clung to the land, we ascended a hill where the sky seemed to stretch out infinitely, the stars shining with an exceptional brightness. Cloaked in a garment woven of leaves and vines by the Astalder, I listened as Kallistos began to share the myths and wisdom of the centarion. Kallistos pointed towards a constellation that we humans know as The Leaves. "That's 'Elnarion', the Frost Whisperer. As Eneioral's nights draw long, Elnarion serves as a beacon, marking Astalar's final solace and the impending rebirth of Atharal." As I listened to Kallistos' words, I was struck by the depth of the centarion's connection with the cosmos. The constellations were not just patterns of stars to them, but symbols of their beliefs, their origins, their identity. They saw themselves not just as inhabitants of Atharal, but as children of the wind, born from its union with the earth.

As the nights passed, Kallistos and I continued our meetings under the starlit canopy of the sky. He shared stories of different constellations, or "celethorin", as he called them. With each tale, I felt more connected to the centarion culture and to Alara itself. One such night, when the month I knew as Elaris began, a new constellation appeared, which I recognized as The Harvest. "Behold 'Broovinalis', Astalar's Beacon," Kallistos explained. "During this season, Astalar, it illuminates our path, its light a promise of the warmth that is to come."

His words resonated within me, making me feel as if I were a part of the natural cycle of seasons. Over the next couple of months, Kallistos taught me how to navigate by the stars. I learned how the constellations moved across the sky, and how this movement was connected to the changing seasons. On another night, he gestured towards the Wings. "Reldanar, meaning Fluttering Spirit, always points North. By finding Reldanar in the sky, you can always know which way is North," he explained. As I continued learning from Kallistos, time passed. The darkness that I had first seen over a cycle prior had not returned, and I began to wonder if it had been a terror of sleep, a misplaced memory, or a childhood fear. What I did see, however, was the changing season around me.

By the time Sylthal arrived, the sky was adorned with a constellation shaped like a young fawn taking its first steps, that I recognized as what we humans referred to as The Archer, "This is 'Sylfara', Theladra's Dance," Kallistos said with a smile. "In Theladra, Atharal bursts forth in bloom and life, a symphony of colors and vitality, much like the lively steps of a fawn.". I felt the wind beginning to beckon me onwards again. Eudora and the Astalder invited me to stay, at least until their upcoming celebration, the Festival of Atharal's Embrace, had concluded. I accepted their invitation, eager to experience this celebration and to spend more time with my centarion friends.

The Festival of Atharal's Embrace, known as "Nahovrelia", celebrated the zenith of Aravell and the full bloom of life, and was an extravagant event that spanned five days, each filled with its own unique rituals and celebrations. The first day, known as "Haynooria", the Gathering of Leaves, saw us journeying to a sacred grove where the Saela-Hathir, the Whispering Leaves, grew cycle-round. Together with the astalder, I joined in the collection of the purple, grassy leaves. Kallistos took this opportunity to educate me further about these remarkable leaves. While they served primarily as a method of communication, they also played an integral role in the festival. Each centarion in the astalder wore a headdress fashioned from an intricately interwoven ring of vines and Saela-Hathir. The sight of these headdresses, fresh and vibrant, was an emblem highlighting the centarion's deep connection with nature. When we returned to the encampment, I saw that the centarion children had painted vibrant patterns on large pieces of cloth, which were then draped over homes and trees, turning the village into a kaleidoscope of colors. As each centarion donned their freshly woven headdress, the "Huralon", the elders, of the astalder, began to sing. Their song, "Lorbrr Atharal" - "An Ode to Alara", was a melody that had been sung since the dawn of creation. It was believed to resonate within the earth itself, a harmonious echo of Alara's heartbeat. As their voices rose in unison, the sacred grove seemed to pulse with the rhythm of their song, the earth itself joining in their celebration.

Atharal, neilrrahn Atharal rhor virthaeih
Valthar trirtheih hrah brrelmeih, valthar zaleih
Brrulneih brralrrah nelthorar neilrreih braihthar
Neilrrahn Atharal, neilrrahn gelheibrrol zalthar
Nir zelrinar, nir zihnor qirthal neilrreih sirthor
Brralrru talamir zoreih, eln brralrrah brilthor
(Alara, our beautiful Alara)
(In fields and plains, within our reach)
(Your spirit guides us everywhere)
(Our Alara, our bright star)

(No evil no hate may drag us down)
(My hooves journey with you and I will be well)

The second day, I witnessed the "Tralmin rohr Trelmin" - the "Dance of Bloom Breeze". Young centaurs, their bodies adorned with fresh flowers and vines, performed a mesmerizing dance, moving gracefully to the rhythm of drums, mimicking the gentle sway of flowers in a breeze. The festivities of the night were marked by a grand display of archery, a spectacle that was as symbolic as it was breathtaking. The centarion shot arrows into the sky, each adorned with small luminescent gemstones tied to the shaft. As the sun glinted off the hundreds of gemstones, it created a light display unlike anything I had ever seen. It was a dance of light and color, a spectacle that was truly magnificent. But this display was more than just a showcase of skill or a dazzling light show. It was a symbolic gesture, a representation of the connection between the earth, the seasons, and the stars. Each arrow was a symbol, an exhibit exemplifying the centarion's deep connection with the natural world and the cosmos. I was invited to participate in this grand display. While my skills were nowhere near as adept as the centarion's, they applauded my attempts and determination, cheering me on with a choir of brays, shouts, and whinnies. Their encouragement was a strong indication of their kindness and their belief in the importance of effort and engagement. As I watched the arrows soar into the sky, their gemstones catching the light and creating a spectacle of color and light, I was struck by the beauty of the moment. It was a reminder of the centarion's deep connection with the world around them, their reverence for the natural world, and their celebration of the cycles of the seasons and the stars.

The third day of the festival was a day of feasting, aptly named "Mirbrreih Brrulneih Selthorin Gelthar" - "The Feast of the Earth". Members from many families within the astalder contributed their culinary skills to the feast, preparing an array of foods sourced directly from the land. The feast was a demonstration revealing their mastery of the culinary arts, their deep knowledge of the land's bounty, and their ability to transform simple ingredients into a symphony of flavors.

Tables overflowed with seasonal fruits and fresh greens, a celebration of the harvest and nature's generosity. I tasted various delicacies, each one a new experience, a journey of flavors that was as surprising as it was delightful. Ingredients I had never seen or even imagined existed were transformed into dishes that were as flavorful as they were nourishing. It was a feast for the senses. But the feast was more than just a meal. It was a celebration, a gathering of the astalder around one large, central bonfire. There was music, the rhythmic beat of clapping hands and stomping hooves, the melodic strains of hums and neighs filling the air with a harmony that echoed the rhythm of the earth. There was dancing, the centarion moving with a grace and fluidity that was as mesmerizing as it was beautiful. And there was storytelling, tales of the centarion history and beliefs shared around the fire, their words weaving a tapestry of stories that was as rich and vibrant as the feast itself.

The fourth day of the festival was marked by the "Tar Dralthen Zoreih" - the "Skyward Race", a traditional event that was as much a test of physical prowess as it was of navigational skills. On this day, the centarion competitors raced across the plains under the night sky. The sight of the centarion, their bodies strong and agile, racing under the starlit sky was a sight to behold. The centarion's deep knowledge of the stars, their ability to navigate by them, was on full display during the race. It was a showcase laying bare their connection with the cosmos, their ability to read the stars and use them as a guide. As their guest, I was given a special place of honor to start the race. I was given the honor of shooting an arrow into the sky, the signal for the race to begin. As I released the arrow and watched it soar into the sky, I felt a sense of awe and excitement. I was not just a spectator, but a participant, a part of this grand celebration.

The festival concluded on the fifth day with the events of the "Sirthbrreih Vaelaen" - the "Harmonious Union". This day was the most spiritual of the festival days, a day of unity and connection. The centarion gathered in a circle, placing me in the center. They were unsure of where else to have me stand, but they wanted me to experience the ritual firsthand. They raised their hands to the sky, and the Huralon, the elders, began chanting. The Saela-Hathir crowns they wore glowed brightly, their luminescence lasting far longer than when Eudora had whispered to them. I felt a surge of magic envelop the centarion, a palpable energy that seemed to resonate with the rhythm of the earth and the cosmos. The centarion believe this ceremony strengthens the bond between them, the earth, and the cosmos. It was a powerful ritual, an attestation bearing witness to their deep connection with the natural world and the cosmos, their belief in the unity and harmony of all things.

As the ceremony concluded, the astalder, as one, offered me a Saela-Hathir crown as a parting gift. Eudora, acting as the emissary, presented the crown to me, signifying my honorary inclusion into their culture. They expressed their hope that the paths of the stars would guide me safely on my journeys. Moved by the experience, I thanked them and promised to carry their wisdom with me. As I held the Saela-Hathir crown, I felt a sense of connection, a sense of unity with the centarion, the earth, and the cosmos. Before my departure, Eudora once again whispered into the Saela-Hathir. The purple leaves glowed softly with a blue light, a gentle luminescence that slowly faded. The enchantment would not last long, but Eudora placed the headpiece atop my head nonetheless. It was a precaution, a safeguard in the chance that I might encounter another race whose language I did not understand before the enchantment faded.

Our farewells were heartfelt, filled with well-wishes and hopes for future meetings. I wished them well on their travels, and in return, they offered me their traditional parting phrases. "Velarethir," they said, meaning "May the winds guide you." "Thalranis," they intoned, which meant "Until the leaves meet again." And "Rhoranal," they whispered, meaning "May our paths cross again." Each phrase was a signal making evident their culture, their beliefs, and their hopes for our future encounters.

I took my leave five months after I had met the centarion, having traveled with them from Duravorn through Sylthal. The wind whispered the wisdom of Alara, one cycle and three months since my journey began, its soft voice carrying the secrets of the earth and the cosmos. Each step I took was a step into the unknown, a journey into the vastness of Alara and its children.

VII

Goblikar

The enchantment on my Saela-Hathir headdress did not last long enough for me to encounter another group of sentient beings. It took several hours for the enchantment to dissipate, a fact I only realized upon encountering a small group of creatures that I assumed were the "thazrik" that the centarion had spoken of. I noticed them, one sunny day in Orendar, before they noticed me, a circumstance that I'm not entirely sure worked in my favor. I believe I startled them, my sudden appearance catching them off guard. I approached them warily, mindful of the centarion's warnings about the thazrik's mischievous and unpredictable nature. Yet, despite these warnings, I was hopeful to learn more about them.

As I moved closer, I could smell them - their repugnant odor an amalgamation of dirt, sweat, rotten fruit, and fecal matter - before I saw them and their small, green forms more clearly. They were unlike any creatures I had encountered before, aside from that snow-swept day in the plains just prior to meeting the centarion astalder, their appearance as intriguing as their reputation. I was stepping into unknown territory, a meeting with a race that the centarion had spoken of with caution. Yet, despite the uncertainty, I was driven by a desire to learn, to understand, and to connect with the diverse children of Alara that Takka had woven tales about. Observing their thin, short, frail builds,

I couldn't help but find myself smiling at the sight of the thazrik. They were odd-looking creatures, donning weapons and armor that seemed far too large for their small green bodies. The sight was almost comical, yet there was a certain charm to their determination and bravado. As I drew near to their encampment, the lead thazrik noticed me. He leapt to attention, shoving his crude spear at my chest. He held it with both hands, struggling to keep it level. He began shouting in his garbled, guttural language, a tongue I could not even begin to understand.

"GOBB throk! Gobb shiknik zozznik, greeggnik gobb snaggik gobb gob skabzibbiknik!" he yelled, his voice echoing through the air. As he shouted, his companions took notice as well, coming over to us and brandishing weapons of their own. I took note of a small thazrik, possibly a child, scoop up a fistful of dirt and begin making his way behind me at a distance. He was readying himself for if the need arose to temporarily blind or confuse me, already showcasing the warnings provided by the centarion of the thazrik's resourcefulness and cunning, their ability to adapt and use their environment to their advantage.

Despite the tension of the situation, I couldn't help but feel a sense of fascination. Here I was, face to face with a group of thazrik, a race I had only heard about from the centarion. Despite their small stature and seemingly comical appearance, they were a force to be reckoned with, their determination and resourcefulness evident in their actions. I was at a loss on how to refresh the enchantment on my Saela-Hathir headdress. The language of the thazrik was beyond my comprehension, their words a garbled mix of sounds that I couldn't decipher. In the face of this language barrier, I could only hope that a universal gesture of peace as I had used several times before would be enough. I extended my arms to my sides, my hands open and empty. It was a simple gesture, but one that I hoped would convey my intentions. I was not there to fight or to cause harm. I was a traveler, a stranger in their land, seeking understanding and connection.

As I stood there, arms outstretched, I could only hope that they would see my gesture for what it was. I hoped that they would lower their weapons, that they would see me not as a threat, but as a visitor, a fellow inhabitant of Alara seeking to learn and understand. The tension hung in the air, a palpable force as I waited for their response. As I extended my arms, the thazrik who first noticed me spoke again. His eyes narrowed with apparent frustration.

"Zubb?! Gobb zubb roggik?! Gobb skabbik shnikthrok?! Gob shniksnaggik gobb guum!" he barked, his voice filled with confusion and irritation. For a moment, he held his club in place. Then, with a grunt of frustration, he lowered his club a bit, and the others followed suit. "Gobb zubb snaggik?" He asked in a defeated tone, his voice echoing in the stillness.

I breathed a sigh of relief, the tension in my body easing slightly. And on that sigh, came the words, previously unknown to me, "*Threl-Vysh-Pax*". As the words left my lips, my Saela-Hathir began to emanate its soft blue glow once again. The thazrik looked on in utter amazement, their eyes wide as they took in the sight. The glow of the Saela-Hathir cast a soft light on the scene, illuminating the faces of the thazrik. Their expressions of surprise and awe were a sight to behold, a sign underscoring the power and mystery of the Saela-Hathir. As the light danced in their wide eyes, I felt a sense of hope. Perhaps, with the help of the Saela-Hathir, I could bridge the gap between us, and find a way to communicate and understand each other.

"What... what you do?! What you is?!" Shrieked the thazrik, his voice filled with surprise and confusion. His words were still a bit difficult to understand due to the informal and atypical way they structured their sentences, but with my discovery of these new spell words, my Saela-Hathir came to life, allowing me to converse with the thazrik.

I learned that they call themselves a "*goblikar*", or a "Shadowborn". Their language was filled with guttural tones and clicks, a unique and complex system of communication that was unlike anything I had encountered before. Due to the complexity of their language, I simply referred to them as "Gobble-kin", or "goblins", a term that seemed to capture their unique nature and culture. The goblikar I had first encountered was named Snikkelgrom. The goblins, a race of creatures known for their rough exterior and wild laughter, welcomed me into their encampment, a haven from the blistering winds of Solara. The camp was a haphazard collection of makeshift tents, the structures patched together from various materials, an indicator hinting at the goblins' resourcefulness. The air was thick with the scent of roasting meat and the earthy aroma of the goblins themselves, a smell not pleasant, but that came to be rather a comforting reminder of their rugged lifestyle.

We gathered around a small but fierce campfire, the flames dancing and flickering, casting long, distorted shadows on the faces of the goblins. Their eyes sparkled with mirth and mischief in the firelight, their gruff voices filling the air with laughter and camaraderie.

The goblins were a humorous race, their jokes a complex play on words that often got lost in translation. Yet, their laughter was infectious, their joy palpable, and I found myself laughing along, the sound echoing in the cold night air.

One goblikar, a burlier creature with a mischievous glint in his eyes, stood up, clearing his throat dramatically. He began, "Zubb goblikar gobbik skabbik gobz thrivikgobniknik blikk skribbnikkik nik?" The others roared with laughter as he delivered the punchline, "Gob shnik gobgob!" The joke played on the varied use of the word "gob" for I/we and you, implying the dark was so thick the goblikar couldn't even find himself. The absurdity of the situation, coupled with the goblikar's animated delivery, had everyone in stitches. The joke roughly translates to say, "What did the goblikar say when he couldn't find his brother in the dark? 'I've lost us!'"

Another goblikar, this one smaller but with a wicked, broken-toothed grin, chimed in with his own joke. "Gobz snobb skrab grob. Zubb? Skrab skrigg rukk!" The joke was a playful jab at their own living conditions and diet, which often involved scavenging or hunting vermin. The idea that even goblins, who regularly consumed putrid meats, found rats too dirty to eat, was met with uproarious laughter. This one crudely translates to, "Why did the goblikar smell the rat before eating it? Because rats are food too dirty even for a goblikar!"

The night wore on, filled with more jokes, each one more absurd and hilarious than the last. The goblins' humor was a reflection of their lifestyle - chaotic, unpredictable, and full of mischief. Despite the linguistic differences, their laughter was a universal language, one that spoke of shared joy and camaraderie. As I sat there, surrounded by the warmth of the fire and the hearty laughter of the goblins, I felt a sense of belonging. I was a stranger in their land, yet they had welcomed me with open arms, sharing their food, their drink, and their humor. It was a night I would remember for a long time, a night filled with laughter and the simple joy of shared companionship.

The goblins' culinary practices were an absolute differentiation to their jovial nature. Their food, a collection of meats left to age in dark, underground pits, was a test of endurance for my palate. The meats, left until maggots began to infest the supply and the carcasses began to putrefy, were a staple in their diet. The smell was overpowering, a pungent aroma that filled the air and clung to the back of my throat. As I bit into the meat, I was hit with a wave of strong, gamey flavors. The texture was tough, the meat having lost its tenderness during the aging process. Yet, as I chewed, I began to find subtle flavors beneath the initial onslaught. There were hints of earthiness, a smoky undertone that, if I focused on it particularly hard, was somewhat tasteful. It was a fleeting moment of palatability amidst the overwhelming taste of decay. Their drinks were no better. They were concocted from water gathered from streams and lakes, which was then left to sit for months in pits they had dug out. The water, once fresh and clear, became stagnant over time, its surface covered with a thin layer of green algae. The smell was musty, a stark reminder of the water's long journey from freshness to stagnation. I took a few large swigs, the water's taste as unpleasant as its smell. My stomach rebelled, and I found myself retching, much to the amusement of the gobble-kins. Their laughter echoed around the camp, a remarkable divergence to my discomfort. Seeing my distress, they fetched water from their most recently dug pit. This water was far fresher, most of it having come from a recent rainfall. The difference was palpable. The water was clear, its taste crisp and refreshing. It was a welcome relief from the earlier ordeal, a reminder of the simple pleasure of fresh water. Despite the challenging culinary experience, the goblins' company more than made up for it. Their laughter, their camaraderie, their acceptance of me into their fold - it was a gauge providing a measure for their spirit, a spirit that thrived amidst the harsh conditions of their lifestyle. As I sat there, sipping the fresh water, I couldn't help but smile. The goblins, with their rough exterior and hearty laughter, had taught me a valuable lesson - that joy can be found even in the most challenging of circumstances.

The goblins had a peculiar practice of fermenting a mixture of sweet plants, fruits, and vegetation they found during their explorations. These pits, filled with a colorful array of nature's bounty, were left untouched for months, allowing nature to work its magic. The result was a thick, potent-smelling, dark brown liquid they affectionately called "gobslop." The sight of the gobslop was not for the faint-hearted. The liquid was a murky brown, its surface occasionally disturbed by bubbles rising from the depths. The smell was overpowering, a heady mix of fermentation and decay, the sweetness of the fruits now a distant memory.

I watched as several goblins gathered around a pit, their faces lit up with anticipation. They each held a crude cup, the excitement palpable as they prepared to compete in their gobslop drinking contest. The goblins were a competitive race, their games a reflection of their wild and unpredictable nature.

The contest began, the goblins downing the gobslop with gusto. Their faces contorted with the effort, the potent liquid proving to be a challenge even for them. The air was filled with their grunts and laughter, the contest a spectacle of their camaraderie and spirit.

One by one, the goblins succumbed to the gobslop's potency, their laughter turning into groans as they joined me in the unpleasant experience of regurgitation. Yet, even in their discomfort, they found humor, their laughter echoing around the camp. As I joined them in their laughter, I felt a sense of camaraderie. Despite our differences, we shared a moment of shared discomfort and humor.

The goblins' revelry was a sight to behold. As the night wore on, the consumption of gobslop took its toll. One by one, the goblins succumbed to the potent brew, their laughter fading into soft snores. They lay strewn about the encampment, their bodies contorted into a variety of strange positions, a reflection capturing the spirit of the night's festivities. I found myself a spot next to the fire, its warmth a comforting presence against the chill of the Solara night winds. The fire crackled and popped, its flames dancing in the night, casting a warm glow on the sleeping goblins. The sound of their soft snores filled the air, a soothing lullaby that lulled me to sleep. As I drifted off, I couldn't help but feel a sense of contentment. The night's festivities, the hearty laughter, the shared camaraderie - it was a refreshing experience, a reminder of the simple joys of life.

My stay with the goblins was brief, lasting only a few days. Yet, each day was a repeat of the last - filled with laughter, shared meals, and the occasional gobslop drinking contest. During my stay, they revealed that it was indeed their scouts who were watching me in the ravine. They had never seen a human before, their encounters mostly limited to the centarion and a small, sprite-like creature they called a "*griz*". My presence had intrigued them, a strange creature wandering in the ravine with a coming storm. Yet, despite their initial apprehension, they had welcomed me into their fold, sharing their food, their drink, and their humor. As I left the goblikar encampment, I carried with me memories of their hearty laughter, their rugged lifestyle, and their infectious spirit. It was an experience I would remember for a long time, a reminder of the joy and camaraderie that can be found even in the most unexpected of places.

During my time with the goblins, I was privy to a deep dive into their rich culture. Snikkelgrom, a goblikar with a twinkle in his eye and a wealth of knowledge, shared with me the intricacies of their societal structure. Their clans, or "ṣḵrêḵḵṇîḵ" as they called them, were more than just a group of individuals. The term ṣḵrêḵḵṇîḵ conveyed a sense of mischievous camaraderie, collective cunning, and a shared code of conduct among the goblins. It was a term that embodied the spirit of goblikar unity and their inclination towards clever tricks and pranks.

The goblikar language, while simplistic in structure, was fascinating in its complexity. The prefix "kree-", short for "kreeg", which means "quick" or "multiple", was added to the beginning of a goblikar word to make it plural, much like how we humans and the dwarrin add an "-s" or "-es" to the end of a word. Their language also had markers to denote past or near-future tenses. For instance, "Gob shiksnaggik" meant "I wanted", with "shik-" being the marker for past tense, and "snaggik" being the word for "to want". The language was a reflection of the kreegoblikar practical and efficient nature, their words tailored to their lifestyle and needs.

The term ṣḳrêḳḳṇîḳ also encompassed the concept of both clan and tribe in Goblish. It carried cultural nuances that were unique to goblikar society, reflecting their close-knit and communal nature. Within a ṣḳrêḳḳṇîḳ, kreegoblikar found belonging, protection, and a shared sense of identity. It was a demonstration making clear their interdependence, their survival hinging on their ability to work together and rely on each other.

Zigwortle, the elder of the ṣḳrêḳḳṇîḳ, was a figure of respect and wisdom among the kreegoblikar. His eyes, though aged, sparkled with a youthful mischief, a witness bearing testimony to his spirit. He took an immediate liking to me, his gruff exterior softening into a warm smile whenever our paths crossed. It wasn't long before he began to share with me their most sacred myths of Alara, or "Grex" as they called it. The term "Grex" in Goblish referred to a labyrinth or maze, a reflection of the kreegoblikar's view of the world as a playground for their capricious antics. It was a term that encapsulated their love for mischief and trickery, their zest for life and adventure.

One evening, as the fire crackled and the stars twinkled overhead, Zigwortle gathered the kreegoblikar around him. His voice, gruff and gurgly, yet still somewhat soothing, filled the air as he began to tell the story of their creation. "Kreegoblikar, gather! Listen close, younglings, as I tell you the story of the Whispering Shadows, about how we, the kreegoblikar, came to be in the land of Grex."

The kreegoblikar, young and old, huddled around Zigwortle, their eyes wide with anticipation. The firelight danced on their faces, casting long shadows that flickered and danced with the flames. The air was filled with a sense of reverence, a shared respect for the sacred myths of their people. As Zigwortle began his tale, the kreegoblikar listened in rapt attention, their faces reflecting the flickering firelight. The night was filled with the sound of Zigwortle's voice, his words weaving a tapestry of their history and culture.

"Once, when night was new, the Skunthar was alone in the sky," Zigwortle began, his voice echoing in the stillness of the night. His words painted a picture of a time long past, a time when the world was young and full of secrets. "She whispered to the kreegobburd, and they danced and delighted. The Skunthar shone on them and gave them Flazzik, and with her, the first kreegoblikar were born, filled with kreesekrath and a love for those kreesekrath."

The kreegoblikar listened intently, their eyes reflecting the flickering firelight. The tale was a tribute giving due recognition to their origins, a story of their birth from the whispers of the Moon, "Skunthar", and the dancing shadows, "kreegobburd". It spoke of Flazzik, the first goblikar, of their love for secrets, "kreesekrath", their zest for exploration, and their kinship with the Skunthar.

"We kreegoblikar ran and played, seeking kreesekrath and exploring. We spoke to the Skunthar, and she showed us the great secret of Grex. We saw the beauty and the kinship of all. We told the other kreegoblikar, and they listened, and their hearts were moved," Zigwortle continued, his voice filled with a sense of reverence and awe.

The tale was a reflection of the kreegoblikar's spirit, their love for exploration and discovery. It spoke of their role as Keepers of Shadows, guardians of the beauty of the night. It was a reminder of their duty, their purpose, and their love for Alara.

"Kreegoblikar, go forth and explore, for Grex awaits!" Zigwortle concluded, his words echoing in the stillness of the night. The kreegoblikar, young and old, listened in silence, their faces reflecting the firelight and the wisdom of Zigwortle's words. As I listened to Zigwortle's tale, I was reminded of my own yearning for exploration, the thrill of discovering things previously unknown. The kreegoblikar story, their love for secrets and exploration, resonated with me. It was a reminder of my own promise to explore the wonders of Alara, to preserve the delicate balance within its primal forces. The kreegoblikar, with their love for secrets and their duty as Keepers of Shadows, were an affirmation confirming the beauty of the natural world. Their story inspired me to cherish and honor our natural world even more deeply, just as the kreegoblikar cherished the secrets of our shared land.

During my stay with the ṣḳrêḳḳṇîḳ, Zigwortle, the elder, became a storyteller, his tales a window into the rich tapestry of goblikar culture and tradition. Each story was a gem, filled with adventure, lessons, and the spirit of the kreegoblikar. He told the tale of "The Muddy Skrabb's Secret", a story set during the season of "Grobkash" or Verindal in my tongue. It was a tale of a clever goblikar named Riklash who discovers a hidden tunnel called Gibnak. Intrigued, he uncovers a magical zikk, or treasure, but learns a valuable lesson about true riches and the importance of kinship. The tale highlighted the kreegoblikar love for exploration and their strong sense of community.

Zigwortle also wove the legend of "The Dance of the Shimmering Shadows". During the season of "Naknik" or Aravelle, the kreegoblikar gather for a grand celebration, performing the enchanting dance of Thrivik. The dance, a mesmerizing display of unity and grace, embodies the beauty of the night and the bond between the kreegoblikar as Children of the Moon. It was a tale that captured the spirit of the kreegoblikar, their love for celebration and their strong sense of community.

On my final night with the ṣḳrêḳḳṇîḳ, Zigwortle told me the tale of the "Zibzab's Whisper". Set in the frosty season of Hargnak, or Isendur, the story follows a cunning goblikar, Haggniknik, who embarks on a journey to confront the Zibzab - a giant, poisonous, armored insect. With its poison, he discovers the power to transform secrets into whispers, teaching the kreegoblikar the importance of trust and the responsibility of guarding secrets.

After a final night of revelry, filled with laughter, shared stories, and the warmth of the kreegoblikar's company, I awoke early the next morning. The encampment was still, the kreegoblikar lost in their dreams, their bodies strewn about once more in a variety of strange positions, as they were every night. The kreegoblikar, with their unique customs and traditions, didn't really say "farewell" or "goodbye". Instead, they expressed their parting sentiments with a grunt or a wave, their actions a reflection of their practical and straightforward nature. As I left their encampment, the memories of my time with the kreegoblikar filled my mind. The laughter, the shared meals, the stories - they were an indicator providing evidence of the kreegoblikar spirit, their love for life and their strong sense of community. Amidst the warmth of these memories, and all the ones I'd made along my journey thus far, I had all but forgotten the vision of destruction I'd had at the start of my adventure.

VIII

Faelari

The wind blew at my back, its warm touch a reminder of the path ahead. I felt an urgency swelling inside me, a sense of purpose that was stronger than ever before. The kreegoblikar, with their love for secrets and their duty as Keepers of Shadows, had taught me valuable lessons. They had shown me the importance of community, the joy of exploration, and the delicate balance between discovering secrets and protecting them. The hot air of Solara burned into my skin, bringing me to pant warm, heavy breaths. The words "*Vis-Kae*" rolled off my tongue, escaping my lips with one such breath. As the last syllable faded into the silence of Solara, a peculiar phenomenon unfolded before my eyes.

A single snowflake, not only an oddity in the month of Orendar, but an absurdity, caught in its gentle descent, seemed to snag on an unseen thread in the fabric of reality. It tore a thin, almost imperceptible line in the air, a rift that began to expand slowly, like a wound being opened. The world around me seemed to ripple and distort, as if I were peering through a veil of water. As the veil lifted, a scene of utter devastation unfurled before me. The once bright and verdant fields of Solara were now a charred wasteland, the emerald green and harvest yellow replaced by the black of burnt earth. The once towering forests, their canopies a sign giving credence to the relentless march of time, were reduced to skeletal remains, their grandeur lost to the insatiable flames. The air was thick with the acrid smell of smoke, the scent of life turned to ash. The sky, once a canvas of brilliant blues, was now a murky gray, choked with the remnants of what had been. The once vibrant world was now a monochrome painting of despair. Among the ruins, I saw the inhabitants of Alara - kreegoblikar, centarion, elandari, dwarrin, and humans alike. Their faces were etched with pain, their eyes reflecting the flames that had consumed their homes. Their bodies were hunched, weighed down by the overwhelming despair that clung to them like a shroud.

At the epicenter of the destruction, a dark silhouette stood, a portrait of horror against the backdrop of flames. The figure of a creature - a monstrous, otherworldly abomination, its form outlined by the inferno, stood tall amidst the chaos. Its posture was one of triumph, its silhouette seeming to drink in the devastation around it. Its presence was like a black hole, absorbing the light and life around it, leaving only destruction in its wake. The scene was a symphony of destruction, each note a symbol giving voice to the power of the monstrosity at its center. The world around me was burning, and at the heart of it all, the conductor of this macabre orchestra reveled in the discordant melody it had created. I began to choke on the heat and ashes that had begun to slowly fill my lungs.

As abruptly as it had appeared, the vision of destruction vanished. The world snapped back into focus, the veil of despair lifting to reveal the familiar surroundings of Alara. I found myself standing at the edge of the forest, the goblikar encampment just a stone's throw away. The sounds of the encampment, the crackling of fires and the distant chatter of kreegoblikar, were an unmistakable split from the eerie silence of the vision. The world around me had returned to normal, but the echoes of the devastation I had witnessed still reverberated in my mind. The spell words "*Vis-Kae*" seemed to hang in the air, their resonance a chilling reminder of the power they held. The image of the dark figure, standing amidst the ruins, was etched into my mind's eye, his silhouette a haunting specter.

Questions began to swirl in my mind, like a whirlwind of confusion and fear. What was the meaning of these new spell words? Who was the dark figure? What connection did he have to the destruction I had witnessed? The questions spiraled out of control, each one spawning a dozen more, their weight pressing down on me. A sense of panic began to creep in, its icy tendrils wrapping around my heart. My breath hitched in my chest, each inhale becoming a struggle as the fear took hold. The world around me seemed to spin, the trees and the encampment blurring into a whirl of colors. A sense of impending peril washed over me, a tidal wave of dread that threatened to pull me under. The fear was a living entity, its grip tightening around me, its whispers of danger echoing in my ears. I felt a desperate yearning for the comforting presence of Tornu, his wisdom and guidance, a beacon in the storm of my fear.

I stood there, at the edge of the forest, the world around me an indelible contrast to the chaos within. The encampment, with its warmth and laughter, seemed a world away. The vision had shaken me to my core, leaving me grappling with the fear and uncertainty it had stirred. How I wished for Tornu's steady presence, his wisdom a guiding light in the darkness that had descended upon me. As the edges of my vision began to blur, the world around me fading into a haze of darkness, a sudden flash of light cut through the gloom. A wisp of green and blue light danced in the air above me, its ethereal glow casting an otherworldly shadow on the sun-kissed ground. It moved with a life of its own, darting back and forth above me, its luminescence a vivid variance from the encroaching darkness. Just as the wisp made another pass over me, my consciousness began to slip away. The world around me faded into nothingness, the warmth of the grass beneath me and the fires of the Solara air becoming distant sensations. The last thing I remembered was the mesmerizing dance of the green and blue light, its glow a mystery in the darkness.

When I awoke, it felt as though days had passed. The dry heat of Solara was replaced by the humid warmth of a rainforest. The yellow dry grass was now a carpet of vibrant green foliage, the sweltering hues of orange replaced by a riot of colors. I was deep within a vast rainforest, the canopy above a patchwork of green, the sunlight filtering through in dappled patterns. The silence of the Maruvial air was replaced by the symphony of the rainforest. The calls of unseen creatures echoed through the trees, a chorus of life that filled the air. The rustle of leaves, the distant trickle of water, the hum of insects - the grove was alive with the sounds of nature. Despite the cacophony of sounds, I seemed to be alone. There was no sign of any other presence, the rainforest seemingly untouched by any other. The lush greenery stretched out in all directions, a world away from the goblikar encampment.

Confusion washed over me as I tried to piece together how I had ended up here. The last thing I remembered was the wisp of green and blue light, its dance a haunting memory. How had I traveled from the burning sun of Solara to this vibrant rainforest, seemingly in the height of Aravell? How long had it been? The questions hung in the air, their answers as elusive as the path that had led me here. Just as I was grappling with the mystery of my sudden displacement, a flash of light caught my eye. The same wisp of blue and green light that had danced above me in Orendar now fluttered in front of my face. It moved with a grace that was almost hypnotic, its ethereal glow illuminating the space around me. This time, however, it came to a halt, hovering in mid-air just at the tip of my nose. As I focused on the light, I realized it was not merely a wisp of light, but a creature! It was ethereal, its form almost translucent, its body radiating a soft glow of blue and green. Its shape was fluid, constantly shifting and changing, like a flame flickering in the wind. It was a creature unlike any I had ever seen, its existence straddling the line between reality and the ethereal.

The creature attempted to communicate with me, its voice a high-pitched melody that filled the air. The sounds it made were unlike any language I had ever heard, the syllables a complex tapestry of sounds that my mind struggled to comprehend. Its voice was like the tinkling of tiny bells, each word a note in a song that was both enchanting and incomprehensible. I strained to understand, to decipher the meaning behind the melody, but the language was too foreign, too alien. The creature's words washed over me, their meaning lost in the symphony of sounds that filled the rainforest. Despite the barrier of language, the creature's intent was clear - it was trying to communicate, to share something with me. But what that something was, I could not decipher. With a sense of purpose, I called upon the enchantment that had served me well during my time with the kreegoblikar. The spell words "*Threl-Vysh-Pax*" rolled off my tongue once more, their resonance filling the air around me. I felt I had spoken these words countless times before, their power enabling me to converse freely with the kreegoblikar during my brief stay among them, despite our different languages. As the last syllable of the spell echoed through the rainforest, my Saela-Hathir responded. The headpiece, a constant companion during my travels, began to glow with a familiar blue light. The glow was a comforting sight, an essence capturing the power of the enchantment. As quickly as it had appeared, the glow faded, the headpiece returning to its normal state. With the enchantment restored, I turned my attention back to the ethereal creature. Its form flickered in front of me, its body radiating the same blue and green light. I spoke gently, my voice a soft whisper amidst the chorus of the rainforest. My words were a question, an inquiry about my current location.

The creature's response came in a melody of sounds, now comprehensible thanks to the enchantment on my Saela-Hathir. She introduced herself as Ilyafae, her name a beautiful note in the symphony of her language. She explained that she had witnessed my collapse at the edge of the forest, her ethereal form a silent observer of my plight. In her recounting, Ilyafae spoke of Alara, or "Eledhin", as she referred to it in her language, with a reverence that was palpable. She had called upon Eledhin to bring me to safety, her plea answered by a weightless bed of air that had carried me away. She had followed me, her form a wisp of light trailing behind the invisible carriage. The grove where I found myself was a nexus of Alara's primal forces. The air was heavy with magic, its presence a tangible force that pulsed with life. The grove was a collection of thousands of trees, their roots intertwined in a complex network, their canopies reaching towards the sky in a silent prayer. It was as if all the magic of Alara converged here, reaching a climactic harmony that resonated with the very essence of the world.

Ilyafae revealed that she was far from her home, on a quest to find Eledhin's protector. Her journey had brought her across vast distances, her path guided by a purpose that was as strong as the magic that coursed through the grove. Intrigued by her tale, I found myself asking her a multitude of questions. I wanted to know more about her quest, about her people, about the world she came from. Each question was a step towards understanding, a bridge that connected our vastly different worlds. As Ilyafae answered, her words painted a picture of a world that was as fascinating as it was foreign, a world that I was eager to learn more about. With a gentle flutter of her ethereal form, Ilyafae began to share the story of her people. She spoke of the faelari, her voice carrying a note of pride as she uttered the name. The term was unfamiliar to me, but she quickly explained that most who encountered her kind referred to them as "Fae" or "Fairies". The names were a simplification, a way for others to understand her people, but the term faelari held a depth of meaning that the other names could not capture. Ilyafae painted a picture of faelari society, a matriarchal community where the wisdom of the females guided their path. Although matriarchal in nature, the faelari form allows a fairy to enter a seven month long hibernation inside a cocoon shaped by weaving the threads of Alara's primal forces together. This hibernation could be undertaken at any time of their choosing, and upon resurfacing seven months later, the faelari would have changed from either male to female, or female to male. Their communities were known as Lünafælen, a term that resonated with the essence of the faelari. The name, she explained, roughly translated to "Moonlit Faelari Haven", a proclamation of their deep connection to the moon and the natural world. The term Lünafælen was a reflection of their beliefs, a symbol of their reverence for the moon and nature. The faelari saw themselves as part of the natural world, their lives intertwined with the cycles of the moon. The moonlit haven was more than just a home, it was a sanctuary, a place where the faelari could connect with the primal forces of the world.

As our conversation continued, I asked about the term "Eledhin", a word that Ilyafae had used earlier. She explained that in the Faelish tongue, Eledhin roughly translated to "All-Song". The All-Song was the melody of the world, a song that the faelari were attuned to, their lives a harmonious note in the grand symphony of Eledhin. As our conversation deepened, Ilyafae seemed to sense my genuine curiosity and interest in her people. Her form shimmered with a brighter intensity, the ethereal light dancing around her as she began to share more about the faelari culture. Her words painted a vivid picture of a society deeply connected to nature, their lives guided by the rhythms of the natural world. She spoke of the faelari's profound bond with Eledhin, their lives intertwined with the All-Song that resonated through every aspect of the world. Their understanding of life and time was cyclical, a reflection of the natural cycles they observed in the world around them. The changing seasons, the shifting constellations, each was a symbol of the cyclical nature of existence.

Ilyafae began to speak of the constellations, her words weaving a tapestry of stars and celestial bodies. Each constellation held a special significance in the faelari culture, their positions in the night sky guiding their calendar and their rituals. The constellations were more than just clusters of stars; they were stories written in the heavens, their patterns a celestial map that guided the faelari through life. As she spoke, Ilyafae interwove details about the faelari calendar, explaining how the positions of the constellations marked the passing of time. Each shift in the celestial pattern signaled a change in the calendar, a new phase in the cyclical journey of life. As I listened, I found myself drawn into the world of the faelari, captivated by their deep connection to Alara and the natural world. Ilyafae began to speak of specific constellations, their stories illuminating the rich tapestry of faelari culture and beliefs. The first she mentioned was Sylphara's Diadem, a constellation that mirrored our own Peaks constellation. It held prominence during the month of Lysawen, or Tavarin in human terms, a period of renewal and rebirth.

The constellation was named after Sylphara, a revered faelari queen who had led her people to Eledhin when their original home among the stars was threatened. The story of Sylphara was a tale of courage and leadership, her journey an example of the resilience of the faelari. The ascension of her Diadem in the night sky was a symbol of the perseverance that all faelari strived to embody, a beacon of hope that shone brightly during the month of renewal.

Following Sylphara's Diadem was the constellation of Baelnorn's Grasp, a celestial pattern that correlated with our Knots constellation. It became visible during Falathir, the third month in the faelari calendar, a time of introspection and learning. This period corresponded with the human month of Loriven, a time when the faelari turned inward, seeking wisdom and understanding.

Baelnorn's Grasp was named after a faelari sage known as Baelnorn. His story was one of acceptance and transformation. Instead of suppressing his shadow, Baelnorn had embraced it, turning it into a source of wisdom. The constellation served as a reminder of his journey, its presence in the night sky a lesson about the power of introspection. It symbolized the necessity of balance between light and dark, a signal to the faelari belief in the cyclical nature of life and the interconnectedness of all things.

Ilyafae continued her celestial narrative, her voice a soft melody that wove tales of heroes and lessons from the stars. She spoke of Silvariel's Whisper, a constellation that mirrored our Totem, dominating the sky during Laelari, or Orendar in human terms. Silvariel was a faelari who could sing to plants, coaxing them into unique, wondrous forms.

Next, she told me of Aeolan's Dance, corresponding to our Hearth constellation. It rose during the frosty month of Thaelen, or Thalindor for humans. Aeolan was a faelari who danced upon Isendur winds, crafting ice into fantastical shapes and bringing warmth and cheer during the cold. His tale underscored the importance of joy and creativity in the face of hardship.

Taelimara's Arrow was the next constellation, corresponding to our Branch. It ascended during Sylthara, or Valandar in human terms.

Taelimara was a faelari huntress who could shoot arrows of moonlight, guiding those who lost their way in the night. Her story celebrated the values of guidance, accuracy, and the quest for wisdom.

Brumil's Touch, corresponding to our Axe constellation, shone brightly during the month of Erendel, or Sylthal for humans. Brumli was a fairy who could soothe and heal wounded animals with a mere touch, turning potential enemies into allies. His constellation reminded the faelari of the power of empathy and kindness.

Thistli's Loom, the faelari equivalent of our Wheels constellation, was visible during the month of Ithilwen. Thistli was a faelari who spun threads of morning dew into intricate patterns, contributing to the ethereal beauty of the Lünafælen. Her tale emphasized the importance of innovation and the intricate, interconnected workings of the world.

During Telorin, or Ithendar for humans, the tale of Lunafae's Flight was told. Lunafae was a faelari blessed with butterfly wings, spreading life and joy wherever she flew. Her tale was a mirror reflecting transformation, the transient beauty of nature, and the freedom of spirit.

Glimmerlain's Glow, or Ruknak's Hoard in human terms, dominated the sky during Maellis, or Nolariel for humans. Glimmerlain was a faelari who turned dewdrops into radiant gems, but instead of hoarding them, she shared her treasures with everyone. Her tale warned against greed and encouraged generosity.

Lastly, Ilyafae told me the tale of Blythaela's Grace, corresponding to our Halar's Bounty constellation. It ascended during Staraelin, or Duravorn for humans. Blythaela was a faelari who could make any plant she touched bloom, leading to an era of plenty. Her tale embodied gratitude, abundance, and the joy of sharing.

As Ilyafae continued to share the tales of her people, I began to understand their profound significance. These were not just stories; they were the moral and societal compass of the faelari. The tales spoke of harmony with Eledhin, of the deep connection between the faelari and the world around them. They emphasized the balance between light and dark, a benchmark of the cyclical nature of life and the importance of accepting all aspects of oneself. Creativity was celebrated, a reminder of the beauty that could be created when one allowed their imagination to take flight. Guidance was a recurring theme, a nod to the importance of helping others find their way. Empathy was valued, a lesson in the power of understanding and kindness. Innovation was praised, a disclosure of the importance of constantly seeking new ways to interact with the world. Transformation was a key lesson, a symbol of the constant change that was a part of life. Generosity was encouraged, a reminder of the joy that came from sharing with others. And gratitude was a central theme, a call to appreciate the abundance that life offered. Each faelari child grew up hearing these tales, the stories a constant presence in their lives. They learned the lessons that the tales taught, striving to embody the virtues represented by the constellations. The tales were a guide, a map that helped the faelari navigate the journey of life, their lessons a beacon that illuminated the path ahead.

Over the course of the following months, our conversations deepened, expanding beyond the tales of the constellations to encompass a myriad of topics. Ilyafae and I found ourselves exchanging stories and experiences, our conversations a bridge that connected our vastly different worlds. I found myself drawn to her tales of the faelari culture, my curiosity piqued by the unique society she described. I asked her more about the protector she was in search of, intrigued by the purpose that had brought her so far from home. Her quest was a mystery, a puzzle that I was eager to understand - one that her people had been searching for and prophesying about for the last three hundred cycles. In return, I shared my own experiences with her. I spoke of my travels, of the lands I had seen and the people I had met. I told her about the spell words I had learned, and the power they held. I spoke to her of my quest to explore, of my desire to understand the world around me. My journey was a path of discovery, a journey that had led me to this grove and to Ilyafae. Our conversations were a meeting of minds, a sharing of experiences that transcended the boundaries of our different cultures.

As the time passed, a sense of trust and camaraderie developed between Ilyafae and me. This newfound comfort allowed me to delve into the more perplexing aspects of my journey, particularly the visions that had haunted me. These visions, filled with destruction and despair, were enigmas that I had struggled to comprehend. I began to share these visions with Ilyafae, my words painting a picture of the devastation I had witnessed. The burnt fields, the forests reduced to ash, the silhouette of an abomination standing amidst the ruins - each detail was a piece of the puzzle that I was unable to solve. Ilyafae listened with rapt attention, her ethereal form shimmering with curiosity. The visions were a mystery, a riddle that sparked her interest. Her eyes, glowing with the same blue and green light that made up her form, reflected a keen desire to understand, to help decipher the meaning behind the visions.

Our conversations took on a new depth as we delved into the enigma of the visions. Each discussion was a step towards understanding, a journey into the unknown that we embarked on together. The visions that had once been a source of confusion and fear became a shared quest for understanding, a mystery that we sought to unravel together.

Ilyafae began to share more of her world with me, taking me through nearby faelari groves, each residing within the larger rainforest, that were seasonally abandoned. These groves were an embodiment of the faelari's deep connection with Eledhin, their layout and design a reflection of the natural world. Ilyafae showed me the beautiful dances her people performed under the constellations, their movements a graceful interpretation of the celestial patterns. The dances were accompanied by enchanting melodies, their notes a harmonious echo of the All-Song, resounding directly from Ilyafae's semi-corporeal form, that resonated through Eledhin. I was enthralled by her harmony with Alara, by her reverence for the seasons and celestial bodies. Her movements were a dance with nature, a celebration of the world around her. Ilyafae invited me to join her in their dances, an invitation that I initially declined. I was content to watch, to learn, to take note of the intricate movements and melodies. But Ilyafae was insistent, her ethereal form shimmering with a playful light as she encouraged me to join her. She stood before me and began to move in slow, sinuous motions, her arms undulating like the branches above us. I mimicked her motions, feeling awkward and clumsy. The movements were so unnatural to my human frame. Ilyafae glided as if swimming through the air, while I stumbled about stiffly. She spun and leapt with otherworldly grace, her ethereal feet never touching the earth, as I lumbered in circles. But as we continued, my self-consciousness faded. I surrendered myself to the dance, letting my body flow and bend in unfamiliar ways. The dance awoke something primal within me - it was as if my spirit recognized movements my body had forgotten. I knew how to dance - that much was not new to me. The tribal dances of my people have always been grounded, stomping affairs - feet pounding in rhythm, bodies swaying and twisting. Our dances convey raw emotion and community spirit. But dancing with Ilyafae was something entirely different. Her movements were fluid and ethereal, unbound by gravity. She didn't so much walk as glide, her steps smooth as a breeze. When she leapt, she took flight for a moment. I felt heavy and oafish in comparison, my limbs incapable of such delicate motions. Yet as we danced, our differences seemed to matter less. I felt an uncanny synchronicity with Ilyafae, as if we moved as one organism. Her eyes would lock with mine, emerald green meeting earth brown, and an understanding passed between us that transcended our disparate forms. As I danced under the constellations, I began to understand the faelari's deep connection with Eledhin. The dances were more than just movements; they were a celebration of the world around them, a specimen of their harmony with Eledhin. And as I moved to the rhythm of the All-Song, I felt a connection with Eledhin that I had never experienced before. I cannot recall for how long we danced. Time seemed suspended. But I remember the exhilaration I felt...and the pang of loss when the dance ended, as I lamented the gulf between us. Ilyafae shone before me, her ethereal skin alight with blue and green hues and swaying with the gentle breeze, faintly translucent, always shifting. She was a creature of the stars, not entirely tethered by physical form. I was confined by sinew, bone and muscle. But for a blissful moment, the dance had made us kin. The memory of it lingered even as we parted - lingers still to this day - a reminder that the soul within pays no heed to outward differences.

As our bond deepened, Ilyafae began to share more of the faelari's sacred spaces with me. She led me deeper into the enchanted grove, a place where the magic of Alara pulsed with a power that was almost tangible. Each site was a symbol representing the faelari's deep connection with the natural world, their sacred spaces a reflection of their reverence for Eledhin. She showed me the ancient trees, their towering forms a realization of the passage of time. Their roots delved deep into the heart of the world, their presence a constant since the time of creation. Ilyafae led me to streams that crisscrossed the grove, their waters carrying pure magical energies. The streams were a lifeline, their waters a conduit for the magic that pulsed through Eledhin. As I watched the waters flow, I could almost see the magic swirling in the currents. She took me to meadows filled with star-touched flowers, their petals glowing with a soft light. Each site was a window into the world of the faelari, a glimpse into their deep connection with Eledhin. As I followed Ilyafae through the grove, I began to understand even deeper the reverence the faelari held for the natural world, their sacred spaces.

As I stepped away from the bustling kreegoblikar camp, the world around me had been in the heat of Orendar, the middle of the season. Alara had shed her vibrant Aravell cloak, now donned in the bright, burning attire of Solara. The trees stood scorched and dry, their twisted branches reaching out to the cloudless sky like gnarled claws. The air was thick with a suffocating heat that made my lungs burn, a silent proclamation of the relentless march of the seasons. Yet, past the invisible threshold of the Faelari Grove, it was as if I had stepped through a portal into another time. Here, it was perpetually Aravell. The grove was a sanctuary, a pocket of eternal Aravell untouched by the flaming fingertips of Solara or the icy grasp of Isendur. It was a vibrant oasis amidst the scorching Solara landscape, a vivid splash of color against the blinding tableau outside. Flowers bloomed in abundance, their petals unfurling in a riot of colors. Scarlet poppies, azure rillydids, and golden daffodils carpeted the ground, their sweet fragrance hanging heavy in the air. Emerald leaves rustled in the gentle breeze, their glossy surfaces catching the sunlight and casting a dappled pattern on the forest floor. The grove was alive with the hum of bees, the chirping of birds, and the rustle of small creatures in the undergrowth. It was a symphony of life, an apparent chasm to the silent stillness of the world outside. The vibrancy of the plant life was unchanging, a constant in this ever-evolving world. The leaves did not wither, the flowers did not wilt, and the grass remained a lush green, as if time itself had been ensnared within the grove. Ilyafae had explained this to me, her voice a soft whisper amidst the rustling leaves. The grove was under the protection of faelari magic, a potent force that defied the passage of time and the changing of seasons. It was a sanctuary, a haven where life thrived amidst whatever seasons passed outside. As I stood there, amidst the eternal Aravell of the grove, I couldn't help but marvel at the power of faelari magic; and as I breathed in the sweet, floral air, I felt a sense of peace envelop me, a feeling of being at one with the vibrant life force of the grove.

As we journeyed from one site to another, I could feel the pulsating rhythm of Eledhin's magic. It was a powerful, resonant force that seemed to seep into the very marrow of my bones. Each location was steeped in ancient magic. The air was thick with it, a tangible force that hummed with energy and vibrated with unseen power. At each site, I could sense a change in Ilyafae. It was subtle, a shift in her aura that was almost imperceptible. Yet, I could feel it, a swelling tide of emotion that seemed to radiate from her. Was it pride? There was a certain lift to her chin, a spark in her eyes that spoke of a deep-seated pride in her heritage, a reverence for the magic that was an intrinsic part of her being. Or perhaps it was amusement? There was a playful glint in her eyes, a soft chuckle that escaped her lips as she watched me grapple with the overwhelming power of Eledhin's magic. It was as if she was privy to a private joke, a shared secret that was hers alone to understand. Excitement, too, was a palpable force around her. It was in the quickening of her breath, the restless energy that seemed to crackle around her. But above all, I believe it was hope that I sensed in Ilyafae. It was a quiet, resilient force that shone in her eyes, a beacon that guided us through our journey. Each site, each resonance with Alara's magic, seemed to fuel this hope, to fan the flames of a dream that was slowly taking shape. It was a hope for understanding, for connection, for a future where the magic of Eledhin would not just survive, but thrive.

As we journeyed together, I couldn't help but be drawn to Ilyafae's radiant spirit. Her emotions - pride, amusement, excitement, hope - were a magnetic force. And as I stood beside her, feeling the resonance of Alara's magic, I could not help but share in her emotions, swept up in the tide of her unyielding spirit. After some time, Ilyafae, the enigmatic faelari with eyes that shimmered like emerald depths of a forest pool meeting the azure sky on a clear summer day, told me that she was growing confident that I was the protector she - and her entire Lünafælen - had been seeking for centuries. The words hung in the air between us, heavy with implications that I could barely begin to comprehend. She shared with me a prophecy, a cryptic verse in the lilting, melodic Faelish language. The words were like a song, a symphony of sounds that seemed to dance in the air. The rhythm, the nuance, the linguistic context, and the rhyme structure were lost in translation, but the essence of the prophecy remained. It was a tale of stars and ancient trees, of flowers and winds, of ancient creatures and songs. It was a tale of a mortal born with the soul of a regal one, a small yet delicate being with the strength of a flower.

The translation into my native tongue did little to dispel the mystery of the prophecy. It was a riddle wrapped in an enigma, a puzzle that seemed to defy understanding. Yet, as I listened to the words, I could not shake off a sense of awe. The prophecy spoke of a protector, a beacon of hope in a world shrouded in strife. It spoke of a wanderer, a seeker, an explorer who would breathe life into the world.

Original Faelish Prophecy:

"Vanaethae ilasaeli Selinve,
Luthaeli til-Thaenalorin, haela sylin la-Lysael.

Ani sylin la-Lysseli, laraelyssae lara-lyndae.
Daevalae thaelorae, ilasaeli Syllithaen.
Borni sylin vanaethae, theli sylin ilaelyrae,
Ani sylin lysseli, theli sylin Lysaelara.
Vorae til-thaelorae, vorae til-ilaesyl.
Haela sylin la-Lysael, lara-lyssae lara-lyndae.
Thaelorae laraelyssae, lara-Lysaelara,
Haela sylin Selinve, lara-lyndae lara-Lysael.
Thaelorae til-thaelorae, vorae til-ilaesyl,
Ani sylin la-Lysseli, theli sylin la-Lysael.
Vanaethae sylin Lysaelara, theli sylin la-Lysael,
Ani sylin la-Lysseli, theli sylin la-Lysael.
Daevasae til-thaelorae, sylin Lysaelara til-ilaesyl,
Teli sylin la-Lysael, lara-lyndae la-Lysaelara."

Human Translation:
"When stars in abundance are born,
Dream of the ancient tree, call for the flower.
I, the small yet delicate one, am embraced by the wind.
The ancient creatures rise, the stars sing.
Born of mortal form, with the soul of a tall and regal one,
I, the small yet delicate one, sing the flower's song.
Across the vast lands, across the deep seas.
Call for the flower, embraced by the wind.
Ancient creatures embraced, flower's song sung,
Call to the small yet delicate, embraced by the wind.
From ancient creature to ancient creature, across the deep seas,
I, the small yet delicate one, with the strength of the flower.
In the abundance of stars, the strength of the flower,
I, the small yet delicate one, with the strength of the flower.
When the shadow descends, and the flower shrouds in strife,

He will raise the beacon of hope, breathing the world to life."

The concept was overwhelming, to say the least. I was just a wanderer, a seeker of knowledge, an explorer of the unknown. The idea of being a prophesied protector on such a grand scale was intimidating. It was a mantle of responsibility that I had never sought, a destiny that I had never imagined. Yet, as I recalled my visions, my encounters with the wind's embrace, the way it seemed to guide me to places unknown, I could not ignore the signs. The prophecy, though cryptic, seemed to resonate with my experiences. It was a path that I could not ignore, a destiny that seemed to be calling out to me.

"Me... a protector?" I stammered, the words feeling foreign on my lips. The idea seemed too grand, too far-reaching for someone like me. I glanced around at the mystical faelari surroundings, as if seeking reassurance from Alara itself. "I..." My eyes settled back on Ilyafae, the green-and-blue-eyed faelari who had become a constant companion over the last few months. Her conviction was palpable, a force as tangible as the magic that seemed to hum in the air around us. "Why me? I'm no warrior. No hero. I am... was... just a member of a small human tribe. A dreamer. A wanderer. A human who did not even know we could be so attuned to Eledhin's forces so as to affect the world around us..." Yet, as I voiced my doubts, I could not ignore the truth that was slowly dawning on me. The prophecy, the visions, the wind's embrace - they were all pieces of a puzzle that seemed to be falling into place. I was a wanderer, yes, but perhaps I was also a protector, a beacon of hope in a world shrouded in strife. It was a destiny that I had never sought, but one that I could not ignore. In the wake of my words, a profound silence descended upon us. It was a silence that seemed to stretch on for an eternity, a silence so deep that it seemed to swallow up the world around us. The only sound that punctuated the quiet was the whispering wind, its soft murmurs growing louder in the absence of other sounds. It echoed the words that Ilyafae had once spoken to me on our travels through the grove - '*Ani kaela.* The wind chooses...'

The wind. It had always been there, a constant companion on my journey. It had guided me, embraced me, whispered secrets in my ear.

And now, it seemed to be affirming the path that lay before me. It was a path that I had not chosen, but one that had been chosen for me by the Bringer of Dawn. "If this is the path that the Bringer of Dawn has set out for me, then I shall strive to honor it," I declared, my voice steady despite the turmoil within me. The wind seemed to respond to my words, wrapping around me in a gentle embrace. It was a comforting presence, a reassuring touch that seemed to lend me strength. This time, the wind's embrace was unprompted. I had not called upon Alara, had not sought the wind's guidance with the spell words '*Su-Tha*'. Yet, it was there, an attestation to the bond that had formed between us. It was a bond that transcended language, a connection that was as deep as it was profound. Yet, even as resolve hardened within me, doubt lingered at the edges of my thoughts. It was a shadow that clung to me, a whisper of uncertainty that threatened to undermine my resolve. But I pushed it aside, focusing instead on the path that lay before me. It was a path that I had not chosen, but one that I was willing to walk. For the Bringer of Dawn, for Alara, for the world that I had come to love.

In that moment of quiet resolve, my thoughts drifted to Tornu. His image came to me as clear as day, his familiar features etched in my mind's eye. I could almost hear his voice, a comforting, raspy baritone that had guided me through many a storm. I wondered what he would say if he were here, what words of wisdom he would impart. I imagined his pride, the warmth in his eyes as he acknowledged how far I'd come. From a simple member of a small human tribe to a wanderer, a seeker, an explorer, and now, potentially, a prophesied protector. I could almost feel his hand on my shoulder, a reassuring weight that spoke of his unwavering faith in me. His belief in my strength, my resilience, my ability to rise to the challenges that lay ahead.

Yet, before I could dwell too long on those thoughts, a sinister presence intruded upon my reverie. It was a palpable shift in the atmosphere, a sudden chill that seemed to seep into my bones. The whispering wind fell silent, replaced by an ominous stillness that seemed to hang heavy in the air. The tranquility of the moment was shattered, replaced by a sense of foreboding that sent a shiver down my spine.

The world around me seemed to hold its breath, as if bracing for an impending storm. The peaceful faelari surroundings, which moments ago had offered solace, now seemed fraught with an unseen danger. As we prepared to leave the sanctuary of the faelari grove, a sudden transformation took hold of our surroundings. The vibrant oasis that had once stood as a microcosm of the power of faelari magic was now a scene of utter decimation. The visions I'd had before were vivid, so real that they had left me breathless. But this... this was something else entirely. This was not just a vision; it was a sensory onslaught. The heat of the flames was a searing inferno that licked at my skin, the smell of blood-soaked earth and burning flesh filled my nostrils, a sickening mixture that turned my stomach. Ash coated my tongue, my throat, my lungs - a bitter taste of the devastation around me. The faelari grove, once a haven of eternal Aravell, was now a burning hellscape. The flowers that had bloomed in vibrant colors were now charred remnants, the trees that had stood tall and proud were now skeletal figures consumed by the flames. In the midst of this chaos, a figure emerged from the smoke and flames. The shadowed figure from my last vision. Even from a distance, I could feel the intensity of his gaze, a piercing stare that seemed to see right through me. He moved with a slow, deliberate pace, unsheathing a greatsword from his back and brandishing it in my direction. I tried to run, to escape the impending doom, but my feet were rooted to the spot, as if they had become one with Alara's surface. My breaths came in shallow gasps, my heart pounded in my chest like a war drum, and sweat trickled down my skin in rivulets. The figure was closing in, his eyes locked onto mine. Fear gripped me, a primal terror that I had never known before. As he raised his mighty blade, ready to bring it down, I braced myself for the end.

And then, just as the flames were about to consume me, just as the figure was about to strike, he vanished. The world around me seemed to freeze, the flames paused mid-dance, the smoke hung suspended in the air. The figure was gone, leaving behind only the echo of his presence and the fear that still clung to me. In the blink of an eye, the world righted itself. The flames that had consumed the grove were gone, replaced by the vibrant colors and lush greenery that had been there before. The air was once again filled with the sweet scent of blooming flowers, the gentle hum of bees, and the rustle of leaves. It was as if the devastation had never happened, as if the world had been reset. I stood there, gasping for breath, my heart pounding in my chest. I took in deep lungfuls of the fresh air, savoring the sweet, floral scent that filled my nostrils. I looked around, drinking in the sight of the faelari grove in all its glory. The flowers bloomed in a riot of colors, the trees stood tall and proud, and the wildlife went about their business, unperturbed by the chaos that had unfolded moments ago.

Everything was as it should be. Everything, except... I looked down at my clothing, a gift from the dwarrin. The edges were singed, the fabric charred and blackened. Blood stained the bottoms of my leggings, a defined break from the vibrant colors of the grove. It was a jarring reminder of the vision, a tangible proof of the devastation that had unfolded. As I took in the sight of my damaged clothing, a sense of unease settled over me. The visions I'd been having, they were more than just figments of my imagination. They were real, as real as the singed edges of my clothing and the blood stains on my leggings. I was left with more questions than answers. What were these visions? Why were they so vivid, so real? And most importantly, what did they mean? As I stood there, amidst the beauty of the faelari grove, I couldn't help but feel a sense of foreboding. With a heavy heart, I turned to Ilyafae, recounting the harrowing vision that had just unfolded before me. Her green and blue eyes, usually so full of light and life, were clouded with concern as I spoke. The vibrant glow that usually surrounded her, a beautiful blend of blues and greens, seemed to dim as I described the devastation I had witnessed.

IX

Hook-Stick

Her expression was somber, an observable juxtaposition to her usual vibrant demeanor. The playful glint in her eyes was replaced by a deep-seated worry, her radiant smile giving way to a tight-lipped frown. As I spoke of the shadowed figure, the greatsword, and the impending doom, her glow seemed to fade, as if the words were draining the life from her. The typically vibrant hues of her aura seemed to lose their intensity, replaced by more muted shades. The bright blues and greens gave way to softer, faded tones, mirroring the concern etched on her face. It was as if she was absorbing the gravity of my words, the vibrant energy that usually surrounded her dimming in response to the grim tale. As I finished my account, a heavy silence hung between us. The lively faelari grove, usually filled with the sounds of nature, seemed to hold its breath, as if the world itself was reacting to the ominous vision.

From the depths of her pocket, Ilyafae produced a small pendant. It was a beautiful piece of craftsmanship, made of a crystal-clear teardrop-shaped stone. The stone was cradled in an intricate metal frame, wrought from the finest silver. The frame was twined with a delicate vine pattern, each leaf and tendril meticulously crafted. Dotted along the vines were tiny gems that glowed with a soft luminescence, like dewdrops catching the first light of dawn.

"This," Ilyafae began, her voice a melodious whisper that seemed to blend with the rustling leaves and the humming of bees, "is the Lunasil." Her blue and green eyes glowed as she held up the pendant, the light catching on the crystal and scattering into a myriad of colors. The Lunasil was a faelari crystal, forged from the very essence of Eledhin itself. It was not just a piece of jewelry, but a conduit, a channel through which the faelari could tap into the magic of the Fae. The crystal was infused with the energies of the moon and stars, a paragon of the deep connection between the faelari and the celestial bodies. As Ilyafae spoke, the pendant seemed to come alive in her hand. The crystal glowed with a soft light, the luminescent gems twinkled like distant stars, and the silver frame seemed to shimmer in the dappled sunlight. It was a piece of the Fae, a piece of Eledhin, a piece of the magic that was an intrinsic part of the faelari. It was a symbol of their heritage, their connection to the natural world, and their ability to channel the magic that flowed through Alara. Ilyafae continued her explanation, her voice a soothing melody that seemed to blend with the rustling of the leaves and the chirping of the birds. The Lunasil, she explained, was as old as the faelari themselves. It had been in her Lünafælen, her lineage, since the dawn of creation. The Lunasil was not just a conduit for faelari magic, but also a key to their language. Its bearer could speak Faelish fluently, the words flowing as naturally as a native speaker. It was a bridge between cultures, a tool that allowed for communication and understanding.

However, the use of the Lunasil was not without conditions. It was a living entity, a crystal that needed to be nourished by the energy of the moonlight to keep its magic alive. It thrived under the soft glow of the moon, the celestial energy feeding its magic and keeping it vibrant. Moreover, the Lunasil resonated with the purity of intent of its user. It was a crystal of balance, of harmony, and it responded to the inner state of its bearer. Should its bearer ever falter toward a path of darkness and imbalance, the Lunasil would react. It was a guardian of sorts, a sentinel that kept a watchful eye on the path of its user. The Lunasil was not just a tool, but also a test. Should it be used to combat a darkness of purest evil, the Lunasil would also shatter. It was a reminder of the delicate balance of the world, a warning against the misuse of power.

"Take this, Yoran." Ilyafae's voice was soft, yet there was a determination in her tone that was impossible to ignore. She held out the Lunasil, the crystal pendant glowing softly in the dappled sunlight. As I reached out to take it, I could feel a surge of energy, a tangible force that seemed to hum with unseen power. "With this, you'll be able to weave Eledhin's melodious and dissonant forces just as the faelari," she continued, her green and blue eyes meeting mine. There was a seriousness in her gaze, a gravity that underscored the importance of her words. "I will teach you a few of our verses in hopes that it will prepare you in some way for your journey to come." Her words hung in the air between us, a solemn promise, a pledge of guidance and support. But remember," she added, her voice dropping to a whisper, "as the Lunasil responds to the heart of the bearer, it thrives on pure intentions, love for nature, and the willingness to protect. Do not stray from this path - for if you do, or even if you should use it to combat a power of purest evils, the Lunasil will be rendered useless, split into a thousand shards."

"Fear not, for I believe your heart is true; and worry not for me," she reassured, a gentle smile playing on her lips. "Though the Lunasil strongly enhances my peoples' connection to Eledhin, it has long become mostly a relic, as we have attuned ourselves more closely with Eledhin since we were first born." Her words were a comfort, a reassurance that I was not taking something vital from her. The Lunasil was a relic, a symbol of the faelari's ancient connection to Eledhin. But it was also a gift, a tool that would allow me to tap into the magic of the Fae, to weave the melodious and dissonant forces of Eledhin just as the faelari. Under Ilyafae's patient guidance, I began to learn the Faelish spell words, or "verses". Each one was a key that unlocked a different aspect of the faelari magic, a tool that allowed me to tap into the natural world in ways I had never imagined.

Thae'liara, she explained, was a verse that allowed one to understand the language of plants. It was a window into a world that was usually silent, a way to perceive the basic sensations and feelings expressed by the flora around us.

Valæris was a verse that summoned a small sphere of bioluminescent light. It was a beacon in the darkness, a gentle illumination that could guide one through the darkest of nights.

Ilÿsįl'æn was a verse that allowed one to momentarily glimpse into the spirit realm. It was a bridge between the physical and the ethereal, a way to reveal the unseen presences that surrounded us.

Élærän'drå was a verse that allowed one to communicate with animals. It did not make them any more intelligent, but it allowed for a basic understanding and interaction, a way to bridge the gap between species.

Lünthårä was a protective charm that could deflect harmful energies and intentions away from the caster. It was a shield, a barrier that could protect one from harm.

As I practiced with the Lunasil, I could feel it responding to me. The crystal seemed to grow brighter, its glow intensifying with each spell I cast. It was as if the Lunasil was attuning itself to me, enhancing my affinity with nature and Alara's primal forces. The Lunasil was more than just a tool for casting spells. It was a constant reminder of the role I had committed to, a symbol of my pledge to protect Alara. Each time I held it, each time I called upon a faelari verse, I was reminded of the path I had chosen, the responsibility I had accepted. It was a weight, yes, but it was also a source of strength in the face of the challenges that lay ahead.

After months of journeying together, the wind began to call to me once more on a frigid day in Ithendar, the first month of Isendur. It was a gentle whisper at first, a soft murmur that tugged at the edges of my consciousness. But with each passing day, the call grew stronger, a compelling force that beckoned me to follow. As we prepared to part ways, Ilyafae turned to me, her blue-green eyes reflecting the soft glow of the setting sun. "*Aelinna lyst moriel,* Yoran," she said, her voice carrying the soft lilt of the faelari language. It was a farewell, a phrase that echoed the cycles of life and the promise of reunion. It was a reminder that even as we parted ways, our paths were intertwined, bound by the shared journey and the promise of a future meeting. She explained that she had hoped to bring me with her, as she hoped to introduce her family to the protector of Eledhin they had prophesied about for so long, but needed to return to her Lünafælen. She had found Eledhin's protector, and it was her duty to inform them of this discovery. It was a responsibility she bore with grace, a corroboration of her commitment to her people and to the balance of Alara. And so, understanding my promise to Tornu, and my need as Alara's supposed protector to follow the wind's guidance, under the gaze of the shimmering stars and silently falling snowflakes, we parted ways. It was a quiet farewell, a moment of shared understanding and mutual respect. As I watched her figure recede into the distance, I felt a sense of peace, and a pang of regret. I remembered that evening in which we shared a faelari dance, forever connecting our souls in a way that, while faelari experience it with many others in their lifetime, forming familial, romantic, and platonic bonds, no mortal like myself had ever experienced before. Our paths may have diverged, but our journey was far from over.

As I stepped out of the enchanted faelari grove, leaving behind the sanctuary where Ilyafae and I had spent the last four months, I was greeted by the familiar sights and sounds of Isendur. The stars and constellations served as a celestial calendar, marking the passage of time. By their positions, I could tell that we were in the month of Ithendar. As I left the grove, I knew there were still many sights to see, many wonders to discover. The wind was calling, beckoning me to follow, and I was ready to answer. With the Lunasil in my possession and the teachings of Ilyafae in my heart, I was ready to face whatever lay ahead. The journey had been long, I had set out one cycle and nine months prior, but it was not over.

Stepping out of the enchanted faelari grove, I found myself on the edge of vast, verdant plains. They stretched out before me, a sea of green, not yet frozen by the newly transforming Isendur winds, that mirrored the expanse I had journeyed with the centarion. It was a familiar sight, a reminder of the five months I had spent engrossed in their culture, beliefs, and practices. The plains were vibrant, a rolling carpet of green sprinkled with wildflowers of every imaginable color. Herds of wild animals roamed freely, their movements a dance of life and survival. Over the several days it took me to traverse the plains, I was a silent observer of the natural order, a cycle of life, death, and rebirth that the centarion had often spoken of. One wildflower caught my eye, a bloom of unrivaled splendor that I had never seen before. I named it the "Dawnbloom", a tribute to its radiant beauty and the time of day when it bloomed. One morning, I woke to find dozens of these 'dawnblooms' near my bedroll. With the first rays of Isendur's pale sun, the flower buds pushed through the thin layer of snow and bloomed, displaying an array of dazzling colors. By noon, the flowers had matured, their seeds dropping back down to the soil. As the sun began to set, the flowers withered and died, their vibrant display fading with the slightest heat of the day. But under the light of the moon, something incredible happened. The fallen seeds began to germinate in the soft, fertile soil of the plains, nurtured by the snow and moonlight. By midnight, new sprouts had taken root, the cycle of life beginning anew. Observing this process, I was reminded of the tales the centarion people wove about the interconnected process of life. It was a recognition of the resilience of nature, a symbol of the cycle of life, death, and rebirth. As I watched the dawnblooms, my thoughts turned to Tornu, my mentor. My uncle. I found myself hoping that there was something more for him after his passing, a place where he could roam and adventure without reservation. The cycle of the dawnblooms, their vibrant life and inevitable death, was a reminder of the natural order of things.

Leaving the now-snowy expanse of the plains behind, I was drawn by a remarkable, melodious sound. It was a soft, almost musical whistle that seemed to waft on the breeze, a siren's call that I couldn't resist. Following the sound, I found myself at the edge of a serpentine river. Its curving flow cut a path through the snowy landscape, winding its way through patches of trees that gradually thickened into a lightly populated forest. The forest stretched up and over the distant, rugged hills, a white blanket that draped over the landscape. The river, I realized, was one that Ilyafae had mentioned in passing. The faelari called it the "Singing River", or the "*Tälindra Eirælī*". As I approached, I understood why.

The river was filled with strangely shaped stones, each one carved and shaped by centuries of water flow. The stones, with their hollows and grooves, coupled with the icey structures that had begun to form along them, interacted with the wind to produce a symphony of soft, whistling tones. It was a natural orchestra, a harmony of wind and water that created a melody unlike any I had heard before. The harmonic hum of the stones, combined with the gentle rustling of the reeds, the high crystalline whistle of the ice, and the babbling of the water, created a serene atmosphere. It was a place of peace, a sanctuary where the music of nature took center stage. As I stood there, listening to the symphony of the Singing River, I felt a sense of peace penetrate my heart. It was a moment of tranquility, a reminder of the beauty and harmony of the natural world.

Having replenished my water supplies with the frigid river water, I turned my attention to the teeming life within the river. It had been a day, perhaps two, since I had last eaten a solid meal. A meager variety of fish, their scales glinting like tiny mirrors in the sunlight, swam in the icy water, darting between the river rocks and floating twigs. With a determined leap, ensuring my camp fire was lit and ready for me to warm and dry myself beside afterwards, I plunged into the cold water, my hands reaching out to try and catch a fish. I spent several long hours in the water - in several spurts of only a few minutes at a time, interspersed by time next to the fire - my attempts to catch a single fish proving futile. My frustration grew with each unsuccessful attempt, the elusive fish always just out of reach. As I grappled with my frustration, I heard the sound of laughter. It was a chortle, the sound of an adolescent child finding amusement in my struggle. Turning to look at the source of the laughter, I found myself looking at an amused little man.

He was a curious sight, with soft, red, curly hair and a stubbly beard that marked him as an adult, despite his small stature. He was no taller than any of the dwarrin I had spent time around, and far less hairy, with the exception of his toes. He wore simple cloth leggings, a thick cloak, and a shirt, his feet bare. He was chuckling loudly, an unlit pipe clenched between his lips, his eyes squeezed shut in laughter. As his laughter caught my attention, he quickly realized he had given himself away. He dropped his pipe, clamping his hand over his mouth, his eyes shooting wide open in shock. With a swift movement, he darted off through the trees, disappearing from my sight as quickly as he had appeared.

What an odd little character, I thought, a smile tugging at the corners of my mouth. The little man had left behind a curious item - a stick with a long, thin strand of yarn or rope attached to it, a neat hook tied to the other end. I picked it up, turning it over in my hands, my mind quickly piecing together its purpose. I wondered if I might be able to use it to my advantage in catching one of the fish. My previous attempts, with their splashing and grabbing, had only served to scare the fish away. They were nimble creatures, their movements too quick for me to anticipate. But perhaps the shiny hook might draw their attention?

The little man was nowhere to be seen, and I reasoned that he would likely not be back this way anytime soon. If he did return for his hook-stick, I would gladly return it. But for now, it seemed like a tool that could be put to good use. And indeed, it proved to be quite handy. With the hook stick, I was able to catch four large fish - enough for a hearty meal. I built a fire in the style of the kreegoblikar - small but intensely hot - to cook my catch. The fire crackled and popped, the heat searing the fish and filling the air with the mouthwatering aroma of cooked food. As I sat down to eat my hard-earned meal and thaw myself by the fire, I couldn't help but feel a sense of satisfaction. The day had been full of challenges, but it had also brought unexpected solutions and rewards. The little man's forgotten hook-stick had turned out to be a blessing, a tool that had provided me with a much-needed meal. And for that, I was grateful.

I continued my journey from the afternoon until the sun set, the world around me bathed in the soft glow of twilight. As night fell, I made my bed under the open sky, the stars twinkling overhead like a blanket of tiny, shimmering lights, dancing across my vision with the flakes of snow gently descending from their heavenly realm.

A week had passed since my time with Ilyafae, and my journey had brought me to a marshland. The ground crunched before giving way and squelching under my feet with every step, the soft, wet earth yielding beneath my weight. A thick mist cloaked everything, turning the world into a landscape of shadows and silhouettes. The marshland was a world of its own, a place where the earth and water met in a delicate balance. Much of the water was frozen over, but not so thick as to prevent one from falling through the disgusting, green and black ice that sat upon the surface. The air was heavy with the scent of damp earth and the faint, tangy smell of decaying vegetation. The sounds of the marsh filled the air - the distant call of a bird, the rustle of reeds in the wind, the soft splash of water as a creature moved through the marsh, the crash of a large icicle plummeting down to the repugnant earth below. The marshland was a realm of mystery and wonder, teeming with a variety of wildlife that brought the landscape to life. Fireflies danced in the night sky, their tiny lights flickering like stars against the dark canvas of the night. Rare herbs and plants, their forms unfamiliar to my eyes, grew in abundance, their leaves glistening with ice in the soft moonlight. Navigating through the marshlands was a challenge, the terrain unfamiliar and the path often obscured by the thick mist and snow. But I moved with caution and determination, guided by the soft glow of the Lunasil. Its light danced on the water's surface, casting a soft glow on the surrounding vegetation. It illuminated the path ahead, revealing the hidden beauty of the marshland. The sight of the fireflies, the scent of the rare herbs, the sound of the marshland's nocturnal creatures - it was a sensory symphony that filled me with awe and wonder, if not a twinge of repulsion.

After several days of navigating the marshlands, my path led me to a series of canyons, known to the centarion as "*Saela-Felrin*" - the "Whispering Canyon". The canyons were a broad gulf to the marshlands, with rocky terrain and towering walls. The wind echoed through the narrow passages, its voice bouncing off the rocky walls to create a sound like hushed whispers. It was as if the canyon itself was speaking, its voice a soft murmur that beckoned me ever onwards. At night, the moon cast its soft glow over the canyons, its light illuminating the icy terrain. The moonlight created long shadows that danced on the canyon walls, their forms shifting and changing with the movement of the clouds. It was a sight of ethereal beauty, the moonlight and ice creating a mesmerizing dance of light and darkness in the shadows before me. The canyons, while devoid of the vibrant life of the marshlands, provided a different kind of challenge. The rocky terrain and slippery cliffs required careful navigation, each step a test of my balance and agility. It was a challenging climbing experience, one that pushed my survival skills to the limit.

I had never climbed anything like this before, and I knew that it would be a dangerous journey. But I had no choice. I had to follow the wind, and the wind was guiding me up the canyon walls. I took a deep breath and started to climb. The ice on the rocks was slippery, and I had to be careful not to slip and fall. I clung to the rocks with my bare hands, my fingers aching from the cold. I climbed for hours, my arms and my legs growing tired. I was almost beginning to lose hope and wonder if I should venture back down, when I finally saw a ledge above me. I pulled myself up onto the ledge and collapsed, exhausted. I lay there for a while, catching my breath. Then I looked out over the canyon below. The sight was magnificent, taking away the breath I had just regained. The ice sparkled in the moonlight, and the shadows danced on the canyon walls.

The next day, the climbing became even more difficult. The ice was steeper, and the cliffs were more slippery. I had to use all of my strength and agility to keep from falling. At one point, I lost my grip and started to slide down the ice. I reached out for a rock and managed to grab it just in time. i hung there for a moment, my heart pounding in my chest. Then I slowly pulled myself up.

I climbed for days, until I finally reached the top of the canyon. I stood there for a long time, looking out at the mountain range below me. I had done it. I had survived the climb.

As I emerged from the confines of the Whispering Canyon, I found myself on the outskirts of a desert. A vast sea of sand and dunes stretched out before me, their undulating forms resembling the waves of an ocean frozen in time. Sparse, hardy shrubs dotted the landscape. The sun hung high in the sky, its faint heat casting a shimmering haze over the desert. The heat was intense, the air dry and parched, the sand hot underfoot, though not as harsh as it would have been in Solara. The winds guided me into the heart of the desert, their whispers a constant companion amidst the silence of the sand, ice, and sun. The transition from the cool, shaded canyons to the harsh, open desert was abrupt and jarring. The sheltered, whispering passages of the canyons gave way to the relentless expanse of the desert, its vast sea of sand stretching out as far as the eye could see. The contrast was stark, a sudden shift that served as a formidable introduction to the challenges that lay before me.

X

Řazzbłûd

The desert, with its harsh conditions and relentless heat, despite being in the throes of Isendur, was a formidable adversary. Yet, it was also an indicator of the resilience of life, a landscape that demanded respect and perseverance. As I navigated the shifting sands, guided by the stars above and the winds of Alara, I was reminded of the strength within me, the resilience that had carried me through the marshlands and the canyons, through storms and battle, and would now guide me through the desert. I took a moment to appreciate just how far I had come - from the scared and innocent boy, barely 16 cycles old, to now almost my eighteenth cycle - having walked across almost the entire width of Alara, having spent time amongst so many cultures, having seen so much, having fought alongside the dwarrin, wandered under the stars and hunted alongside the centarion, I had been heralded as a prophesied protector of this diverse world, and my journey was still not yet at an end.

As I journeyed across the vast expanse of the desert, a small village appeared on the horizon. It was a welcome sight, a promise of respite from the relentless heat of the sun. With renewed hope, I continued on my way, the village growing larger with each step I took. However, as I drew closer, a sense of unease began to creep over me. Scattered across the sands were the bones of various creatures, their sizes ranging from small to large. The sight was disconcerting. The quantity of these skeletal remains seemed to increase the closer I got to the village, a chilling welcome that made me question the safety of my destination. The sun beat down relentlessly, its heat intensifying with each passing hour. I had not found any food or water in several long, tiring days, and the exhaustion was beginning to take its toll. My options were limited - I could either continue on my path and risk the unknown dangers of the village, or succumb to the harsh conditions of the desert. Despite the ominous sight of the bones, I decided to press on. The need for food and water was urgent, and the village was my only hope. As I approached the outskirts of the village, I couldn't help but wonder about the fate of the creatures whose skeletons now littered the sands. I could only hope that I would not become the next victim of whatever had claimed their lives. Among the skeletal remains scattered across the sands, I noticed carefully placed stone cairns. These miniature mountains of stones were meticulously arranged, marking certain spots in the vast expanse of the desert. Their presence added an air of solemnity to the landscape, as if they were silent guardians keeping watch over the remains of the fallen.

As I neared the village, I was met with an imposing sight. Tall trees, likely cut and hauled from a nearby forest or perhaps the canyons I had just traversed, formed a tall palisade around the settlement. The trees had been sharpened to points, creating a formidable barrier against potential threats. Guarding the entrance were several large figures, their bulging muscles and heavy armor making them appear even more formidable. Their skin tones varied, ranging from different shades of grays to greens and blues. They stood like statues, their imposing forms casting long shadows on the sandy ground. The figures' eyes were completely black, deeply set beneath their prominent brows. Their gaze was intense, adding to their already formidable appearance. Their lower jaws jutted out, housing large, fang-like teeth that stood tall. These teeth extended up and out past their upper lips, giving them a fierce, predatory appearance. Their ears, though shorter than those of the elandari, also came to pointed tips. The combination of these features made them quite intimidating creatures. Their visage was striking, a blend of beastly and humanoid traits that was both fascinating and terrifying.

As I took in their appearance, I was reminded of the beast-men from Takka's tales. The stories had described them as fierce warriors, their strength and ferocity unmatched. Seeing these figures in person, I could see the truth in those tales. Their imposing presence was a reflection of their strength, their fierce appearance a clear warning to any who might pose a threat. Before I had a chance to reconsider my approach, the creatures began moving towards me, their movements deliberate and menacing. With each breath they took, a low snarl escaped their lips, a sound that echoed ominously in the vast expanse of the desert. Their solid black eyes were fixed on me, their gaze as sharp as the points of their towering fang-like tusks. I could feel a surge of adrenaline coursing through my veins as I began to whisper to my Saela-Hathir, seeking its communicative properties.

"*Threl-!*"

But before I could finish, they were upon me. Their hands, strong and unyielding, grabbed me by my arms. Their grip was like vorgrund, their strength evident in the way they effortlessly lifted me off the ground.

They began to drag me away, their strides long and purposeful. I could feel the rough sand scraping against my skin, the heat of the desert sun beating down on us. As they hauled me away, I tried to focus on the rhythm of my breath, the feeling of the Saela-Hathir in my hand, and the resolve within me. As they hauled me towards the back side of their walled camp, I managed to whisper "*Threl-Vysh-Pax*", reigniting the enchantment on my Saela-Hathir. The familiar hum of the enchantment brought a small measure of comfort, a reminder that I was not entirely defenseless.

"Please," I began, my voice steady despite the fear that gripped me, "I mean you no harm! I simply come to learn from you - or even just to quench my thirst and then I'll be-"

"Bah!" The largest of the creatures cut me off, his voice grating like stones being dragged across each other. He towered over me, his imposing figure casting a long shadow in the harsh desert sun. "Shaddup! We no care. You walk on our ground. We no let no one walk on our ground. This ground belong to us blâdur." His words were harsh, his tone dismissive. It was clear that they saw me as an intruder, a trespasser on their land. Despite their intimidating presence and the threat they posed, I knew I had to try and reason with them. I had come too far and faced too many challenges to give up now.

"Please, I beg of you, I will leave; simply spare my life and allow me to be on my way!" My voice echoed in the vast expanse of the desert, my words a desperate plea for mercy. I clung to the hope that my journey would not end here, not like this.

"Ugbrog, maybe we take him to Kharok? We never see a no-tusk that talk Skaragg'ha," another creature snarled. His voice was filled with uncertainty, a hint of fear at the prospect of opposing the larger one.

"Kill the no-tusk!" The words rang out, a harsh growl from another of the hulking creatures. His gray skin was a patchwork of scars, a chronicle of a life of battle and survival.

"Take to Kharok!" An older creature croaked, his voice raspy with age and countless battles. Almost before I knew what was happening, a brawl had broken out amongst the onlookers and the guards that had been dragging me away. The air was filled with the sound of snarls and grunts, the clash of fists against flesh. Dust and sand were kicked up into the air, obscuring my vision.

"Blâdur! Stop now! What this mean?" A gutteral, bestial voice boomed out, commanding and authoritative. An older, more battle-worn creature stepped out from the encampment behind the palisade walls. His skin was a patchwork of scars, each one a testimony to a battle survived, a challenge overcome. At his command, the brawl ceased as abruptly as it had begun. Each of the creatures turned to face him, their expressions a mix of respect and fear. The dust settled, revealing the imposing figure of the elder creature.

"What this I hear 'bout he talk Skaragg'ha?" He spoke again, his gravelly voice echoing in the silence that had fallen over the camp. His gaze turned to me, a spark of curiosity in his otherwise stern expression.

"Kharok," another of the creatures began, his voice hesitant as he addressed the elder. "We thought we take him out and kill him - as sacrifice to Grûmak'Tûrg. What you say?"

The words hung in the air, heavy with the weight of my fate. I could only watch, my heart pounding in my chest, as the elder creature, Kharok, considered the proposal.

The figure before me, known as Kharok, came to a halt, his imposing presence casting a long shadow in the sunlight. His eyes, one as hard and unyielding as obsidian, the other as icy cold as frigid Isendur snow, bore into mine, their intensity amplifying the terror that had already taken root in my heart. He scratched his scruffy black beard, a thoughtful gesture that contrasted with the raw power he exuded. His gaze was unwavering, a predator assessing its prey, and I found myself unable to break away from the hypnotic hold it had on me. His good eye was the color of a stormy night, and both eyes held an ocean of unspoken tales, tales of battles won and lost, of lives taken and seldom spared. What caught my attention next were his tusks, fang-like and protruding from underneath his lower lip. They were not just mere appendages but works of art, their ivory surface etched with intricate carvings that ran along their length. The carvings were like ancient hieroglyphs, their meaning known only to their creator, each one a badge of Kharok's life and his journey. Adorning these magnificent tusks were two finely crafted gold rings, their lustrous sheen a clear demarcation to the rugged ivory. The rings were nestled in small engravings along his tusks, just deep and wide enough to hold them in place without jutting out past the sides of his tusks. The sight was both intimidating and awe-inspiring, an assertion of the beast-man's taste for the grandiose. Underneath each of Kharok's eyes was a tattoo, as dark as the night sky, and as intricate as a woven basket. The ink had aged with time, the lines wrinkling and fading, yet they held a certain allure, a mystery that added to his enigmatic persona. A large scar marred his right brow and cheek, a stark white line against his weathered skin. His right eye was a milky white, the sightless orb a silent narrator of a past battle, a story of survival etched onto his face. His body was a canvas of scars, each one a different size, a different depth, a different tale. His arms, in particular, bore the brunt of these battle wounds, the skin marred by countless encounters. It was evident that his leadership was not handed to him on a silver platter, but earned, carved from the bodies of his enemies - a stamp of his battle prowess. Each scar was a badge of honor, a symbol of his strength and resilience, a measure of the formidable warrior that was Kharok.

The silence was deafening, a palpable entity that seemed to exist for an eternity. The only sound was the harsh rasp of Kharok's breath, a steady rhythm that echoed ominously in the tense air. Then, without warning, his voice shattered the silence, a rough, booming sound that resonated across the open desert.

"Řazzblûd."

The single word rolled off his thick, grayed-green lips, a guttural utterance that seemed to reverberate in the air long after it was spoken. The word was foreign to my ears, its meaning shrouded in mystery, yet it held a power that was impossible to ignore. It was as if the word itself was a living entity, a force that commanded attention and respect. As the echoes of his voice faded, I dared to tear my gaze away from Kharok, my eyes darting around the clearing. The creatures that had gathered around us were an assortment of fearsome beings, their forms bathed in the light. Their faces, once twisted into snarls, now transformed, their expressions morphing into cruel grins and smirks. Their eyes, black as the abyss, glinted with a malicious glee, their teeth gleaming in the eerie light as they bared them in wicked smiles. The atmosphere shifted, the tension giving way to a sense of anticipation, as if the utterance of that single word had set something in motion. The grins were not of joy, but of cruel amusement, a shared understanding that I was not privy to.

The clearing, once filled with an oppressive silence, was now alive with a sinister energy. The creatures' cruel grins and the echo of

Kharok's booming voice painted a chilling picture, a scene that sent a shiver of dread coursing down my spine. The single word, "Řazzbłûd," hung in the air, a harbinger of an unknown fate that was yet to unfold. Kharok's hand extended in my direction, a silent command hanging in the air between us. His gaze remained locked onto mine, a relentless scrutiny that seemed to pierce through my very soul. His one eye like a shard of obsidian, the other a ball of white ash, together, their unwavering stare an affirmation of his indomitable will. The silence stretched on, each passing second amplifying the awkward tension that had descended upon us.

In my confusion, I found myself on the verge of reaching out to grasp his outstretched hand, a desperate attempt to break the uncomfortable silence. But before I could act on this ill-advised impulse, a new figure emerged from the shadows, inadvertently saving me from a potentially fatal mistake. The newcomer was somewhat smaller, its form still quite tall and hardy, yet frailer than Kharok's imposing figure. Its skin was a striking shade of blue, a hue that seemed to absorb the light of the sun. It moved with a certain grace, its relative frailty belying a hidden strength. In its hand, it held a black stone blade, gnarled and jagged, its surface gleaming with an ominous black sheen. The creature placed the blade into Kharok's outstretched palm, its movements precise and deliberate. With a dismissive wave of his other hand, Kharok sent the smaller beast-man away, his gaze never straying from me. Then, with a swift, calculated movement, he tossed the blade onto the ground before me. The blade landed with a soft thud, its black surface gleaming ominously in the desert light.

"You do Řazzbłûd. You live, you come back. Do this ruk moons, we talk. You die in Řazzbłûd, you dead. We no talk. Yeah?" His voice was a low rumble, the words heavy with an unspoken challenge. The terms "*Řazzbłûd*" and "*ruk*" were foreign to me, their meanings lost in translation. Yet, the implication was clear. I was to survive in the desert and then return to these creatures. I could escape, run far away, and continue on my journey. But the allure of the unknown was too strong to resist. These beast men, with their intriguing customs and mysterious language, had piqued my curiosity. I was far too fascinated to pass up the opportunity to learn more about their culture, their beliefs, and their connection to Alara. The challenge had been laid before me, a test of survival and a promise of knowledge. And I was ready to accept it.

"Yes..." I responded, my voice barely more than a whisper, the uncertainty clear in my tone. "But... could you explain what 'Řazzblûd' is? I'm not familiar with the phrase-"

"No." The word was a blunt dismissal, a wall erected against my curiosity. Kharok's voice was as unyielding as stone, his refusal leaving no room for negotiation.

"Oh. I see... Could you tell me what 'ruk' is, then? How do I know what moons to look for?" I pressed on, my determination outweighing my fear. I needed to understand, to know what I was agreeing to. Kharok's patience seemed to be wearing thin, his scowl deepening into a fierce grimace. His irritation was palpable, a storm brewing beneath his stern exterior. Yet, despite his growing impatience, he responded to my question. He held up both hands, one displaying all five of his large, meaty fingers, and the other only two. Seven. The number was clear.

"Now grab blade and go. No want see you till after ruk moons. Kharok no want see no-tusk. But you strange... Strange not bad all time. Go. You come back, you strange be good. Not, you strange be bad. But you gone anyway. Now go."

His words were a mix of dismissal and challenge, a final decree that marked the end of our conversation. His gaze was as hard as ever, his eyes reflecting a strange mix of annoyance and curiosity. I was an enigma to him, a puzzle he was unsure of how to solve. But for now, he was willing to let the mystery unfold on its own. With a final nod, I reached down to pick up the blade, its cool surface an unmistakable delineation from the heat of the desert. As I turned to leave, Kharok's words echoed in my mind, a reminder of the task that lay ahead. I was to survive, to return after the 'ruk' moons, and prove that my strangeness was not a threat. The challenge was daunting, but I was ready to face it.

XI

Lünthårä

Seven days stretched out before me, a daunting expanse of time that I was to spend in the burning expanse of the desert. Isendur was just beginning its rule, casting a cold, silvery light over the rest of the world. The current month, Ithendar, was just starting, its initial days marked by the decreasing temperature and the rising frost. Ithendar was the first month in Isendur, a time of transition and stillness. The world was preparing for the arrival of Nolariel, which would see even colder days, its approach heralded by the icy winds and the pale moon. Nolariel was a time of deep cold, a test of resilience abd survival for all who dared to venture too far into the distant northern or southern expanses. I was in neither. The desert sand I tread still burnt hot from the sun, though I was grateful it was not Solara.

The next seven days would be a test of my resilience and my will to endure. The desert was a relentless warden, but I was ready to confront it, to brave its tests, and to emerge unbroken. As the initial days of Ithendar introduced the embrace of Nolariel, I fortified myself for the challenges that loomed, ready to face the desert and all its tribulations. As the sun began its ascent, illuminating the sky with hues of orange and white, I began my quest called the "Řazzbłûd." The term remained enigmatic to me, its full meaning as intangible as the fleeting sand in the wind. Yet, I was resolute to meet whatever challenge it encompassed.

The desert was soon shimmering in the sun's furious glow, the oncoming day carrying a sense of stillness. The desert was merciless during the day, its serene allure morphing into a scorching inferno that presented overt dangers under the blazing sun. I needed to find shelter, a sanctuary from the relentless heat that threatened to overwhelm me. Guided by the shimmering waves of the midday mirage, I pressed on through the desert, my eyes scanning the horizon for any sign of respite.

Luck was with me, for I soon stumbled upon a small cluster of abandoned huts, but the scene whispered of more than mere desertion. They were relics of a bygone era, their sun-baked clay bricks a testament to the passage of time. The huts were crafted with remarkable attention to detail, their beige bricks contrasting starkly against the desert's golden sands. Scattered around were remnants of a fierce battle — broken weapons made of a dark rock - the same dark rock that the blade given to me by Kharok was made of - that shimmered under the blazing sun, discarded wooden shields, and stains of a deep hue on the sand that suggested a battle. They were weather-beaten, their structures succumbing to the relentless wear of time and harsh desert winds, yet they provided the shelter I so desperately needed. Shattered arrows and broken pottery lay scattered, remnants of a battle that had once raged here. The huts stood vacant, their previous inhabitants long gone, leaving behind only silent echoes of their existence and traces of conflict. A melancholic aura lingered, heavy with memories of a time when this place had echoed with the cries of war. It felt like sacred ground where brave souls once defended their home. But amidst it all, there was peace, a tranquil solitude contrasting the desert's scorching heat and the history it hid. I chose the hut farthest from the beast-men's outpost I had set out from, its sheltered coolness a balm against the desert's heat and history's weight. As I settled in for the night, feeling the weathered clay bricks beneath me, I pondered the upcoming trial. The "Řazzbłûd" remained a mystery, its meaning as elusive as ever. But as sleep took me, within the confines of the age-old hut and under the watchful glow of the stars, a renewed determination sparked within.

As the first rays of dawn stretched across the horizon, the desert stirred from its nocturnal tranquility. Even though it was the onset of Isendur, the heat was still blistering, the sunlight transforming the landscape into a searing expanse. The desert, once enveloped in the gentle coolness of the night, was now a stark, desolate stretch under the blazing caress of the sun.

The desert's heat was oppressive. The sand, once cool and smooth, was now scorching, each grain a tiny mirror reflecting the blazing sunlight. The air was filled with heatwaves, the once gentle night breezes now hot gusts that bore the desert's scalding breath. As I trekked through this blistering realm, I sought shade in the lee of tall sand dunes. These natural barriers provided a brief shelter from the searing sun, their protected side a haven in the heart of the desert. The dunes resembled the waves of a golden ocean, their shifting sands reflective of the desert's ever-changing character. Now and then, I would stumble upon a rock formation, a rare spectacle in the vast sandy expanse. These formations stood like red sentinels in the sea of sand, their steadfast shapes a stark contrast to the fluid sand dunes. They offered refuge from the sun, their leeward sides a much-needed shield from the relentless heat.

The desert was a challenge, a test of endurance and resilience. But as I navigated through the dunes, seeking shelter in their shadows and behind the rare rock formations, I found myself adapting to its harsh conditions. As the sun ascended to its zenith, its fiery light grew harsher, casting the desert into a stark, blistering realm. The heat was suffocating, a ceaseless adversary that drained the moisture from my body and made each inhalation burn. Faced with such severe elements, I found myself adapting, altering my tactics to endure. I minimized my exposure, each movement, each action thought out to retain hydration and stay as cool as possible. The desert became a battleground, and survival a game of resilience and strategy. I sought shelter from the sun, seeking solace in any shade I could discover. The towering sand dunes and the occasional rock formations became my refuges, their sun-protected sides a sanctuary from the ruthless heat. I nestled in their cooling embrace, the heat a distant foe kept at a distance by the enveloping shelter.

In my contest against the heat, the dwarrin chainmail emerged as a steadfast ally. This chainmail, with its elaborate design and robust build, offered a layer of defense against the scorching sun. It wasn't the most useful shield against the sun's attacks, but in the desert's stern conditions, even minor shade was invaluable. As the heat intensified and the desert bared its hottest demeanor at midday, I found my fatigue growing. I adapted, I endured, and I survived. The desert was a rigorous overlord, but I was overcoming its challenges, one scorching day at a time. The initial nights in the desert tested my adaptability. I had with me a modest stash of supplies, remnants from my sojourn from the faelari grove and subsequent travels. These reserves were my lifeline, a tiny solace in the stark expanse of the desert. However, as the days progressed, my stock began to diminish. While the desert seemed inhospitable, it wasn't entirely barren. Small critters, desert owls, and the occasional hare thrived here. For this, I leaned on the survival techniques taught by my tribe, skills crafted over generations of harmonious living with the wild. I constructed snares, their designs a fusion of ancestral methods and on-the-spot ingenuity. I hunted with a combination of stealth and precision, each motion a meticulous part of the survival dance. The desert was a demanding hunting ground, its residents skittish and astute. Nonetheless, I prevailed, my snares procuring modest but crucial bounties. Each owl, each hare signified a win, a minor success in the enduring struggle to subsist. Along with my tribal wisdom, the tools and knowledge from my journey also found their application.

With each passing day, the heat grew more scorching, its fiery breath converting the desert into a blistering wasteland. The heat was stifling, a relentless adversary that made every footfall an ordeal. Confronted by such formidable elements, I discovered adaptability in myself, modifying my tactics to persevere. The nighttime hours, which I formerly used for resting, became my time for travel and exploration. I chose the guidance of the moon for my nocturnal journeys, its gentle luminescence a beacon in the warm embrace of night. This celestial navigation was another skill imparted by the centarion, a gift for which I remained ever thankful. The stars served as my directional cues, their patterns forming a celestial chart that steered me across the expansive desert.

My attire, a woven tunic and leggings, yet another gift bestowed by the centarion, proved invaluable in the scorching climes. The fabric was light and breathable, providing protection against the blistering heat and warding off the daytime sun. The tunic and leggings showcased the centarion's masterful craftsmanship, their design an impeccable mix of coolness and functionality. The blade gifted by the beast-men became a vital component of my survival. I employed it to prepare my sustenance, its razor edge efficiently processing the occasional game I had trapped. I was cautious not to overuse the dwarrin blade, Faelthorn, reserving its potency for moments of dire need. Armed with the beast-man's blade and the traditional knowledge from my tribe, I adeptly prepared my meals.

The month of Nolariel in Isendur arose during my Řazzblûd, taking Ithendar's place in the great continuum. This shift was underscored by the air getting slightly crisper, with the cold embrace of Isendur creeping up onto even this heat-drenched expanse. With the advent of Nolariel, a notable juncture was achieved. Almost two cycles had passed since my departure from the comforts of my homeland, venturing into the uncharted with a heart brimming with resolve and a soul seeking novelty. The expedition was a tapestry of encounters, a mingling of challenges and victories that molded me into an adept traveler. The elapsed time had unveiled a plethora of adventures and experiences, each serving as a marker on the trajectory of my quest. As I stood amid the embrace of the warm night air, the sand-covered ground extending before me, I found myself contemplating the bygone moons. In the tranquility of the sandswept landscape, under the boundless canopy of the starry night, I was enveloped in memories of Tornu. His recollection was a consoling touch, a recognizable anchor amidst the ever-changing surroundings. His voice seemed to resonate gently within, guiding and emboldening me to persevere.

I wished he was here, by my side, to witness the transformation I had undergone. From a boy, unsure and hesitant, to a survivor, resilient and determined. I wished he could see the adventures I had embarked upon, the trials I had overcome, and the strength I had discovered within myself. A part of me, a growing ember in the depths of my heart, thirsted for vengeance. The celestriker, the entity responsible for Tornu's absence, had become a symbol of my anger, my grief. I yearned for justice, for a chance to utilize my newfound strength and avenge my mentor, to make the celestriker pay for the pain it had caused. Yet, another part of me, a softer, more vulnerable part, simply yearned for Tornu's presence. I missed his guidance, his wisdom, his comforting presence. I missed the sound of my uncle's voice, the warmth of his smile, the reassurance of his presence. I wanted my mentor back, the man who had taught me so much, who had been a constant source of support and encouragement. As I stood beneath the starlit expanse, the warm wind gently brushing against my skin, I let the depth of my emotions surface. The sorrow, the rage, the yearning - they epitomized the connection I once held with Tornu, a link that defied the limits of time and distance. And as I looked up at the stars, I made a silent promise to myself - I would honor Tornu's memory, I would continue my journey, and I would become the person he believed I could be.

Water, the lifeblood of survival, was a scarce commodity in the desert. Yet, it was not entirely absent. The desert, for all its harshness, held secrets, hidden treasures that could mean the difference between life and death. I remembered Kallıstos' teachings, his words echoing in my mind. Certain stars, he had said, always pointed towards running water. It was a lesson I had held onto, a beacon of hope in the harsh reality of the desert. With hope in my heart and the stars as my guide, I set out to find water. I wasn't sure if Kallistos' teachings would hold true in the desert, but I had to try. And whether it was the guidance of the stars or a stroke of luck, each time I sought water, I found it. The desert, in its warm guise, concealed secrets beneath its scorching sands.

These covert oases were frequently guarded by venomous vipers or stinging scorpions, their lethal presence serving as a warning to intruders. Yet, I was not deterred. Armed with my dwarrin dagger, Faelthorn, I ventured into the viper's den, my determination outweighing my fear. Faelthorn was not just a weapon, but a tool, its elandari moonstones a guide in my quest for water. The moonstones, sensing my thirst, would glow a subtle blue when water was nearby, and a deep crimson whenever danger lurked nearby. It was a magical phenomenon, an exhibit of the mystical properties of the elandari moonstones.

As I navigated through the desert, guided by the stars and the glow of the elandari moonstones, I found myself marveling at the resilience of life. One night, under the watchful gaze of the stars, I found myself face to face with one of the desert's most formidable inhabitants - a Tailsinger. The creature was a master of stealth, its presence concealed by the shadows of the night. It was only when its barbed tail lashed out towards me that I became aware of its presence. Caught off guard, I reacted instinctively. Faelthorn, my trusted dwarven dagger, was in my hand in an instant. The dagger, with its mystical connection to the wind, lent me a swiftness that was beyond my natural human capabilities. I moved with a speed and agility that defied the laws of nature, my movements a blur as I blocked the Tailsinger's attack. The Tailsinger was a formidable opponent, its deadly stinger a constant threat. Yet, I was not deterred. I fought back, my movements a dance of precision and speed. The struggle was brief but intense, a battle of survival in the harsh reality of the desert. In the end, I emerged victorious, the Tailsinger defeated. Yet, the encounter was a stark reminder of the ever-present dangers of the desert. As I continued my journey under the starlit sky, the encounter with the Tailsinger etched in my memory, I found myself more alert, more aware.

The desert was a land of extremes, its beauty often marred by sudden and unpredictable dangers. Wild beasts were a constant threat, their presence a reminder of the harsh reality of the desert. Yet, they were not the only dangers I encountered during my solitary journey. In its merciless demeanor, the desert posed countless natural dangers.

At dusk one evening, as I roused from my day's reprieve and the sun aggressively descended below the horizon, tranquility was abruptly disrupted by the onset of a fierce sandstorm. Emerging from the desert's depths, this immense force blanketed the world in a whirling flurry of sand. Everything transformed into a tumultuous storm; the air was thick with swirling sand particles, and the winds bellowed with wild might. Confronted with this overpowering foe, I turned to the faelari magic. Harnessing the "*Lünthårä*" chant, powered by the Lunasil pendant, I summoned a protective barrier. The spell cast a shelter around me, shielding me from the scorching winds and piercing sand. Though the storm continued its relentless surge, I remained secure within the spell's cool embrace. Recognizing the invaluable defense the Lunasil pendant provided, I chose to keep it within arm's reach. Instead of stowing it away, I attached it to a strand from my woven leggings, wearing it as a necklace, allowing the enchanted faelari relic to rest close to my heart.

As I journeyed through the vast expanse of the desert, I made a conscious effort to tread lightly, to respect the delicate balance of this harsh landscape. Every trace of my existence, every piece of waste I produced, was carefully buried, hidden beneath the shifting sands. The desert was now my temporary home, my battlefield, and I was determined to leave it as untouched as possible. Water was a precious commodity. Each source I encountered was treated with reverence, used sparingly and with utmost care. I was careful not to contaminate them, preserving their purity for the creatures that called the desert home. As I continued along my Řazzbłûd, I felt a profound connection with Alara. The winds, Alara's breath, seemed to embrace me, their gentle caress a source of comfort in the harsh reality of the desert. I felt a sense of confidence, a reassurance that Alara was pleased with the respect I showed for its domain. Alara's wind was a constant companion, its whispers a soothing melody in the silence of the desert. It told tales of the desert, its voice carrying the stories of the sands, the creatures, and the trials they faced. The wind was a teacher, its lessons a guide in my journey through the desert. Even in the harsh landscape of the desert, I found comfort in the familiar presence of Alara's wind. It was a guiding force, a beacon of hope in the face of adversity. Through all my trials, through all the challenges I faced, I was not alone. Alara's wind was with me.

As the seventh day of my Řazzbłûd dawned, a sense of anticipation filled the air. The desert, once a vast expanse of trials and tribulations, was now a familiar landscape, its harsh beauty a manifestation of my journey. I found myself drawn back towards the beast-man palisade, my steps guided by the promise of the end of my trial. Excitement welled up within me, a bubbling spring of anticipation and curiosity. I was eager to learn, to delve into the mysteries of the beast-men. Their culture, at first glance seemingly simplistic, held a certain allure. If it was anything like goblikar society, I knew there would be layers upon layers of complexity hidden beneath the surface. The beast-men were a fascinating race, their customs and traditions an emphatic difference to my own. I yearned to understand them, to learn about their beliefs, their values, their way of life. I wanted to unravel the threads of their culture, to explore the tapestry of their society.

As I made my way back towards the palisade, the desert stretching out behind me, I found myself reflecting on my journey. The Řazzbłûd had been a trial, a test of my resilience and determination. Yet, it was also a journey of self-discovery, a mirror of my strength and my will to survive. As the end of my trial neared, I felt a sense of accomplishment, a pride in the journey I had undertaken. I was ready to face the beast-men, to learn from them, to understand them. Lost in a reverie of anticipation and curiosity, I found myself wandering through the desert. My mind was preoccupied with thoughts of the beast-men and the knowledge they held. The subtle sizzle of sun-scorched sands beneath my boots went unnoticed as I lost myself in contemplation, having decided to make my return during daylight, despite the potent heat the day time offered. Faelthorn, my trusted dwarrin dagger, was the first to alert me to the impending danger. Its elandari moonstones began to glow an eerie crimson, casting a soft luminescence over the sandy dunes. So engrossed was I that their gentle warning eluded me. The desert, with its stark beauty, had yet another challenge prepared.

Concealed by a ripple in the dunes, a dune lion lay in ambush. Its tawny fur was almost indistinguishable from the sand, its silent presence hidden by the deceptive calm of the desert landscape.

Before I could react, the lion pounced. It was a streak of tawny fury, a blur of graceful agility and bared fangs. I was taken off-guard, the swiftness of the assault leaving me momentarily disoriented. The dune lion, a stunning manifestation of the desert's wild essence, descended upon me with a growl that cut through the heated silence. Its lithe body, an embodiment of its survivalist instincts, toppled me, plunging me into the hot, sand-covered dunes. The world tilted, the bright desert sky blending with the golden sand in a dizzying dance. Clutched in my hand, Faelthorn's moonstones pulsed with an urgency that echoed my pounding heart. Their crimson luminescence stood out vividly against the sandswept landscape, their rhythmic light serving as a stark reminder of my perilous situation. The moonstones, with magic attuned to the heartbeats of Alara, became my beacon, their warning offering a sliver of hope amidst the lion's ambush.

Pain shot through my shoulder where the lion's claws had scratched. The wounds were deep, the sharp claws leaving behind a trail of pain that mirrored the intensity of its assault. Yet, even amidst the throbbing pain, I recognized my fortune. A beat slower, a mere blink of an eye's delay, and the lion's teeth would have found my throat. Facing this immediate danger, I mustered my strength, pushing aside the dizziness and the burning sting from my shoulder. With a surge of adrenaline, I stumbled backwards, the hot sand crunching and shifting beneath me, creating a gap between the lion and myself. The dune lion, with its unwavering predatory stare, readied itself for another leap. Confronted with such peril, I leaned into the faelari magic that had guarded me against the desert's challenges. The verse, Lünthårä, resounded again in my thoughts, a sacred chant imparted to me by Ilyafae. Swiftly, I chanted the verse, my voice an urgent invocation to the Lunasil for a shield. As I voiced the incantation, a potent energy surged within, harmonizing with the pulse of the Lunasil. A gleaming barrier sprang into existence in front of me, its otherworldly glow contrasting starkly against the sun streaked desert. This barrier, born of faelari magic, stood as my bulwark against the lion's next strike.

The dune lion lunged once more, its agile form a blend of tawny fur and coiled strength. But instead of striking flesh, it met the mystical barrier. The unexpected blockage elicited a startled yowl from the lion, which recoiled from the unseen force. The shield remained unwavering, its luminous exterior unperturbed by the lion's attempt. Using this fleeting moment of the lion's bewilderment, I grasped the chance to steady myself. I rose from the sand, the raw scratches on my shoulder a piercing reminder of the lion's assault. Blood trickled from the gashes, dotting the golden sand beneath with dark drops. However, despite the pressing pain, my attention veered towards the Lunasil, more than my dagger. Murmuring words of peace and solace, I aimed to pacify the creature rather than wound it further. The moonstones, though unintentional recipients of my words, responded, resonating with my purpose, and started to radiate a gentle blue hue. This tranquil aura from the stones spread, casting the surrounding wilderness in its pacifying glow.

The lion, its keen amber eyes mirroring a mix of perplexity and inquisitiveness, observed me with caution. Its muscles remained tensed and its hunter's poise persisted, but, swayed by the moonstones' ambiance, it withheld from striking again. In this lull of confrontation, my gaze drifted back to the Lunasil, the mystic faelari artifact symbolizing a glimmer of hope amidst looming peril. I began reciting another faelari incantation, "*Élærän'drå*", the chant being a supplication for harmony, a quest for mutual understanding. As the tones of the faelari verse resonated, the Lunasil pendant nestled against my chest subtly resonated. A gentle silvery luminescence burst forth from its heart, the amulet responding to the enchantment-laden song. The Lunasil, an emblem of faelari mysticism, was crafting a nexus of comprehension between the lion and me. The calming blue of the moonstones enveloped the area, setting a tranquil scene for the budding bond. However, it was the Lunasil that truly captivated the dune lion. The amulet pulsed in tandem with the faelari incantation, disseminating ripples of empathic energy towards the majestic feline. In this fleeting span, communication evolved beyond mere words, morphing into a melody of sentiments and purposes, a profound link binding me to the wild lion. The pendant, with its silvery radiance piercing through the desert expanse, facilitated this profound rapport, its enchantment connecting the realms of man and wild.

The lion, its amber eyes mirroring the silvery sheen of the Lunasil, appeared to comprehend. The once dominant and intimidating posture began to relent, its gaze mellowing as it absorbed the understanding waves radiating from the pendant. In the midst of the sun-drenched desert of early Isendur, a unique connection was blossoming, a testament to the might of faelari magic and the ties it could weave between two seemingly disparate souls. Engaged in this wordless communion with the dune lion, I channeled serenity and assurance through the empathic bridge the Lunasil offered. The bewilderment in its amber orbs seemed to wane. It wasn't an exertion of dominance but an entreaty for harmony. I stood not as a target but as another traveler of the desert, wishing for unobstructed passage across its realm. The lion's reply, although mute, was deep. Signaled by a gentle dip of its head and the easing intensity in its gaze. Its eyes, previously blazing with potential onslaught, now echoed the serene blue of the moonstones, suggesting a newfound clarity. It seemed to grasp my petition, sensing the kinship the Lunasil had fostered. Offering a concluding, mellowed growl, more out of inquisitiveness than menace, it acknowledged our mutual respect. Then, with an elegance contrasting its daunting might, it ambled away. Vanishing amidst the sun-tinged desert, its tawny frame effortlessly merging with the sandy terrain, it left me in solitude. Awed by Alara's splendor and the elemental magic intertwining all its beings, I watched the lion fade into the distance, feeling an intense bond with the harsh yet mesmerizing expanse of the desert.

XII

Orukuthûndar

With the departure of the dune lion, a sense of calm descended upon the desert landscape. I found myself slowly sinking to my knees, the adrenaline that had fueled my encounter with the beast now leaving me feeling drained. The Lunasil pendant, its glow dimming, returned to its passive state. Yet, it still felt warm against my chest, its residual heat a comforting reminder of the magic it held. The pendant, a relic of faelari magic, had been my shield, my bridge to understanding the dune lion. My breaths came in slow and deep, each exhale a release of the tension that had gripped me during the encounter. I took a moment to recover, to process the events that had unfolded. The imprint of the creature's mind, its confusion and eventual understanding, was still vivid in my own.

With the encounter with the dune lion behind me, I turned my steps back towards the beast-men's camp. The journey was a quiet one, the desert landscape stretching out around me a portrayal of the trials I had faced. As I walked, I restored the enchantment on my Saela-Hathir, the magical artifact a comforting presence in the face of the challenges that lay ahead. As I approached the camp, the imposing figures of the beast-men standing guard came into view. Their incredulous stares met me, their eyes wide with surprise. I could almost sense their disbelief, their doubt that I would return from the desert's trials. Yet, here I was, standing before them, signifying my resilience and determination. Their surprise was understandable. The desert was a harsh and unforgiving landscape, its trials a test of one's strength and will to survive. Yet, I had faced its challenges, survived its trials, and returned to tell the tale. As I stood before the beast-men, their incredulous stares, a blatant discordance to the respect I had earned in the desert, the weight of my endeavors lifted. I had faced the desert's trials, survived its challenges, and returned to continue my journey. The beast-men's surprise was a welcome validation of the trials I had faced and the strength I had shown. The smallest guard, a muscular creature with a fierce glint in his eyes, scrambled inside the palisade walls, his voice echoing through the air, "Kharok! *Kharok!*" His call was urgent, a clarion call that pierced the stillness of the night, bouncing off the rough-hewn wooden walls and the towering mudstone watchtowers.

Within moments, the beast-man elder, Kharok, emerged from the shadows of the inner sanctum once more. His towering figure was silhouetted against the flickering torchlight, his broad shoulders hunched, and his tusks gleaming ominously in the dim light. His eyes, like two glowing embers, as black as the stone blade he had given me, fixed on me, assessing my bloodied state with a penetrating gaze. He approached me, his heavy footfalls resonating against the packed sand, each step a representation of his formidable strength. His face was a mask of stern authority, but as he drew closer, he gave a single, solemn nod of his head. The gesture was simple, yet it carried the weight of his approval.

"You come back. Bloodied from krugûl. Take great strength to do Řazzblûd." His voice was a deep rumble, strong and gravelly, echoing off the walls of the palisade. It was a voice that commanded respect, a voice that had led his people through countless battles and hardships. Yet, beneath the stern exterior, there was a hint of pride. Pride at seeing a "no-tusk" - a term they used for outsiders - successfully complete their Řazzblûd, a grueling rite of passage.

"We have zûg'mok watch you. You follow orukuthûndar ways strong. You keep lûr clean. Leave no truk'grut. You show honor to rok'gar of Brâġa, and to Grûmak'Tûrg. You come in. We talk." His words, though foreign to my ears, were spoken with a sincerity that transcended language barriers. His approval was evident, not just in his words but in the way his eyes softened, the way his stern demeanor eased. Though I had no grasp on some of their words, the pride in Kharok's voice, the respect in his gaze, stirred something within me. Deep within my heart, a tapestry of pride and fulfillment was woven, a sense of belonging that I hadn't expected. Pride welled up inside me, a warm, invigorating sensation that spread through my veins, igniting a newfound determination. I had passed their test, earned their respect, and in doing so, I had found a piece of myself I hadn't known existed.

At that moment, a brutish looking beast-man, his muscles rippling under his coarse fur cloak, and his tusks gleaming menacingly, pushed his way forward. His eyes were ablaze with indignation, and his nostrils flared as he snarled, "You no let no-tusk in our walls! Say this not true!" His voice was a thunderous roar, echoing through the silent crowd and challenging the authority of his leader. The leader, Kharok, who had just moments ago commended me for completing the Řazzbłûd, turned on him. His eyes were now ablaze with a silent fury. His gaze was a storm, a tempest of unspoken wrath that sent a shiver down the spine of every beast-man present.

"We *never* let no-tusk in! You do this now, maybe you no fit to lead us no more!" The beast-man continued, his voice rising in volume and intensity. He was openly berating his leader, his words a blatant challenge to Kharok's authority. Kharok, however, was not one to be easily intimidated. He stood his ground, his towering figure an illustration of his unyielding resolve.

He corrected his follower, his voice a low growl that reverberated through the silent crowd. "You question my word, you question my place. You think you lead better, face me in fight." His words hung in the air, a dare, a challenge to any who opposed him. The crowd fell silent, the tension palpable. The beast-man who had questioned his leader was taken aback. He glared at Kharok, his eyes burning with defiance, but he didn't respond. Instead, he pushed his way back through the crowd, his shoulders hunched and his fists clenched. He disappeared into the throng, his departure leaving a ripple of whispers in his wake. His challenge had been met with a counter-challenge, and he had retreated. The crowd watched him go, their eyes wide with a mixture of fear and respect for their leader. Kharok had asserted his authority, and in doing so, had reinforced the hierarchy within the tribe.

I followed Kharok through the imposing, wooden double-gates that marked the entrance to their camp. My heart pounded in my chest, but it was no longer a rhythm of fear. Instead, it was a beat of anticipation, curiosity, and a newfound respect for the beast-men. As I stepped through the gates, I was able to take better note of the things I saw, my eyes no longer clouded by the fear for my life.

Hanging ominously from the large log walls, which had been sharpened to deadly points, were an array of bones and skulls. They were stark warnings, a grim echo reverberating the fate of those who dared to encroach on their territory. The sight was chilling, yet it spoke volumes about the beast-men's fierce protectiveness of their home. Upon crossing the threshold, the sounds were what first assaulted my senses. It was a cacophony of harsh voices, the clashing of stones, and animalistic grunts. The settlement was a hive of activity, a living, breathing entity that pulsed with the rhythm of life. Broad, muscular beast-men toiled under the harsh desert sun, their bodies slick with sweat. Some were honing weapons, their movements precise and practiced. Others were tending to animals, their hands gentle yet firm. Still, others were engaged in various tasks, each contributing to the overall functioning of the camp. The air was thick with the smell of roasting meat, the musky scent of sweat, and the dry, earthy aroma of dust. Over an open fire, a beast-man cook could be seen stirring a large, bubbling cauldron, his muscles straining with the effort. Nearby, others were roasting hunks of meat on spits, the sizzling sound and tantalizing smell adding to the sensory overload. Beast-women, recognizable by their less-bulky forms, worked diligently. Some were skinning hunted animals with practiced ease, their hands moving swiftly and surely. Others were grinding grains, their movements rhythmic and steady.

Some were carrying water in heavy leather bladders from a nearby well, their strength evident in their steady strides. The beast-children, bare and dirt-streaked, ran amok, their boisterous laughter and yells adding to the overall tumult. They chased each other around the camp, their small forms darting between the adults, their joyous energy a compelling discrepancy to the serious work of the adults.

The camp was a microcosm of life, a representation underscoring the beast-men's resilience, strength, and community spirit. It was a sight that was both awe-inspiring and humbling, a sight that I would carry with me for the rest of my life. As I ventured deeper into the camp, my eyes were drawn to a multitude of red mud huts. They were just like the ones I had taken shelter in on the first night of my Řazzbłûd, their familiar shapes a comforting sight amidst the unfamiliar surroundings. However, seeing them in such a large congregation was nothing short of astonishing. To the east, the landscape was dominated by rows upon rows of these huts. They were stacked on top of each other with an efficiency that spoke volumes about the beast-men's ingenuity. The arrangement was a motif recurring in honor of the challenges of limited space and a high population. I found myself wondering just how many hundreds of these creatures lived inside this, from the outside, seemingly small village. The huts were built ingeniously, one atop the other, in a haphazard manner that was both chaotic and harmonious. Their walls were contiguous, each hut sharing a wall with its neighbor. Their roofs served as the base for the hut above, creating a multi-tiered structure that was both practical and efficient. They were laid side by side, their raw, earthy exteriors almost blending into one another. From a distance, the village looked like a single, massive structure, its red hue a categorical distinction against the barren desert landscape. Despite the seeming lack of individual privacy, I realized that this setup reflected a deep sense of community and collective living ingrained in these peoples' culture. It was a portrayal vividly capturing their adaptability, their resilience in the face of the harsh desert environment. The arrangement optimized space and provided shared shelter from the scorching suns and raging windstorms, a symbol resonating with their survival instincts.

To the north of the huts lay a vast central gathering area. It was the communal heart of the beast-men's settlement, pulsating with the rhythm of daily life. The square was a flurry of activity, a living, breathing entity that was both chaotic and harmonious. The corners of this square were laden with roughly woven baskets of varying sizes, each filled to the brim with goods. Carts were loaded with wares, their colorful displays a reflection giving a clear picture of the bustling trade within their community. The sight was a vibrant mosaic of colors and textures, a visual feast that spoke volumes about the beast-men's resourcefulness and communal spirit. Beast-men of different shades - gray, green, and blue - were engrossed in their daily chores. They moved about in an organized chaos, their movements fluid and purposeful. The trading of goods was a spectacle in itself. Beast-men haggled and bartered, their voices a cacophony of different gravelly tones and volumes. The sharing of meals was a communal affair, a time for bonding and camaraderie. Beast-men gathered around fires, their barking laughter and boisterous conversation filling the air. The aroma of roasting meat wafted through the square, a tantalizing scent that spoke of shared meals and shared stories. The training of younglings was a sight to behold. Older beast-men instructed the young in the art of combat, their movements precise and practiced. The younglings watched and mimicked, their dark eyes wide with awe and determination. Every action, every interaction, was a seamless blend of individual effort and communal spirit.

In the western part of the village, a majestic tent stood tall and proud. It was a grand structure, constructed from a blend of leather, wood, and mudstone. The materials, though simple, were put together in a way that evoked an aura of authority and reverence. The tent was an attestation giving weight to the beast-men's craftsmanship, their ability to create something grand from the most basic of materials. This tent, larger and more ornate than the others, seemed to be the abode or meeting place of the beast-man leaders. It was a symbol of their authority, a beacon of power and respect amidst the hustle and bustle of the village. Encircling the tent were stone cairns, similar to the ones I had seen on my arrival. Each cairn was a towering structure, its stones stacked with a precision that spoke volumes about the beast-men's attention to detail. I speculated that each cairn might symbolize an important event or figure in their history.

In the center of the settlement, a large, raised platform commanded attention. It was made of rough-hewn logs and stones. The platform, with its rugged charm and imposing presence, appeared to be a communal meeting area or perhaps a place for the clan's leaders to address their kin. It stood as a symbol of unity, a place where the beast-men could gather to discuss, debate, and make decisions that affected their community. Near the platform, a tall, stone monument reached towards the sky. It was a towering structure, its surface intricately carved with symbols and images. The carvings depicted scenes of their battles, their brave warriors locked in combat with formidable foes, from other beast-men to great zephryans. Other carvings depicted their migration from the mountains, a journey that seemed fairly recent - if I had to guess, probably within the last 150 cycles - fraught with challenges and hardships. The images told a story of resilience, of a people who had braved the elements and the unknown to find a new home. There were also carvings that possibly depicted their creation, their origins as a people. These images were more abstract, their meanings shrouded in mystery. Yet, they spoke of a deep reverence for their past, for the thunder, and for a mountain which seemed to be exploding from the peak, a respect for their origins that was deeply ingrained in their culture.

Kharok, the towering figure with a stern countenance, guided me through the labyrinthine pathways of their settlement. The air was thick with the scent of burning wood and roasting meat, mingling with the dry, arid aroma of the surrounding desert. The settlement was a hive of activity, with tribespeople going about their tasks, their movements a well-practiced dance of survival. Our destination was the westernmost tent, a massive structure that stood out against the backdrop of smaller dwellings. It was encircled by a ring of cairns, each meticulously stacked stone a silent echo of the tribe's reverence for their ancestors. The tent's entrance was flanked by two large, intricately carved totems, their grotesque figures illuminated by the flickering light of nearby torches.

As we stepped inside, the atmosphere changed dramatically. The noise from the bustling settlement outside was muffled, replaced by a heavy silence that seemed to hang in the air. The interior was dimly lit, the only light coming from a small fire pit in the center, casting dancing shadows on the leather walls. The walls themselves were adorned with large tapestries, each one a canvas of chilling imagery. They were painted in a dark, rusty red hue, the color so vivid it could only have been blood. The scenes they portrayed were of great slaughter, each one more gruesome than the last. One tapestry depicted the elegant elandari, their poised forms riddled with despair and anguish as they met their merciless doom. Another showed stalwart dwarrin, their strong frames crumbling beneath the weight of an overwhelming force. The sight was enough to send a shiver down my spine. These tapestries were a stark reminder of the tribe's brutal history, each one a chapter in a blood-soaked saga. The air in the tent felt heavy, the weight of countless lives lost hanging oppressively. As I followed Kharok deeper into the tent, I couldn't shake off the feeling of unease.

Kharok led me into the heart of the tent, where a large, mud-stone table dominated the space. The table's surface was rough yet meticulously shaped. It was adorned with an array of bones and pelts of various sizes, each one a trophy from a successful hunt. The bones were bleached white, polished to a shine, and arranged in intricate patterns. The pelts, still bearing the vibrant hues of their original owners, were draped over the table's edges, their soft fur contrasting with the hard stone. The centerpiece of the table was a shining black blade, its surface gleaming ominously in the firelight. It was similar to the one I had been given for my Řazzblûd. The blade was embedded deep into the table, having gouged a large chunk of mud-stone with its insertion. The sight of it, so casually displayed, was a stark reminder of the tribe's strength and ferocity. Kharok dismissed his guards with a curt nod, and they retreated outside, leaving us alone in the dimly lit tent. The atmosphere was tense, the silence broken only by the crackling of the fire and the occasional rustle of the tapestries.

As we settled down, Kharok's stern expression softened, his obsidian eyes reflecting a genuine interest. At his insistence, I spent the next several hours regaling him with tales of my travels. I spoke of the vast landscapes I had traversed, the creatures I had encountered, and the challenges I had overcome. Kharok listened intently, his gaze never leaving my face, his silence encouraging me to continue. The fire flickered and danced, casting a warm glow on the mud-stone table and the gruesome tapestries. The shadows danced on Kharok's face, highlighting his strong features and the lines of age and experience. The shining black blade stood as a silent observer, its gleaming surface reflecting the firelight. As the hours passed, the tent became a cocoon, shielding us from the world outside. The gruesome images on the tapestries seemed less intimidating, the chilling silence replaced by the rhythm of my storytelling. Despite the initial unease, a sense of camaraderie began to form, the shared tales bridging the gap between our cultures. Despite the violent and aggressive nature of his people, Kharok exuded an unexpected air of wisdom and discernment. His rough, scarred skin bore a depiction underscoring the depth of countless battles, a silent proclamation of his strength and physical prowess. Yet, as he listened to my tales, his demeanor was one of quiet contemplation, his eyes reflecting a depth of understanding that belied his rugged exterior. He listened intently, his gaze never wavering from my face. He never interrupted, except to grunt in understanding or to ask me to elaborate on certain events that piqued his interest. His fascination was particularly evident when I recounted tales of the primal magic that permeated the other races of Alara. As I spoke of the faelari, the centarion, and the elandari, and the ways in which they harnessed Alara's magic with grace and power, Kharok's eyes would take on a distant look. It was as if he was transported to another place, his mind lost in a daydream. His gaze would soften, staring almost longingly into the flickering firelight, his thoughts seemingly elsewhere.

Over the course of a week, Kharok continued to invite me into the large tent. Each time, he would listen with rapt attention as I shared the stories of all that I had seen and experienced in my last cycle of journeying Alara. At the end of the week, Kharok finally broke his silence. His voice, deep and resonant, echoed in the tent, a definite diversion from the hours of quiet listening. His words, when they came, were measured and thoughtful, reflecting the wisdom and discernment that had become so apparent over the course of our conversations.

"Your stories impress me. You not as easy broken as most no-tusks. You have quiet strength. Me see you now as *blâdur*. Kin. Yoran, the no-tusk orukuthûndar," Kharok's voice rumbled, his words echoing in the vastness of the tent. His declaration, calling me one of their own, was a profound honor. I tried to repeat the term, to accept his honor in their tongue, but found myself choked on the swell of emotions that welled up within me. My throat tightened, the words sticking like a lump, refusing to come out. All I managed was a strangled "orc", the word hanging in the air of the tent, a choke amplifying the overwhelming emotions coursing through me. Kharok let out a bark of a laugh, a sound that echoed around the confines of the tent. His hand clapped roughly on my back, a gesture of camaraderie that sent a jolt through me. He drew the rough, black blade from the mud stone table, its surface gleaming ominously in the dim light. With a nod, he led me back outside the large leather tent.

As we stepped into the evening light, the world seemed to transform. The sky was painted with the hues of twilight, a canvas of purples, pinks, and oranges. The setting Isendur sun cast long shadows over the settlement, the last rays of the day bathing everything in a warm, golden glow. Kharok roared a word in his harsh, guttural language, the sound resonating like a thunderclap. "Blâdur!" The word echoed through the settlement, a command that demanded attention. Instantly, the hubbub of the orukuthûndar camp hushed, the sounds of daily life coming to a sudden halt. Every eye turned towards their

Chieftain and the strange, no-tusk outsider. The air was thick with anticipation, the silence punctuated only by the crackling of nearby fires. Once Kharok was certain he held the attention of every orukuthûndar in the settlement, he raised the black stone blade high above his head. The blade seemed to drink in the dying light, its surface shimmering eerily. The assembled orukuthûndar fell silent, their gazes fixed on the blade and the orukuthûndar who wielded it.

"This no-tusk," Kharok roared, his voice carrying across the settlement, "Yoran. He show great strength. Great courage. Great mind. He did Řazzblûd. He live. He tell Kharok of many things around Břâġa. Kharok honor Yoran. Blâdur. Kin. Orukuthûndar!" His declaration echoed through the settlement, a proclamation of my acceptance into their tribe. The blade, still held high, pointed directly at me. The orukuthûndar watched, their eyes reflecting a mix of surprise, curiosity, and respect. The setting sun cast long shadows, the twilight sky a fitting backdrop for this momentous occasion. For a few heartbeats, silence hung over the encampment, a tangible stillness that seemed to hold its breath. The orukuthûndar stood frozen, their gazes locked on Kharok and me, the weight of the Chieftain's words hanging in the air. Then, as if a dam had broken, a deafening roar of approval erupted from the orukuthûndar crowd. The sound was like a tidal wave, a powerful surge of noise that swept across the settlement. Some beat their chests, the thumping rhythm a primal anthem of acceptance. Others clanged their weapons together, the stoney clash a cacophony showcasing their warrior spirit. Still others howled their approval into the setting sun, their voices rising in a wild chorus that echoed across the landscape. The noise was chaotic and powerful, a symphony of sounds that embodied the wild spirit of the orukuthûndar people.

Amidst the revelry and celebration, I noticed a small group of orukuthûndar standing apart. They were not participating in the jubilation, their stern expressions a bold incongruity to the joyous faces around them. Their silence was a loud proclamation amidst the cacophony, their stillness a noticeable anomaly in the sea of movement. The one in the foremost center of their group was particularly striking. His face was set in a hard, unyielding line, his eyes cold and calculating. I recognized him as the one who had challenged Kharok's authority when I returned from the Řazzbłûd. His presence was like a dark cloud, casting a shadow over the celebration. Without a word, he turned and left the celebrating crowd, his movements deliberate and unhurried. His cronies followed behind, their loyalty to him evident in their synchronized movements. Their departure was a silent protest, a clear indication of their disapproval. As they disappeared into the encampment, the celebration continued unabated, the orukuthûndar's joyous roars drowning out the silent dissent. Yet, their departure left a lingering unease.

In the wake of the declaration, I found myself being swept up in the ensuing procession. The orukuthûndar circled around me, a whirl of muscular bodies moving in a rhythmic dance. They pushed me towards a towering cairn, their hands firm on my shoulders. Kharok stepped forward, an ochre paste in his hand. With a solemn expression, he smeared the paste onto my forehead, marking me as a member of their tribe - their "blâdur". The paste was cool against my skin, its earthy scent filling my nostrils. The procession then moved through the camp, a living river of bodies. Each tent we passed added more orukuthûndar to the throng, their numbers swelling with each step. The rhythm of our march seemed to shake the very earth beneath our feet, a validation speaking volumes about our combined strength. Upon reaching the edge of the camp, I was handed a bowl of a potent, smoky brew, the traditional drink of the orukuthûndar. I took the bowl, its contents swirling ominously. The aroma hit me first—a heady blend of fermented cactus, scorched desert herbs, and a hint of aged animal hides. The brew's color was as deep as the night, with the consistency of liquefied sand. I hesitated for a moment, then braced myself and took a sip. The taste was overpowering—salty like the sweat on a warrior's brow, combined with the bitterness of sun-baked roots. It felt gritty, almost abrasive, against my tongue. Downing the rest of it in one gulp, I felt the liquid burn down my throat, its strength nearly buckling my knees. Yet I remained standing, the cheers and roars of approval from the crowd bolstering my resolve. Finally, I was led back to the center of the encampment, to the large raised platform. Kharok presented me with a heavy bone necklace, a symbol of my acceptance into the blâdur. I accepted the bone necklace, feeling its weight settle around my neck. It was a tangible reminder of my new status, a symbol of the bond I now shared with the orukuthûndar.

As I looked around at the assembled orukuthûndar, I saw their fierce faces carrying a different expression - one of acceptance and respect. I was one of them now. A part of an orukuthûndar blâdur. An honor no other no-tusks had ever received. As the sun finally finished setting at the end of my first week in the orukuthûndar deserts, the night filled with the echoing roars and rhythmic beats of the blâdur. Their celebration carried on deep into the night, the sounds of their joy marking my initiation into the tribe, and cementing my place as one of their own.

XIII

Snaga'Mok

In the months that followed my initiation, Kharok took me under his wing. He became my mentor, my guide in this new world of the orukuthûndar. He taught me everything he could about his people, their customs, their beliefs, and their way of life. His lessons were not just about survival, but about understanding and respecting the orukuthûndar's rich culture and history. Kharok even went so far as to teach me their language, Skaragg'ha. He explained the meanings of their words, their syntax, and their unique expressions. His lessons were patient and thorough, his dedication to my learning evident in his meticulous teaching. Over time, I began to grasp the nuances of Skaragg'ha, the rhythm and guttural inflections of the language becoming more familiar with each passing day. I practiced constantly, repeating the words and phrases until they felt natural on my tongue. The orukuthûndar were patient with my efforts, their encouragement a constant source of motivation. By the time I left the blâdur, I had become well-versed enough in Skaragg'ha that I no longer used my Saela-Hathir for communicating with them.

Beginning with the word "orukuthûndar", Kharok broke down its meaning for me. "Orra" meaning "blood", and "thûndar" being "mountain" - they referred to themselves as "Blood of the Mountains". Skaragg'ha, their language, was as rugged and raw as the orukuthûndar themselves. It was full of guttural sounds and hand gestures, shaped by life in the harsh mountains. The language was rich in nouns, verbs, adjectives, and numbers, each word carrying a depth of meaning that reflected the orukuthûndar's way of life. They had specific words to denote essential concepts. 'Kruk' for stone, 'Grut' for flesh, and 'Râg' for horn. Each word was a piece of the puzzle, a key to understanding the orukuthûndar's worldview.

Kharok stressed the importance of understanding and correctly pronouncing their language. Certain words, such as "Kruk", meaning "Stone", and "Krûk" being the season of "Aravell", were easily confused. Less difficult, but still easily missed in conversation if one was not paying attention, were "Rûkash", meaning "Armor", and "Drûkash", meaning "Night".

One of the most challenging aspects of Skaragg'ha to master was the tonal grunting. This unique feature of their language added a layer of complexity, with each nuanced grunt subtly shifting the context of words. It was a form of communication that was as much about the sound as it was about the words themselves. For instance, the word "Grak", meaning "sword", when written, loses all contextual meaning. Without the tonal grunting with which it was spoken, the depth of its meaning is lost. If the orukuthûndar talking about a "grak" imposes a higher-pitched grunt on the word, its meaning deepens. It becomes not just a "sword", but a ceremonial sword, specifically one used in their ritualistic massacres, which are referred to as "Gâth'mûrg". Conversely, using a deeper grunt with the word would turn its meaning to a "battle-worn sword". The tonal grunting, therefore, was crucial in conveying the full meaning of the word. Another example of this nuance is found in the word "Mok", or "Warrior". The pronunciation of the 'k' sound significantly alters the meaning of the word. A soft 'k' would be referring to a common warrior, whereas a forceful 'k' would signify that you are speaking of a great warrior or a champion. Mastering these nuances was a painstaking process, requiring careful listening and constant practice. Yet, it was a necessary part of understanding Skaragg'ha and, by extension, the orukuthûndar.

In the human tongue, we often have a single word, or possibly a few, to describe a particular action or concept. However, for the orukuthûndar, certain words that are much more commonplace have many variations. The concept of "kill" was a prime example of this linguistic diversity. While we have "kill" and "murder", the orukuthûndar have a plethora of terms, each carrying a unique connotation. "Gâth" was the basic term, simply meaning "to end life". It was a neutral term, devoid of any additional context or emotion. "Dûr'gâth" was a darker term, meaning a "dark/evil kill". It carried a negative connotation, often used to describe acts of violence that were seen as dishonorable or cruel. "Kugûl'gâth", on the other hand, meant "victorious kill". It was a term of honor, used to describe a kill that was achieved through skill and bravery. "Mok'gâth" translated to "warrior's kill", a term reserved for the orukuthûndar warriors. It was a symbol of their strength and skill, an indicator of their prestige within the tribe.

"Rok'gâth" translated to "battlefield kill", a term used to describe kills made during large-scale battles. It was a term that carried a sense of gravity and respect, acknowledging the chaos and danger of the battlefield. Finally, "tûr'gâth" meant "king's kill". It was a term of great honor, used to describe a kill made by a king or a leader, typically the kill that granted them the title of leader. It was a term that carried a sense of authority and power, testifying to the leader's strength and skill. These variations in the word "kill" reflected the orukuthûndar's complex relationship with violence and death.

Kharok often referred to me as "snaga'mok", or "one warrior". The term "one" in this context referred to the start of someone's journey as a warrior. It was a term of endearment, usually used to refer to orukuthûndar children. Yet, in the context of my journey, it was more akin to "youngling", a nod to my status as a newcomer to their ways. This contrasted with the term the blâdur used to refer to Kharok - "Krân'mok", or "Bone Warrior". This term referred to his age, as Kharok was the eldest orukuthûndar in the blâdur. It was a term of respect, acknowledging his cycles of experience and wisdom. Kharok was not just the eldest, but also the most accomplished warrior. He had the most awe-inspiring reputation in Gâth'mûrg, a clear indication of his skill and bravery. His achievements had earned him the ranks, first of tûr'mok, or "champion", and then eventually "orûk'tûrg" - "orukuthûndar chief". This was a title he had laid claim to many cycles ago, a symbol of his leadership and authority.

Kharok was usually forthcoming with his teachings, but there was one topic he remained reticent about - the krâzgar, or battle, in which he earned his tûr'gâth. When I broached the subject, a shadow seemed to pass over his face, his usually expressive eyes becoming distant and guarded.

Upon my inquiries, he would instinctively turn his head, placing his scarred, blind eye further removed from my line of visibility. It was a subtle gesture, yet it spoke volumes. The scar was a silent reminder of the battle, of the past that he carried with him. His reluctance to discuss the battle was palpable, a wall of silence that I did not dare to breach. I respected his privacy, understanding that some memories were too painful to revisit. I did not continue that line of questioning, choosing instead to focus on the lessons he was willing to share. The orukuthûndar who had questioned Kharok's leadership upon my arrival, a burly figure named Mugrak, overheard our conversation. Unlike me, he did not share the same respect for Kharok's silence. His voice cut through the air, a harsh interruption to our quiet exchange.

"What wrong, Krân'mok? Why you no tell new snaga'mok how you gâth you brother for title? You no find honor in dûr'gâth?" His words were like a slap, another blatant challenge to Kharok's authority. He pushed, his voice laced with scorn and defiance, clearly grating on Kharok's nerves. Mugrak's words hung in the air, his challenge a blatant disregard for the unspoken rules of respect and honor among the orukuthûndar. Not just a challenge to Kharok, but a disruption to the harmony of the tribe. Orukuthûndar all around began to halt their tasks, listening in on the brewing conflict. The tension in the air was palpable, the silence that followed Mugrak's challenge heavy with anticipation. All eyes were on Kharok, waiting to see how the bone warrior would respond to this blatant disrespect. In the tension, I could not help but feel a sense of unease. Mugrak's words had revealed a hidden rift within the tribe, a conflict that threatened to disrupt the unity of the orukuthûndar. After a moment of heavy silence, Kharok turned, his gaze meeting Mugrak's defiant stare. His voice, when he spoke, was calm and steady, a glaring split from the tension that hung in the air.

"You push much, Mugrak," he began, his words echoing in the silence. "You right. Oneeg was orûk'tûrg. Oneeg get sick. Oneeg threaten blâdur. I kugûl'gâth Oneeg. Become new orûk'tûrg. Set blâdur right." His admission was met with a hushed silence, the orukuthûndar hanging onto his every word. He continued, his gaze never leaving Mugrak's. "Last challenge you made, I say face me, how I face Oneeg. You strong enough - orukuthûndar enough - to kugûl'gâth Kharok? You too weak last time. You too weak now?" His words were a direct challenge to Mugrak, a clear assertion of his authority. The crowd watched in anticipation, the tension in the air palpable. Mugrak seethed, his face contorting with rage. Yet, despite his anger, he seemed to understand that the crowd was not swayed by his taunting of their leader. With a final glare at Kharok, he turned and left, his departure met with a collective exhale from the crowd.

Mugrak's defiance was becoming increasingly apparent, his challenges to Kharok's authority growing bolder with each passing day. It was clear that he was not content to remain in the shadows, his ambition a constant undercurrent in his interactions with Kharok. The tension between them was like a simmering pot, threatening to boil over at any moment. The tribe was aware of this growing rift, their unease palpable in the hushed whispers and wary glances that followed Mugrak and Kharok. Sooner or later, this tension would come to a head. It was an inevitable clash, a storm brewing on the horizon. I found myself hoping that I wouldn't be caught in the middle of it, but it seemed a bit too late for that. With my status as a "snaga'mok", I was a part of the orukuthûndar tribe. I had earned their respect and their acceptance, but with it came the complexities of their social dynamics. I was now a part of their world, and that included the brewing conflict between Kharok and Mugrak. As I watched the tension between them escalate, I couldn't help but feel a sense of apprehension. I had come to respect Kharok, his wisdom and leadership a guiding force during my time with the orukuthûndar. Yet, I also understood Mugrak's ambition, his desire for power a common trait among the orukuthûndar.

As the days passed, Kharok continued teaching me, but the tension between them continued to grow, a silent specter looming over the tribe. I could only hope that when the storm finally broke, the orukuthûndar would weather it together, their unity stronger than any conflict. After ensuring I had a solid understanding of Skaragg'ha, Kharok moved on to teaching me about the orukuthûndar rites of passage. These were trials that every snaga'mok must undertake in order to be considered an adult and a full-fledged member of the blâdur, their tribe. The Řazzbłûd was the last of these rites, with the first three being performed at ages five (prūk), ten (mûrg), and eighteen (mûrg'zût). The Řazzbłûd was performed at the age of twenty-five (dû'mûrg'prūk). Each rite was a step in the journey of a snaga'mok, a test of their strength, endurance, and survival skills. During the first and second trials, snaga'mok would be given a pack, filled with various resources and materials that would assist them in their survival. For the third, they received only a small pouch. Then, for the Řazzbłûd - the only rite with a specific name - the snaga'mok would only be given a shining black blade, whose base was wrapped in leather. These black, stone blades, called "bûrz'kruk", served a dual purpose in orukuthûndar society. On one hand, they were the primary tool with which nearly all rituals requiring a blade were performed. On the other hand, they were a symbol of status and achievement. To join the ranks of Krân'mok, a title few in a blâdur ever strive for but is greatly honored and respected, the orukuthûndar must face another rite of passage. They must have survived at least fifty cycles in their entirety. In this rite of passage, the orukuthûndar must travel, alone and by foot, to a mak'gor'thûndar - a fire mountain. There, they must find a large boulder of pure, shining bûrz'kruk, touched by the thûndar'mak'gor (mountain fire) itself. They must then haul the bûrz'kruk back to their blâdur, and perfectly craft three weapons from it - first, the ritual dagger, followed by the head of a greataxe, and finally, a weapon of the orukuthûndar's choosing. Kharok, for instance, crafted a large greatsword. These rites of passage served as a symbol of the orukuthûndar's immense strength and endurance. They were a journey of growth and self-discovery, each trial a step closer to becoming a full-fledged member of the blâdur. As I learned about these rites, I gained a deeper understanding of the orukuthûndar's values and their way of life. Their rites were not just trials, but a celebration of their strength, their survival skills, and their deep connection to the land and the elements.

After carefully instructing me on the orukuthûndar rites of passage, Kharok swiftly moved onto imparting knowledge of the orukuthûndar beliefs. His teachings shifted from the physical trials of their culture to the spiritual beliefs that underpinned their society. He delved into the orukuthûndar outlook, explaining how they view the mountain elements as sacred entities. Their reverence for the natural world was deeply ingrained in their culture, their beliefs a reflection of their close relationship with the land and the elements. They held a particular reverence for the Spirit of Thunder, referred to as the Thunder King, or "Grûmak'Tûrg". They believed that this powerful entity carried the voices of their ancestors, a spiritual connection that linked the past, the present, and the future. Kharok enlightened me about their rituals, which included sacrifices and ritualistic combat. These rituals were often performed on mountaintops during turbulent storms, a sign of their utmost respect for the Thunder King. This ritual was called Thunder's Trial, or Grûmak'Grōldūn - an intense spiritual journey and physical challenge all at once. As I listened to Kharok's stories, my appreciation for the orukuthûndar's religious practices grew. Their rituals and beliefs showcased their profound connection with nature, their admiration for the elements a manifestation of their respect for the power and beauty of nature. Their beliefs were not just a part of their culture, but a part of their identity, a guiding force that shaped their way of life. Kharok then shifted his teachings to the orukuthûndar mok, warrior, tradition, emphasizing that strength (grothuk) and courage (yud - also meaning "honor") were the defining attributes of an orukuthûndar's worth. He painted a vivid picture of their warrior culture, illustrating how they were trained from a young age to use various weapons and tactics for survival and battle (krâgzar). This was not just a lesson in their culture, but a practical training session. Kharok took the opportunity to teach me how to wield some of these weapons, guiding me through their skirmishes. These were seen as a measure of valor, not senseless acts of aggression. Every clash of weapons, every decision made, showed off their strength, courage, and expertise. We spent several weeks honing my combat abilities with a hand-axe and the black blade, the bûrz'kruk, which came more naturally to me than the hand-axe, after having spent time training with the dwarrin dagger under Thrumir's tutelage. Each day was a test of my strength and endurance, each training session a step closer to becoming a proficient warrior. Kharok was a patient teacher, his guidance invaluable in my journey to becoming a mok.

XIV

Blâdur'Grōldūn

By the end of our training, I was proficient in wielding the hand-axe and the bûrz'kruk. Yet, I was acutely aware that I was nowhere near as skilled as a true orukuthûndar mok. Their skill and prowess was a result of their cycles of training, their strength and courage a reflection of their warrior heritage. Kharok seemed to be pleased with my progress, his approval a clear sign of the skills I had acquired. Mugrak, on the other hand, was not. His disdain for me was as palpable as the tension that hung in the air whenever we crossed paths.

One evening, as I made my way towards the empty hut that the blâdur had afforded me to sleep in during my stay with them, I was abruptly grabbed by one of the orukuthûndar who hung around with Mugrak. His grip was like vorgrund, his intentions clear as he dragged me down an empty side path near the huts on the eastern side of the encampment. He threw me in front of Mugrak, who stood there with a wicked grin, his features highlighted by the flickering flames of the small campfire burning behind him. The fire cast long, dancing shadows around us, creating an eerie backdrop for the confrontation.

"I see you been learn mok ways, no-tusk. Show Mugrak how strong you is," he taunted, his words a clear challenge. With those words, he attacked. I tried to fight back, but Mugrak and his three companions wailed on me relentlessly. It was four orukuthûndar against one human, a fight that was impossibly skewed in their favor. Despite my training, I was no match for their combined strength. Each blow was a painful reminder of the gap in our skills, their attacks relentless and unforgiving. My fate that evening seemed quite grim, the odds stacked heavily against me. Yet, I refused to back down, my determination fueled by the lessons I had learned from Kharok. The world seemed to spin as I staggered back, my body aching from the relentless blows. I lifted my gaze, and through the haze of pain, I saw Mugrak unsheathing his bûrz'kruk. The firelight danced upon the black, jagged blade, casting ominous shadows that seemed to mock my predicament. The air around us thickened with anticipation, the crackling fire the only sound breaking the silence.

Mugrak's companions, who had been relentless in their onslaught, now stepped back, forming a crude circle around us. Their grunts and snarls ceased, replaced by a palpable tension that hung heavy in the air. I reached for my own bûrz'kruk, its familiar weight offering a small comfort. I was no seasoned warrior, and my encounters with combat were few and far between. Now, weakened and battered, I was to face Mugrak, a formidable orukuthûndar, in a one-on-one fight. The odds were still not in my favor. Mugrak circled me like a predator, his eyes gleaming with cruel amusement.

"You *weak*, no-tusk. You no belong here," he taunted, his voice a low growl. His bûrz'kruk danced in his hand, making small incisions on my skin as he passed. I parried a few strikes, my own weapon crashing against his with a harsh clack. But for every strike I blocked, two more found their mark, leaving me bloody and gasping for breath. My life would surely have ended at that point had it not been for the dwarrin harndûreng I wore on my chest. I could feel the magic of Alara, as well as the Lunasil, both pulsing, one from within me and the other against the skin of my chest, aching to be unleashed. But I held back, honoring the orukuthûndar ways I had been taught. Unfair as it was, this was a fight of strength and skill, not of magic.

As the fight wore on, I stood my ground, my body screaming in protest with every movement. My blood seeped into the earth beneath my feet, a grim sign of the ferocity of the fight. The crowd of orukuthûndar grew, their hulking forms casting long shadows in the firelight. Whispers rippled through the crowd, some calling for Kharok to intervene, their voices laced with concern. Others, however, were not as sympathetic. "Kill the no-tusk!" they sneered, their words a harsh reminder of my first encounter with the blâdur. The scene was eerily reminiscent, the same hostile crowd, the same sense of dread, the same mixed cries - some for my death and others for the Krân'Mok. But this time, I was not a helpless outsider. I was an honorary orukuthûndar, fighting for my place, my yud. And I would not go down without a fight.

Just as Mugrak lunged towards me for a strike that would have been sure to end my life, a primal roar filled the air. A large, previously unseen fist shot out, catching Mugrak square in the jaw. The force of the blow sent him sprawling onto his back, his bûrz'kruk clattering to the ground. The crowd gasped, a ripple of shock echoing through the onlookers. Stepping forward from the shadows, Kharok emerged. His massive form towered over Mugrak's prone figure, his eyes blazing with a fierce determination. He unsheathed his own bûrz'kruk, the obsidian blade gleaming ominously in the firelight.

"Stand, Mugrak," Kharok commanded, his voice echoing through the silent crowd. His tone was not of anger, but of a deep, resounding disappointment. He looked down at Mugrak, his gaze hard. "You *weak*," he taunted, his words a mirror of Mugrak's earlier remark towards me. "Need grî orukuthûndar to dûr'gâth snaga no-tusk?" His words hung heavy in the air, a damning indictment of Mugrak's actions. The crowd murmured, their whispers a low hum in the tense silence.

"Mugrak, you be pest too long," Kharok continued, his voice resonating with authority. "Time to smush." With a final, resolute look at Mugrak, Kharok uttered a single phrase that sent a shiver through the crowd.

"*Blâdur'Grōldūn.*"

The word echoed through the night, a chilling declaration of a '*Tribe's Trial*'. It was a duel to the death, a challenge issued by an orukuthûndar who believed another posed a threat to their tribe, their blâdur. The same trial that Kharok had challenged his brother, Oneeg, to, many cycles past. With that single word, Kharok had challenged Mugrak, not just for his actions against me, but for the fate of their tribe. The crowd fell silent, the tension palpable as they awaited Mugrak's response. The fire crackled ominously, casting long, dancing shadows over the scene, as the fate of the blâdur hung in the balance.

Mugrak slowly rose to his feet, his face a mask of fear, anger, and embarrassment. The crowd watched in silence, their eyes wide with anticipation. He reached for his fallen bûrz'kruk, his hand trembling slightly as he gripped the weapon. With a roar, Mugrak charged towards Kharok, his bûrz'kruk raised high. The firelight glinted off the blade, casting a menacing shadow as he closed the distance between them. Kharok stood his ground, his own weapon held steady, his eyes never leaving Mugrak. Their bûrz'kruks clashed with a resounding clack, the sound echoing through the silent night. Shards and sparks flew as shining black stone met shining black stone, illuminating their faces in a harsh, flickering light. Mugrak was flailing away with his weapon, attacking with a wild, frenzied desperation. His strikes were powerful but imprecise and clumsy. Kharok, on the other hand, was moving gracefully and with an even temper; every action a dwelling for his training and expertise. The two men clashed together in epic combat for what felt like hours, Mugrak ultimately unable to keep up with the skillful movements of Kharok's swordplay. They danced around each other, their movements a deadly ballet. Mugrak lunged, his bûrz'kruk slicing through the air towards Kharok. But Kharok sidestepped, his own weapon coming up to parry the blow. Their bûrz'kruks met with another loud crack, the force of the impact sending a shudder down their arms. Kharok retaliated, his bûrz'kruk swinging towards Mugrak in a swift, fluid motion. Mugrak barely managed to block the strike, his weapon coming up just in time to deflect Kharok's attack. The crowd watched in rapt attention, their breaths held as the two orukuthûndar fought.

Neither seemed to gain the upper hand, their fight a constant back and forth of strikes and parries. Sweat glistened on their bodies, their breaths coming out in harsh pants as they pushed their limits. The fire crackled in the background, its light casting long, dancing shadows that mirrored their deadly dance.

The battle made for an astonishing display of strength and skill, a clear indication of the power of the orukuthûndar ways. Each clash of their weapons, each narrowly avoided strike, each grunt of effort, added to the tension that hung heavy in the air. The fate of the blâdur hung in the balance, the outcome of the fight a deciding factor in the tribe's future, and my fate. The duel raged on, a relentless dance of strength and skill. Both Kharok and Mugrak bore the marks of the fight, their bodies adorned with slashes that painted a grim picture of the battle. Their grunts of effort echoed through the night, punctuated by the harsh impact of their weapons.

Then, in a moment that seemed to stretch into eternity, Kharok's bûrz'kruk struck Mugrak's with a force that resonated through the silent crowd. There was a sharp, ear-piercing crack, and Mugrak's bûrz'kruk shattered. The black stone shards flew in all directions, glinting ominously in the firelight. The crowd gasped as the shards rained down on the combatants. The sharp fragments cut into their faces, drawing blood and obscuring their vision. One particularly large shard embedded itself in Mugrak's eye, eliciting a guttural scream of pain from him. The pain seemed to ignite a berserker fury within Mugrak. He roared, his voice echoing through the night, his remaining eye blazing with a wild, untamed rage. Kharok, his own vision marred by the scar across his left eye, stood his ground, his face a mask of determination.

In a surprising move, Kharok dropped his bûrz'kruk, the weapon clattering to the ground. The crowd watched in stunned silence as he continued the fight unarmed. His fists clenched, his stance steady, Kharok faced the berserk Mugrak, ready to continue the fight. The duel took on a new intensity, the stakes higher than ever. The two combatants, both blind in one eye, circled each other, their movements cautious yet determined. The crowd watched in rapt attention, their breaths held as the fate of the blâdur hung in the balance. The fire crackled in the background, its light casting an eerie glow over the brutal scene.

With a sudden burst of speed, Kharok lunged at Mugrak. His fist shot out, aiming for Mugrak's midsection. Mugrak sidestepped, his own fist swinging towards Kharok. But Kharok was quicker. He ducked, Mugrak's fist whistling harmlessly over his head. Kharok retaliated, his fist connecting with Mugrak's side. The impact sent Mugrak staggering, a grunt of pain escaping his lips. But he quickly regained his footing, his face twisting into a snarl. The fight was a blur of movement, a whirlwind of punches and kicks. Kharok moved with a fluid grace, his strikes precise and calculated. Mugrak, on the other hand, fought with a wild desperation, his attacks erratic but forceful. They traded blows, their grunts of effort echoing through the silent night. Sweat glistened on their bodies, their breaths coming out in harsh pants. Blood ran down their faces in rivers, a gut-wrenching visage of the strenuous battle they were engaged in. Its crimson hues sparkled against their skin, a vivid portrayal of the anguish they had both suffered. Every drop that spilled to the floor was an indication of how far they had pushed themselves.The fight raged on, neither Kharok nor Mugrak showing any signs of backing down. Their bodies were slick with sweat and blood, their breaths coming out in ragged gasps. The crowd watched in tense silence, their eyes wide with anticipation.

Suddenly, Kharok lunged forward, his fist connecting again with Mugrak's torso. Kharok didn't let up. He continued his onslaught, his movements ferocious and precise. With a swift uppercut, Kharok's fist connected with Mugrak's jaw. The force of the blow sent Mugrak's head snapping back, his body following suit. He fell to the ground, his body convulsing from the impact. Kharok stood over Mugrak's prone figure, his chest heaving with exertion. His face was a mask of determination, his eyes hard. He reached down, his hand closing around Mugrak's throat. With a final, resolute look at Mugrak, Kharok tightened his grip. The crowd watched in stunned silence as Kharok lifted Mugrak off the ground, his hand still around Mugrak's throat. Mugrak struggled, his hands clawing at Kharok's arm, but it was in vain. Kharok's grip was unyielding, his resolve unwavering. With a final, brutal, crackling squeeze, Kharok ended it. Mugrak's struggles ceased, his body going limp in Kharok's grip. Kharok released him, Mugrak's body collapsing to the ground in a lifeless heap.

The crowd erupted into cheers, their voices echoing through the night. Kharok stood victorious, his body sickeningly battered but unbroken. The fire crackled in the background, its light casting long, dancing shadows over the brutal scene. As I watched the brutal end of Mugrak, a mix of emotions coursed through me. Relief washed over me, followed closely by a strange sense of sorrow. I had survived. The sight of Mugrak's lifeless body was a stark reminder of the harsh reality of the orukuthûndar ways. I could feel the crowd's excitement, their cheers echoing in my ears. But all I could focus on was the throbbing pain in my body and the metallic taste of blood in my mouth. I was alive, but barely.

Kharok's voice cut through the cheers, his command echoing through the night. "Clean up this *truk'grut*," he ordered, his gaze fixed on Mugrak's lifeless body. His words were met with immediate action, a few orukuthûndar moving forward to carry out his command and remove the "worthless flesh". Then, Kharok turned towards me. He walked over, his steps steady despite the brutal fight. He looked me over, his gaze assessing. "You live," he stated, his voice gruff. "You show worth." His words, simple as they were, held a weight that settled heavily on my shoulders. Though I hadn't won my encounter with Murgrak and his minions, I stood strong against them, never backing down. I had proven myself, again earning an air of respect and belonging among the orukuthûndar.

I slowly made my way back to my hut, each step a painful reminder of the brutal fight. The cheers of the crowd were a distant echo, their excitement a marked divide to the exhaustion that weighed heavy on my shoulders. Inside the relative peace of my hut, I sank to the floor, my body screaming in protest. My wounds throbbed with a relentless intensity, the pain a constant reminder of my encounter with Mugrak.

I closed my eyes, taking a moment to gather my strength. Then, I recalled two of the spell words Alara had taught me through my listening to her whispers in the wind. "*Eg-Cur*," I whispered, the words a soft murmur in the silent hut. As the words left my lips, I could feel the magic stirring within me. It was a gentle warmth that spread through my body, soothing the pain and mending my wounds. I could feel my strength returning, the exhaustion slowly fading away.

The process was slow, the magic working its way through my body, healing each wound one by one. But with each passing moment, I could feel myself getting stronger, the pain becoming more bearable. By the time the spell had done its work, I was left feeling drained but healed. My wounds were gone, replaced by a faint, tingling sensation that was an evident gulf to the pain I had felt earlier. I leaned back against the wall of my hut, a sigh of relief escaping my lips. I had survived, proven myself worthy, and lived to tell the tale. As I closed my eyes, the events of the night replayed in my mind, a grim reminder of the brutal world I was now a part of. But for now, I was safe, healed, and alive. And that was enough.

As dawn broke one morning, several months after that night, I felt a familiar stirring. The wind, a constant companion on my journey, seemed to beckon me onward. I had spent nearly a full cycle with the orukuthûndar, learning their ways, earning my place among them. But now, it was time to continue my quest of exploration. I had almost forgotten the visions of doom that had plagued me before my time with the orukuthûndar. The urgency of those visions seemed distant now, overshadowed by the immediate trials and tribulations of life with the tribe. But the wind's call was a stark reminder of my purpose, my quest, my promise to Tornu.

I sought out Kharok, finding him overseeing the morning activities of the tribe. "Kharok," I began, "I must leave. The wind calls me." Kharok turned to me, his gaze understanding. He had heard my story countless times over the past cycle, and he knew of my quest, my purpose.

"Yoran," he said, his voice gruff but not unkind, "you follow wind. You go." His blessing was a weight lifted off my shoulders. I had not realized how much I had wanted his approval, his understanding. But his next words were a surprise, a heartfelt farewell that I had not expected. "Yoran," he said, his gaze meeting mine, "you help fix problem in blâdur. You show strength much over cycle. You earn place here. You always welcome." His words, simple as they were, held a weight that settled heavily on my heart. I had made a difference here, had earned my place among the orukuthûndar. As I turned to leave, Kharok's farewell echoing in my ears, I knew that I would carry a piece of the tribe with me, wherever the wind might lead.

As the sun began its ascent, casting long shadows across the orukuthûndar stronghold, I prepared to depart. Kharok, along with a select few of their mok, accompanied me. Their presence was a final symbol of respect, a portrayal of the bond we had formed. They had come to view me as snaga'mok no longer, but *mok*, a title I wore with pride. The morning air was crisp, the wind carrying the faint scent of the desert beyond. The stronghold, which had been my home for nearly a full cycle, was slowly coming to life, the orukuthûndar beginning their daily tasks. But for me, it was time to say goodbye.

We walked in silence, the only sound the crunch of sand under our feet. The stronghold slowly receded behind us, its imposing walls a stark reminder of the life I was leaving behind. As we reached the outskirts of their territory, I turned to face Kharok and the gathered mok. They raised their fists in a salute, a sign of respect among the orukuthûndar. I returned the gesture, my heart heavy with the weight of the farewell. Their green, grey, and blue faces were stoic, but their black eyes held a warmth that spoke volumes.

With a final nod, I turned away, setting off into the wilderness. The group watched in silence as I walked away, their figures slowly shrinking in the distance. The wind rustled through the trees, a gentle whisper that seemed to carry their silent farewell. I didn't look back, my gaze fixed on the horizon. The stronghold, Kharok, and the mok, they were all behind me now, a part of a chapter that had come to an end. But ahead lay the unknown, the next part of my journey. As I disappeared beyond the horizon that Nolariel day, two and a half cycles since the onset of my journey, I knew that while this chapter had ended, my story was far from over.

XV

Xolesh

Several days after beginning my trek across Alara once again, after having crossed the desert, coming to a small patch of plains and forest, covered in Isendur snow. I came across a figure in the distance. As I drew closer, I realized it was a human, a young man about my age. He was clad in a tattered black cloak that fluttered in the wind, its edges frayed and worn. Beneath the cloak, he wore simple gray woven clothing, the fabric stained with the telltale signs of travel. His boots, a pair of dark black matte, were scuffed and dust-covered, bearing the marks of a long journey. As I approached him, I couldn't help but wonder what had brought him so far from home, into the heart of the wilderness. I had never known of any human tribes so far from the land Takka settled. As I drew nearer, I noticed that the young man was hunched over a peculiar structure. It was a monolith, a natural formation that seemed to have been thrust up from the very crust of Alara itself. The monolith stood tall and imposing, its surface weathered by the elements, yet it held an air of intrigue.

The young man was engrossed in his task, oblivious to my approach. He was muttering something under his breath, his voice barely a whisper against the rustling of the leaves. The words, though similar in sound to the spell words I had grown accustomed to, were unfamiliar, a language or perhaps a code that I had not encountered in my travels. At first, nothing happened. His words seemed to dissipate into the air, swallowed by the vast expanse of the plains. But as he repeated the phrase for the third time, varying his pronunciations each time, a remarkable transformation began to take place. The monolith, once solid and unyielding, began to shift. It was as if its very existence had become fluid, its form wavering like a mirage under the desert sun. From its surface, shadowy tendrils began to emerge, pouring forth like dark smoke. They swirled around the monolith, their forms constantly shifting and changing, creating a mesmerizing spectacle.

I watched in awe as the monolith continued to transform, its solid form giving way to a fluid, shadowy existence. The sight was both fascinating and unsettling. In the blink of an eye, the tranquil world around me was replaced by a scene of utter devastation. The once verdant plains were now ablaze, the flames reaching skyward in a furious dance. The air was filled with the acrid smell of smoke and the crackling of burning wood, a notable variance from the peaceful serenity that had prevailed just moments ago. Images began to flash across my mind, each one more horrifying than the last. I saw villagers and tribesmen, their faces etched with fear and despair. elandari, orukuthûndar, humans, kreegoblikar, dwarrin, centarion - all of them fallen, their bodies strewn across the burning landscape. The sight was a chilling reminder of the vision I had experienced long ago, a vision of destruction wrought by a shadowed behemoth. The behemoth loomed large in my mind, its form shrouded in darkness. It was a creature of nightmares, its very presence a harbinger of death and destruction. I could see it now, striding across the burning plains, leaving a trail of devastation in its wake.

Suddenly, a firm hand on my shoulder jolted me back to reality. The hellish scene of destruction faded away, replaced by the familiar sight of the snowy plains and the monolith. I blinked, disoriented, and turned to see the young man standing beside me. "Are you alright?" he asked, his voice filled with concern. His eyes, a deep shade of brown, were wide with worry. "You seemed... somewhere else."

"I... I saw..." I stammered, still reeling from the vision. But how could I explain the destruction, the fallen children of Alara, the towering abomination?

His eyes widened in realization. "You saw it, didn't you?" he asked, his voice barely a whisper. "The darkness..."

I nodded, my heart pounding in my chest. "Yes," I admitted, "I saw it all." For a moment, panic flashed across his face. But before he could say anything, I reached out with my hand, calling on the primal magic of Alara. "*Su*," A soft wind rose from the ground, enveloping my hand, a tangible proof of my ability to wield Alara's power.

His eyes widened in surprise, then relief. "You... you can wield Alara's power *too*," he said, a note of awe in his voice. "I... I'm Xolesh," he introduced himself, his voice steadier now. "It seems we have much to discuss." As we sat beneath the shadow of the monolith, the world around us bathed in the soft glow of the setting sun, we shared our stories. I began, recounting my adventures thus far. I spoke of my time with the elandari, the graceful elves whose wisdom and serenity had left a profound impact on me. I told him about the dwarrin, the stalwart dwarves whose resilience and craftsmanship were unparalleled. I shared tales of the centarion, the noble centaurs whose strength and honor were as vast as the plains they roamed. I omitted my encounters with the goblins, sensing that Xolesh grew weary of hearing me drone on endlessly about culture and society. Instead, I finished with my recent tale of the time I spent with the orukuthûndar, with which Xolesh took great interest, though something seemed to tug at his focus.

As I finished my tale, Xolesh was silent for a moment, his gaze distant. Then, with a deep breath, he began to share his own story. His voice was soft, tinged with a sadness that tugged at my heart. He spoke of his family tribe, a vibrant community that had been his home. His eyes darkened as he recounted the fateful day when an orukuthûndar raiding party, had attacked his tribe. His words painted a vivid picture of the chaos and destruction that had ensued - a scene whose description fit the tales of Gâth'mûrgs that Kharok had regaled me with, not so long ago. Xolesh spoke of the bravery of his tribesmen, their desperate fight against the invaders. But the orukuthûndar had been too ruthless. His tribe had been slain, their home reduced to ashes, with Xolesh barely escaping with his life. As he finished his tale, the air between us was heavy with shared sorrow of having lost our parents.

As our conversation continued, my curiosity piqued and I turned to Xolesh. "What were you doing with the monolith?" I asked, my gaze drifting to the towering structure. Xolesh followed my gaze, a thoughtful look on his face.

"I was trying to bend it," he said, his voice quiet. "Using these... *words*... I don't know how I know them, but over my travels, they have just come to me."

I nodded, understanding entirely. I was familiar with the concept, having learned several spell words from the wind myself at this point. Xolesh seemed to sense my understanding. "Let me show you," he said, turning back to the monolith. He took a deep breath, his gaze focused on the towering structure. Then, he began to speak. The words that left his lips were unfamiliar, unlike any spell words I had heard before. They were heavy, laden with a power that seemed to resonate with the very air around us. The words felt dark, their energy contrasting harshly to the spell words I had come to know.

"*Eich-Vol...*"

As Xolesh spoke, I watched him closely, trying to decipher the unfamiliar spell words. I could feel their power, their potential to reshape the world around us. As Xolesh continued his demonstration, I couldn't help but wonder what these unfamiliar spell words meant, and what they could do to the world of Alara. Despite the unease that Xolesh's spell words stirred within me, I found myself drawn to him. He was, like me, a wanderer, a seeker of knowledge navigating the vast expanse of Alara. There was a kinship in our shared experiences, a bond that transcended our different paths.

As the sun began to dip below the horizon, we settled down for a meal. Xolesh had caught a couple of rabbits earlier, their bodies now roasting over a fire I had ignited with a simple '*Nis*' spell word. The flames danced and crackled, casting a warm glow over us as we shared our meal. The food was simple, the weather frigid, but it was made enjoyable by the stories we shared. I spoke of my mentor and uncle, Tornu, his wisdom and guidance a constant source of inspiration during my journey. I recounted tales of our adventures together, our explorations of Alara, and the lessons he had taught me. Xolesh, in turn, shared stories of his mother, Cira. His voice softened as he spoke of her, an echo of the love and respect he held for her. He spoke of her strength, her wisdom, and the lessons she had imparted on him. Despite the tragedy that had befallen his tribe, his memories of his mother were filled with warmth and love. As we shared our stories, the fire crackling in the background, I felt a sense of camaraderie with Xolesh. We were both products of our tribes, shaped by the wisdom of our elders and the experiences of our journeys. In that moment, under the starlit sky of Alara, we found solace in our shared experiences and heritage.

After a few days of shared stories and companionship, the time came for us to part ways. Xolesh was following his own path, a journey guided by a purpose I could only guess at. As for me, I was following the guidance of the wind, its gentle whispers leading me across the vast expanse of Alara. We stood at the edge of the plains, the rising sun casting long shadows over the landscape. Xolesh turned to me, his gaze serious. "May your journey be safe, Yoran," he said, his voice carrying the weight of our shared experiences.

"And yours, Xolesh," I replied, meeting his gaze. With a final nod, Xolesh turned and walked away, his figure soon disappearing into the veil of falling snow in the distance. I watched him go, a sense of melancholy settling over me. His companionship, however brief, had been a welcome respite in my journey. But as the wind picked up, rustling the leaves and whispering in my ear, I knew it was time to move on. With a final glance at the spot where Xolesh had disappeared, I turned and continued my journey, the wind guiding my steps across the vast expanse of Alara.

Two weeks into my journey, the tranquility of my travels was shattered by the onset of a ferocious storm. I had left the barren expanse of the desert far behind and, after passing through the snow swept plains, traded it for the lush, verdant canopy of a rainforest capped in blankets of snow. The air was thick with the scent of damp earth and the vibrant chorus of wildlife, a striking incongruence with the arid silence of the desert.

A storm hit without warning, the sky darkening as ominous clouds rolled in. Thunder rumbled in the distance, a low growl that echoed through the dense foliage. Lightning streaked across the sky, illuminating the rainforest in a harsh, flickering light. I was grateful for the cover of the rainforest, the thick canopy providing some protection from the elements. But the storm was relentless, the rain cascading from the sky in a torrential downpour. The thunder grew louder, the sound deafening as it reverberated through the trees. The lightning was a terrifying spectacle, the bolts striking with a ferocity that left me breathless. There was no delay between the thunder and lightning, a clear sign that the storm was directly overhead. Several large trees were struck, their trunks splintering under the force of the impact. The sight of the trees, mere meters from where I ran, being struck by the ferocious hammer of nature, was a chilling reminder of the storm's power.

Ice-wrapped twigs and vines slapped me across my face as I sprinted through the rainforest, my heart pounding in my chest. The rain soaked through my clothes, the wind whipping through the trees. My only goal was to find shelter, to escape the wrath of the storm. The storm raged on, the thunder and lightning a terrifying symphony of nature's fury. But despite the danger, there was a certain beauty to it, a raw, untamed power that was awe-inspiring. As I ran, the rainforest a blur around me, I couldn't help but marvel at the spectacle, even as I sought refuge from the storm. In the midst of the storm's fury, I tried to call upon Alara, the magic pulsing within me. "*Hav!*" I cried out, my voice barely audible over the roar of the thunder. I sought shelter as I had so long ago, a refuge from the relentless storm. But this time, Alara remained silent, its presence a faint whisper against the storm's wrath.

Or perhaps, its answer was lost in the chaos. As I called out, a large boulder dislodged from a cliff overlooking the rainforest floor. It plummeted towards me, a terrifying spectacle amidst the rain and lightning. But just as it seemed to spell my doom, it was caught in mid-air by two bowed, intersecting trees. For a brief moment, I was sheltered from the storm, the boulder and trees forming a makeshift refuge. But the respite was short-lived. As quickly as the shelter had arrived, it passed, leaving behind a trail of destruction. The trees, strained beyond their limits, buckled under the weight of the boulder. They shattered at their weakest points, the sound of splintering wood echoing through the rainforest. The boulder dropped with an earth-shaking thud in the snow, landing directly where I had been standing moments before. I rolled away just in time. It would have obliterated me, had I not moved at the last moment. I lay on the snow-covered ground, my heart pounding in my chest, the storm's fury a stark reminder of nature's power.

I continued my desperate sprint through the rainforest, the dense trees a blur around me. My footing was uncertain on the snowy ground, the ice beginning to form a crust atop the soft white blankets causing me to slip or stumble every few steps. The storm showed no signs of letting up, the thunder and lightning a relentless assault on my senses. Suddenly, amidst the chaos, I spotted a small crevice in the cliffside. It was narrow, barely wide enough for me to fit through if I crouched low. Peering through the opening, I noticed a small cave on the other side. It wasn't much, but it offered a chance at shelter, a refuge from the storm. Without a second thought, I made my way towards the crevice. Rain, snow, and sleet pelted down, soaking me to the bone as I crouched low and squeezed through the narrow opening. The cave was small and dark, but it was dry, a welcome respite from the storm outside.

The darkness inside the cave was thick, almost suffocating. It reminded me of the marshland mud I had trudged through over a cycle ago, on my way to the orukuthûndar desert. It was a darkness that seemed to swallow all light, leaving me in a world of shadows. But despite the darkness, the cave offered a sense of safety, a sanctuary amidst the storm. As I settled in, the sound of the rain a constant drumming against the cave entrance, I couldn't help but feel a sense of relief. I had found shelter, a place to wait out the storm. For now, I was safe. With the storm raging outside, I began to explore the cave, my hands trailing along the cold, damp walls. The cave was larger than it had initially seemed, the darkness making it difficult to gauge its size. I moved slowly, carefully, my senses heightened in the near-total darkness.

Time seemed to stretch out, each minute feeling like an eternity. What felt like half an hour was likely closer to five minutes. But in the darkness of the cave, time seemed to lose its meaning. As I made my way towards the back of the cave, I could feel a cool moisture building on my palms and fingertips. The walls were slick with condensation. I followed the curvature of the wall around the back of the cave, expecting it to lead me back towards the entrance. But then, the wall suddenly disappeared. My hand met empty air, a startling contrast to the cold, damp stone. I paused, my heart pounding in my chest. A small tunnel seemed to open up at the back of the cave, its presence a surprise in the otherwise circular cavern.

The discovery sparked a sense of curiosity, a desire to explore further. But for now, the tunnel remained a mystery, its secrets hidden in the darkness. As the storm continued to rage outside, I found myself wondering what lay beyond the tunnel, what secrets the cave held. The curiosity gnawed at me, a persistent itch that I could no longer ignore. Besides, wouldn't Tornu find it fascinating enough to explore? After a few minutes of contemplation, I made up my mind. I reached for the Lunasil, its familiar weight a comfort against the uncertainty of the unknown.

"*Valæris*," I chanted, the faelari verse echoing softly in the cave. As the word left my lips, I could feel the magic stirring within me, a gentle warmth that spread through my body. Within moments, the cave was bathed in a soft, bioluminescent light. The light danced across the jagged stone walls, casting long, flickering shadows. It emanated from a dimly glowing sphere of pure energy, a manifestation of the primal forces of Alara. The sphere floated behind me, its light a comforting presence in the darkness. With the newfound light guiding my way, I ventured into the tunnel. The walls were narrow, the air cool and damp. But the light from the sphere illuminated the path ahead, revealing the rough stone and the path that lay ahead.

As I made my way down the corridor, the light from the sphere casting long shadows on the walls as the air grew warmer, I couldn't help but feel a sense of anticipation. The tunnel was a mystery, its secrets hidden in the darkness. As I ventured deeper into the tunnel, I noticed a subtle change in my surroundings. The rough, damp walls of the cave began to transition, slowly giving way to a different texture. The rugged stone was gradually replaced by a soft, perfectly smooth surface. I ran my fingers along the stone, marveling at the transformation. The stone was cool to the touch, its smooth surface a profound difference from the rough, jagged stone of the cave. The transition was gradual, almost imperceptible, but unmistakable nonetheless. The light from the sphere of essence cast a soft glow on the walls, highlighting the smooth stone. The walls seemed to shimmer in the light, the stone taking on an almost ethereal quality. I traced the patterns on the stone, my fingers following the gentle curves and lines. The change in the stone was a mystery, its cause unknown. But it added a sense of wonder to the exploration, a reminder of the unknown that lay ahead.

As I continued my journey down the corridor, the minutes melded into one another as I moved slowly, my attention captivated by the walls around me, becoming more and more evident that these walls were crafted by some intelligent being. The craftsmanship was exquisite, the precision with which the walls had been hewn a validation of the unknown artisans' skill. The further I ventured, the more intricate the designs became. Patterns began to emerge on the smooth stone, their complexity increasing with each step. They were a mix of geometric shapes and abstract designs, each one unique and intricately detailed. The light from the sphere danced across the designs, casting a soft glow on the stone. The designs seemed to come alive in the light, their details standing out in sharp relief. I traced the patterns with my fingers, marveling at the smoothness of the stone and the intricacy of the designs. As I moved further down the corridor, the designs continued to evolve, each one more intricate than the last.

Venturing deeper into the tunnel, a new element began to emerge. Stone columns, chiseled straight from the mountain stone itself, started to appear at regular intervals. They were carved with swirling structures, their intricate designs a reminder of their creators' skill. These columns provided support to the tunnel's ceiling, their bases and tops perfectly transitioning from the floor and ceiling. It was as if stalagmites and stalactites had grown together in perfect harmony, forming a seamless union. They appeared every twenty or so steps, standing like sentinels on either side of the tunnel. The tunnel itself was beginning to widen, the stone columns marking the transition. The columns were a marvel of craftsmanship, their presence adding a sense of grandeur to the tunnel. As I moved further down the tunnel, the stone columns continued to appear, their presence a constant reminder of the unknown artisans who had crafted this marvel. The beauty of the columns, their intricate designs illuminated by the faelari light sphere, was a sight to behold.

The initial stretch of the tunnel was a study in the raw, unadorned beauty of nature. The columns, hewn from the very stone of the earth, stood in their natural state, untouched by any artifice. Their rough, unpolished surfaces bore the marks of time and the elements, a silent chronicle of the ages that had passed. The air was cool and damp, carrying the scent of stone and earth, a mark signifying the tunnel's subterranean nature. As I ventured deeper into the tunnel, a subtle transformation began to unfold. The columns, once bare, began to be adorned with stones that shimmered with an inner light. These were no ordinary stones. They were luminescent, glowing with a soft, warm, orange light that seemed to emanate from their very core. The light they cast was gentle, bathing the surroundings in a warm, inviting glow that softened the stark, raw beauty of the stone columns. The stones were placed with an artistry that spoke of a careful, deliberate hand. They were not merely strewn about but arranged in intricate patterns, their luminescence casting a play of light and shadow on the stone columns. The effect was mesmerizing, transforming the once austere tunnel into a spectacle of light and stone. The floor, too, underwent a transformation. What was once a rough, uneven path strewn with pebbles, debris, and dirt, had become a finely polished surface. The stone floor was now as smooth as a calm lake at dawn, its surface reflecting the warm, orange hues from the luminescent stones. It was a sight to behold, the stone floor glistening under the soft light, devoid of any dust or imperfection. The tunnel had transformed from a raw, natural formation into a crafted masterpiece. The luminescent stones, the polished floor, the intricate patterns - all spoke of a craftsmanship that was both meticulous and artistic. It was as if the tunnel was not merely a passageway, but a work of art, a signature of the skill and creativity of its unknown creators.

The journey through the tunnel was no longer just a trek through a stone passage. It was an exploration of artistry and craftsmanship, a journey through a gallery of stone and light. The warm, orange glow of the luminescent stones, the glistening, polished floor, the intricate patterns - all combined to create an ambiance of tranquility and awe. The tunnel, in its transformed state, was a marvel to behold, a spectacle of light and stone that left me in a state of wonder and admiration. As I ventured further into the depths of the tunnel, the simplicity of stone and light gave way to a landscape of complexity and intrigue. Scattered around were various contraptions and devices, remnants of a time and purpose unknown. Each device bore the mark of meticulous craftsmanship, their intricate designs a testimony underlining the ingenuity of their creators. They lay strewn about, silent and still, their purpose a mystery waiting to be unraveled. The tunnel, once a silent passage of stone and light, was now filled with the symphony of mechanical sounds. From the depths of the perfectly carved hallway, the rhythmic creaking and groaning of ropes and chains echoed off the stone walls. The sounds were methodical, a mechanical cadence that resonated in the confines of the tunnel. It was as if the tunnel had come alive, its silence replaced by the symphony of movement and mechanics. Intermingled with the rhythmic sounds were the noises of heavy objects being lifted. The sounds were distinct, a note marking the weight and size of the objects. Each lift was punctuated by the clank of metal on stone, a stark reminder of the tunnel's stone confines. The sounds echoed off the stone walls, a cacophony of movement and mechanics that filled the tunnel. The tunnel had transformed once again. From a passage of stone and light, to a gallery of artistry and craftsmanship, it was now a mechanical symphony. The contraptions and devices, the rhythmic sounds, the echoes of movement - all combined to create an ambiance of complexity and intrigue.

The deeper I ventured into the tunnel, the more the soundscape evolved, adding new layers to its mechanical symphony. The rhythmic creaking and groaning of ropes and chains, the clank of metal on stone, were now accompanied by the whirring and clicking of gears and cogs. The sounds were precise, an indicator pointing to the intricate mechanisms at work. They blended seamlessly with the hissing of steam, the low hum of magic-infused mechanisms adding a mystical quality to the mechanical symphony. Interwoven with these mechanical sounds were the occasional chimes and whistles. They were distinct, their tones cutting through the mechanical symphony with their clarity. Each chime, each whistle, was an indication of intelligent life at work. They were not random sounds, but signals, a form of communication that echoed in the confines of the tunnel. The tunnel was now a blend of mechanics and magic, a symphony of sounds that filled the cavernous space. The whirring of gears, the hissing of steam, the low hum of magic-infused mechanisms, the occasional chime or whistle - all combined to create an almost musical ambiance. The tunnel was alive with sounds, its silence replaced by a symphony that resonated in the stone confines.

As I pressed on, I found myself continuously admiring the construction and inventions along the way. Each device, each contraption, was a marvel of craftsmanship and ingenuity. The constant symphony of sounds, the marvel of the constructions, the intrigue of the inventions - all filled me with a sense of awe and admiration as I ventured deeper into the tunnel. I continued on, finding myself continuously admiring the construction and inventions along the way. Each device, each contraption, was a marvel of craftsmanship and ingenuity. Upon reaching the end of the cavern, a sight most unexpected greeted my eyes. A multitude of small, frail-looking bipeds busied themselves in the warm, orange glow of the luminescent stones. Their forms were delicate, their movements precise, a clear disparity to the robust, mechanical surroundings of the tunnel.

XVI

Gnomarik

These creatures were unique, their features unlike any I had encountered before. They possessed large noses, prominent features that stood out on their small faces. The noses were not merely large, but intricately shaped, their contours and lines adding character to their faces. Atop their heads were little tufts of hair, sparse and delicate. The hair was not merely a covering, but a crown of sorts, adding a touch of softness to their otherwise stark features. It swayed gently as they moved, a chronicle recounting their delicate nature. Their ears were long and pointed, a distinct feature that set them apart. The ears were not merely appendages, but expressive features that twitched and moved with their emotions. They added a layer of expressiveness to their faces, their movements a silent form of communication. The sight of these creatures was entrancing. Their delicate forms, their unique features, their expressive ears - all combined to create a spectacle of life amidst the mechanical symphony of the tunnel. They were an exhibit of the diversity of life, a reminder of the wonders that lay hidden in the depths of the earth. As I stood at the end of the cavern, I found myself captivated by these small, frail-looking bipeds, their presence adding a touch of life to the mechanical marvel of the tunnel.

As I stood at the edge of the cavern, observing the delicate creatures, I felt a sense of curiosity welling up within me. Their studious nature, their constant engagement with the devices and contraptions around them, spoke of a deep-seated passion for knowledge and discovery. It was a passion I shared, a common thread that connected us despite our differences. With a sense of purpose, I stepped forward, my footsteps echoing softly in the cavernous space. The sound caught the attention of the nearest creatures. Their pointed ears twitched, their large noses sniffed the air, and their eyes, previously focused on their work, turned towards me. For a moment, there was a silence, a pause in the symphony of sounds that filled the cavern. Then, one of the creatures stepped forward. It was smaller than the others, its tuft of hair a lighter shade. It approached me with a cautious curiosity, its eyes studying me intently. In its hand, it held a small device, a blend of technology and magic. The device hummed softly, its surface glowing with a soft, magical light. The creature extended the device towards me, its eyes never leaving mine. It seemed to be an invitation, a gesture of trust.

I reached out and gently took the device. It was lighter than it looked, its surface warm to the touch. The device hummed louder, its glow intensifying. It was a marvel of technology and magic, an emblem of the ingenuity of these creatures. The other creatures watched the exchange, their eyes wide with curiosity. Slowly, they returned to their work, their movements more animated. The symphony of sounds resumed, the cavern once again filled with the whirring of gears, the hissing of steam, and the low hum of magic-infused mechanisms. As I held the small device in my hand, its soft hum resonating with the rhythm of my heartbeat, I realized the need for a bridge of communication. The creatures and I shared a common passion for discovery, but our means of communication were as different as our forms. It was then that I remembered the Saela-Hathir headdress, a gift from the Centaurs, resting atop my head.

With a sense of purpose, I reached up to touch the headdress. It was cool to the touch, its surface smooth and unblemished. Closing my eyes, I whispered the spell words, "*Threl-Vysh-Pax*". The words echoed in the cavern, their resonance blending with the symphony of sounds. As the last syllable of the incantation faded, its signature glow enveloped the headdress. It was a cool, inviting light, a tribute to the magic infused within it. The glow intensified, spreading from the headdress to envelop my entire form. I could feel the magic coursing through me, a warm, comforting presence that filled me with a sense of understanding.

Opening my eyes, I turned to face the creature that had offered me the device. Its eyes were wide with curiosity, its form still as it watched the transformation. The device in my hand hummed louder, its glow matching the intensity of the headdress. It was then that I understood the purpose of the device. The device was a tool of research, a means to study the blend of technology and magic. As I stood there, the device humming in my hand, the creature suddenly darted forward. With a swift, precise movement, it snatched the device from my grasp. Its small, nimble fingers closed around the device, its large nose twitching as it studied the glowing object. The creature's eyes were wide, its gaze focused intently on the device. It turned the device over in its hands, its fingers tracing the intricate patterns etched on its surface. The device hummed louder, its glow intensifying under the creature's scrutiny. Then, with a suddenness that took me by surprise, the creature pulled out a small piece of parchment and a writing tool from a pouch at its side. It began to jot down notes, its hand moving in quick, precise strokes. The creature's focus was unwavering, its attention completely absorbed by the task at hand. The notes were detailed, a hallmark of the creature's meticulous nature. It sketched the device, its lines precise and accurate. It jotted down observations, its script neat and organized. The creature was a scholar, its actions a declaration of its studious nature. Once it was done, the creature looked up at me, its eyes gleaming with a sense of accomplishment. Then, without a word, it scurried away, disappearing into the crowd of its kin, the device once again in its possession.

As the small creature disappeared into the crowd, I found myself alone once again in the cavernous expanse. The hum of activity resumed, the symphony of mechanical sounds filling the air. I took a moment to truly take in my surroundings, to appreciate the marvels of the creatures' architecture. Their constructions were not merely functional, but aesthetic as well. They had managed to blend form and function in a way that was both practical and pleasing to the eye. The structures around me were a signature of their ingenuity, their ability to harness the power of nature and technology in harmony. Windmills stood tall and proud, their large blades turning slowly in the gentle breeze that flowed through the cavern. They were not merely structures, but works of art, their design intricate and detailed. Large windmills harnessed the power of the wind that wove itself through the tunnels and caverns within, their blades turning the gears and cogs that powered the machinery around them. Waterwheels spun in the underground streams that flowed through the cavern, their rhythmic motion a soothing sight. They harnessed the power of water, their constant rotation driving mechanisms that powered various contraptions scattered around the cavern. Telescopes and observatories aimed at the sky through small holes bored into the stone ceiling of the cavern, their lenses gleaming in the soft, orange light. They were an expression of the creatures' curiosity, their thirst for knowledge. The telescopes were not merely tools, but windows to the universe, their lenses capturing the wonders of the cosmos.

With a sense of wonder, I began to walk through the creatures' settlement. The path was lined with a variety of rudimentary inventions. Simple machines like pulleys and levers were scattered around, their practicality evident in their usage. They were used in construction and transportation, their simple design belying their effectiveness. The pulleys lifted heavy objects with ease, their ropes and wheels working in perfect harmony. The levers moved large structures, their simple design amplifying the force applied. A series of tubes and pipes crisscrossed the settlement, a rudimentary plumbing system that carried water from a nearby underground stream. The system was ingenious, its design simple yet effective. The water flowed through the pipes, its journey guided by the gentle slope of the tubes. It was a marvel of engineering, a manifestation of the creatures' understanding of fluid dynamics. The water from the stream was not merely a resource, but a lifeline. It was carried to the various homes and workshops, its flow controlled by a series of valves and switches. The sound of flowing water was a constant in the settlement, a soothing backdrop to the symphony of mechanical sounds. All in all, I was overtaken by amazement at the advanced nature of these small creatures. As I continued my exploration of the settlement, I came upon an area where a group of these creatures was huddled around a mechanical contraption. The contraption was a complex assembly of gears and springs. The creatures worked in harmony, their movements precise and coordinated. Each gear, each spring, was placed with a meticulousness that spoke of their dedication and skill. The contraption was a marvel of engineering, its design intricate and detailed. The gears interlocked perfectly, their teeth meshing with a precision that was mesmerizing. The springs were coiled tightly, their tension controlled by a series of levers and switches. The creatures worked on the contraption with a focus that was unwavering, their attention completely absorbed by the task at hand. In another part of the settlement, I saw a creature carefully inscribing a spell word onto a piece of golden metal. The creature's hands moved with a precision that was awe-inspiring, whispering words of magic to the metal surface. The words were not merely an string of language, but an infusion of magic. As the creature completed the incantation, the metal glowed softly, a declaration of the magic infused within it. The creature was not merely a craftsman, but a mage. Its understanding of magic was evident in its work, its skill an embodiment of its mastery. The piece of metal was not merely a material, but a conduit of magic, its surface bearing the spell word that infused it with power.

The creatures were constantly busy, their hands always in motion. They tinkered with their inventions, their fingers moving with a precision that was awe-inspiring. They adjusted the gears, tightened the springs, and fine-tuned the mechanisms with a meticulousness that spoke of their dedication and skill. Their eyes sparkled with intelligence and curiosity, their gaze focused and intense. They studied their inventions with a keen eye, their attention completely absorbed by the task at hand. Their eyes were not merely organs of sight, but windows to their minds, their sparkle an affirmation to their intelligence and curiosity. The creatures spoke in a rapid, excited manner, their words a blend of technical jargon and spell words. Their language was not merely a means of communication, but a stamp of their understanding of technology and magic. They discussed their inventions, their words filled with terms and phrases that spoke of gears, springs, levers, and magic. Despite their small stature, the creatures were a marvel of grace and precision. Their movements, their work, their language - all combined to create a spectacle of intelligence and curiosity that was awe-inspiring.

The small creature who had hurriedly handed and retrieved the strange device from me scurried back in my direction, his eyes gleaming with excitement. He was devoid of the strange device he had previously handed to me, however, his hands now empty but his demeanor full of anticipation. "Apologies for the abrupt departure," he said, his voice high-pitched and excited. "I'm Zanmin, an apprentice Spellweaver. I had to rush off to record some findings." He gestured towards where the device had been, his small fingers tracing the air. "That device you held, it's a *Lindiknik Drin'tik*. It measures magical and technological lindiknik'n. Yours... well, they were unlike any I've seen before." Zanmin's eyes sparkled with curiosity as he looked at me. "Your magical lindiknik'n are unique, different. I had to take the readings to my master, a Spellweaver. He's intrigued, to say the least." He extended a small hand towards me, his gesture friendly and welcoming. "Welcome to our home. There's much to learn, and much to share, if you're going to be here a while?"

After introducing myself, Zanmin's eyes twinkled with a mischievous light as he leaned in closer, his voice dropping to a lighthearted whisper. "Tell me, Yoran," he began, his words slow and deliberate, "have you encountered gnomarik'n before?" The unfamiliar term hung in the air between us, a strange melody in the symphony of our conversation. "Gnom... arik... gnom-whats?" I echoed, my tongue stumbling over the unfamiliar syllables. I tried to mimic the peculiar "pop" sound Zanmin had made when pronouncing the "m" in "mar", and the guttural "click" at the end of "rik", but the sounds felt alien and awkward in my mouth. A soft chuckle escaped Zanmin as he watched my attempts, his small body shaking with mirth.

"Gnomarik'n," he repeated, his laughter subsiding. "But you may just call us gnomes, if you prefer. We often shorten it this way. The engineering mind always looking for a way to make things more efficient, and all." His words, spoken with a warm humor and a touch of pride, brought a smile to my face. With a wave of his hand, Zanmin beckoned me to follow him deeper into the cavern. As we delved further into the heart of the gnomish city, the air buzzed with an energy that was both electric and magical. The cavern was alive with the sounds of tinkering and the hum of machinery, punctuated by the occasional cheer of success or groan of frustration.

Everywhere I looked, gnomes were engrossed in their work. Some were huddled over intricate devices, their fingers deftly manipulating tiny gears and levers. Others were engrossed in spellcasting, their hands weaving intricate patterns in the air as they chanted spell words. The city was a hive of activity; of relentless pursuit of knowledge and innovation.

"Welcome to the heart of our society," Zanmin said, his voice filled with pride. "Here, we experiment, we learn, we create. Nothing is 'standard issue' as you might say. Everything is in a constant state of evolution." We passed by a group of gnomes working on a large, clockwork device. Its gears whirred and clicked, steam puffing from its joints. Zanmin explained that it was an early prototype of a mining machine, designed to extract precious minerals from the earth without causing harm to the environment. Further along, we came across a Spellweaver, her hands glowing with a soft light as she manipulated a floating orb of greenish water. She was experimenting with spell words, trying to find a new way to purify contaminated water sources. As we continued our tour, I was struck by the gnomes' dedication to their work, their unwavering commitment to improvement and innovation. Despite being a relatively young society, as all the children of Alara were first born only around five centuries before this time, they were making strides in technology and magic that were truly impressive.

"This is us, Yoran," Zanmin said, his eyes reflecting the vibrant energy of the city. "Always experimenting, always improving. We are the gnomes, the children of innovation and magic." Continuing the tour, Zanmin led me through a labyrinth of tunnels, each one bustling with activity. We first came across a large, open space filled with gnomes hunched over workbenches, their hands a blur as they worked on various contraptions. "These are our Master Inventors," Zanmin explained, "They are the minds behind our technological advancements." Next, we passed a vast library, the air heavy with the scent of parchment and ink. Gnomes were scattered throughout, some engrossed in thick tomes, others scribbling furiously on scrolls. "Our Knowledge Keepers," Zanmin said, his voice filled with reverence. "They maintain our libraries and educate our young." Speaking of the young, we soon came across a group of apprentice gnomes. They were in a separate chamber, practicing their spell words under the watchful eyes of their mentors. The air crackled with magic, the apprentices' faces lit with determination and focus. Finally, we passed by the Rik'n, the general populace of gnomes involved in various tasks. They were mining for resources, maintaining the machinery, and performing other manual work. "Each one, like a cog, a 'rik', plays a small but critical part in the functioning of our society," Zanmin explained.

Just as our tour was concluding, a new gnome appeared. He was taller than Zanmin, his face stern and his eyes sharp. "New one," he said, his voice echoing in the cavern, "the Grand Arcanist wishes to speak with you." Zanmin turned to me his expression serious. "You should hurry, Yoran. The Grand Arcanist doesn't like to be kept waiting. Meet me back in the Spellweaver quarters when you're done. I'll be convening with my master." I nodded at Zanmin, then turned to follow the new gnome. As we walked, the sounds of the gnomish society filled the air - the rhythmic clinking of tools, the soft hum of machinery, the distant murmur of gnomes engrossed in their work. The air was heavy with the scent of oil and metal, intermingled with the faint, underlying aroma of earth and stone. The ground beneath my feet was uneven, due to the natural formation of the caverns, but the paths were paved to be perfectly smooth and polished. I could feel the subtle vibrations of the machinery through the soles of my boots, a constant reminder of the technological prowess of the gnomes.

The new gnome led me through a series of tunnels, each one more intricate than the last. As we walked, he introduced himself. "I'm Hisdri, an aide to the Grand Arcanist," he said, his voice echoing off the stone walls. "When speaking with the Grand Arcanist, be respectful and concise. He values knowledge and efficiency above all else." Hisdri's words hung in the air as we continued our journey, the anticipation building with each step. The tunnel eventually opened up into a grand chamber, the walls lined with intricate machinery and glowing crystals. At the far end of the chamber, seated behind a large, stone desk, was the Grand Arcanist.

The Grand Arcanist was an imposing figure, even while seated. He was taller than most gnomes, his frame lean but sturdy. His skin was a deep, earthy brown, like the rich soil of the caverns, and his eyes were a vibrant emerald green, sparkling with wisdom and a hint of arrogance.

His hair was a shock of white, standing out starkly against his dark skin. It was wild and untamed. His face was lined with age, each wrinkle a mark of cycles filled with knowledge and experience. He was dressed in a robe of deep blue, adorned with intricate silver patterns that glowed faintly in the dim light of the chamber. Around his neck hung an amulet, a large crystal set in a complex clockwork setting, its inner workings visible and constantly moving, a symbol of the gnomish blend of magic and technology. In his hands, he held a staff, its surface etched with countless runes. The staff was topped with a large, glowing crystal, its light pulsating in rhythm with the Grand Arcanist's heartbeat.

The Grand Arcanist looked up as I approached, his emerald eyes studying me intently. "What is your name, stranger?" he asked, his voice deep and resonant for a gnome.

"Yoran, sir," I replied, meeting the Grand Arcanist's gaze.

"And what brings you to our society, Yoran?" the Grand Arcanist continued, his fingers tapping rhythmically on his staff.

"I wish to learn, sir," I answered honestly. "I wish to understand your society, your magic, your technology."

The Grand Arcanist considered this for a moment, his eyes narrowing slightly. "If you mean to stay and learn, then you must make yourself useful," he said finally. "Tell me, Yoran, are you more skilled in engineering or spellcrafting?"

I hesitated, unsure of how to answer. "I... I'm not particularly experienced in either, sir," I admitted.

The Grand Arcanist let out a sigh, a sound of mild annoyance. "Then you will spend time with both our Master Inventors and our Spellweavers," he decided. "See if you can be of any assistance to them. We value knowledge and efficiency here, Yoran. If you wish to stay, you must contribute."

I nodded, taking in the Grand Arcanist's words. "I understand, sir," I said, my voice steady. "I'm eager to learn and contribute in any way I can."

The Grand Arcanist looked up at me again, his emerald eyes seeming to pierce right through me. "Good," he said, a hint of approval in his voice. "Remember, Yoran, knowledge is the greatest asset one can possess. Use it wisely."

"Thank you, sir," I replied, feeling a sense of determination welling up within me. "I'll do my best."

The Grand Arcanist nodded, then turned his attention back to his work. "Now, off you go," he said, waving me away. "Hisdri will show you to the Master Inventors and Spellweavers. Learn well, Yoran. We have much to teach you." Hisdri led me back through the labyrinth of tunnels, our path illuminated by the soft glow of the crystals embedded in the walls. The air was filled with the increasingly familiar hum of machinery and the distant murmur of gnomes at work. We eventually arrived at the Spellweavers' quarters, a large chamber filled with gnomes engrossed in their magical studies. The air crackled with energy, the soft glow of spell words illuminating the room. Zanmin was there, his face lighting up as he saw me. "Yoran!" he exclaimed, rushing over. "I see you've met the Grand Arcanist. How did it go?"

Before I could answer, another gnome approached us. He was older than Zanmin, his hair a silvery white and his eyes a deep, vibrant blue. His aura was powerful, an attestation of his skill and knowledge in spellweaving.

"I am Felkur," he introduced himself, his voice soft yet commanding. "I am a master Spellweaver, and I will be your mentor in spellweaving." I nodded, extending a hand towards Felkur.

"I look forward to learning from you, Felkur," I said, my voice steady.

Felkur smiled, a warm, welcoming smile that put me at ease. "And I look forward to teaching you, Yoran," he replied. "Welcome to the world of spellweaving."

I looked at Felkur, a hint of surprise in my eyes. "I just came from the Grand Arcanist," I said, my voice filled with curiosity. "How did you know already I would be coming?"

Felkur chuckled, a soft, warm sound that echoed through the chamber. "Ah, that would be thanks to a device our Master Inventors have come up with," he explained. "In tandem with a few spell words, it allows for instant communication within short distances."

He held up a small, intricate device, its surface etched with countless runes. "We use the spell words '*Hael*', '*Vis*', and '*Threl*'," he continued. "Together, they allow us to whisper visions and connect with each other, no matter where we are in the city."

I looked at the device, my eyes wide with awe. With tools like this, it was no wonder the gnomes were making such strides in their society. Felkur looked at me, his eyes twinkling with curiosity. "Tell me, Yoran, what do you know of spellcasting?" he asked, his voice gentle.

I hesitated, considering my words carefully. "I know a few spell words," I admitted. "I learned '*Su-Tha*', '*Flux*', '*Eg-Cur*', and '*Threl-Vysh-Pax*' during my journey here."

Felkur nodded, his expression thoughtful. "Those are good words to know," he said. "They are versatile and can be used in many different combinations. But spellcasting is not just about knowing the words. It's about understanding their essence, their true meaning. It's about weaving them together in harmony, creating a symphony of magic." I listened, my eyes wide with awe. I had learned the spell words, yes, but I had never known their meanings. I was eager to learn more, eager to delve deeper into the world of spellweaving.

"I look forward to learning from you, Felkur," I said, my voice filled with determination. "I want to understand the true essence of spellcasting."

Felkur smiled, pleased with my eagerness. "Good," he said. "We will begin your lessons tomorrow. For now, rest and prepare yourself. The world of spellweaving awaits you, Yoran."

As Felkur left, Zanmin approached me, a wide grin on his face. "So, you're going to be a spellweaver, eh?" he said, his eyes twinkling with amusement. "I can't wait to see you weaving spells with the best of us."

I chuckled, feeling a sense of camaraderie with the small gnome. "I'm looking forward to it," I replied. "But for now, I think I need some rest."

Zanmin nodded, understanding. "Of course, of course," he said, waving his hand dismissively. "Follow me, I'll show you to our guest house. It's built for gnomes from neighboring *vendoktoris* - enclaves - but I think it'll suit you just fine."

XVII

Spellweaver

As we walked, I couldn't help but marvel at the gnomish city. Despite its size and the coldness of the stone, it was filled with a sense of community as warm as the steam escaping the bronze vents that lined the city tunnels and streets. The guest house was a small, cozy structure, its walls lined with glowing crystals that cast a soft, warm light.

"It's a bit small for your human height," Zanmin admitted, his eyes twinkling with amusement. "But I think you'll find it quite comfortable." I looked around, taking in the cozy interior of the guest house. Despite its size, I'd stayed in less comfortable places.

"It's perfect, Zanmin," I said, a smile on my face. "Thank you." As Zanmin left, I found myself alone in the small guest house. Despite its size, the space was cozy and inviting, filled with the soft glow of the crystals embedded in the walls. The air was cool and crisp, a delightful respite to the warm, bustling energy of the gnomish city outside. The guest house had a distinct scent, a blend of earthy stone and the faint, metallic tang of machinery, with a hint of something warm and inviting, like freshly baked bread.

I moved around the space, my head nearly brushing against the low ceiling. The furniture was gnomish-sized, each piece meticulously crafted and surprisingly sturdy. I found a small bed tucked away in one corner, its frame made of polished stone and covered with a thick, plush blanket which, despite its simple appearance, held a myriad of scents. It smelled of the deep, rich earth from which the gnomes had sprung, mixed with the faint, sweet scent of the moss that grew in the darker corners of the caverns. There was also a hint of something else, something uniquely gnomarik - the subtle, spicy scent of their favorite tea, perhaps? Or the crisp, clean smell of their meticulously maintained machinery? Sitting on the bed, I could feel the coolness of the stone seeping through the blanket, a comforting sensation after the day's events. I lay down, my body stretching out across the length of the bed. My feet hung off the edge, but I didn't mind. The blanket was warm and soft, a welcome comfort in the unfamiliar surroundings. I wrapped the blanket around myself, and I was struck by its texture. It was surprisingly soft against my skin, like the downy feathers of a bird, yet it held a certain weight, a comforting heaviness that grounded me. It was as if I was being enveloped in a warm, gentle hug.

As I lay there, I could hear the distant hum of the gnomish culture, a soft lullaby that echoed through the cavernous city. I could feel the subtle vibrations of the machinery through the stone bed, a constant reminder of the gnomarik technological prowess. Despite the unfamiliar surroundings and the cramped space, I found myself feeling surprisingly at ease. The gnomes had welcomed me into their society, had offered me a place to stay and a chance to learn without a moment's hesitation. I was a stranger in a strange land, yet I felt a sense of belonging here. With those comforting sensations enveloping me, I drifted off to sleep, my dreams filled with the soft glow of crystals and the rhythmic hum of machinery, the comforting scent of the guest house and the soft touch of the blanket against my skin.

The morning came with a soft knock at the door, pulling me from the depths of a dream-filled sleep. The rhythmic hum of the gnomarik city had been replaced by a symphony of new sounds - the distant clinking of tools, the soft murmur of gnomes starting their day, the gentle rustle of parchment.

As I stirred, the scent of the guest house filled my senses. The earthy aroma of stone, the faint tang of machinery, the warm, inviting scent of freshly baked bread. It was a comforting blend, a reminder of the unique society I had found myself in. I stretched, feeling the cool stone of the bed beneath me, the soft, downy texture of the blanket against my skin. My calves and feet hung off the edge of the bed, a reminder of the gnomish-sized accommodations. Despite the cramped space, I felt rested, the peaceful slumber having rejuvenated me for the day ahead. Opening my eyes, I was greeted by the soft glow of the crystals embedded in the walls. Their light danced across the room, casting intricate patterns on the stone walls. The guest house, with its cozy warmth and earthy scent, felt like a sanctuary, a small slice of home in this strange, new world.

The knock came again, more insistent this time. "Yoran, are you awake?" came Zanmin's voice, muffled by the door. "We have a big day ahead of us!" I smiled, pulling myself out of bed. My first day as an apprentice Spellweaver was about to begin, and I was eager to learn, eager to contribute, eager to become a part of gnomarik society. With a sense of anticipation, I opened the door to greet Zanmin, ready to start my day in this vibrant, bustling city.

As Zanmin and I made our way towards the Spellweaver quarters, the city was alive with activity. The rhythmic clinking of tools and the hum of machinery filled the air, a measure of the gnomes' industrious nature. The scent of oil and grinding stones was stronger now, mixed with the earthy aroma of the caverns and the faint, underlying scent of magic. We were stopped by a new gnome, his skin a deep, earthy brown and his eyes a vibrant blue. He was shorter than Zanmin, his frame sturdy and his hands calloused from cycles of work. He approached us with a wide grin, his eyes twinkling with amusement.

"Ah, Orrick!" Zanmin exclaimed, his face lighting up at the sight of the new gnome. "What brings you here?"

Orrick turned to me, extending a hand. "You must be Yoran," he said, his voice deep and resonant for a gnome. "I've heard much about you."

I shook his hand, feeling the rough texture of his palm against mine. "Nice to meet you, Orrick," I replied, meeting his gaze.

Orrick nodded, a hint of approval in his eyes. "The Master Inventors have been informed that you've chosen to spend time with the Spellweavers first," he said. "They're eagerly awaiting your arrival once your time with the Spellweavers is concluded."

I nodded, feeling a sense of anticipation welling up within me.

With a final handshake and a nod of his head, Orrick took his leave. "I'll see you later, Zanmin," he said, his voice filled with warmth. "We'll meet up for drinks, as usual."

Zanmin nodded, a wide grin on his face. "Looking forward to it, Orrick," he replied. "Take care." With that, Orrick disappeared into the bustling city, leaving Zanmin and me to continue our journey. As we walked, I found myself taking in new sights that I hadn't noticed the day before. To our right, a group of gnomes were working on a large, intricate piece of machinery, their hands moving with practiced ease as they adjusted gears and tightened bolts. The machine hummed with energy, its surface glowing with a soft, magical light. To our left, a young gnome was practicing spell words, her voice echoing through the cavern as she weaved magic into the air. Her spells shimmered in the air, their light casting intricate patterns on the stone walls. Above us, the ceiling of the cavern was adorned with glowing crystals, their light illuminating the city below. The crystals pulsed with energy, their rhythm matching the heartbeat of the city.

As we neared the Spellweaver quarters, the hum of machinery gave way to a different kind of energy. The air seemed to crackle with magic, the subtle vibrations of spell words resonating in the cavernous space. The scent of parchment and ink mingled with the earthy aroma of the caverns, a testimony to the scholarly pursuits of the Spellweavers. The Spellweaver quarters were located in a large, open chamber, its walls lined with shelves filled with scrolls and tomes. Crystals of various colors hung from the ceiling, their soft glow illuminating the room. Each crystal pulsed with a different rhythm, their light dancing across the room in a mesmerizing display. Gnomes of all ages were scattered throughout the room, their attention focused on their studies. Some were engrossed in tomes, their eyes scanning the pages as they whispered spell words under their breath. Others were practicing their spellcasting, their hands moving in intricate patterns as they weaved magic into the air. The gnomarik people seemed to have a much more intimate grasp on the workings of Alara's primal magics than I had. In the center of the room was a large, circular table, its surface covered with scrolls and parchments. A group of older gnomes were gathered around it, their voices low as they discussed their findings.

As we entered the room, all activity paused for a moment, the gnomes turning to look at us briefly before returning to their work. Zanmin led me through the room, weaving between the tables and gnomes engrossed in their studies. The air was filled with the soft rustle of parchment and the murmuring of spell words, a soothing symphony of scholarly pursuits. We eventually reached Felkur, who was seated at his own large, circular table in the back of the room. He was engrossed in a large tome, his eyes scanning the pages as his fingers traced the intricate runes etched into the parchment. Zanmin cleared his throat, drawing Felkur's attention.

Felkur looked up, his deep blue eyes meeting mine. A hint of a smile tugged at the corners of his mouth. "Ah, Yoran," he said, his voice soft yet commanding. "Welcome. We have much to learn today."

With that, Zanmin gave me a reassuring pat on the shoulder. "I'll leave you to it, Yoran," he said, his voice filled with warmth. "I need to find my master and begin my work for the day. We'll meet up later, alright?"

I nodded, watching as Zanmin disappeared into the bustling room. Felkur, his eyes twinkling with anticipation, held up a small glass orb. "Today, Yoran," he began, his voice echoing softly in the quiet room, "we will learn a new combination of spell words. This is *'Bex-Threl-El-Cii'*." I watched as he held the orb up to the light, its surface gleaming with a soft, ethereal glow. "*Bex*," he said, his voice steady, "refers to the object, in this case, the orb." He then moved his hand in a complex pattern, his fingers tracing invisible lines in the air. "*Threl-El*," he continued, "'Connect' and 'Light', respectively, connect light to the object."

Finally, he placed his other hand over the orb, his palm barely touching its smooth surface. "*Cii*," he concluded, "finalizes the enchantment on an object, binding the enchantment to it." As he spoke the final word, the orb began to glow, a soft, warm light emanating from its core. It was a mesmerizing sight, the light dancing within the orb, casting intricate patterns on the stone walls.

Felkur handed me the orb, its light pulsing in rhythm with my heartbeat. "This orb," he explained, "will be sent to the Master Inventors. Their apprentices will attach it to a short metal rod with a switch, creating a device that can be turned on and off at will." He paused, a hint of a smile tugging at the corners of his mouth. "Imagine," he said, his voice filled with wonder, "being able to illuminate your path with a flick of a switch. No need for torches or lanterns. Just pure, magical light, at your fingertips." I held the orb in my hand, its light warm against my skin. It was a simple object, yet it held so much potential. It was a vindication of the gnomarik peoples' ingenuity, their ability to blend magic and technology in ways I could never have imagined. As I looked at the orb, I felt a sense of awe and excitement. I was eager to learn more, eager to delve deeper into the world of spellweaving. With Felkur as my guide, I knew I was just beginning to scratch the surface of what was possible.

I turned the glowing orb over in my hands, my mind filled with questions. "Felkur," I began, my voice echoing softly in the quiet room, "how did your people discover their affinity for magic?"

Felkur looked at me, his deep blue eyes twinkling with curiosity. "Ah," he said, his voice filled with warmth, "that is a question that has been asked by many gnomarik'n." He paused, his gaze distant as he delved into the annals of gnomarik history. "We gnomarik'n," he began, "have always had a deep connection with Rikklin. We were born from it, after all. But our affinity for magic... that is a different story."

He explained that the gnomes did not know of their attunement to the primal forces of the world. They could not cast spells without the use of spell words, nor did they have a language that functioned as a secondary spell language like the centarion. His explanation resonated with me, remarkably similar to the connection I had - that, possibly, all humans may have - with the primal magic of Alara - 'Rikklin' in gnomarik.

"Instead," Felkur continued, "we discovered our affinity for magic through our love for invention. We noticed that certain combinations of words had an effect on our creations. They would move on their own, or glow with light, or even change shape. It was... fascinating." He paused, a smile fully crossing his cheeks, "So, we began to experiment. We tried different combinations of words, observed their effects, and recorded our findings. Over time, we discovered the spell words and learned how to use them to enchant our creations." I listened, captivated by his words. The gnomarik journey into the world of magic was not entirely unlike what I had known. It was not a natural gift, nor a divine blessing, but a discovery born out of curiosity and a love for invention - in my case, a love for learning and exploration, listening to the whispers of Alara.

After we had practiced a few more spell word combinations, *Bex-Su-Cii*, for enchanting an object to become lighter; *Bex-Nis-Cii*, for enchanting an object to generate heat; *Bex-Flux-Qar-Cii*, for channeling a stream of water through an object; and *Bex-Sil-Cii*, for enchanting an object to absorb sound; Felkur leaned back in his chair, his eyes twinkling with anticipation. "Now, Yoran," he began, his voice echoing softly in the quiet room, "we move onto a more complex aspect of spellweaving - understanding magical *lindiknik'n*." He reached into a drawer and pulled out a small, intricate device, similar to the one Zanmin had handed me. "Every being, every object, every place," he explained, "has a unique magical *lindiknik*. It's like a signature, a unique rhythm that distinguishes it from everything else." He activated the device, and it began to hum softly, its surface glowing with a soft, ethereal light. "This device," he continued, "is designed to measure these lindiknik'n. It helps us fine-tune our spell words, aligning them with the lindiknik'n of the objects we wish to enchant." He handed me the device, its light pulsing in rhythm with my heartbeat. "Understanding these lindiknik'n," he said, "is key to effective spellweaving. It allows us to work in harmony with the natural rhythms of the world, enhancing our magic and making our enchantments more efficient."

After our lesson on magical "*lindiknik'n*" - frequencies - Felkur rose from his chair, his eyes gleaming with excitement. "Come, Yoran," he said, his voice echoing softly in the cavernous room. "Let's move on to the experimentation chambers." We left the main quarters, walking down a long, winding corridor. The air grew cooler as we descended deeper into the cavern, the hum of magic growing stronger with each step. The scent of parchment and ink gave way to a different aroma - a mix of earth, metal, and something else I couldn't quite place. Finally, we arrived at a large, circular chamber, its walls lined with shelves filled with various tools and devices. In the center of the room was a large table, its surface covered with scrolls, parchments, and a variety of strange-looking objects.

"This," Felkur announced, his voice filled with pride, "is where we experiment. Here, we push the boundaries of what we know, seeking new spell words and new combinations." He led me to the table, picking up a small, metallic object. "For instance," he continued, "this device was enchanted with a new combination we discovered just last week. It can detect changes in temperature and adjust its own heat accordingly." As he spoke, I could see the passion in his eyes, the excitement in his voice. We stood in the experimentation chamber, and Felkur pointed towards a group of gnomes huddled around a table. "Watch," he said, his voice barely above a whisper. "They're attempting to discover a new spell word."

The group was focused on a small, bronze cube placed in the center of the table. One of the gnomes, a young female with bright, eager eyes, was moving her hands in an intricate pattern as she recited their experimental spell word.

"*Quis!*" she intoned.

The cube began to vibrate, a soft hum filling the room. The gnomes watched in anticipation, their eyes glued to the cube. The hum grew louder, the cube vibrating more intensely. Suddenly, with a loud pop, the cube transformed. But instead of a new shape or form, it turned into a small hare. The hare, seemingly unharmed and unfazed, hopped off the table and scurried away, leaving the gnomes staring in disbelief. The room was silent for a moment, the gnomes exchanging confused glances. Then, as if on cue, they all burst into laughter. The sound echoed through the chamber. Felkur chuckled, shaking his head in amusement. "Well," he said, his eyes twinkling with mirth, "that was certainly unexpected. I believe they had been expecting the word to 'reveal' something. Unless they were trying to reveal a hare, I would say they need to revisit their notes."

Still chuckling, the group of gnomes regrouped, replacing the previous bronze cube, which was now hopping around the tunnels somewhere in the gnomarik city, with a new one from a nearby shelf, their faces a mix of amusement and determination. The young female Spellweaver, her cheeks flushed from laughter, cleared her throat and once again began to recite the spell word, her hands moving in the same intricate patterns as before.

"*Quis!*"

This time, the metallic cube began to glow, a soft, ethereal light emanating from its core. The light grew brighter, filling the room with a warm, golden glow. The gnomes watched in anticipation, their laughter fading into a tense silence. Suddenly, the cube shattered, fragments of metal flying in all directions. But instead of the expected loud crash, the fragments hung in the air, suspended in time and space. The room was filled with a strange, eerie silence, the fragments glowing like tiny stars in the dim light. As the fragments hung suspended, an ethereal energy began to build at the center of where the cube had been. Bolts of electricity, shards of ice, spouts of flame, all began to shoot from the center of the cube for a few moments, sending everyone in the room scampering for cover, before suddenly ceasing.

The gnomes stared in disbelief, their faces pale. This was not what they had expected either. This was not a harmless, amusing surprise like the hare. This was something different, something serious. Something had gone wrong both times. With a sense of urgency, they began to scurry around, taking notes and discussing in hushed tones. The laughter was gone, replaced by a palpable tension. Something was wrong, but they didn't know what. Felkur, his face grave, turned to me. "This," he said, his voice barely above a whisper, "is why we experiment. Magic is unpredictable, and sometimes, it surprises us in ways we don't understand."

As the room buzzed with hurried activity, a senior Spellweaver, a stern-looking gnome with a silver beard, turned to a young apprentice. "Take these notes to the Grand Arcanist," he ordered, his voice firm. "And be quick about it." The apprentice nodded, clutching the parchment tightly as he scurried out of the room. Around us, other orders were being given, notes being passed around, and discussions being held in hushed, urgent tones.

Suddenly, a commanding voice echoed through the chamber, silencing the room. A tall gnome, her hair a fiery red and her eyes sharp and focused, stepped forward. "Enough," she said, her voice resonating with authority. "We need to regroup and figure out what's happening." She was the lead Spellweaver, a respected figure known for her wisdom and leadership. "I want everyone to take the rest of the day off," she announced, her gaze sweeping across the room. "I will be meeting with the head Master Inventor to discuss these developments." The room was silent, the gnomes exchanging worried glances. The lead Spellweaver's orders were met with nods of agreement, the gnomes slowly filing out of the room.

As we left the chamber, I turned to Felkur, my mind buzzing with questions. "Felkur," I began, my voice echoing softly in the quiet corridor, "what do you think-" But before I could finish, Felkur held up a hand, cutting me off. "Not now, Yoran," he said, his voice strained. His usual warm demeanor was replaced by a look of frustration, his brows furrowed in deep thought. "We'll meet again in the morning," he continued, his gaze distant. "For now, let's just... let's just take a break." I nodded, acknowledging his desire for silence to contemplate today's happenings.. The day's events had taken a toll on Felkur. After having cast several spells on multiple occasions along my journey here,

I had never encountered anything so complicated. The world of spell-weaving was proving to be more complex and unpredictable than I had imagined.

XVIII

Training

As I stepped out of the Spellweaver quarters, I was met by a familiar face. Zanmin was waiting for me, his eyes wide with curiosity. "Yoran!" he called out, a hint of excitement in his voice. "I heard about what happened. Let's go to the drink house, I could use a good brew after today." I nodded, welcoming the distraction. Zanmin led the way, his steps quick and eager. The drink house was a lively place, filled with the chatter of gnomes, the clinking of glasses, and the rich, sweet aroma of gnomish brew. As Zanmin and I stepped into the drink house, a wave of warmth washed over us, a pronounced dissension from the cool air of the cavernous city. The room was dimly lit, the soft glow of enchanted lanterns casting long shadows on the wooden tables and stools.

The drink house was quieter than I had expected. A few tables were occupied by older gnomes, their faces etched with lines of wisdom and experience. Their voices were soft, their conversations filled with laughter and reminiscence. At another table, a group of Spellweavers were huddled together, their heads bowed in quiet discussion. The barkeep, a stout gnome with a bushy beard, was busy behind the counter, his hands expertly pouring brew into large mugs. The sound of liquid hitting the mugs, the clinking of glasses, and the low hum of conversation created a soothing melody, a comforting backdrop to our own discussion.

We settled into our corner table, mugs of gnomish brew in hand. Visually, the drink was enchanting. The liquid was translucent, but it sparkled with iridescent hues of blues, purples, and silvers, mimicking the appearance of an underground starry night. Tiny, luminescent flecks floated within, creating a swirling galaxy right in my palm. Drawing the glass closer, I took a moment to appreciate its aroma. It was unexpectedly fresh for something brewed underground, bearing the invigorating scent of cool, moss-covered stones mixed with the sweetness of ripe underground berries and a hint of earthy undertones, perhaps reminiscent of aged oak barrels. Taking a cautious sip, I was greeted with a dance of flavors. Initially, there was the gentle sweetness of a rare subterranean flower the gnomarik'n called "Vippidil", followed by a refreshing minty coolness derived from "Ludlin" - a fern that grows just above the subterranean city. The finish, however, was what truly made it a marvel — a warm, lingering spicy sensation, thanks to the infusion of "Fedlixil", an underground herb known for its fiery zest. The glimmering brew was not just a beverage; it was an experience. With each sip, I could feel a delightful tingling sensation, starting from the tip of my tongue and spreading warmth to the rest of my body. It left me with a light-headed, euphoric feeling, making the surroundings appear even more magical than before. The room seemed to pulse with energy, the laughter and music around me taking on a melodious, dreamy quality. I realized then why the gnomes held this drink in such high regard. It wasn't merely for its taste, but for the otherworldly experience it promised, a momentary journey through the wonders of their underground realm, all captured within a single, mesmerizing mug.

As I relished in the experience of my drink, Zanmin leaned in, his eyes gleaming with curiosity. "You know, Yoran," he began, his voice barely above a whisper, "I've been thinking about what happened today." He took a sip of his own brew, his gaze thoughtful. "What if," he continued, "this wasn't an accident? What if someone *sabotaged* one of the devices?"

I raised an eyebrow, intrigued by his theory. "You mean, a Master Inventor?" I asked, my voice echoing his hushed tone.

Zanmin nodded, his eyes serious. "It's not unheard of," he said. "Rivalries can run deep, especially when it comes to innovation and discovery." We sat in silence for a moment, considering the possibility. It was a chilling thought, the idea of sabotage within a society that thrived on cooperation and shared knowledge "But," Zanmin added, breaking the silence, "there's another possibility. What if they stumbled upon a spell word that causes random effects?"

I considered this, sipping my brew. "A wildcard spell word?" I mused. "That would be... unpredictable."

Zanmin nodded, his gaze distant. "Indeed," he said. "But it's just a theory. For now, all we can do is speculate." As we delved deeper into our theories, the drink house around us faded into the background. The day's events had sparked a flurry of questions, of possibilities. And as we sat there, discussing the complexities of spellweaving, I couldn't help but feel a sense of excitement. This was a mystery, a puzzle to be solved. And I was eager to uncover the truth. As the night wore on, Zanmin and I continued our discussion, our theories growing more elaborate with each passing hour. The drink house gradually filled up, the soft hum of conversation growing louder, the clinking of glasses more frequent.

Eventually, the door swung open, and in walked Orrick, his face flushed from the cool night air. He spotted us in our corner and made his way over, a friendly grin on his face.

"Evening, Yoran, Zanmin," he greeted, pulling up a stool. "What's the topic of discussion tonight?" We filled him in on the day's events and our theories, watching his face for any sign of recognition. But Orrick shook his head, his brow furrowed in confusion. "I haven't heard anything about it," he admitted. "But it's rightly intriguing. I'll ask around tomorrow, see if any of the Master Inventors know anything."

As the night drew to a close, we parted ways, each of us lost in our own thoughts. The streets were quiet, the city bathed in the soft glow of the moonlight. I made my way back to the guest house, the day's events replaying in my mind. The guest house was just as I had left it, the small room welcoming in its simplicity. I crawled into the small bed, the blanket soft against my skin. As I drifted off to sleep, my mind was filled with questions, theories, possibilities. The world of spellweaving was proving to be more complex and unpredictable than I had imagined.

The following morning, I awoke to the sound of the city coming to life. The hustle and bustle outside was an undisguised differentiation from the previous day's tension. As I made my way to the Spellweaver quarters, Zanmin joined me, a cheerful grin on his face. "Back to normal, I hope," he said, his eyes twinkling with amusement. When we arrived at the quarters, Felkur was waiting for us. "We're attempting the spell word again," he informed us, his voice steady. "We need to see if yesterday's events were an anomaly." We both followed him to the experimentation chamber this time, the room buzzing with a mix of anticipation and apprehension. The same group of Spellweavers from the previous day were gathered around the table, their faces a mask of concentration. The room was filled with a palpable sense of anticipation as the young female Spellweaver prepared to recite the sound once more. The metallic cube sat innocently on the table, oblivious to the eyes fixed on it.

"*Quis*," she pronounced clearly, her voice echoing in the silent room.

As the word left her lips, the cube began to shimmer, a soft glow emanating from its surface. Suddenly, intricate patterns and symbols, previously invisible, appeared on the cube's surface. The room erupted in cheers, the gnomes clapping and congratulating each other.

They had discovered a new spell word, "*Quis*", which, they decided, did mean "Reveal". The experiment had gone exactly as planned this time, and the cube had revealed hidden symbols, an assertion of the power of this new spell word. As the cheers echoed around the room, Felkur clapped once, a clear, sharp sound that cut through the celebration. He turned to me, his eyes gleaming with a sense of accomplishment. "Come, Yoran," he said, his voice steady. "We have much to learn."

I followed him out of the experimentation chamber, the sound of the gnomes' celebration fading behind us. Zanmin gave me a quick nod, a grin on his face. "See you later, Yoran," he called out before disappearing into the crowd, off to meet his own master. Felkur led me to a quiet corner of the Spellweaver quarters, a space filled with scrolls and tomes. "Today," he began, his voice echoing softly in the quiet room, "we will focus on pronunciation, gestures, and energy management." Felkur began the lesson on pronunciation with a simple statement. "Pronunciation," he said, "is the heart of spellweaving. The slightest mispronunciation can alter the effect of a spell word, sometimes with drastic consequences." He then proceeded to demonstrate, using the spell word "*Vap*" as an example. "Pay heed," he directed, the serenity of the enclave amplifying his voice's resonance. He articulated "*Vap*" with precision: a gentle 'V', the 'a' almost clipped, and the 'p' crisp, akin to a droplet meeting water. He reiterated, beckoning me to replicate. "Grasp this," he stressed, "exactness is vital. Spell words aren't mere utterances; they're the keystone. Each must align immaculately with its purpose." Felkur's eyes gleamed with anticipation, eager to showcase the myriad manifestations of a single spell.

He began softly, stretching out the 'a', "*Vahp.*" The room stilled as a gentle waft of steam spiraled from his palm. It danced gracefully in the air, curling and twisting as if it had all the time in the world, before fading into nothingness.

Without missing a beat, he continued, emphasizing the 'a' with an accent, "*Váp.*" The response was instantaneous. An explosive jet of steam burst forth, its energy so potent that it almost seemed eager to prove its might before retracting back into obscurity as swiftly as it had emerged.

Capturing my undivided attention, Felkur then laid stress on the 'V', uttering, "*Vvap.*" The ambiance was transformed as a thick, dense fog of steam emerged. It hung in the air, refusing to budge, creating a veil that seemed to separate us momentarily from the world outside.

Lastly, with a gleam of mischief, he exclaimed, "*Vap!*", popping the 'p' sharply. A brisk, assertive jet of steam pierced the atmosphere, reminiscent of a steamy whistle declaring its presence, before it too, like all the others, dissipated, leaving me in awe of the power of pronunciation. "Remember," he said, "the pronunciation must be precise. The spell words are not just words, they are keys. And each key must fit perfectly into its lock to work." We spent the rest of the morning practicing pronunciation, Felkur correcting me gently whenever I mispronounced a word. It was a challenging task, but with each repetition, I could feel myself improving, the spell words rolling off my tongue with increasing ease.

After the lesson on pronunciation, Felkur moved on to the topic of gestures. "Gestures," he began, "are not necessary for casting spells, but they can enhance the power of a spell or cause variations in its effects." He demonstrated by casting a simple light spell, "*El*". First, he cast it without any gesture, simply pronouncing the spell word. A soft light appeared, illuminating the room. Then, he cast it again, this time making a sweeping gesture with his hand as he pronounced the spell word. The light that appeared was noticeably brighter, and it seemed to pulse in time with his hand movements.

"Gestures," Felkur explained, "help to channel your energy into the spell. They can make a spell more powerful, or they can subtly alter its effects." He showed me several different gestures, explaining their meanings and effects. There was the sweeping gesture he had used for the light spell, which increased power. A circular motion could cause a spell to affect a wider area. A sharp, cutting gesture could focus a spell's effects on a single point.

As the day wore on, Felkur moved on to the final part of our lesson: magical energy management. "Spellweaving," he began, "is not just about saying the right words and making the right gestures. It's also about managing your energy." He explained that every spell we cast draws on our personal energy. "Think of it like a reservoir," he said. "Every time you cast a spell, you're drawing water from that reservoir. If you draw too much, too quickly, you'll drain the reservoir.

And if you don't give it time to refill, you'll find yourself unable to cast spells." He taught me how to feel the flow of my own energy, how to draw on it without depleting it. He showed me exercises to replenish my energy, techniques to conserve it, and ways to increase my overall energy capacity.

"Remember," he said, "spellweaving is not a sprint. It's a marathon. You need to pace yourself, manage your energy wisely. That's the key to becoming a successful spellweaver." As Felkur's final words of wisdom echoed in my mind, a familiar figure scurried over to us. It was Zanmin, his face flushed from a day's work, but his eyes sparkling with the same infectious enthusiasm I had come to associate with him.

"Finished for the day?" he asked, his gaze flitting between Felkur and me. Felkur nodded, a small smile playing on his lips. "Indeed, we have covered much ground today."

With a farewell nod to Felkur, Zanmin and I made our way out of the Spellweaver quarters. The sun was setting, casting long shadows across the gnomish city. As we stepped outside, we saw Orrick waiting for us, leaning against a nearby wall.

"Kept you waiting, didn't we?" Zanmin called out, a playful grin on his face.

Orrick shrugged, a good-natured smile on his face. "A few minutes, nothing more." As we walked, the city around us began to settle into its evening rhythm. The hum of machinery softened, replaced by the distant clinking of glasses and the murmur of conversation. The drink house was our destination, a place where gnomes gathered after a day's work to unwind and share stories. The drink house was nestled in a cozy corner of the city, its warm light spilling out onto the cobblestone streets. As we approached, the scent of brewed herbs and the faint hint of ground stone and oil filled the air, a unique blend that was becoming familiar to me.

We entered, the door creaking slightly in welcome. Inside, the drink house was a symphony of sounds. The soft hum of conversation, the clinking of glasses, the occasional burst of laughter. It was a warm, inviting space, filled with gnomes of all ranks, from Master Inventors to Rik'n, all sharing the camaraderie of a day's work done. We found a table near the back, away from the bustle. As we settled down, I couldn't help but feel a sense of contentment. Here I was, in a city deep underground, surrounded by gnomes, learning about magic and technology. It was a far cry from where I had started, and I was eager to see how it would continue.

As we settled into our seats, Zanmin wasted no time in bringing up the topic that had been on all our minds. "So," he began, his eyes flicking to Orrick, "any news from the Master Inventors?"

Orrick took a sip of his drink before responding. "Well," he started, "I can confirm that it wasn't the Master Inventors who sabotaged the Spellweavers. We've been noticing strange occurrences too. Unexpected results, inventions behaving oddly, that sort of thing." A hush fell over our table as we digested this information. If it wasn't a rivalry or a random spell, then what could it be?

"But what could cause such a thing?" I asked, my mind racing with possibilities. "Could it be an external force? Or maybe something within the city?"

Orrick shrugged, his expression thoughtful. "I don't know," he admitted. "As an apprentice, I'm not privy to all the details. But it's clear that something is happening, something that's affecting both our magic and our technology." We fell silent, each lost in our thoughts. The jovial atmosphere of the drink house seemed a world away as we contemplated the implications of Orrick's words.

Zanmin was the first to break the silence. "Yoran," he said, his voice serious, "I think you should try to get Felkur to talk about what happened. If he won't, then maybe you should try to speed up your lessons. Get to a point where you can be of help to the Spellweavers. Maybe then you can find out more."

I frowned, feeling a knot of unease in my stomach. "But they're the Master Spellweavers and Master Inventors," I protested. "We're just apprentices... and I'm an outsider. Shouldn't we let them handle whatever's going on?"

Orrick shook his head, his expression resolute. "The Spellweavers and Inventors may work together to create our society, but they have deep-rooted rivalries. They don't see eye-to-eye on most things. If something is affecting both our magic and our technology, we're going to need a solution that considers both sides. Something neither group is able or willing to do." He paused, looking at me and Zanmin in turn. "I think we might be the perfect ones to handle this." His words hung in the air, a challenge and a call to action. I looked at Zanmin, then back at Orrick. They were right. We were in a unique position to bridge the gap between the Spellweavers and the Inventors. And if there was a chance we could help, then we had to take it.

The next morning, I found myself standing before Felkur, my mind filled with questions. "Felkur," I began, my voice steady, "about the spell that went wrong a couple of days ago…"

Felkur's eyes flicked to mine, a hint of surprise in his gaze. He paused, seeming to weigh his words carefully. "Yoran," he said after a moment, "that incident… it's something we're still trying to understand." I waited, hoping he would continue, but he didn't. Instead, he changed the subject. "Today," he said, "we will continue our lessons."

I felt a pang of disappointment, but I didn't press him. It was clear that Felkur wasn't ready to discuss the incident. So, I nodded, pushing my questions aside for the moment. "Alright," I said, "let's get started." As we delved into the day's lessons, I couldn't help but feel a sense of urgency. If Zanmin and Orrick were right, then we needed to understand what was happening, and soon. But for now, all I could do was learn, and hope that I would be ready when the time came.

Felkur began the day's lesson with a solemnity I hadn't seen before. "Today," he said, "we will discuss the Gnomarik Ethics of Spellcasting." He paused, looking at me with a serious expression. "Spellcasting is not just about power or control. It's about responsibility. As spellweavers, we have a duty to use our abilities wisely and ethically." He went on to explain that the Gnomarik Ethics of Spellcasting were a set of principles that guided their use of magic. "These principles," he said, "are not just rules. They are a reflection of our values as a society. They remind us that our magic is a gift, and that we must use it for the betterment of all gnomarik'n, not just for our own personal gain." As he spoke, I could see the passion in his eyes, the conviction in his voice. This was clearly a topic close to his heart, and I found myself drawn in by his words. I realized then that spellweaving was more than just a skill or a tool. It was a way of life, a philosophy that shaped the very fabric of gnomarik society.

As the day wore on, Felkur delved deeper into the principles of the Gnomarik Ethics of Spellcasting. He spoke of the importance of intention, of understanding the potential consequences of a spell before casting it. "A spellweaver must always be mindful," he said, "of the ripple effects their magic can cause. Even the smallest spell can have far-reaching consequences." He then moved on to the principle of respect. "Respect for the magic itself, for the natural world that gives us our power, and for the individuals and communities affected by our spells," he explained. "We must always remember that our magic is a part of the world, not separate from it. We are stewards, not masters."

The third principle he discussed was that of restraint. "Magic is a powerful tool," Felkur said, "but that doesn't mean we should use it for every task. Sometimes, the non-magical solution is the best one. Knowing when to use magic, and when not to, is a key part of being a responsible spellweaver." As Felkur spoke, I found myself nodding along, completely engrossed in his words. The principles he was teaching were not just about magic, but about life itself. They spoke of responsibility, respect, and restraint, values that were as relevant to a human like me as they were to the gnomes. I realized then that these lessons were not just about becoming a better spellweaver, but about becoming a better person. As Felkur continued, I found my mind drifting back to my mentor, Tornu. The way Felkur spoke about magic, the lessons he was imparting, they reminded me of the way Tornu used to teach me about life through exploration.

Tornu would often say, "Exploration is not just about discovering new places, Yoran. It's about understanding our place in the world, about learning to respect the natural order of things." Now, as I listened to Felkur, I realized that his teachings about magic were strikingly similar. Just as Tornu used exploration as a medium to teach me about life, Felkur was using spellweaving to impart lessons about responsibility, respect, and restraint. I felt a pang of nostalgia, a longing for the simpler times when my biggest concern was what new place Tornu and I would explore next. But I also felt a sense of gratitude. Gratitude for Tornu, for all the lessons he had taught me, and for Felkur, who was now guiding me on this journey.

As the day began to wane, Felkur moved on to the final principle of the Gnomarik Ethics of Spellcasting: the principle of growth. "Spellweaving is a journey," he said, his voice echoing in the quiet room. "It's a process of constant learning and growth. We must always strive to improve, to understand more about the magic we wield and the world we live in." He paused, looking at me with a thoughtful expression. "But growth is not just about gaining more power or learning more spells. It's about deepening our understanding, about becoming more attuned to the magic around us and more aware of our place in the world." As he spoke, I felt a sense of understanding wash over me. As I looked at Felkur, I realized that this was what it meant to be a spellweaver. It was not just about casting spells or wielding magic. It was about growing, learning, and understanding.

As the lesson drew to a close, Felkur turned to me, a thoughtful expression on his face. "Yoran," he began, "I think it's time you learned more about our history. Go to the House of Gnardok and speak with the Knowledge Keepers. Ask them for a gnardok about the first gnomish Spellweavers. It will give you a deeper understanding of our magic and our society."

I nodded, grateful for the guidance. "I will, Felkur. Thank you."

As I stepped outside the Spellweaver quarters, I found Zanmin waiting for me. His eyes lit up as he saw me, and he was about to speak when Orrick joined us. "Let's head to the drink house," Orrick suggested, a smile on his face.

"I'll meet you there shortly," I replied, "I have to visit the House of Gnardok first."

As I mentioned my need to visit the House of Gnardok, Orrick and Zanmin exchanged a glance. "Would you like some company, Yoran?" Orrick asked, his eyes twinkling with curiosity.

Zanmin nodded in agreement. "The House of Gnardok can be a bit overwhelming on your first visit. We could help you navigate."

I was touched by their offer. "I'd appreciate that," I responded, grateful for their companionship. And so, we set off together, leaving the drink house for later and heading towards the grand library. As we walked, the air was filled with the sound of our laughter and the hum of speculation. The camaraderie between us was palpable, a comforting presence as we navigated the winding paths of the gnomish city.

XIX

House of Gnardok

As the grand building came into view, I found myself intrigued by its name. "Is '*Gnardok*' an important gnomarik family or figure?" I asked, looking between Zanmin and Orrick. At my question, Orrick let out a chuckle, while Zanmin's eyes twinkled with amusement.

"No, Yoran," Zanmin replied, a smile playing on his lips. "A gnardok is... well, it's like a keeper of tales and knowledge. Imagine many pieces of parchment, bound together, each imprinted with symbols and signs that convey stories or wisdom."

As Zanmin explained, I felt a spark of understanding. "Oh," I uttered, wonder illuminating my features. So, a 'gnardok' is like a... knowledge holder? A tangible reflection of thoughts and tales?"

Zanmin nodded, his smile growing warmer. "Precisely. We're essentially venturing to the House of these Knowledge Holders."

Upon grasping the concept, a light laugh escaped my lips. "Ah, now the pieces come together," I mused, feeling a mix of fascination and amusement. And so, there we stood, in the midst of the gnomish city, a trio bound by laughter and newfound understanding. It was a pure, radiant moment, testament to the burgeoning camaraderie amongst us.

As we approached the doors of the House of Gnardok, our laughter subsided, replaced by a sense of awe and anticipation. The grandeur of the library, even from the outside, was impressive. Our grins remained, however, a silent echo of the laughter that had just filled the air. With a shared look of excitement, we pushed open the doors, stepping into the hushed reverence of the House of Gnardok. As the doors of the House of Gnardok swung open, a wave of scents washed over me. The musty aroma of aged parchment mingled with the crisp, clean scent of new paper. Underlying it all was a hint of oil and metal, a standard of the gnomish love for machinery, and a faint, elusive whiff of petrichor, the telltale sign of magic at work. The library was hushed, but not silent. The soft rustle of turning pages, the quiet murmur of gnomes engrossed in their studies, the faint hum of magical devices, and the occasional whirr and click of some mechanical contraption filled the air. It was a symphony of sounds, each note contributing to the unique melody of knowledge and discovery. My eyes widened as I took in the sights. Towering shelves, filled to the brim with gnardoks and scrolls, stretched as far as the eye could see. Tables laden with gnardoks, parchment, and an array of strange devices were scattered throughout the room. gnomes were everywhere, engrossed in their reading, scribbling notes, or tinkering with some gadget. The walls were adorned with intricate diagrams and maps, and the ceiling was a marvel of gnomish engineering, a complex network of gears and pulleys, with enchanted lights floating like stars in a mechanical sky. Stepping into the House of Gnardok was like stepping into another world, a world where magic and technology danced together in a beautiful ballet of knowledge and discovery. It was overwhelming, awe-inspiring, and utterly captivating.

With a nod to Orrick, who veered off towards a section filled with intricate blueprints and mechanical diagrams, Zanmin led me towards a grand staircase. The steps were carved from a gleaming stone, each one worn smooth by countless feet. As we ascended, I could see the library unfolding below us, a vast expanse of knowledge stretching out in all directions. We climbed several flights, passing by shelves filled with gnardoks of all shapes and sizes. Some were bound in leather, others in metal or wood. Some were small and delicate, others large and imposing. Each one was a tangible representation of the gnomarik thirst for knowledge.

Finally, we reached a landing where a group of gnomes were gathered. They were older than most I had seen, their faces lined with age and their eyes filled with wisdom. They were deep in conversation, their voices a low murmur that echoed softly in the vast space. These, Zanmin explained, were the Knowledge Keepers, the custodians of the gnomish wisdom - the guardians of the House of Gnardok. As I approached the Knowledge Keepers, Zanmin busied himself with the gnardoks and scrolls lining the myriad of shelves. Their eyes, filled with a wisdom that seemed to span the ages, turned to me. I was an anomaly in their midst, a human in the House of Gnardok, and their gazes held a mix of intrigue and curiosity.

"I seek knowledge of Gnomarik Spellweaving," I began, my voice echoing in the vast expanse of the library. "Can you guide me to the gnardoks that hold this history?" The Keepers exchanged glances, their eyes flickering with an unspoken conversation. Then, they huddled together, their voices a soft murmur in the otherwise silent room. I waited, my heart pounding with anticipation. The Keepers were the gatekeepers of knowledge, and I was at their mercy. After what felt like an eternity, they turned back to me. One of them, a gnome with a long, silver beard and eyes that twinkled like stars, stepped forward.

"Three gnardok'n hold the knowledge you seek," he said, his voice a soft echo in the grandeur of the library. "The first is a collection of spellweavers' notes, spanning nearly the last 500 cycles - since the dawn of creation. It holds the wisdom and experiences of those who have woven magic into the fabric of our society." He paused, his gaze thoughtful. "The second gnardok is a chronicle of our history over the same period. It tells the story of our people, our triumphs and failures, our discoveries and losses."

"The third," he continued, "is a history of the higher ranks of our society. It traces the line of succession of the Grand Arcanists and provides a detailed account of the Spellweaver and Master Inventor groups." He looked at me, his gaze piercing. "Each gnardok holds a piece of the puzzle you seek to solve. Read them with an open mind and heart, and you may find the answers you seek."

With the Keepers' guidance echoing in my mind, Zanmin and I set off into the labyrinthine expanse of the library. The air was thick with the scent of parchment and ink, a criterion of the centuries of knowledge housed within these walls. The library was a maze of towering shelves, each filled with gnardoks of varying sizes and colors, their spines inscribed with intricate gnomish script.

We spent hours navigating the library's many floors, our footsteps echoing in the vast silence. Zanmin, with his innate gnomish sense of direction, led the way. His small form darted between the shelves, his eyes scanning the gnardoks with an intensity that was almost palpable. The first gnardok we found was the collection of spellweavers' notes. Thankfully, my Saela-Hathir also seemed to allow its user to read foreign languages, not only speak and understand them. It was a massive tome, its cover etched with intricate symbols that shimmered in the library's soft light. The gnardok was a treasure trove of knowledge, each page a window into the minds of the spellweavers who had shaped gnomarik society. The second gnardok, the chronicle of gnomarik history, was found in a secluded corner of the library. It was a series of smaller gnardoks, each one detailing a specific era. The third gnardok was the most elusive. We searched for it high and low, scouring the library's many floors. It was Zanmin who finally found it, tucked away in a dusty alcove. It was a slender volume, its cover adorned with the symbols of the Grand Arcanists. As I leafed through it, I was struck by the depth of the history it contained, the lineage of the Grand Arcanists stretching back to the dawn of creation.

As we sat amidst the towering shelves, the gnardoks spread out before us, I felt a sense of awe. Here, in the heart of the House of Gnardok, I was touching the threads of history, tracing the path of the gnomarik people. After hours of searching, Zanmin and I had finally found the three gnardoks we were looking for. They were heavy and filled with the wisdom of centuries, their pages worn from countless hands that had turned them over the cycles. I could feel the weight of the knowledge they contained, and was eager to delve into them. We made our way back to the entrance where we found Orrick waiting for us. He was engrossed in a gnardok of his own, its title embossed in gold on the cover - The Balance of Magic and Technology.

"Ah, Yoran, Zanmin," Orrick greeted us, looking up from his gnardok. His eyes twinkled with excitement. "I've found something interesting. This gnardok is written by one of the few gnomes who had ever mastered both Spellweaving and Inventing - Rigtin Felwor. I really admired him as a kid. Glist, I still do."

Zanmin's eyes widened in recognition. "I've heard of him!" he said, his voice filled with respect. "His work is what inspired me to get into Spellweaving!"

I looked at the gnardok with interest. "I look forward to reading it," I said, my voice filled with anticipation. "There's so much to learn."

As the three of us stood there, the weight of the gnardoks in our hands, we realized how late it had become. The library's many candles had burned low, their flickering light casting long shadows across the room. The idea of heading to the drink house now seemed less appealing.

"Perhaps we should skip the drink house tonight," Orrick suggested, his gaze shifting between Zanmin and me. "And maybe tomorrow night as well. These gnardoks aren't going to read themselves."

Zanmin nodded in agreement. "I think that's a good idea. We've got a lot of reading to do."

I found myself agreeing with them. "I think that's a wise decision," I said, my fingers brushing against the gnardoks' worn covers.

With our plan for the next few days set, we parted ways. Orrick and Zanmin disappeared into the labyrinthine city, their forms soon swallowed by the shadows. I made my way to the small guest house in the living quarters of the city, the gnardoks heavy in my arms. The next morning, I made my way to the Spellweaver quarters. The quarters were already bustling with activity, gnomes engrossed in their magical studies. I found Felkur in his usual spot, engrossed in a gnardok of his own.

"Felkur," I greeted him, my voice echoing in the vast room.

He looked up, his deep blue eyes meeting mine. "Ah, Yoran," he said, his voice soft yet commanding. "Did you have a chance to read the gnardok I asked you to?"

I hesitated, then shook my head. "The Keepers advised me to find three separate gnardoks," I explained. "It took quite some time to find them." Felkur's expression shifted slightly, a hint of disappointment flickering in his eyes. He muttered something under his breath, a soft complaint about the Keepers and their need to be thorough.

Then, he looked at me, his gaze thoughtful. "Perhaps you should spend the day reading one of the gnardoks the Keepers gave you," he suggested.

I nodded, grateful for his understanding. With Felkur's words echoing in my mind, I left the Spellweaver quarters, ready to delve into the gnardoks I had obtained from the House of Gnardok.

The morning light streamed through the small window of the guest house as I settled down with the first gnardok, the collection of spellweavers' notes from the last five centuries. As I delved deeper into the gnardok, I discovered a wealth of information about the various methods the gnomes had used to find new spell words. Each method was meticulously documented, providing a fascinating insight into the gnomes' relentless pursuit of knowledge. One method involved observing the natural world. The gnomes believed that the world around them was imbued with magic, and by observing it, they could uncover new spell words. For instance, the spell word "*Su*," meaning "Wind," was discovered by a spellweaver who spent days observing the wind, its patterns, and its effects. He noticed that when he channeled his magic while focusing on the wind's essence, a new spell word resonated within him. Meditation was another method used by the gnomes. They would meditate in silence, their minds clear of all thoughts, their senses attuned to the magic around them. This method led to the discovery of the spell word "*Es*," meaning "Essence/Being." A spellweaver, deep in meditation, felt a profound connection with his own essence and that of the magic around him, leading to the birth of this new spell word.

The gnomes also conducted complex rituals to find new spell words. These rituals often involved intricate patterns, specific materials, and precise timing. The spell word "*Nis*," meaning "Fire," was discovered during a ritual involving a circle of fire and a night of full moon. The spellweaver conducting the ritual felt a new word resonate within him as he channeled his magic through the flames. Trial and error was another method used by the gnomes. They would experiment with different combinations of existing spell words, different intonations, and different ways of channeling their magic. This method was often time-consuming and required a lot of patience, but it led to the discovery of many new spell words - "*Quis*" was one such word.

One experiment that stood out was the use of a metallic cube as an object of focus in their experimentation to find new spell words. The cube, made of a unique alloy that resembled bronze in appearance, was said to resonate with the magic, amplifying the spell words' power. The gnomes had discovered that by focusing their magic through the cube, they could uncover new spell words, their magic resonating with the cube in unique ways. One experiment detailed in the gnardok involved the spell word "*Tac*," meaning "Touch." A spellweaver chanted the word while focusing his magic through the cube. The cube resonated with the magic, and the spellweaver reported feeling a tactile sensation, as if he was touching a variety of textures, from rough stone to smooth silk. Another experiment involved the spell word "*Mor*," meaning "Break." A group of spellweavers chanted the word in unison, their magic focused through the cube. The cube vibrated violently, and a small object placed near it suddenly cracked, as if an unseen force had struck it. The gnardok also mentioned an experiment with the spell word "*Vest*," meaning "Footprint." A spellweaver chanted the word, her magic flowing through the cube. The cube pulsed with a soft light, and a series of footprints appeared on the ground, leading away from the cube. As I read, I was filled with a sense of awe. The gnomes' dedication to their craft. They had spent centuries honing their skills, pushing the boundaries of what was possible with magic.

The day slipped away as I read, the gnardok's pages turning under my fingers. I realized it was about the end of the workday, and it was time to meet up with Zanmin and Orrick. I gathered the gnardoks, their weight a comforting presence in my arms, and made my way down to the entrance of the Spellweaver quarters. The quarters were quieter now, the bustle of the day giving way to the calm of the evening. As I reached the entrance, I saw Zanmin and Orrick waiting for me. They were deep in conversation, their voices a soft murmur in the quiet of the evening. As I approached, they looked up, their faces lighting up in recognition.

"Yoran," Zanmin greeted me, his voice warm. "How was your day?"

I smiled, the gnardoks in my arms. "It was enlightening," I said, my voice filled with the excitement of the day's discoveries.

"I learned a great deal about the Gnomarik history of experimentation with spell words," I told Zanmin and Orrick, my fingers brushing against the gnardoks' worn covers. "The methods they used, the discoveries they made... it's all fascinating."

Zanmin's eyes twinkled with interest. "That sounds like a productive day," he said, his gaze shifting to the gnardoks in my arms.

I nodded, then turned to Orrick. "What about you?" I asked. "Did you find anything useful in your gnardok?"

Orrick's smile widened, a hint of excitement in his eyes. "Let's go to the drink house," he said, his voice filled with anticipation. "I'll tell you all about it." With Orrick's words hanging in the air, we made our way to the drink house. The city was quiet, the bustle of the day giving way to the calm of the evening. The drink house, usually a hub of activity, was unusually quiet when we arrived.

Zanmin and I exchanged confused glances. The drink house was usually filled with gnomes, their voices a lively hum in the background. But today, it was mostly empty, the usual patrons noticeably absent. Orrick, who had been lost in thought, seemed to suddenly remember something. "Ah, I forgot to mention," he said, his voice slightly sheepish. "Something went wrong at the Master Inventor quarters today. Everyone but the apprentices are being kept late to repair the damages."

His words explained the unusual quiet of the drink house. With the majority of the gnomes busy at the Master Inventor quarters, the drink house was left mostly empty. Despite the unexpected quiet, we settled down at our usual spot, ready to delve into the knowledge he had gained from his gnardok.

One groundbreaking theory, or *"brizglim"*, Orrick mentioned was the concept of "Lindivorti Drevfint." This theory proposed that certain spell words, when spoken in the presence of specific technological devices, could create a resonance, or *"lindivorti"*, effect, amplifying the power of both the spell and the device. This could potentially lead to the development of new, more powerful spells and technological advancements. An intriguing hypothesis, or *"brizvorti"* was the "Zilnik Trivdrev Brizvorti." This theory suggested that a spellweaver and an inventor, working in tandem, could act as dual conduits - *"zilnik trivdrev'n"* for magic and technology, respectively. This could potentially allow for the creation of spells and devices of unprecedented power and complexity. Orrick also discussed the "Lindiglim Lindiknik Brizglim." This brizglim proposed that every spell word and every piece of technology has a unique harmonic frequency, or *"lindiglim lindiknik"*. If these lindikniks could be matched, it could lead to a significant increase in the efficiency and effectiveness of both magic and technology. Finally, Orrick touched on the "Zilfint Drevfintel Brizglim." This cutting-edge brizglim suggested that magic and technology could be entangled, meaning that a change in one could instantaneously affect the other, regardless of distance. This could potentially revolutionize long-distance communication and transportation.

As Orrick finished explaining the brizglims, his excitement palpable, we sat in thoughtful silence, our minds buzzing with possibilities. The drink house was quiet around us, the usual hum of conversation replaced by the soft crackling of the fire.

"Could it be a lindivorti issue?" Zanmin finally broke the silence, his brow furrowed in thought. "Maybe the spell words and the devices are not drin'tin properly, causing the malfunctions."

Orrick nodded, considering Zanmin's words. "That's a possibility," he said. "The Lindivorti Drevfint brizglim does suggest that a lack of lindivorti could lead to inefficiencies and malfunctions."

"But what about the Zilnik Trivdrev Brizvorti?" I chimed in. "Could it be that we need a spellweaver and an inventor working in tandem to solve this issue?"

"That's an interesting thought," Orrick said, his eyes lighting up. "It would certainly explain why neither magic nor technology alone can solve the problem - and with the rivalries between groups, would also explain why no solution has been found yet."

We continued to speculate, using the brizglims as our guide. Could it be a mismatch in harmonic frequencies, as suggested by the Lindiglim Lindiknik Brizglim? Or could it be a disruption in the entanglement, as proposed by the Zilfint Drevfintel Brizglim? The three of us continued brainstorming, using our collective knowledge to try and solve the issue at hand well into the night.

The following morning, I returned to the Spellweaver quarters, the insights from the gnardok fresh in my mind. The quarters were already bustling with activity, the air filled with the soft hum of magic. I found Felkur in his usual spot, again engrossed in a gnardok.

"Ah, Yoran," he greeted me. "Did you find the gnardok enlightening?"

I nodded, eager to share what I had learned. "I did," I said, my voice filled with excitement. "I learned about the various methods the gnomes used to find new spell words. They observed the natural world, meditated in silence, conducted complex rituals, and even used trial and error."

Felkur's eyes twinkled with interest. "And what did you learn from these methods?" he asked, leaning back in his chair.

I thought for a moment, then said, "I learned that the gnomes are relentless in their pursuit of knowledge. They're not afraid to experiment, to try new things. And they understand that failure is just a stepping stone to success."

Felkur's face broke into a smile, his eyes filled with pride. "That's a valuable lesson, Yoran," he said, his voice filled with approval. "One that will serve you well in your journey as a spellweaver."

Felkur nodded, his gaze thoughtful. "Now that you have a deeper understanding of our history and the methods we've used to discover spell words," he began, "I think it would be beneficial for you to spend the day experimenting with combining different spell words."

I looked at him, surprised. "You mean, create my own spells?" I asked, my voice filled with a mix of excitement and apprehension.

Felkur smiled, his eyes twinkling with anticipation. "Yes, Yoran," he said, his voice filled with encouragement. "You've learned from the past, now it's time to create the future. Remember, spellweaving is not just about using established spells. It's about innovation, about pushing the boundaries of what's possible with magic."

With Felkur's encouragement, I stepped into the spellcrafting room. The room was filled with a sense of calm, the air humming with latent magic. I took a deep breath, steeling myself for the task ahead. For my first experiment, I decided to combine the spell words "*Tac*," meaning "Touch," and "*Vis*," meaning "Vision." I wanted to create a spell that would allow me to see what I touch, a sort of tactile vision.

I stood in the center of the room, the metallic cube in my hand. I focused my magic, feeling it flow through me, and chanted the spell words.

"*Tac... Vis...*"

As I chanted the spell words, the cube in my hand began to resonate, vibrating with an energy that was both subtle and profound. It felt as if it were alive, pulsating in rhythm with my heartbeat. The cube's surface began to glow, emitting a soft, ethereal light that bathed the room in a gentle luminescence, casting long, dancing shadows on the walls. Slowly, I reached out, my hand moving towards the table in front of me. The air seemed to thicken, time stretching out in the moment before my fingers made contact with the wood. The moment my skin brushed against the rough surface, a rush of sensory information flooded my mind. I could see the intricate grain of the wood, each line a proclamation of the cycles it had lived, each whorl a unique signature of its existence. Minute scratches, invisible to the naked eye, appeared before my inner vision, each a story of use and wear. I could see the faint traces of magic lingering in the air, swirling around the table like invisible smoke, a residue of the spells that had been cast in the room. The world around me faded away, replaced by this tactile vision. It was as if I was seeing with my fingers, each touch translating into vivid images in my mind. The sensation was overwhelming, yet exhilarating. As I pulled my hand back, the images faded, leaving behind a sense of wonder. I looked at the cube, its glow dimming, and I couldn't help but marvel at the magic it had helped me unleash. I had not just touched the table, I had seen it - felt it - in a way I never had before.

I spent the rest of the day experimenting with different combinations of spell words. I combined "*Mor*," meaning "Break," with "*Vit*," meaning "Life," hoping to create a spell that could mend broken things. I combined "*Vad*," meaning "Go," with "*Vin*," meaning "Come," trying to create a spell that could move objects. Each experiment was a learning experience, a step towards understanding the limitless possibilities of spellweaving. And with each success, a profound satisfaction settled in my soul, a sense of pride in my progress. As the day came to an end, I looked back at my experiments, my mind buzzing with ideas for new spell combinations. I found Felkur waiting for me at the entrance of the spellcrafting room. His deep blue eyes were filled with a sense of pride as he looked at me.

"Yoran," he said, his voice filled with warmth. "I've been observing your experiments. You've made remarkable progress."

I felt a flush of pride at his words. Coming from Felkur, they meant a lot. "Thank you, Felkur," I said, my voice filled with gratitude.

Felkur smiled, then reached into his robe and pulled out a stack of parchment. "I took some notes while you were experimenting," he said, handing me the parchment. "They might be useful for your future experiments." I took the parchment, my fingers brushing against the rough surface. The pages were filled with Felkur's neat handwriting, detailing my experiments, the spell words I used, and the results I achieved. With Felkur's notes in hand, I made my way to the drink house, eager to meet up with Zanmin and Orrick. The city was bathed in the soft glow of the setting sun, the streets quiet as the day gave way to the evening.

As I entered the drink house, I saw Zanmin and Orrick waiting for me. They were deep in conversation, their heads bent together over a gnardok. As I approached, they looked up, their faces lighting up in recognition.

"Yoran," Zanmin greeted me, his voice warm. "How was your day?"

I smiled, the notes in my hand. "Eventful! I think, once I finish reading these gnardoks, I will be ready to continue onto whatever help Felkur might need from me."

"Wonderful!" Came Orrick's excited response.

As we settled down with our drinks, we began to speculate once again. We discussed the theories Orrick had shared, the experiments I had conducted, and the potential solutions to the malfunctions in the magic and technology. As the evening wore on, I found myself lost in thought, reflecting on the past few days. I had come to the gnomarik people as a stranger, an outsider. But in just shy of a week, I had learned so much, not just about magic and technology, but about the gnomarik people themselves. I thought about the Spellweavers, with their relentless pursuit of knowledge and their innovative approach to magic. I thought about the Master Inventors, with their ingenious inventions and their unwavering dedication to their craft. I thought about the Keepers, with their wisdom and their deep respect for the gnardoks. But most of all, I thought about Zanmin and Orrick. They had welcomed me into their world, shared their knowledge with me, and immediately treated me as one of their own. We had spent hours together, discussing theories, conducting experiments, and speculating about the future. In the process, we had formed a bond, a friendship that I had not expected but was deeply grateful for.

As I sat there, surrounded by the soft hum of conversation and the warm glow of the fire, I felt a sense of contentment. I had found a place among the gnomarik people, a place where I could learn, grow, and contribute. I had found friends who shared my passion for discovery and my curiosity about the world. I looked at Zanmin and Orrick, their faces lit by the soft glow of the fire, and I couldn't help but feel a sense of anticipation. I was excited about the journey ahead, about the discoveries we would make and the challenges we would overcome. And I knew, with absolute certainty, not feeling the wind beckoning me anywhere else at that moment, that I was exactly where I was meant to be.

Our conversation shifted over the course of the night, further from speculations and over to jokes and tall tales. In the midst of a particularly light-hearted tale from Orrick about a misadventure involving a misfiring spell and a floating teapot, I felt a nudge of realization. With a sheepish grin, I interrupted, "You know, as wonderful as our conversations have been, there's something I haven't admitted."

Zanmin raised an eyebrow, curiosity glinting in his eyes. Orrick simply took another sip of his drink, waiting for me to continue.

"I actually don't *know* how to speak gnomarik," I confessed with a chuckle.

Orrick almost choked on his drink, and Zanmin burst into hearty laughter. "That explains why you babble like a fool!" Zanmin managed to say between fits of laughter.

Joining in their mirth, I added, "You see, since my arrival, I've been using my Saela-Hathir headdress." I tapped the ornate band around my head for emphasis. "It's a magical crown that translates other languages for me. And when I speak, it translates my words into a language that listeners can understand."

Orrick wiped a tear from his eye, still chuckling. "So, all this time, you've been magically speaking in our native tongue? Clever headdress!" He gave a mock bow, adding, "I'm impressed. Although, now I'm wondering how genuine my jokes sound in translation."

Zanmin grinned, "I suppose you'll have to learn gnomarik the traditional way then, Yoran. Through endless hours of tedious study and practice."

I laughed, "Oh, joy. But for now, I'm quite thankful for my trusty translator. Although, if you're willing, maybe you both could teach me a phrase or two."

Zanmin and Orrick exchanged amused glances before launching into a series of hilariously misguiding lessons, each phrase more absurd than the last. And as the evening wore on, the drink house echoed with our combined laughter, bringing with it a deeper sense of camaraderie

Sitting in the quiet of the drink house, my mind wandered back over the past six days. I had been immersed in a world so different from my own, yet I was beginning to feel a sense of familiarity with the gnomarik way of life. I thought about the intricate mechanisms of their technology, the way the stone gears and cogs ground and clicked in harmony, the soft glow of magic-infused crystals embedded in their walls. I was fascinated by their ingenious inventions, from the self-watering plants in their gardens to the magically heated stones that kept their homes warm.

I thought about their food, the unique flavors and textures, the way they combined ingredients in ways I had never imagined. I remembered the first time I tasted a gnomarik dish, a blend of sweet and savory that was like witnessing a mythical creature, nimble and graceful, darting through a subterranean grove bursting with luminescent flora. It was a delicate, flaky pastry stuffed with finely diced *"Ikklesprit"* - a chubby, pale creature that thrived in the cool, damp corners of underground caverns. This amphibian, despite its unassuming appearance, boasted meat that was succulent and mildly nutty in flavor. The ikklesprit had been marinated in an infusion of moonlit mushrooms and sunlit honey. These rare fungi, which glowed faintly in the darkness, imparted a unique, earthy sweetness to the meat, elevating its inherent flavors. Yet, what truly took me by surprise were the pockets of wild berry compote nestled within the pie. The burst of sweet tanginess from the compote, combined with the savory richness of the ikklesprit, created a symphony of flavors that played out on my palate. The dish was garnished with a sprinkle of crushed "rikkut", a nut native to the lands just outside their underground city. These nuts emitted a soft luminescence, making the entire dish shimmer under the dim lights, adding a touch of magic to an already unforgettable meal. The whole experience was emblematic of gnomarik culture: innovative, full of wonder, and deeply connected to the land they called home.

I thought of the way they communicated, not just with words, but with gestures and expressions, a subtle language of the body that spoke volumes. I was still learning to decipher these cues, but each day brought me closer to understanding their silent conversations.

I thought about their respect for knowledge, the way they treasured their gnardoks, the reverence in their voices when they spoke of the Keepers. The hush that fell over the room when a Keeper entered. As I sat there, lost in my thoughts, I realized how much I had learned in just six days. I had not just observed the gnomarik way of life, I had experienced it, lived it. And with each passing day, I was becoming more and more a part of this fascinating world.

XX

The Gnardoks of Time

Over the coming weeks, I delved into the other two gnardoks. The first was a detailed account of the gnomarik culture over the last 468 cycles. I had been told it spanned 500 cycles, but the gnomes had only started recording their history about 32 cycles after their existence began. I read, allowing myself to be transported back in time, witnessing the evolution of the gnomarik people. I learned about their early struggles, their triumphs, and their failures. I read about their discoveries, their inventions, and their advancements in magic. I saw their society grow and change, adapting to the challenges and opportunities of each new cycle. As I delved into the gnardok detailing the history of gnomarik society, a few key events stood out, each marking a significant turning point in their history.

The first was the Great Unearthing, occurring around 50 cycles into their recorded history. The gnomes, in their relentless pursuit of knowledge, had discovered a vast underground network of caverns rich in magical crystals. These crystals, they found, could be harnessed to power their inventions. This discovery revolutionized their society, leading to a period of rapid technological and magical advancement, as this was how they initially powered their devices. Crude in comparison to their enchanting process, but it certainly paved the way for them to develop such a finely tuned process.

Another significant event was the Time of Division, about 200 cycles in. A philosophical divide had emerged between those who believed in the primacy of magic (the Spellweavers) and those who championed the power of technology, holding on to the methods of crystal embedding (the Master Inventors). This led to a period of strife and conflict, but ultimately resulted in the formation of the two distinct groups within gnomarik society, each contributing to the society in their own unique way.

The final event I found particularly noteworthy was the recent Invention of the Metallic Cubes, just 33 cycles ago. These cubes, when infused with magic, resonated with the spell words, providing a new way to discover and understand the power of spellweaving. This discovery was still shaping the course of gnomarik society, its full implications yet to be understood.

The second gnardok was equally fascinating. It detailed the histories of the Spellweaver and Master Inventor groups within gnomarik society, each contributing to the rich tapestry of gnomarik history. I read about the individuals who had shaped these groups, their contributions, and their legacies. I learned about the traditions and rituals of these groups, their values, and their beliefs.

One of the earliest Spellweavers, a gnome named Jormin, was known for her pioneering work in spell word discovery. She was the first to propose the idea of combining spell words, leading to the creation of more complex and powerful spells. Her contributions laid the groundwork for the advanced spellweaving techniques used today.

Another key figure was Valpip, a Spellweaver who made significant advancements in light manipulation spells. Her work led to the development of the gnomes' unique lighting system, which uses magically infused crystals to illuminate their underground cities.

In the Master Inventors' history, a gnome named Warbis stood out. He was the inventor of the first magic-infused machinery, a breakthrough that revolutionized gnomish technology. His inventions, though rudimentary by today's standards, were the precursors to the intricate devices that now power gnomarik society.

Additionally, the gnardok detailed the contributions of Calji, a Master Inventor known for his work on the gnomes' transportation system. His invention of the gear-driven carts significantly improved the gnomes' mobility within their vast network of caverns, making travel faster and more efficient.

The gnardok also detailed the line of succession of the Grand Arcanists. One particularly notable Grand Arcanist was Lantor. He was known for his balanced approach to magic and technology, advocating for a harmonious coexistence of the two. His tenure saw a period of peace and prosperity in gnomarik society, a display of his wise and balanced leadership.

The current Grand Arcanist, a gnome named Urilin, had a unique path to his position. Urilin was not a typical choice for the role of Grand Arcanist. He was neither a Master Inventor nor a Spellweaver, but rather a Keeper, a guardian of the gnardoks and a scholar of gnomarik history. Urilin's appointment was a result of a period of turmoil in gnomarik society. The previous Grand Arcanist had passed away unexpectedly, and the Spellweavers and Master Inventors were locked in a power struggle, each group pushing for one of their own to take up the mantle. In an unprecedented move, the Keepers intervened, proposing Urilin as a neutral candidate. Urilin's main contribution to gnomarik society was not through groundbreaking inventions or powerful spells, but through his wisdom and his deep understanding of gnomarik history. He was known for his ability to mediate conflicts, his decisions often drawing from the lessons of the past. His leadership style was characterized by a focus on maintaining the knowledge and histories of the past, to better prepare for the future.

As I read, I felt a deep sense of respect for the gnomarik people. They had faced many intellectual and philosophical challenges, yet they had persevered, driven by their relentless pursuit of knowledge and their unwavering belief in the power of magic and technology.

During those weeks of reading the gnardoks, my days fell into a rhythm. Each morning, I would make my way to the Spellweaver quarters, where Felkur awaited me. Under his guidance, I continued to learn about the art of spellweaving, each day bringing new insights and understanding. Felkur was a patient teacher, his deep knowledge of spellweaving evident in every lesson. He guided me through the complexities of combining spell words, his explanations clear and concise. I could feel myself growing more confident, my understanding of Alara's primal forces deepening with each passing day. In the evenings, I would meet with Zanmin and Orrick at the drink house. We would share our experiences of the day, our conversations filled with laughter and speculation. Zanmin's enthusiasm was infectious.

As we sat in the drink house, Zanmin would often regale us with tales of his Master, a Spellweaver named Quovyn. Quovyn was known for his eccentricities, and Zanmin's stories never failed to bring a smile to our faces. One such story was about the time Quovyn decided to experiment with a new spell word combination in the middle of the night. "He woke me up at the crack of dawn, his eyes wide with excitement," Zanmin began, his eyes twinkling with amusement. "He had spent the entire night experimenting with a new spell word combination. But instead of the expected result, he had accidentally turned all his hair bright pink! It took a week for the effect to wear off." Another tale involved Quovyn's peculiar habit of talking to his plants. "He insists they, not only grow better when he converses with them, but that they develop their own form of communication to reciprocate," Zanmin explained, trying to suppress his laughter. "He has full-blown conversations with them, discussing everything from the weather to the latest developments in spellweaving. It's quite a sight to behold."

Zanmin also shared a story about the time Quovyn misplaced his magical staff. "He was in a panic, searching high and low for it," Zanmin recounted. "He was convinced it had been stolen. Turns out, he had used a vanishing spell on it by accident and forgotten about it. The staff reappeared a day later, right in the middle of the Spellweaver quarters!" Each of Zanmin's stories painted a vivid picture of Quovyn, his eccentricities making him all the more endearing. Despite his quirks, it was clear that Quovyn was a dedicated and skilled Spellweaver, his unconventional methods often leading to unexpected breakthroughs.

Stories of Zanmin's Master brought much humor and laughter to our trio, Orrick, on the other hand, while quite humorous and mirthful, was more reserved, his comments thoughtful and insightful. He was less forthcoming about his master, a Master Inventor known as Urigim. From the few comments Orrick made, I gathered that Urigim was a stern and rigid individual, his approach to teaching as precise and unforgiving as the intricate devices he created.

"He doesn't tolerate mistakes," Orrick once said, his voice carrying a hint of respect mixed with frustration. "Every gear, every spring, every crystal has to be in its exact place. One wrong move and you have to start all over again."

Despite his strictness, it was clear that Urigim was highly respected among the Master Inventors. "He's a genius," Orrick admitted one evening, his tone begrudgingly admiring. "His inventions are unlike anything I've ever seen. They're complex, efficient, and incredibly precise. Just like him."

Urigim's strictness extended beyond his work. "He expects punctuality, efficiency, and absolute dedication," Orrick told us. "There's no room for idle chatter or unnecessary breaks. Every moment is dedicated to our craft." Despite the demanding nature of his master, Orrick never complained. It was clear that he respected Urigim, even if he didn't always agree with his methods. And from what I could tell, Orrick was learning a great deal under Urigim's tutelage.

One evening, as our laughter died down from Zanmin's latest Quovyn tale, Orrick leaned forward, swirling the sweet, shimmering liquid in his cup thoughtfully. "Yoran," he began, "you've been to so many places. What's the most fascinating landscape you've ever encountered?"

I thought for a moment, reminiscing about the vast stretches of land I'd crossed. "The orukuthûndar desert was something to behold," I replied. "Miles of golden sand, shimmering under the sun, with occasional oases springing up like mirages."

Orrick's eyes widened in awe. "I've always wanted to explore places like that. My adventures have been limited to the outskirts of

Vindelkor, but there's something equally mesmerizing about the forest beyond our city walls."

"*Vindelkor.*" A week in the city, and I realized this was the first I'd heard it called by name. I recalled the stormy night I found refuge in Vindelkor, nodding in agreement. "That forest, with its whispering trees and dancing shadows, is quite a sight. It's how I stumbled upon this hidden city."

A glint of excitement sparkled in Orrick's eyes. "Ah, that forest! I've mapped it, you know." He reached into his bag, pulling out a carefully rolled parchment. As he spread it out on the table, intricate details of the forest were revealed, showing pathways, clearings, and even some hidden groves. "This is my pride and joy," he said with evident pride. "Every nook and cranny of the forest, right up to the crack in the cliffside wall you entered through."

I looked at the map in amazement. "Your work is impeccable, Orrick. This is a treasure."

Zanmin nodded in agreement. "It's impressive how both of you, from different worlds, have such a thirst for exploration. It's as if the universe brought together two kindred spirits." We all raised our mugs in a toast, our bond of friendship and shared love for adventure deepening.

On my fifth week with the gnomes, Felkur seemed particularly thoughtful. He watched me as I practiced the spell word combinations he had taught me, a faint smile on his face. When I finished, he nodded, seemingly satisfied with my progress.

"Yoran," he began, his voice serious. "I believe you have learned a great deal in these past days. You have shown dedication and a quick understanding of our ways. I think it is time for you to assist me with a problem I've been working on." He led me to a corner of the Spellweaver quarters, where a large metallic cube sat on a table. The cube was similar to the ones I had seen before, but it was larger and covered in intricate runes. Felkur explained that this was a Master Cube, a more powerful version of the metallic cubes used in spell word experimentation.

"For some time now, I've been trying to unlock a new level of power from the Master Cube," Felkur explained. "I believe it holds the potential for more complex spell word combinations, ones that could greatly advance our understanding of magic. However, despite my efforts, I've been unable to make any progress." Felkur's problem was a complex one. The Master Cube was a mystery, its full potential yet to be unlocked.

For the next several days, Felkur and I dedicated ourselves to the Master Cube. We spent hours each day in the Spellweaver quarters, surrounded by the soft glow of the magic-infused crystals, the air filled with the hum of concentrated magic. Felkur led the experiments, his hands moving with practiced ease as he chanted spell words, his eyes focused on the Master Cube. I was by his side, quill in hand, meticulously documenting each spell word combination, each reaction from the Master Cube, each theory, each brizglim Felkur proposed. Despite our efforts, progress was slow. The Master Cube remained largely unresponsive, its surface glowing faintly but showing no signs of the increased power Felkur was seeking. Each failed attempt was a setback, but Felkur remained undeterred. His determination was unwavering, his belief in the potential of the Master Cube unshaken.

As the days passed, I found myself growing more invested in the problem. I shared Felkur's frustration with each unsuccessful attempt, and his hope with each new theory. And so, we continued our work, the days blending into one another in a cycle of experimentation and documentation. We were yet to make a breakthrough, but I could feel it. We were on the brink of something significant.

On the final day of this leg of our experiments, the fourth of those several days, something went wrong. We were in the middle of a particularly complex spell word combination when it happened. Felkur was chanting, his voice steady and confident, his eyes focused on the Master Cube. I was by his side, quill poised over parchment, ready to document the results.

"*Threl-Vin-Arg...*"

The combination of spell words, chanted by Felkur, meaning "Connect-Come-Silver", which Felkur anticipated that the intended result of this combination was to call upon the essence of silver, a metal known for its high conductivity, to enhance the connection between the caster and the Master Cube. This was supposed to allow for a deeper and more powerful interaction with the cube's magic. Suddenly, the Master Cube began to glow brighter than I had ever seen before. It pulsed with a powerful energy, the air around it crackling with magic, the familiar aroma of petrichor that I had come to associate with the use of magic. Felkur's chanting faltered, his eyes widening in surprise. Then, without warning, emitting a loud 'POP' accompanied by the split-second blast of lightning, the Master Cube went dark. The glow disappeared, the hum of magic abruptly silenced. Felkur stumbled back, a look of shock on his face. I dropped my quill, my heart pounding in my chest.

We stared at the Master Cube, its surface now dull and lifeless. It was clear that something had gone wrong, something beyond our understanding. The underlying issue that had been causing magic and technology to malfunction in Vindelkor had now affected our experiment. Felkur was silent for a moment, his gaze fixed on the Master Cube. Then, he turned to me, his expression grave. "It seems we have a bigger problem than we thought, Yoran," he said, his voice heavy with concern. "We need to find out what's causing this, and we need to do it quickly."

"Wait," I said, my mind racing. "The master Spellweavers still don't know what's going on?" Felkur looked at me, surprise flickering in his eyes. He seemed to realize that he had shared more with me than he had intended. After a moment, he let out a sigh, his shoulders slumping slightly.

"No, Yoran," he admitted, his voice heavy. "We don't know what's happening. Neither do the Master Inventors." He paused, looking at me with a serious expression. "There's something you should know," he said. "Something that might help you understand the gravity of our situation." He went on to explain about the Chrono-Core, a grand clockwork device that was imbued with magic. It kept time for the gnomes, but more importantly, it connected and powered their underground city and magical mechanisms.

"Recently, the Chrono-Core has begun losing time," Felkur said. "Its magical aura is waning. As a result, our inventions are malfunctioning, and our magical experiments are becoming increasingly unpredictable and dangerous." He looked at me, his eyes filled with worry. "The Spellweavers and Master Inventors are divided on the cause," he said. "Some believe it's a problem with the Chrono-Core itself, while others think it's an issue with the magic that powers it. But the truth is, we just don't know." The gravity of the situation hit me then. The gnomes were facing a crisis, one that threatened their way of life. And I, a stranger in their society, had somehow found myself in the middle of it all.

Felkur looked at me, his expression thoughtful. "Yoran," he began, his voice serious. "I want to thank you for your assistance. You've been a great help, and I appreciate your dedication." He paused, his gaze steady. "However, I believe it's time for you to go and spend some time learning from the Master Inventors, as the Grand Arcanist instructed. I had hoped that we would finally gain some traction with the Master Cube, but until things get sorted out amongst the higher-ranking Spellweavers and Master Inventors and the Chrono-Core is repaired, that doesn't seem likely."

He gave me a small smile, his eyes twinkling with a hint of mischief. "Who knows," he said. "Maybe we just need an outsider's perspective." His smile faded, and he looked at me with a serious expression. "Yoran," he said, his voice low. "I need to ask you not to tell anyone about what I've revealed to you. The nature of the issues we're wrestling with... it's sensitive information. Can I trust you to keep this to yourself?"

I nodded, understanding the gravity of his request. "Of course, Felkur," I said. "You have my word. As the work day came to a close, I found myself filled with a sense of urgency.

XXI

Speculation

Despite my promise to Felkur, I knew I had to share what I had learned with Zanmin and Orrick. I hurried through the winding tunnels of Vindelkor, my footsteps echoing in the quiet. The usual hum of activity had died down, the city settling into the calm of the evening. As I neared the drink house, I could hear the faint sounds of conversation and laughter, a comforting reminder of the camaraderie I had found among the gnomes. As I entered the drink house, I scanned the room for Zanmin and Orrick. I spotted Zanmin at our usual table, a grim expression on his face. In front of him was a drink, thicker and, judging by the whiff I caught of his breath, stronger than what he usually had. Orrick was nowhere to be seen. A sense of unease settled over me as I made my way to the table. Zanmin looked up as I approached, his eyes meeting mine. There was a heaviness in his gaze, a worry that mirrored my own. I took a seat across from him, my mind racing with questions. But for now, I remained silent, waiting for Zanmin to speak. The news I had to share could wait a moment longer.

Zanmin looked at me, his gaze heavy. "Yoran," he began, his voice barely above a whisper. "Something happened today... at the Master Inventor quarters." He paused, taking a deep breath before continuing. "There was a malfunction. A big one. I was with master Quovyn in the

Spellweaver quarters when it happened, I only know what I've heard. But... Orrick was involved."

My heart dropped at his words. "Orrick?" I echoed, my voice tight. "Is he...?"

Zanmin shook his head quickly. "He's alive," he assured me. "But he's been seriously injured. He's in the medical house now. They're not letting anyone in to see him."

I felt a wave of relief at his words, quickly followed by a surge of worry. Orrick was hurt, and there was nothing I could do to help him. I felt a pang of guilt, knowing that I had been so caught up in my own problems that I hadn't even considered that something might have happened to him.

Zanmin was silent for a moment, his gaze distant. "I don't know what went wrong," he admitted. "All I know is that something malfunctioned, and Orrick was caught in the middle of it." He looked at me then, his eyes filled with worry. "Yoran," he said, his voice quiet. "What are we going to do?"

As Zanmin's words sank in, a whirlwind of emotions swept through me. Guilt was the first to hit, a heavy weight in my chest. The malfunction with the Master Cube... could it have somehow caused the accident in the Master Inventor quarters? Was I, in some way, responsible for Orrick's injuries? Duty followed closely behind. We had started this quest together, the three of us. We had pledged to uncover the mystery behind the malfunctions plaguing gnomarik society. Now, with Orrick injured and our progress at a standstill, that duty felt more important than ever. But it was the unexpected memory of Tornu that hit me hardest. My mentor, gravely wounded and bedridden for weeks before his death. I had been by his side, helpless to do anything but watch as he slowly slipped away. The memory was a painful one, a stark reminder of the fragility of life.

I looked at Zanmin, my resolve hardening. "We continue," I said, my voice steady. "We find out what's causing these malfunctions. We do it for Orrick, and for all of gnomarik society." And silently, I added a promise to myself. I would not let Orrick's fate be the same as Tornu's. I would do everything in my power to prevent that.

I took a deep breath, steeling myself for what I had to say next. "Zanmin," I began, my voice steady. "There's something else. Something Felkur told me." Zanmin looked at me, his eyes wide. "What is it?" he asked, his voice filled with apprehension.

I told him about the Chrono-Core, about how it was losing time and its magical aura was waning. I explained how this was causing the inventions to malfunction and the magical experiments to become unpredictable and dangerous. I told him about the division among the Spellweavers and Master Inventors, about how they were unsure of the cause.

As I spoke, Zanmin's expression shifted from surprise to concern. "The Chrono-Core?" he echoed, his voice barely above a whisper. "But that... that powers everything. If it's failing..." He trailed off, the implications of what I had said sinking in. We sat in silence for a moment, the weight of our situation pressing down on us.

Finally, Zanmin spoke. "We need to do something," he said, his voice filled with determination. "We need to find out what's causing this." I nodded, feeling a renewed sense of purpose. We were in this together, and we would face whatever came our way.

The next day, I made my way to the Master Inventor quarters. The air was thick with tension, the usual hum of activity replaced by a somber quiet. I was met by one of the masters, a gnome named Jexif. Jexif was a wiry gnome, his frame lean and his movements quick and precise. His hair was a shock of bright red, standing out starkly against his pale skin. His eyes were a sharp blue, filled with intelligence and a hint of impatience. He was known for his innovative inventions and his no-nonsense attitude.

"Yoran," he greeted me, his voice brisk. "We've been awaiting the completion of your time with the Spellweavers. However, recent events have necessitated a change in plans." He paused, his gaze meeting mine. "You were originally going to be assigned to master Tragrim," he continued. "But given the circumstances, you will now be working with Urigim."

The name was familiar. Urigim was Orrick's master. A sense of unease settled over me, but I pushed it aside. This was my chance to learn more about the Master Inventors, to gain a deeper understanding of their work. And perhaps, in doing so, I could help find a solution to the problems plaguing gnomarik society.

"I understand," I said, meeting Jexif's gaze. "I'm ready to begin." With a nod, Jexif led me deeper into the Master Inventor quarters, my journey into the heart of gnomish technology beginning. Jexif led me through the labyrinthine corridors of the Master Inventor quarters, each turn revealing a new marvel of gnomish technology. Finally, we arrived at a large, cluttered workshop, the air filled with the scent of oil and metal. Seated at a workbench in the center of the room was a gnome, his back to us. He was hunched over a complex piece of machinery, his hands moving with a precision and speed that was almost mesmerizing.

"Urigim," Jexif called out, his voice echoing in the large room.

The gnome at the workbench stiffened, then slowly turned to face us. His face was lined with age, his skin a deep bronze. His eyes were a piercing silver, sharp and focused. His hair was a stark white, contrasting sharply with his dark skin. He was dressed in a simple tunic, stained with oil and grease.

"Yoran," Jexif introduced me. "Your new apprentice."

Urigim studied me for a moment, his gaze assessing. Then, with a nod of approval, he turned back to his work. "Welcome, Yoran," he said, his voice gruff. "I hope you're ready to work." Urigim didn't look up from his work as he spoke, his hands continuing their precise movements over the intricate machinery in front of him. "And I hope you're tired of reading and babbling.," he said, his voice gruff. "Because it's time to learn valuable things now."

I blinked in surprise, taken aback by his blunt words. "I... I've learned a lot from the Spellweavers," I began, but Urigim cut me off with a dismissive wave of his hand.

"Spellweavers," he scoffed, finally looking up at me. His silver eyes held a spark of challenge. "Always with their heads in the clouds, lost in their gnardoks and their magic. They forget the value of real, tangible work. Of creating something with your own two hands." He gestured around the workshop, at the various pieces of machinery and tools scattered about. "This," he said, his voice filled with pride, "this is where real progress is made. Not in some dusty library, but here, in the heart of invention."

I could see the rivalry between the Spellweavers and the Master Inventors firsthand, the tension between the two groups clear in Urigim's words. But I also saw the passion in his eyes, the dedication to his craft.

"I understand," I said, meeting his gaze. "I'm ready to learn."

Urigim nodded, a hint of approval in his eyes. "Good," he said. "Then let's get to work." Urigim started the day by showing me several different technologies, each one already enchanted by the Spellweavers. He explained the purpose of each device, from a clockwork bird that could deliver messages to a small, handheld device that could produce light or heat at the utterance of a spell word.

"These are the basics," Urigim said, his voice gruff. "The Spellweavers have started the process, now it's up to us to do the work." He showed me how to assemble the pieces, his hands moving with a precision and speed that was mesmerizing to watch. He explained the importance of each component, from the smallest cog to the largest gear, and how they all worked together to create a functioning piece of technology.

The rest of the day was spent in tedious work, assembling the devices under Urigim's watchful eye. It was a far cry from the theoretical work I had done with the Spellweavers, but there was a certain satisfaction in seeing the tangible results of my efforts. By the end of the day, my hands were covered in oil and my back ached from hunching over the workbench, but I had successfully assembled several of the devices. Urigim gave a gruff nod of approval, a rare compliment from the stern Master Inventor.

"Tomorrow, we'll move on to more complex devices," he said tersely. Exhausted but satisfied, I left the workshop, ready for a well-deserved rest.

After a long day of work, I made my way to the drink house, my mind buzzing with the day's lessons. Zanmin was already there when I arrived, a somber expression on his face.

"Yoran," he greeted me, his voice subdued. "How was your first day with the Master Inventors?" I shared with him the day's events, from the gruff introduction to my new master, to the satisfaction of assembling the devices. Zanmin listened attentively, his eyes lighting up at the mention of the enchanted technologies.

"But enough about me," I said, once I had finished recounting my day. "How's Orrick?"

Zanmin's expression darkened. "No change," he said, his voice heavy. "He's still unconscious. The healers are doing everything they can, but..." He trailed off, his gaze distant. The usually lively gnome seemed weighed down by worry, his usual spark dimmed.

"We just have to hope," I said, placing a hand on his shoulder. "Orrick is strong. He'll pull through."

Zanmin nodded, managing a small smile. "You're right, Yoran," he said. "We just have to keep hoping." Zanmin and I sat in silence for a moment, the noise of the drink house fading into the background. Finally, I broke the silence.

"Urigim is my new master," I said, watching for Zanmin's reaction.

Zanmin's eyebrows shot up in surprise. "Urigim?" he repeated. "Orrick's master? That's... unexpected."

I nodded, taking a sip of my drink. "He's a tough one," I admitted. "But I think I can learn a lot from him."

Zanmin nodded, his expression thoughtful. "Urigim is one of the best," he said. "If anyone can teach you about gnomarik technology, it's him."

We fell into silence again, our thoughts turning to the problems plaguing gnomarik society. "Zanmin," I began, "what do you think is wrong with the Chrono-Core?"

Zanmin sighed, running a hand through his hair. "I don't know, Yoran," he admitted. "It's like nothing we've ever seen before. The Chrono-Core has always been reliable, a constant source of power for our city. For it to start malfunctioning... it's unprecedented."

"But there must be a reason," I insisted. "Something must have caused it."

Zanmin nodded, his expression serious. "You're right," he said. "And we need to find out what it is. Before it's too late." We spent the rest of the evening discussing theories, trying to piece together the puzzle of the Chrono-Core.

XXII

Master Inventor

The next few weeks passed in a blur of activity. Each day, I would rise with the sun, make my way to the Master Inventor quarters, and spend the day under Urigim's watchful eye. He had me working on basic technologies, each one a lesson in precision and patience. One such device was a clockwork messenger bird. The process began with the assembly of the bird's intricate clockwork body. Each tiny gear and cog had to be carefully placed, their movements synchronized to mimic the flapping of wings and the tilt of the head. Once the body was assembled, I moved on to the addition of a small compartment for carrying messages.

Another device was a light-producing gadget. This was a small, handheld device that, when activated by a switch, would produce a bright light. The construction of this device was a lesson in the integration of magic and technology - it happened to be the same type of device which Felkur had first shown me how to enchant using the glowing orbs. The device was made up of a series of gears and springs that, when activated, would trigger the small orb imbued with a light-producing spell.

In the evenings, I would meet Zanmin at the drink house. He continued to have new stories to share about his eccentric master. One evening, he regaled me with a tale of how Quovyn had attempted to create a spell to instantly clean his workshop. Instead, the spell had backfired, covering everything in a thick layer of dust. The best news came on the fourth day since I had become an apprentice Master Inventor. Orrick had finally awoken from his unconscious state. He was still gravely injured, but the fact that he was awake was a good sign. Zanmin and I visited him in the medical house, relieved to see our friend awake and responsive.

"Orrick," I greeted him, a smile on my face. "It's good to see you awake."

Orrick managed a weak smile. "It's good to be awake," he replied, his voice hoarse. "So, what'd I miss?"

Zanmin and I spent the next hour filling Orrick in on everything that had happened in the past four days. We told him about my work with Urigim, the devices I had been building, and the theories we had been discussing about the Chrono-Core. Orrick listened attentively, his eyes bright with interest despite his weakened state. We also shared Zanmin's stories about his eccentric master, Quovyn. Despite his condition, Orrick laughed at the tale of the cleaning spell gone wrong, his laughter turning into a coughing fit that had the healers rushing over.

By the time we finished, Orrick looked exhausted but satisfied. "I've missed a lot," he said, his voice weak but determined. "But I'll catch up. I promise." After we had filled Orrick in on the past few days, I decided to ask the question that had been on my mind since I heard about his accident.

"Orrick," I began, my voice hesitant, "what happened, exactly? How did you end up here?"

Orrick's expression turned serious. He was silent for a moment, gathering his thoughts. "We were working on a device," he began slowly. "A clockwork automaton, designed to assist with heavy lifting in the workshops."

He paused, taking a deep breath. "Everything was going as planned. We had just finished the assembly and were about to hand it off for the enchantment process. I was handling the automaton, preparing it for the spell, when... it malfunctioned."

His voice grew quieter, his gaze distant. "There was a flash of light, a surge of magic. The automaton activated prematurely. It... it lashed out."

He lifted his hand, showing the bandages that wrapped around his arm. "I was too close. Didn't have time to react." I felt a chill run down my spine. The malfunction had caused the automaton to attack Orrick. It was a stark reminder of the danger we were all in, the urgency of the situation.

"But you're going to be okay, right?" Zanmin asked, his voice small.

Orrick gave a weak smile. "I'll be fine," he assured us. "It'll take time, but I'll recover. And when I do, I'll be back in the workshop, working to fix this mess."

Zanmin's eyes widened as he took in Orrick's story. "The automaton did all *that* to you?" he asked, his voice filled with disbelief. "I know they're strong, but, glist..."

Orrick hesitated, his gaze dropping to his hands. "Well," he began, his voice barely above a whisper, "the automaton... it roughed me up a bit, yes. But it wasn't the only one."

He took a deep breath, his gaze meeting ours. "Urigim... he didn't realize it was a malfunction. He thought it was a mistake I had made. He... he lashed out." A heavy silence fell over the room. I could see the shock on Zanmin's face, mirroring my own feelings. Urigim, for all his strictness and rigidity, was still a master. To think that he could react so violently...

"He knocked me into a machine," Orrick continued, his voice steady despite the heavy topic. "It broke apart, and the pieces... they landed all over me." The image was horrifying. Orrick, injured and helpless, buried under heavy machinery. And all because of a misunderstanding, a moment of anger.

"I'm sorry, Orrick," I said, my voice thick with emotion. "We'll figure this out. We'll fix the Chrono-Core, stop the malfunctions. We won't let this happen to anyone else." As Zanmin and I left the medical house, the weight of Orrick's story hung heavy in the air. The streets of Vindelkor were quiet, the usual bustle of the evening replaced by a somber silence that echoed my thoughts.

As we walked, I found myself lost in thought. Urigim's actions were a glaring divergence from the mentorship I had experienced with Felkur. The thought of working under him, knowing what he had done to Orrick, filled me with a sense of dread. I thought back to my time with Felkur, the patience and understanding he had shown me. He had been strict, yes, but always fair. He had pushed me, challenged me, but he had never been cruel. The thought of Urigim lashing out at Orrick, causing him such harm... it was difficult to comprehend.

As we neared the guest house, Zanmin broke the silence. "Yoran," he began, his voice hesitant, "are you okay?"

I gave a small nod, forcing a smile onto my face. "I'm fine, Zanmin," I assured him. "Just... thinking." He gave me a knowing look, but didn't press further. We said our goodnights, and I retreated to the guest house, my mind still whirling with thoughts of the day's revelations.

As I settled into bed, I couldn't help but wonder what the next day would bring. How was I to face Urigim, knowing what I now knew? How could I continue to work under him, to learn from him? But as I closed my eyes, I made a promise to myself. I would do what I had to do. For Orrick, for the gnomarik people, for myself. I would face whatever challenges came my way, and I would not back down. No matter what.

The following day, I found myself standing in front of a massive contraption that Urigim referred to as the Mining Machine. It was a hulking mass of gears, levers, and pipes, all working in harmony to perform a task that would have taken dozens of gnomes to accomplish manually. Urigim began the day by explaining the purpose of the Mining Machine. "This beast," he said, gesturing towards the towering structure, "is responsible for extracting precious minerals from the earth. It's a crucial part of our society." He led me around the machine, pointing out the various parts. "These are the drill bits," he said, pointing to a series of sharp, rotating tools. "They bore into the earth, breaking apart the rock and soil. We're working on a new machine that should do the same thing, but just extract the metals and minerals, leaving the rest of the earth and stone alone. But for now, this is what we've got." Next, he showed me the conveyor system. "Once the minerals are extracted, they're transported along these belts," he explained. The belts were a complex network of moving parts, carrying chunks of rock and soil from the drill bits to a series of sorting machines. Urigim then took me to the sorting machines. "These separate the valuable minerals from the worthless rock," he said. The machines were a marvel of engineering, using a combination of mechanical and magical processes to sort the materials. Finally, he showed me the control panel. "This is where we control the machine," he said. The panel was a complex array of levers, buttons, and dials, each one controlling a different part of the machine. As Urigim explained the workings of the machine, I could see the pride in his eyes. This was more than just a machine to him. This was his life's work, as if oil pumped through his veins.

Watching the machine in action, I noticed something odd. The flow of magic within the machine was inconsistent. At times, it was strong and steady, powering the machine with an almost palpable energy. But at other times, it was weak and fluctuating, causing the machine to stutter and falter.

I pointed this out to Urigim, but he dismissed it as a minor issue. "The machine is old," he said, "It's bound to have a few quirks." But I wasn't convinced. This wasn't just a quirk. It was a pattern, and it was the same pattern I had noticed in the Master Cube. After Urigim's detailed explanation, the rest of the day was spent working with the Mining Machine. Urigim had me start with the control panel, familiarizing myself with each lever, button, and dial. Each movement I made had an immediate effect on the machine, causing it to hum, whir, or clank in response. It was like a giant, mechanical beast responding to my commands.

Once I was comfortable with the controls, Urigim had me assist with the sorting process. This involved carefully monitoring the flow of materials coming from the conveyor belts, adjusting the sorting machines as needed to ensure the valuable minerals were properly separated. It was a delicate balance, requiring a keen eye and a steady hand. Next, I was tasked with maintaining the drill bits. This involved regular inspections to check for wear and tear, and replacing any bits that were too worn to function effectively. The work was grueling and physically demanding, but it gave me a deeper understanding of the machine's operation. Throughout the day, I kept a close eye on the flow of magic within the machine. I could see the fluctuations, the moments when the magic seemed to falter. Each time it happened, the machine would stutter, its movements becoming less smooth, less efficient.

As the workday came to a close, I found myself outside the Spellweaver quarters, my body aching from the day's labor but my mind buzzing with the thrill of new knowledge. I had spent the day working with the mining machine, my hands now familiar with the intricate gears and levers that powered the impressive piece of gnomish technology. Zanmin was waiting for me, his face lighting up as he saw me approach.

"Yoran!" he exclaimed, his voice echoing in the quiet evening air. "Ready to visit Orrick?" I nodded, a tired smile making its way across my face. Despite the long day, I found myself looking forward to our visit to the medical house.

As we made our way through the winding tunnels of the Vindelkor, we fell into an easy conversation. We talked about our day, shared our discoveries, and speculated about the future of gnomarik society. Our laughter echoed off the stone walls, a plain distinction from the somber silence that usually filled the medical house. When we arrived, Orrick was awake, his eyes bright despite his frail state. He greeted us with a weak smile, his spirit undeterred by his injuries. We spent the evening with him, our conversation filled with the same humor and camaraderie that we would have shared at the drink house. Despite the circumstances, it felt good to laugh, to forget about our worries for a while.

As our laughter subsided, I found myself looking at Zanmin and Orrick, my friends and companions. I took a deep breath, gathering my thoughts. It was time to share my observations, the strange phenomenon I had noticed while working with the mining machines.

"You know," I began, my voice steady, "I noticed something today while working with the mining machines. There were... fluctuations in the flow of magic."

Zanmin's eyebrows shot up in surprise, while Orrick leaned forward, his interest piqued. "Fluctuations?" Zanmin echoed, his voice filled with curiosity.

I nodded, my mind going back to the moment. "Yes, fluctuations. The magic didn't flow smoothly, it... pulsed, almost. It was the same pattern I recognized in the Master Cube during my time with Felkur." A heavy silence fell over us as they processed my words. The implications of what I had said were clear. The fluctuations were not the cause of the malfunctions, but another symptom. We were still no closer to figuring out what exactly was going on, or determining a solution.

Orrick was the first to break the silence. "That's... concerning," he admitted, his voice grave. "But it's also a clue, Yoran. We may not have a solution yet, but every piece of information brings us one step closer." Orrick looked thoughtful, his gaze distant. "All my time working with the mining machines, I've never noticed that," he admitted, his voice filled with a mix of surprise and curiosity. "I've always been so focused on the mechanics, the physical parts... I never paid much attention to the magic flow." I nodded, understanding his perspective. As a Master Inventor, Orrick's focus would naturally be on the tangible, mechanical aspects of the machines. The flow of magic, while crucial, was often seen as a constant, a given.

"I mentioned it to Urigim," I added, my voice carrying a hint of frustration. "But he wrote it off as a 'quirk from being old'."

Orrick let out a dry chuckle at that, his eyes twinkling with amusement. "Sounds like Urigim," he said, a wry smile on his face. "Always quick to dismiss anything that doesn't fit his understanding." Despite the gravity of our conversation, I found myself smiling. It was comforting to know that I wasn't alone in my observations, that my friends were there to listen and understand.

XXIII

Grivzant

The next day dawned bright and early, the city of Vindelkor already buzzing with activity as I made my way to the Master Inventor quarters. Urigim was waiting for me, his stern face softened slightly by the morning light.

"Yoran," he greeted me, his voice gruff. "Today, we'll be working with the Communication Devices." I felt a spark of excitement at his words. I remembered the Spellweaver mentioning these devices when I first arrived in the city, explaining how they knew of my arrival. Now, I would finally learn how they worked. The Communication Devices were small, intricate pieces of technology. They were filled with tiny gears and levers that clicked and whirred in a mesmerizing dance. Urigim explained that these devices allowed for instant communication within short distances, a vital tool in the bustling city of Vindelkor.

He showed me the spell words '*Hael*', '*Vis*', and '*Threl*', explaining how they were used to whisper visions and connect gnomes, no matter where they were in the city. I watched in awe as he demonstrated, his voice resonating with the device and a soft glow emanating from the runes. Urigim's explanation of the spell words was brief and to the point, reflecting his focus on the mechanical aspects of the devices. He handled the Communication Device with a practiced ease, his fingers tracing over the barely perceptible glow of the enchantment on the mechanism.

"'*Hael*', '*Vis*', and '*Threl*'," he said rapidly, his voice carrying a note of dismissal. "These are the spell words used in the enchantment process. '*Hael*' is for connection, '*Vis*' for vision, and '*Threl*' for...distance."

Though his definitions of the words were incorrect, I did not correct him. In truth, '*Hael*' is the spell word for 'Whisper', '*Vis*' he correctly stated was for 'vision', and '*Threl*' is for 'connect'. I was already familiar with these spell words from my studies with Felkur, but I had never seen them used in this combination before. The way they worked together to create a network of communication was fascinating. Urigim, however, seemed less interested in the magic behind the device. "The enchantment process is handled by the Spellweavers," he explained, his tone terse. "Our job is to create the machinery, the physical structure that houses the magic."

As the day progressed, I learned about the clockwork mechanisms that made the device work. It was a complex process, requiring precision and a deep understanding of the mechanics. But under Urigim's stern guidance, I slowly began to grasp the concepts. By the end of the day, I was able to send a simple message to Zanmin, who was across the city in the Spellweaver quarters. It was a small achievement, but it filled me with a sense of pride and accomplishment.

Throughout the day, I worked alongside Urigim, my hands growing more confident with each task. I assembled and disassembled the devices, familiarizing myself with their intricate mechanisms. By the time the day came to a close, I had a newfound appreciation for the work of the Master Inventors. It was a challenging task, requiring both technical skill and a deep understanding of magic. But as I held the finished Communication Device in my hands, a crescendo of achievement echoed through the vast chambers of my being. As the day came to an end, I left the Master Inventor quarters, my mind still buzzing with the day's learnings. I found Zanmin waiting for me, his eyes sparkling with curiosity.

"How did it go, Yoran?" he asked, his voice echoing in the quiet evening air. I shared my experiences, my words painting a picture of the intricate devices. Together, we made our way to the medical house, our footsteps echoing off the stone walls. The city was winding down for the day, but for us, the day had not yet ended. Orrick was propped up on his bed when we arrived, his face lighting up at our presence. Despite his injuries, his spirit was as strong as ever. We filled him in on our day, our words weaving stories of clockwork devices, magical enchantments, and eccentric masters. We spent the evening in Orrick's company, our conversation light and filled with laughter. It was a welcome respite from the day's work, a chance to unwind and enjoy the simple pleasure of friendship.

The next morning arrived with a sense of anticipation. As I made my way to the Master Inventor quarters, I couldn't help but feel a knot of trepidation in my stomach. Urigim was waiting for me when I arrived, his stern face set in a serious expression. "Today, we'll be working with the automatons," he said, his voice echoing in the quiet room. The automatons were mechanical beings that assisted with various tasks in gnomarik society. They were an impressive feat of gnomish technology, a blend of intricate clockwork mechanisms and powerful magic. But they were also a reminder of the accident that had landed Orrick in the medical house. He led me to a large table where several automatons were laid out. They were of varying sizes and designs, each one a benchmark of the ingenuity and skill of the Master Inventors. Urigim explained the basics of their construction and maintenance, his hands moving deftly over the mechanical parts. Despite my apprehension, I found myself drawn to the automatons. Their intricate mechanisms were fascinating, a complex dance of gears and levers that brought them to life. As Urigim guided me through the process of activating and controlling them, I felt a sense of awe.

As the morning wore on, I worked closely with Urigim, learning the ins and outs of the automatons. It was a challenging task, one that required both technical skill and a deep understanding of magic. But with each passing hour, I felt more confident, more capable. Despite the shadow of Orrick's accident, I was determined to master the automatons, to prove that I was worthy of being an Apprentice Master Inventor. As the morning gave way to afternoon, Urigim transitioned from teaching to assigning tasks. He had a list of chores that needed to be done, menial work that was usually assigned to the automatons. Today, however, I would be the one controlling them. The tasks were simple but tedious. There were gears to be polished, tools to be sorted, and parts to be cataloged. Under normal circumstances, these tasks would have been monotonous, but controlling the automatons added a layer of complexity that kept me engaged. Urigim watched as I directed the automatons, his stern gaze assessing my every move. I could feel the weight of his scrutiny, but I didn't let it deter me. I focused on the tasks at hand, guiding the automatons with precision and care. As the day wore on, I found a rhythm in the work. The whirring of gears and the soft glow of magic became a comforting background noise, a sign of my growing familiarity with the automatons.

As I continued to work with the automatons, I began to notice something peculiar. The clockwork mechanisms within the automatons, usually so precise and reliable, were behaving unusually. At times, the gears would speed up, whirring at a pace that seemed too fast for their design. At other times, they would slow down, their movements sluggish and hesitant, even completely losing power more than once. It was as if the automatons were struggling to maintain a steady rhythm, their internal mechanisms fluctuating without any apparent reason. I kept a close eye on the automatons throughout the day, noting down each instance of unusual behavior.

As I continued to observe the erratic behavior of the automatons, I could see Urigim growing increasingly frustrated. He was a Master Inventor, a man who prided himself on the precision and reliability of his creations. To see them malfunctioning was a blow to his pride.

"These blasted machines!" he growled, his hands clenching into fists. "They should be working perfectly!" But as the day wore on, I saw a change in Urigim. His anger slowly gave way to confusion, then concern. He began to watch the automatons more closely, his eyes narrowing as he observed their erratic behavior.

I could see the realization slowly dawning on him. The malfunctions weren't due to any mistakes on Orrick's part. There was something else at play, something that was affecting not just the automatons, but all of gnomarik technology. Despite Urigim's growing understanding, I couldn't help but feel a pang of anger. His realization, while important, was no excuse for his previous actions. He had lashed out at Orrick, causing him harm, all because of a misunderstanding. Yet, as I watched Urigim, I also felt a sense of relief. He was beginning to understand that the malfunctions weren't Orrick's fault. He was starting to see the bigger picture, to realize that there was a deeper issue at play. It didn't absolve him of his actions, but it was a step in the right direction.

As the workday drew to a close, Zanmin and I made our way to the medical house, our footsteps echoing in the quiet tunnels of Vindelkor. I shared my experiences with the automatons, my words painting a vivid picture of the erratic behavior and Urigim's growing understanding. Zanmin listened attentively, his eyes lighting up at the mention of the automatons. "Orrick will be excited to hear about this," he said, a smile playing on his lips. "And he'll be relieved to hear about Urigim's change of heart. It's about time he realized that none of this was Orrick's fault." But as we approached the medical house, our conversation was cut short. A stern-faced gnome stopped us at the entrance, his expression grave. "I'm sorry," he said, his voice heavy with regret. "But you can't visit Orrick today. A medical device malfunctioned, and his condition has worsened."

The news hit us like a punch to the gut. Our smiles faded, replaced by expressions of shock and concern. We exchanged a glance, our minds racing with worry for our friend. The malfunctions were not just affecting the machines and the automatons, they were now directly impacting the health and well-being of the gnomarik'n. The stakes had just gotten higher, and we were more determined than ever to find a solution. With heavy hearts, Zanmin and I made our way to the drink house. The usual hum of conversation and clinking of mugs felt strangely distant as we found a quiet corner to sit. Our thoughts were with Orrick, who was now fighting for his life because of a malfunctioning medical device. We spent the evening discussing the Chrono-Core, the source of magic that powered all of Vindelkor. We tried to piece together the clues we had gathered so far - the inconsistent magic flow, the unusual clockwork behavior, the strange reactions to spell words, and the unexplained malfunctions. Despite our best efforts, the puzzle remained unsolved. The pieces didn't fit together, and we were missing crucial information. But we were not discouraged. If anything, our resolve was stronger than ever. As the evening wore on, our conversation turned into a brainstorming session. We discussed theories and possibilities, each idea leading to another. We didn't find the answers we were looking for, but we were making progress, slowly but surely.

By the time we left the drink house, the city was quiet, its inhabitants lost in dreams. But for Zanmin and me, the night was far from over. Our minds were buzzing with ideas and theories, our determination unwavering. We would find a solution, no matter what it took. With the weight of the day's news still fresh in our minds, Zanmin and I made our way to the House of Gnardok. The grand library was a treasure trove of gnomarik knowledge, its shelves filled with scrolls and tomes that held the wisdom of countless generations. We spent hours poring over the texts, searching for any information we could find about the Chrono-Core. The grand clockwork device was a marvel of gnomarik technology, its intricate mechanisms powered by a potent blend of magic and science. It was the heart of their city, the source of their power, and now, it seemed, the root of our problems.

From the texts, we learned that the Chrono-Core was more than just a power source. It was a symbol of gnomarik ingenuity, an attestation of our ability to harness the power of magic and technology. It was a source of pride, a beacon of their achievements. But now, it was failing. Its magic was waning, its mechanisms faltering. And we didn't know why. Despite the grim circumstances, our search was not in vain. We found clues, pieces of information that hinted at possible causes and solutions. We didn't have all the answers, but we were making progress. Just as we were about to leave the House of Gnardok, Zanmin paused. "Wait," he said, his eyes scanning the shelves. "That last gnardok referenced another that I think I saw somewhere on the shelves. I want to check it out." He moved towards a dusty corner of the library, his fingers tracing the spines of the gnardoks until he found the one he was looking for. He pulled it out, a cloud of dust puffing into the air, and opened it with reverence.

As he read, his eyes widened, and he let out a gasp. "Yoran," he said, his voice barely above a whisper. "Look at *this*."

He handed me the gnardok, his finger pointing to a passage. It was an account of a time when the Chrono-Core had shown similar signs of instability. According to the text, the issue had been looked into by a Master Inventor named Grivzant, who had discovered a flaw in the magical matrix that powered the Chrono-Core. The gnardok didn't provide any details about the flaw - and it was unclear whether Grivzant fixed it. On top of that, he seemed to be quite a controversial figure among those who knew his name. But it was a lead, a piece of information that could be pivotal to our investigation.

"We need to talk to Urigim," I said, my mind racing. "Or maybe even a higher-ranking Master Inventor. They might know more about this."

Zanmin nodded, his expression serious. "You're right," he said. "We need to find out more about this flaw, and what Grivzant found. It could be the key to solving our problem."

With a renewed sense of purpose, we left the House of Gnardok, the gnardok safely tucked under Zanmin's arm. We had a lead, a direction to follow.

XXIV

Confrontation

As we stepped out of the House of Gnardok, the first rays of the sun were beginning to peek over the horizon. We had spent the entire night poring over the gnardoks, our search for answers consuming us. Despite our exhaustion, there was a sense of accomplishment. We had found a lead, a glimmer of hope in our quest to solve the mystery of the Chrono-Core. But for now, we needed to return to our daily duties. Before we went our separate ways, our stomachs rumbled in unison, reminding us of the missed dinner. A small cook house was already bustling a short distance away, with a line of early risers awaiting their turn. We joined them, and in no time, were presented with *"Mizith Jarkim'n"*. These were freshly baked bread rolls, hollowed out and filled with a creamy, herbed mushroom stew, topped with bits of crispy root vegetables. It was a common breakfast in these parts - quick to make, delicious, and incredibly filling. The warmth of the stew, combined with the crunchy vegetables and soft bread, was a comforting start to the day. With our hunger satiated and our spirits lifted, we parted ways. Zanmin headed towards the Spellweaver quarters to assist his master, Quovyn, with his daily tasks. I, on the other hand, made my way to the Master Inventor quarters, ready to face another day of learning and discovery under Urigim's stern guidance.

As I walked, my mind was filled with thoughts of Grivzant and the magical matrix. I needed to find an opportunity to ask Urigim about it. I didn't know how he would react, but I was prepared for any outcome. The information was too important, the stakes too high. The day began with Urigim introducing me to the Water Purification Tank. It was a fascinating device, a copper vat of water that could purify contaminated sources. As I watched the water bubbling, I couldn't help but marvel at the ingenuity of the gnomes.

Urigim explained the mechanical aspects of the device, his hands moving over the vat with practiced ease. He showed me how the device filtered the water, separating the contaminants and purifying it. It was a complex process, one that required a deep understanding of both mechanics and magic. However, as I had come to expect, Urigim's explanation was focused solely on the mechanical side of the device. He didn't mention the spell words that were used to enchant the vat, or how the magic worked in conjunction with the mechanics to purify the water. Despite the incomplete explanation, I was fascinated by the Water Purification Tank. It was another assertion of the gnomes' ability to blend technology and magic, to create devices that were both practical and magical. And while I was eager to learn about the enchantment process, I knew that would have to wait. For now, I was content to learn about the mechanics, to understand how the device worked from a Master Inventor's perspective.

As the day wore on, Urigim assigned me a series of tasks involving the Water Purification Tank. The work was tedious, requiring a level of precision and focus that was difficult to maintain in my exhausted state. My mind kept drifting to the inconsistent flow of magic I had started noticing in the vat. The fluctuations were subtle, but they were there, a pattern that was becoming all too familiar. I found myself trying to come up with a way to ask Urigim about Grivzant, to inquire about the magical matrix and the potential flaw that had been mentioned in the gnardok. In my distraction, I made a mistake. I misaligned a gear, causing the vat to wobble and spill some of its water. It was a minor error, one that could be easily fixed, but it was enough to set Urigim off.

His face turned a deep shade of red as he launched into a tirade of insults. "Careless!" he barked, his voice echoing in the quiet room. "Inattentive! You're supposed to be an Apprentice Master Inventor, not a bumbling fool! They should have known better than to let you spend time learning from those babbling Spellweavers first!" Urigim's harsh words echoed in the room, but I couldn't hold back any longer. My exhaustion, my frustration, and my concern for Orrick all bubbled to the surface.

"Enough!" I snapped, my voice ringing out. "*You're* careless, Urigim! You're the one who put Orrick in the medical house!"

Urigim's eyes widened in surprise, but I didn't stop. "If gnomes like you would put aside your petty rivalry with the Spellweavers, maybe we could *fix* the Chrono-Core! Maybe Zanmin and I wouldn't have had to spend the whole of the night searching through dusty tomes to find out about Grivzant - and *minimal* information at that!"

At the mention of the Chrono-Core and Grivzant - especially Grivzant - Urigim's surprise turned into rage. He lunged at me, his hands reaching out to grab me. But before he could, my dwarrin dagger, Faelthorn, leaped from my belt and into my hand. The dagger was swift as the wind, its blade gleaming in the dim light. The elandari moonstones embedded in its hilt glowed a deep crimson, a warning of the danger that was looming. I held the dagger in front of me, its blade pointed at Urigim.

The room fell silent, the tension thick in the air. Urigim stood frozen, his eyes locked on the dagger. I could see the rage in his eyes, but I also saw something else. Fear. For the first time, Urigim looked afraid. I didn't want to hurt him, but I wasn't going to back down. Not now. Not when so much was at stake. I held my ground, my grip on Faelthorn steady. I was ready to defend myself, ready to fight for what I believed in.

A rush of emotions surged within me. Anger, frustration, fear, and a burning desire for justice. Maybe it was my time with the savage orukuthûndar that brought it on, but a small part of me wanted to strike out, to make Urigim pay for what he had done to Orrick. I wanted to see him suffer, to feel the pain that Orrick was feeling. But I held that part of myself in check. As much as I wanted to lash out, I knew that it wouldn't solve anything. It wouldn't fix the Chrono-Core, it wouldn't help Orrick, and it wouldn't bring us any closer to finding the answers we needed. Noticing a flicker of sadness, possibly guilt, in Urigim's eyes, seeing his shoulders soften ever so slightly, I took a deep breath, steadying myself.

I looked Urigim in the eye, my voice steady and firm. "Your violent methods of instructing and delegating end here and now, Urigim," I said. "If you know anything about the Chrono-Core or Grivzant, tell me. Now." Urigim stared at me, his eyes wide. For a moment, he looked like he was going to argue, to lash out. But then, he seemed to deflate, his shoulders slumping. He looked at me, then at Faelthorn, and I could see the conflict in his eyes.

Defeated, Urigim lowered his gaze, his hands falling to his sides. "Alright," he said, his voice barely above a whisper. "I'll tell you what I know." He explained that the issues with the Chrono-Core were supposed to be kept a secret from the apprentices. "We didn't want to cause panic," he said, his voice heavy with regret. "We didn't want the people to fall into fear - especially not the Rik'n." When I mentioned Grivzant, Urigim's expression hardened. "I don't know what Grivzant has to do with anything," he said, his voice cold. "And I have no respect for that gnome." He told me about Grivzant's attempts to fix the Chrono-Core, about how he had tried to use spellweaving and inventing in tandem. But according to Urigim, Grivzant had failed. "It was a result of engineering that fixed the Chrono-Core," he said, his voice filled with conviction. "Nothing to do with magic."

As he spoke, I could see the disdain in his eyes, the bitterness in his voice. But then, Urigim shared a truth that stunned me.

"Grivzant was kin to me," he said, his voice barely audible. "Raised me as his own. In the eyes of the tribe, he stood tall and honorable. But within the walls of our shelter... he was a storm, unpredictable and fierce." He looked at me, his eyes filled with a mix of anger and sadness. "You're free to have his notes. Keepers should have them," he said, his voice bitter. "Maybe you'll find something useful in them. But don't expect me to help you decipher them."

With that, he turned and walked away, leaving me standing there, Faelthorn still in my hand. I was left with more questions than answers, but I also had a new lead. Grivzant's notes. Maybe they held the key to solving the mystery of the Chrono-Core. And I was determined to find out. As Urigim walked away, he paused at the door, his back still turned to me. "I'll see you in the morning, Yoran," he said, his voice gruff. "We have work to do." His words hung in the air, a stark reminder of the reality we were facing. Despite our differences, despite our heated exchange, we were both working towards the same goal. We were both ultimately trying to fix the Chrono-Core.

As I watched him leave, I couldn't help but feel a sense of respect for Urigim. He was a tough gnome, stern and unyielding. But he was also dedicated, committed to his work and to Vindelkor. And despite his harsh words and actions, I could see that he cared. He cared about Orrick, about the Chrono-Core, about the gnomarik people.

As I sheathed Faelthorn and made my way out of the room, I felt a renewed sense of determination. I had a lead to follow, a path to explore. After the confrontation with Urigim, I made my way to the House of Gnardok to obtain Grivzant's notes from the Keepers, and then to the Spellweaver quarters to meet Zanmin. We were both exhausted, our bodies yearning for rest, but we had one more stop to make. We needed to visit Orrick. We made our way to the medical house, our steps slow and heavy. But once again, we were turned away. Orrick's condition had not improved, and the healers needed peace and quiet to do their work. With heavy hearts, we left the medical house and headed to the drink house. It was a familiar routine, a comforting end to a long and challenging day. We found our regular table, the worn wood and familiar surroundings offering a small measure of comfort. We didn't stay long, our bodies too tired, our minds too full. But we had things to discuss, theories to share, and plans to make. So, we sat there, two friends in a quiet corner of the drink house, our conversation a low hum in the bustling room.

As we sat at our regular table, I recounted my clash with Urigim, revealing the information about Grivzant and the notes I had been given. Zanmin listened intently, his eyes wide with surprise.

"I confronted Quovyn today as well," he said when I finished, his voice quiet. "Well - it wasn't as... exciting as your encounter with Urigim, but it was revealing." He explained how Quovyn, eccentric as ever, tried to deny that anything was wrong with the Chrono-Core. He evaded the question, coming up with wild and conflicting excuses. But Zanmin was persistent, and eventually, Quovyn confessed.

"The Chrono-Core is malfunctioning, this much we knew," Zanmin said, echoing Urigim's words. "No amount of spellweaving seems to be able to fix it. The Spellweavers and Master Inventors are at a standstill, neither side willing to let the other attempt to fix anything."

As he spoke, I could see the stress in his eyes, the weight of the situation pressing down on him. It was clear that the situation had become out of hand for the Master Inventors and master Spellweavers, which might have partially explained the extreme reactions of our masters at finding out their secret was out. Zanmin also revealed that the Spellweavers had a similar story about Grivzant. They believed that he had tried, and failed, to fix the Chrono-Core using a blend of magic and technology. But unlike the Master Inventors, they believed that it was solely the work of magic that had realigned the Chrono-Core.

As we sat there, the pieces of the puzzle slowly coming together, I couldn't help but feel a sense of hope. We had a lead, a direction to follow. After our conversation, Zanmin and I decided it was time to call it a night. We were both exhausted, our bodies yearning for rest. Zanmin headed to his home, while I made my way to the guest house. The guest house was quiet. I made my way to the bedroom, my body heavy with fatigue. I barely had the energy to remove my boots before

I collapsed onto the bed. Sleep came quickly, a welcome escape from the worries and uncertainties of the day. As I drifted off, my mind was filled with thoughts of Grivzant, the Chrono-Core, and the challenges that lay ahead. But for now, all I needed was rest. Tomorrow was another day, another chance to find the answers we were looking for. And so, I closed my eyes and let sleep take me, ready to face whatever the next day would bring.

The next morning, I woke up early and made my way to the Master Inventor quarters. The city was just beginning to stir, the early morning light casting long shadows on the cobblestone streets. When I arrived at the quarters, Urigim was already there, his back turned to me as he worked on a device. I approached him, my heart pounding in my chest. I didn't know what to expect after our confrontation the previous day.

Urigim turned to face me, his expression unreadable. "Yoran," he said, his voice gruff. "About yesterday..."

He paused, his gaze dropping to the floor. It wasn't much of an apology, but coming from Urigim, it was as close as I would ever get. Before I could respond, he quickly moved on, launching into instructions for the day's work. It was as if the previous day's events hadn't happened, as if we were back to our usual routine. But things were different. We both knew it. There was a tension in the air, a silent acknowledgment of the words that had been spoken, the secrets that had been revealed. But for now, we had work to do. And so, we set aside our differences and focused on the task at hand, each of us lost in our own thoughts, our own worries. And so, the day began, just like any other. But beneath the surface, things were changing. We were changing.

The day progressed in a blur of activity. Urigim assigned me a host of tedious tasks, each one more mundane than the last. I worked on adjusting gears, tightening bolts, and checking alignments, my hands moving with practiced ease. As the day wore on, my thoughts began to drift to Grivzant's notes. I found myself wondering what secrets they held, what answers they could provide. The mystery of the Chrono-Core was like a puzzle, and Grivzant's notes could be the missing piece we needed to solve it. I thought about the inconsistencies in the magic flow, the unusual clockwork behavior, the strange reactions to spell words. All these anomalies pointed to the Chrono-Core, but we still didn't know why or how it was malfunctioning. Grivzant had tried to fix it once, and he had failed. But maybe his notes held the key to his failure, a clue to what we were missing. As the day neared its end, my anticipation grew. I was eager to delve into Grivzant's notes, to uncover the secrets they held.

The workday came to an end, and I met Zanmin at the entrance of the Spellweaver quarters. We made our usual trek to the medical house, hoping to see Orrick, but were, once again, turned away. The disappointment was becoming a familiar sting. We decided to head to the drink house, hoping to find some solace in our usual routine. But as we approached, we found the doors closed. A sign hung on the door, explaining that malfunctions with their food preparation devices and drink coolers had forced them to shut down.

As we turned away, we began to notice something unsettling. The usual hum of activity in Vindelkor was quieter, the city's vibrant energy dimmed. Devices were malfunctioning, hubs were closing, and a sense of unease was creeping into the streets.

"We need to figure this out," Zanmin said, his voice filled with determination. "Let's go to my house and start reading through Grivzant's notes." I nodded in agreement, a sense of urgency filling me. The city was falling apart, and we were running out of time. We needed to find a solution, and we needed to find it fast. And so, we set off towards Zanmin's house, Grivzant's notes our only lead.

We made our way through the city streets, the familiar sights and sounds of Vindelkor taking on a different tone in the face of the growing crisis. The clatter of gears and the hiss of steam from the various devices and machines were punctuated by the occasional sputter and groan of a malfunctioning device. The air was filled with the scent of oil and metal, a comforting smell that was now tinged with a hint of worry.

As we approached Zanmin's house, I realized I had never been here before. It was a cozy little place, nestled between two larger buildings. The exterior was adorned with intricate carvings, and a small garden filled with vibrant flowers and herbs added a touch of color to the otherwise stone-hewn surroundings. Inside, Zanmin quickly set to work, igniting a device with a simple spell word. "*El*," he said, and the device sprang to life, casting a warm, soft light that filled the room. The light illuminated the pages of Grivzant's notes, the intricate diagrams and dense text suddenly coming into sharp focus. As we settled in to read, the urgency of our task was ever-present. But in that moment, in the cozy warmth of Zanmin's home, there was also a sense of hope.

As the hours passed, Zanmin and I studied Grivzant's notes, our eyes scanning the dense text and intricate diagrams. Despite our efforts, we found little that seemed immediately helpful. The notes were filled with complex theories and calculations, many of which were beyond our understanding. Suddenly, the device illuminating our reading material brightened significantly. Before we could react, it exploded with a loud pop, plunging us into darkness. We sat in stunned silence for a moment, the sudden darkness disorienting.

"*El*," Zanmin muttered, and another device atop the table sprang to life. It emitted a soft, steady light that filled the room, allowing us to continue our work. We returned to the notes, our determination renewed. Despite the setbacks, we were not ready to give up. The answers had to be there, somewhere within Grivzant's notes. We just had to find them. And so, we continued to pore over the pages, the soft glow of the device casting long shadows as we delved deeper into the mysteries of the Chrono-Core. As the night wore on and the early hours of the morning began to creep in, my eyes grew heavy with exhaustion. But just as I was about to suggest we take a break to rest our eyes, a particular section of Grivzant's notes caught my eye.

I leaned in closer, my tiredness momentarily dispelled. The notes detailed a mechanical device that Grivzant had designed and enchanted. This device was meant to regulate the Chrono-Core's magic flow. However, the notes also mentioned that the enchantment would likely fade over time, leading to the current malfunctioning of the Chrono-Core. But that wasn't all. Grivzant's notes also contained a blueprint for a new device. This device, which Grivzant had been designing before his death, was meant to permanently regulate the Chrono-Core's magic flow. I felt a surge of hope. This could be the solution we were looking for. The blueprint, coupled with my ability to perceive the flow of magic, could provide the key to fixing the Chrono-Core. But we would need the help of both the Master Inventors and the Spellweavers to make it happen.

I looked over at Zanmin, excitement coursing through me. "Zanmin," I said, my voice barely above a whisper. "I think I've found something." I showed Zanmin my findings, and together, we quickly formulated a plan of action. First, we needed to approach the Master Inventors about constructing the device outlined in Grivzant's blueprint. Given Urigim's previous refusal to help, we decided to approach another Master Inventor, one Zanmin had only heard of in passing: Master Inventor Jexif. Jexif was known for his innovative thinking and open-mindedness. He was a bit unorthodox, even by gnomish standards, with a wild shock of hair that always seemed to stand on end, as if charged by static. His eyes sparkled with a constant curiosity, and he was always eager to take on new and challenging projects.

Once we had the device, we would need to find a Spellweaver willing to enchant it. Finally, we would need to convince both the Master Inventor and the Spellweaver to work together to install the device on the Chrono-Core. This would require at least one Spellweaver to constantly channel their magical energies to keep the Chrono-Core stable, while another performed the final enchantments to bind the device to the Chrono-Core while a Master Inventor attached it to the Chrono-Core. This would likely be the more challenging part of our plan, given the current tension between the Master Inventors and the Spellweavers.

It was a daunting plan, filled with uncertainty and potential obstacles. But it was the best chance we had to fix the Chrono-Core and save Vindelkor. With our plan decided, we finally allowed ourselves to rest.

I took the cushion in the hosting chamber, while Zanmin retired to his bed in the bedchamber. As I drifted off to sleep, my mind was filled with thoughts of the challenging day ahead. But now we had a plan, and we were determined to see it through.

XXV

Chrono-Core

The following morning, we found both the Spellweaver quarters and the Master Inventor quarters closed off to all but the masters. They were desperately trying to find a solution to the city-wide shutdown, each group working in isolation, neither making much progress. The tension in the air was palpable, the usually bustling city eerily quiet. Despite the closures, we managed to find a sympathetic Master Inventor who was willing to let us inside to speak with Master Jexif. The Master Inventor, a kindly gnome named Zantifel, understood the urgency of our mission and escorted us through the busy workshop to Jexif's quarters.

As we entered, we found Jexif hunched over a workbench, his wild hair standing on end as he tinkered with a complex-looking device. He looked up as we approached, his eyes sparkling with curiosity.

"What brings you here?" he asked, setting aside his tools and giving us his full attention. We explained our findings to Jexif, glossing over the fact that we weren't supposed to know about the Chrono-Core's issues. As we laid out our plan, Jexif's eyes widened in surprise. He was clearly taken aback by how much we knew and by the audacity of our proposed solution.

"I must admit, I'm impressed," he said, leaning back in his chair. "You've done your homework. But this... this is a monumental task.

I'm willing to help in any way I can, but I'm not sure my skills alone will be enough to design this device." He paused, a thoughtful look on his face.

"You'll need the best Inventor we have," he said finally. "He's a bit of a hothead... I don't know if you've met him or not, but his name is Urigim."

The mention of Urigim's name sent a chill down my spine. After our recent confrontation, I wasn't sure how he would react to our request. But we were running out of options. If Urigim was our best chance at saving Vindelkor, then we would have to find a way to work with him. With Jexif at our side, Zanmin and I navigated through the bustling workshop towards Urigim's quarters. The atmosphere was thick with urgency and tension. Master Inventors moved about with a frantic energy, their faces etched with worry as they tried to rectify the city-wide shutdown.

The normally rhythmic clatter of tools and machinery was replaced by a chaotic cacophony. As we moved deeper into the workshop, I could see Urigim in the distance. He was hunched over a workbench, his focus entirely on the device in front of him. As we approached, I felt a knot of apprehension in my stomach. I had no idea how he would react to our request, but I knew we had to try. For the sake of Vindelkor, we had to try. As we approached Urigim, he looked up from his work, his eyes narrowing as he saw me.

"Only masters are allowed in here," he said gruffly. "There's no work for you until further notice." Zanmin tried to interject, but Urigim quickly cut him off. "I wasn't talking to you, babbler." he snapped. Taking a deep breath, I stepped forward.

"I apologize for the way things have happened. For lashing out at you," I began, my voice steady. "But we believe we've found a way to fix the Chrono-Core."

Urigim scoffed, a bitter smile on his face. "Let me guess," he said mockingly. "Your solution came from my crazy grandfather's notes?" Zanmin nodded, confirming Urigim's suspicion. I winced, knowing this wouldn't help our case. Urigim scoffed again, his expression turning dark. "Are you aware that his crazy ideas are what got him killed?" he asked. "No one knows who did it, but I'm sure it was because of his ideas."

Despite his harsh words, I could see a flicker of pain in Urigim's eyes. It was clear that Grivzant's death still affected him, even after all these cycles. Just as Urigim was about to dismiss us again, Jexif stepped forward.

"Urigim," he said, his voice firm. "I believe Yoran and Zanmin may be onto something. Their plan has the potential to fix the Chrono-Core - for good."

Urigim turned to Jexif, his eyes wide with disbelief. "You can't be serious, Jexif," he said. "You believe in this... glist?" Jexif met Urigim's gaze, his expression unyielding. There was a moment of tense silence, then Urigim let out a sigh of defeat. The look in Jexif's eyes had told him all he needed to know.

"Alright," Urigim said, his voice barely above a whisper. "I'll help you build this device. But I'm doing this for our people; not for you or your crazy ideas. Sure as glist not for my dead, bastard grandfather." Despite his harsh words, there was a glimmer of hope in his eyes. For the first time since we'd met, I felt like we were on the same side.

With a newfound sense of purpose, Urigim and Jexif immediately set to work on building the device. Their hands moved with practiced precision, their focus entirely on the task at hand. It was a sight to behold, two of the most skilled Master Inventors in Vindelkor working together towards a common goal. Leaving them to their work, Zanmin and I made our way to the Spellweaver quarters. As we walked through the city, we couldn't help but notice the escalating chaos. The usually vibrant city was falling into disarray, the malfunctioning devices causing havoc everywhere we looked.

The air was thick with tension and worry. Gnomes hurried past us, their faces etched with concern. The city-wide shutdown had affected everyone and everything. The urgency of our mission weighed heavily on us as we continued towards the Spellweaver quarters, hoping that we could convince them to help us with our plan. As we neared the

Spellweaver quarters, we spotted Quovyn. Zanmin's eccentric master was easy to spot with his wild hair and animated gestures. We approached him, explaining our plan and the urgency of the situation.

To our relief, Quovyn agreed to help us. His usual jovial demeanor was replaced by a serious expression. "Oh, woeful tidings indeed!" he exclaimed, his voice draped in somber hues. "Yet, behold! If within the labyrinth of fate, a minuscule glimmer of hope flickers for the wondrous Chrono-Core's restoration, verily, my dear comrades, we must seize it with unyielding fervor, like enchanted moonbeams weaving through a tapestry of time!" Despite the gravity of the situation, I couldn't help but be captivated by his eccentricity. He had a way of infusing even the most dire of circumstances with a sense of magical possibility, as if the very fabric of reality bent to his extraordinary will.

With that, he led us into the Spellweaver quarters. The air inside was thick with magic, the energy pulsing around us like a living entity. It was a palpable contrast to the mechanical atmosphere of the Master Inventor quarters, but it was a difference that felt comforting in its familiarity. We were one step closer to implementing our plan, and the hope that had been kindling within us grew a little brighter. As we made our way towards the experimentation chambers, we ran into Felkur. The elderly gnome's eyes lit up at the sight of me, but confusion quickly replaced his initial joy. "Yoran, it's good to see you," he said, his gaze flicking to Quovyn. "But why are you here?"

We quickly explained our findings and our plan to Felkur. As we spoke, his eyes widened in surprise, then narrowed in thought. When we finished, he looked at me, a spark of pride in his eyes. "See," he said, a small smile playing on his lips. "I told you it might just need an outsider's perspective." I asked Felkur for his help, and he didn't hesitate in his response.

"Of course, Yoran," he said, his voice firm. "I'll do whatever I can to help." His words filled me with a renewed sense of hope. With Felkur on our side, our plan felt even more achievable.

As we entered the experimentation chambers, I was struck by the sheer amount of magical energy that filled the room. It was like stepping into a storm, the air crackling with raw, untamed power. Felkur and Quovyn seemed to take it in stride, but Zanmin and I exchanged a glance, both of us feeling the weight of what we were about to undertake. We started by laying out Grivzant's notes, the pages filled with complex diagrams and cryptic notes. Felkur and Quovyn began discussing potential spell word combinations, their voices a rapid-fire exchange of ideas and theories. Zanmin and I listened, trying to keep up, but it was like trying to catch a river with a sieve. By the time we reached the experimentation chambers, Felkur claimed to have already figured out and decided on the spell words for preparing the device; but we would need an additional enchantment to get the device to function with the Chrono-Core.

Hours passed in a blur of magic and theory. We tried countless combinations, each one resulting in a different reaction from the magical energies in the room. Some caused the air to shimmer with heat, others made the room grow cold as ice. Each failure was met with renewed determination, the four of us pushing forward, driven by the urgency of our task. As the night wore on, our list of potential combinations grew shorter. We were running out of options, and the tension in the room was palpable. Then, just as the first light of dawn began to filter through the windows, we found it. A combination that seemed to resonate with the magical energies in the room, causing them to stabilize and flow in a steady, controlled manner:

"Bex-Ma-Flum-Es-Kou-Ron-Agn-Cur-Dil-Flux-Cres-Ast-Ex-Tab-Evan-Eg-Endil-Ni-Fin-Ul-Cro-Ep-Flec-Ardha-Fer-Lae-Cii";

We all felt it, a sense of rightness that filled the room. It was as if the magic itself was breathing a sigh of relief, finally finding the rhythm it had been seeking. "Object-Energy-River-Being-Core-Time-Great-Heal-Love- Flow-Grow-Speed-Outside-Stability-Disappear-Self-Shining-Harmony-Enduring-Pulse-Synchronization-Perpetual-Bend- Heaven-Iron-Eternal-Enchant." We looked at each other, a mix of exhaustion and elation on our faces. We had found our enchantment. Now, all we needed was the device.

As we left the Spellweaver quarters, Quovyn suddenly stopped and began rummaging through his pockets. After a moment, he pulled out a small, intricate device that looked like a tiny clockwork bird. He wound it up, whispered something to it, and then let it go. The bird took off, flying in a wide circle around the room before landing back in Quovyn's outstretched hand. He chuckled to himself, a satisfied smile on his face. "Can't leave without checking the flight patterns," he said, before tucking the bird back into his pocket and leading us out of the quarters. Zanmin and I chuckled at his master's inherent quirkiness.

The journey back to the Master Inventor quarters was a quiet one, each of us lost in our own thoughts. As we entered, we were met by Urigim and Jexif, their faces streaked with soot and sweat. Between them, on a workbench, lay the device. It was a complex piece of machinery, full of gears and cogs, but there was a beauty to it, a stamp of the skill of its creators. Urigim, arms crossed, looked at us with a scowl.

"Well, don't just stand there," he grumbled. "Get on with your higgly-wiggly babble. Let's get this over with." Felkur stepped forward, his hands hovering over the device. He began to chant, his voice low and rhythmic. The spell words flowed from his lips, filling the room with a palpable energy. The device began to glow, a soft, pulsating light that grew brighter with each word. Quovyn watched the process with a goofy smile on his face, his eyes wide with childlike wonder. Zanmin and I watched in awe as the enchantment took hold, the device humming with magical energy. Jexif watched in silent wonder, his eyes reflecting the glow of the device. Urigim just rolled his eyes, but I noticed a hint of curiosity in his gaze.

"*Bex...Es-Flux...*"

Felkur began the rhythmic incantation on the device, weaving intricate tapestries with his gesturing hands above the metallic device.

"*Zek-Nor...*" he continued.

Finally, Felkur uttered the last word of the enchantment, "*Cii.*" The device gave a final, bright pulse, then settled into a steady glow. The first enchantment was complete. All that was left now was to take the enchanted device to the Chrono-Core and put everything together.

As we made our way through the city, the smell of oil and ground stones filled my nostrils, a scent that had become familiar during my time with the gnomarik'n. The city was eerily quiet, the usual hum of machinery and the chatter of gnomes replaced by a tense silence. The only sounds were our footsteps echoing off the stone streets and the distant, sporadic clanking of malfunctioning machinery. The city was bathed in an unusual, dim light, the normally bright and vibrant glow of the magical devices and crystals replaced by a dull, flickering luminescence. The buildings, usually bustling with activity, were now mostly deserted, their occupants either at home or gathered in small, worried groups, discussing the ongoing crisis.

Moving deeper into the city, the architecture became more grand and intricate, the buildings adorned with complex mechanisms and glowing runes. The streets were lined with large, mechanical trees, their metallic branches swaying gently in the breeze, the leaves flickering with a soft, magical light. Finally, we arrived at the heart of the city, where the Chrono-Core resided. The massive, spherical structure pulsed with a faint, erratic light, a clear sign of its instability.

As we stood before the Chrono-Core, I took a moment to truly appreciate the marvel before me. The massive sphere was a verification of the ingenuity of the gnomes, a perfect blend of magic and technology. Its surface was a complex network of gears and cogs, all moving in a mesmerizing, rhythmic dance. The core pulsed with a faint, ethereal light, the magic within it flowing like a river, albeit a turbulent one. Even with the crisis at hand, I found myself captivated by the sheer beauty and complexity of the Chrono-Core. It was a symbol of the gnomes' dedication to progress and innovation, a beacon of their indomitable spirit. But now, that beacon was flickering, its light threatened by an unseen force.

I could feel the weight of the situation pressing down on me. I looked at my companions, their faces set with determination. We were ready.

Standing in front of the pulsating Chrono-Core, I turned to Urigim and Jexif, holding out Grivzant's blueprint. "You two need to attach the device here," I pointed to a specific spot on the blueprint, then mirrored the spot on the actual Chrono-Core. It was a small, flat area nestled between a series of rotating gears and pulsating magical conduits. Urigim grunted in acknowledgment, his eyes scanning the blueprint before he and Jexif moved towards the Chrono-Core. They moved with a precision and efficiency that was impressive to watch. Urigim, his strong arms steady, held the device in place against the Chrono-Core. The device, a complex array of gears, cogs, and magical conduits, seemed to fit perfectly against the surface of the Chrono-Core. Jexif, meanwhile, worked quickly to secure the device. His nimble fingers tightened nuts and bolts, ensuring the device was firmly attached. He moved around Urigim, securing latches and checking their work for any errors. The sound of metal on metal echoed through the chamber as they worked.

As they finished, they stepped back, their faces etched with a mix of exhaustion and anticipation. Next. Felkur began the incantation to attach the device to the Chrono-Core and keep the two working in tandem in perpetuity, his voice echoing through the chamber, each spell word resonating with a power that seemed to vibrate the very air around us.

"Bex...Ma-Flum...Es-Kou...Ron...Agn-Cur...Dil-Flux..."

He began. The words flowed from him like a river, each one a drop of magic that fell into the swirling pool of energy surrounding the Chrono-Core. At the same time, Zanmin and Quovyn began their own incantations, their voices intertwining with Felkur's as they worked to maintain the flow of magic. Their hands moved in intricate patterns, weaving a tapestry of energy that seemed to shimmer in the air. As they worked, I watched, my eyes darting between them and the Chrono-Core. Everything seemed to be going as planned, but then I noticed it. A flicker in the flow of magic, a stutter in the rhythm of the Chrono-Core. It was subtle, almost imperceptible, but it was there. Something was going wrong.

"...Cres-Ast...Ex-Tab-Evan...Eg...Endil-Ni..."

Felkur continued, Quovyn and Zanmin maintaining their channeled incantation as well. Urigim's eyes widened in alarm as he too noticed an irregularity in the device. He darted towards the device, his hands moving swiftly over the knobs and levers, his brow furrowed in concentration. But his efforts seemed to be in vain. The magic continued to build, the amalgamation of petrichor and burning oil a pungent odor that threatened to overwhelm my senses, its pressure mounting like a storm ready to unleash its fury.

As I watched, I began to hear something. A whisper, a murmur, a soft hum that seemed to resonate from the Chrono-Core itself. It was a sound I recognized, a sound I had heard before when I listened to the earth, as the centarion had taught me. It was the language of Alara, the primal forces of the world, speaking through the flow of magic. As I listened, I began to understand what was needed, Alara was telling me the adjustments that had to be made. But before I could relay this to Urigim, disaster struck. The pressure within the Chrono-Core reached a critical point, and with a deafening roar, it lashed out. A wave of pure, uncontrolled magic surged outwards, catching Urigim, still frantically fiddling with knobs and levers, in its path. He was thrown backwards, his body colliding with the rock-hard wall of the chamber. His head hit the stone with a sickening crack, and he slumped to the ground.

Time seemed to slow as I watched Urigim fall. But there was no time to waste. I turned to Jexif, shouting over the roar of the magic. "Jexif! Take over for Urigim! I'll tell you what adjustments to make!"

"*...Fin-Ul...Cro-Ep-Flec...*"

As Felkur's voice echoed through the chamber, his words weaving the intricate enchantment, I watched Zanmin and Quovyn. Their faces were etched with concentration, their bodies rigid as they channeled their magic to stabilize the Chrono-Core. I could see the strain beginning to take its toll, their bodies trembling with the effort. In the corner of my eye, I could see Urigim's still form, a harsh reminder of the danger we were in. But there was no time to dwell on it. Jexif was rushing towards the device, his face pale but determined. Everything seemed to slow, the world moving in a surreal, dreamlike pace. And through it all, I could hear the voice of Alara, a gentle whisper in the chaos. It guided me, its words clear and calm amidst the turmoil.

"Jexif!" I called, my voice cutting through the noise. "Turn the third knob to the right, then push the second lever up!" Jexif didn't hesitate. His hands moved swiftly, following my instructions. I continued to relay the adjustments, the voice of Alara guiding me. Each command was met with immediate action, Jexif's trust in me absolute. And with each adjustment, I could feel the magic's flow beginning to stabilize, the pressure slowly easing.

"*...Ardha-Fer-Lae...Cii!*"

As Felkur's voice reached a crescendo, the final words of the incantation echoing through the chamber, something extraordinary happened. The chaotic flow of magic within the Chrono-Core began to calm, the wild currents of energy slowly aligning with the rhythm of the device. It was like watching two separate melodies merge into a harmonious symphony, each note perfectly complementing the other. The pressure that had been building steadily eased, the danger of a catastrophic explosion receding. The Chrono-Core, once a source of chaos and potential destruction, now pulsed with a steady, rhythmic glow. It was a soft light, pure and serene, a conspicuous discrepancy from the volatile energy it had been emanating just moments before.

A sense of relief washed over me, the tension in my body easing. Grivzant's blueprints had worked. The device, a product of both magic and technology, had successfully regulated the magical flow of the Chrono-Core. The threat of imminent disaster had been averted. As the glow of the Chrono-Core stabilized, I rushed over to Urigim, who was now stirring weakly. His eyes fluttered open, a pained grimace on his face. He looked up at me, his gaze flickering to the now harmonious Chrono Core, and a weak chuckle escaped his lips.

"So it worked?" he rasped, his voice barely a whisper. "*Glist*... I guess that old bastard was good for something after all... glist... *glist*, that means..." His voice trailed off, his gaze becoming distant. I could see the pain in his eyes, not just from his physical injuries, but from something deeper, something that had been festering for a long time.

"*I* killed him, you know," he confessed, his voice barely audible. "Grivzant. It wasn't because of his ideas... but because of how he treated me. The beatings, the insults... I couldn't take it anymore." His admission hung in the air, a heavy silence settling over us. I could see the regret in his eyes, the burden of his past actions weighing heavily on him.

"If I hadn't... maybe... maybe all this never would have happened..."

"But *you*," he continued, his gaze focusing on me. "You've shown me something different. You've shown me that there's more to this world than just machines. You've shown me true respect, something I never thought I'd find." With that, his eyes closed, his body going limp. Urigim, the gruff and stubborn Master Inventor, had breathed his last. In his final moments, he had found a new respect for the world, for the Spellweavers, and for me. It was a bittersweet victory, one that came with the cost of the life of the most skilled gnomarik Master Inventor in Vindelkor.

XXVI

Descent

Carrying Urigim's lifeless body, we made our way out of the depths of the gnomish city, heading towards the Grand Arcanist's quarters. The weight of Urigim was not just physical, but emotional as well. His death marked a turning point, a moment of change that would ripple through the city and its inhabitants. As we walked, I noticed the city coming back to life. The once dark and silent streets were now filled with the hum of machinery and the glow of magic. The Chrono-Core, now functioning properly, was breathing life back into the city. The once malfunctioning devices were now working smoothly, the streets were lit with the soft glow of magical lights, and the sounds of the city were returning to their normal rhythm. The gnomes we passed looked on in awe and confusion, their eyes wide as they took in the sight of their city coming back to life. They watched as we passed, their gazes lingering on the lifeless body of Urigim. The news of his death would spread quickly, and with it, the story of what had transpired. Despite the heaviness of the situation, there was a sense of hope in the air. The city was recovering, and with it, the hope that the divide between the Master Inventors and the Spellweavers could be bridged. As we continued our journey, I couldn't help but feel a sense of optimism. The city was healing, and perhaps, so too were its people.

We arrived at the Grand Arcanist's quarters, the grandeur of the place a broad deviation from the somber mood of our group. We laid Urigim's body before the Grand Arcanist, who looked upon his fallen comrade with a mixture of shock and deep sadness. Urigim had been a pillar of the Master Inventors, his loss was a blow to the entire city. Zanmin stepped forward, his voice steady as he recounted the events that had transpired. He spoke of our discovery of Grivzant's notes, our plan to repair the Chrono-Core, and the tragic loss of Urigim. The Grand Arcanist listened in silence, his gaze never leaving Urigim's lifeless form. When Zanmin finished his tale, the Grand Arcanist nodded solemnly.

"Urigim was a great Master Inventor, his loss will be felt deeply," he said, his voice heavy with grief. "We will honor him with a city-wide farewell tomorrow evening. He deserves to be remembered for his contributions to our city." He then turned to us, his gaze softening. "And you," he said, "you have done a great service to our city. You have not only repaired the Chrono-Core but also bridged the gap between the Master Inventors and the Spellweavers. For that, you have my deepest gratitude."

With the Grand Arcanist's words of gratitude still echoing in our ears, we left his quarters, each of us lost in our own thoughts. Zanmin and I made our way through the now bustling city streets, the city coming back to life around us. The magic was flowing smoothly again, and the city's devices were humming with renewed energy. Our destination was the medical house, where our friend Orrick was being treated. The medical house was a flurry of activity, the healers rushing about, their devices working at full capacity once again. We found Orrick in a quiet corner, still unconscious but looking more peaceful than he had in days. A healer approached us, her face breaking into a relieved smile as she saw us.

"He's going to be alright," she assured us. "With the devices working again, we can properly treat his injuries. He's still unconscious, but we expect him to make a full recovery." Hearing those words, a weight lifted off our shoulders. Despite the loss of Urigim, there was a glimmer of hope. Orrick would recover, and the city was safe once more. As we left the medical house, the city was alive with the hum of magic and machinery, a vindication of the unity of magic and technology that we had achieved.

After spending several hours at the drink house, enjoying well deserved drinks and relaxation, Zanmin and I went our separate ways. As I made my way back to the guest house, I couldn't help but reflect on the whirlwind of events that had taken place over the past three weeks. It felt like I had been in the gnomish city for a lifetime, so much had happened. I thought back to my first day, when I had been introduced to Felkur and had begun my studies in spell words. I had learned so much from him, not just about magic, but about the world and its many wonders. I remembered the evenings spent in the drink house, the laughter and camaraderie that I had shared with Zanmin and Orrick. Those were moments I would cherish forever. And then there was the Chrono-Core. I had been a part of something truly extraordinary, something that had saved the city and its people. It was a feat that I would carry with me in my heart. As I settled into the guest house, I felt a sense of contentment wash over me. I had made a difference here, I had helped in a significant way.

The next morning, the city was quiet, a somber mood hanging in the air. The gnomes had gathered in the city square, a large open space in the heart of the city, for Urigim's farewell ceremony. In the center of the square, a large mechanical platform had been erected. On it lay Urigim, his body covered with a shimmering cloth of bronze and copper, the traditional colors of the Master Inventors. Around him, intricate mechanical devices whirred and clicked, a touchstone of his life's work and passion. The Grand Arcanist stood at the foot of the platform, his voice echoing through the square as he spoke of Urigim's contributions to the city, his unmatched skill as an inventor, and his unwavering dedication to his craft. He spoke of the Chrono-Core, and how Urigim's final act had been to help save the city he loved.

As the Grand Arcanist finished his speech, the platform began to hum with energy. Slowly, Urigim's body began to rise, lifted by a beam of light that emanated from the platform. The crowd watched in silence as the body was lifted higher and higher, until it disappeared into the light. Then, with a final burst of energy, the light exploded into a shower of sparks, illuminating the square with a brilliant display of colors. The crowd gasped in awe as the sparks rained down, each one a tiny mechanical device that whirred and clicked as it fell. As the last of the sparks faded, the crowd began to disperse, each gnome carrying a small mechanical spark as a memento of Urigim. The ceremony was a fitting tribute to a Master Inventor, a final farewell that celebrated his life and his work. As I watched the ceremony, I felt a pang of sadness. Urigim had been a difficult gnome, but he had also been a brilliant inventor. His loss was a blow to the city, and to the world of invention. But his legacy would live on, in the devices he had created, and in the city he had helped save.

After the ceremony, Zanmin and I made our way to the medical house. The city was slowly coming back to life, the mechanical devices humming and whirring as they returned to their normal functions. The air was filled with a sense of relief, but also a sense of loss. Urigim's absence was felt everywhere. As we entered the medical house, we were greeted by the sight of Orrick sitting up in his bed, a weak smile on his face. He looked frail, but there was a spark in his eyes that hadn't been there before.

"Yoran, Zanmin," he greeted, his voice weak but steady. "I heard about Urigim. I'm sorry." We sat with him, recounting the events of the past few days. We told him about Zanmin's confrontation with Quovyn, about my clash with Urigim, about Grivzant's notes and the blueprint for the device. We told him about the device, about how we had brought the Master Inventors and the Spellweavers together, about how we had fixed the Chrono-Core.

As we spoke, Orrick listened, his eyes wide with amazement. "You two did all that?" he asked, his voice filled with awe. "You saved the city!" We nodded, a sense of pride welling up inside us. We had done it. We had saved the city. And in the process, we had brought the Master Inventors and the Spellweavers together, even if only for a moment.

"You've done well," Orrick commended us, his voice weak but steady. I thanked him, expressing my gratitude for his friendship and guidance. I told him to take care of himself and to recover soon. His eyes twinkled with a mix of gratitude and sadness as he nodded, promising to do his best.

Having already spent one month with the gnomarik'n, I stayed with them another four after the restoration of the Chrono-Core, working half of my time in the Spellweaver quarters and the other half in the Master Inventor quarters. But one Orendar morning, as I looked out the guest house kitchen window at the city, now humming with life and energy, I felt a familiar tug. The wind was calling to me, whispering of new adventures and experiences waiting just beyond the horizon. I knew that my time in the gnomarik city was coming to an end. The day had finally come when I had to bid farewell to the gnomarik people and the city of Vindelkor. The streets were bathed in the soft light of dawn as I made my way to the entrance of the city, my belongings slung over my shoulder. Orrick and Zanmin had come to see me off, their faces a mix of sadness and warmth.

As I shared my goodbyes, Orrick approached, a mischievous glint in his eye. With a flourish, he presented a brightly illustrated gnardok to me - Gnarvend Gnomarik. The title was written in gnomarik script, but the illustrations unmistakably depicted gnomarik children engaged in playful antics.

"Thought you might want to brush up on your gnomarik in your travels," he said with a wink, clearly recalling our conversation from the drink house. Laughing, I took the gnardok. "A children's gnardok? Is this your way of saying I'm starting from the beginning?"

Orrick grinned. "Well, every expert has to start somewhere!"

But then, his demeanor became more serious, and he handed me another item. It was the map, the very one he'd spent years drawing out, detailing the forest surrounding Vindelkor. "If you ever find your path leading back to Vindelkor, I hope this helps. No more stumbling through stormy nights trying to find a crack in the cliffside."

A lump formed in my throat as I accepted the map. "Thank you, Orrick. This means more than you can imagine."

He clapped me on the back, his eyes glistening. "Remember us, Yoran. And if the winds of fate bring you back, know that the city of Vindelkor will always welcome you."

With my farewells said to Zanmin and Orrick, I made my way to the Spellweaver quarters. The city was alive with activity, the gnomes working tirelessly to restore their city to its former glory. As I entered the quarters, I was greeted by Felkur, his eyes twinkling with a familiar warmth.

"Yoran," he greeted, his voice filled with a sense of pride. "I'm quite proud of all you've achieved, you know." I thanked him, expressing my gratitude for all he had taught me. He showed me the progress he had made on his Master Cube, still not fully functioning with a steady flow of magic, but he had made significant progress. We shared a moment of quiet understanding before I bid him farewell, promising to return someday. Next, I found Quovyn, Zanmin's eccentric master. His farewell was as unique as he was, filled with strange gestures and cryptic words. Despite his oddities, I could tell he was genuinely sad to see me go. Finally, I made my way to the Master Inventor quarters, where I found Jexif. He greeted me with a warm smile, expressing his gratitude for my help in fixing the Chrono-Core. We shared a few words, reminiscing about our recent adventure, before I bid him farewell.

With my goodbyes said, I left the city, the wind guiding me on my next journey. As I looked back at the city one last time, I couldn't help but feel a sense of accomplishment. I had made a difference here, and I knew I would carry these memories with me wherever I went. I exited the gnomarik city through the narrow crevice in the canyon wall, the same one that had served as my gateway to this world of knowledge five months prior. I was met with a profound sense of tranquility. The storm that had driven me to seek refuge among the gnomes had long since passed, leaving in its wake a world washed clean and glistening under the soft glow of the setting sun. The canyon, once a formidable labyrinth of stone and shadow, now lay serene and welcoming. Its towering walls, etched with the tales of time, stood silent guard as I navigated the winding path. The air was crisp and cool that Orendar morning, three cycles and three months since my journey began, carrying with it the faint scent of damp earth and the distant echo of a world awakening from the storm's embrace.

As I emerged from the canyon's embrace, a vast expanse of forested plains stretched before me, a sea of green undulating with the gentle roll of hills. The sight was breathtaking, a chronicle of the unyielding beauty of Alara. The plains, dotted with clusters of trees, stretched as far as the eye could see, their verdant expanse broken only by the occasional glint of a distant stream. For several days, I journeyed through this landscape, my path guided by the sun during the day and the stars at night. The world around me was alive with the sounds of nature, the rustle of leaves, the chirping of birds, the whisper of the wind. Yet, I encountered no other living being, the vast plains seemingly devoid of any presence. Days turned into nights and nights into days as I journeyed across the vast expanse of Alara, guided by the whispers of the wind. The solitude was a constant companion, broken only by the occasional rustle of leaves or the distant call of a bird. But the tranquility of my journey was shattered when my visions struck again.

It came without warning, a sudden onslaught of images that overwhelmed my senses. The scene of destruction was back, more vivid than ever. The once verdant hills were ablaze, the flames reaching skyward in a furious dance. The air was filled with the acrid smell of smoke and the crackling of burning wood. In the midst of the chaos, the behemoth stood, its form shrouded in darkness. It wielded a greatsword, its blade gleaming ominously in the firelight. The creature was a terrifying sight, its very presence a harbinger of death and destruction. But this time, the vision was different. It was more confusing, the images jumbled and disjointed. I saw flashes of faces I didn't recognize, places I had never been. The vision was a chaotic whirl of images and sensations, each one more disorienting than the last. As quickly as it had come, the vision faded, leaving me standing alone on the plains, the peaceful serenity an overt contrast to the hellish scene I had just witnessed. I was left with a sense of unease, the images of the vision etched into my mind. The behemoth, the destruction, the unfamiliar faces - they were all pieces of a puzzle that I was still yet to solve. That Ilyafae, the faelari, believed I was to protect this world from...

When I came back to my senses, the world around me had returned to its peaceful state. The verdant hills stretched out before me, untouched by the flames of my vision. But something had changed. The vision had left an imprint, a shadow that lingered in my waking moments. Images of destruction would flash across my mind's eye without warning. I would be admiring the beauty of a tree, its leaves rustling gently in the wind, when suddenly it would transform. In the blink of an eye, the tree would be engulfed in flames, its leaves curling and blackening under the intense heat. The experience was horrifying. But just as quickly as it had appeared, the image would fade, the tree returning to its original state. Its leaves would be green and vibrant once more, the flames replaced by the gentle sway of the branches. It was as if the vision had never happened, the peaceful scene a sheer differentiation from the hellish image that had just flashed across my mind.

This pattern continued, the peaceful world around me constantly being replaced by images of destruction. It was disorienting, the constant shift between peace and chaos leaving me on edge. Despite the tranquility of the hills, I couldn't shake off the feeling of unease. After several more weeks of travel, I came across a small human tribe. They had set up a village of leather tents, their structures dotting the landscape in a harmonious blend of nature and human ingenuity. The sight of the village, with its smoke curling up from the fires and the sound of laughter echoing in the air, should have been a welcome respite. But as I approached, my mind was once again flooded with horrifying images. In the blink of an eye, the peaceful village was replaced by a scene of utter chaos. I could hear blood-curdling screams, the sound echoing in my ears even as the peaceful hum of the village returned. I saw images of the tents and their inhabitants engulfed in flames, the fire consuming everything in its path. Just as quickly as they had appeared, the images would fade, replaced by the peaceful scene of the village. The tents were intact, their inhabitants going about their daily lives, oblivious to the destruction I had just witnessed.

I found myself stuck between reality and my visions, the line between the two blurring with each passing moment. The peaceful village and the horrifying images of destruction seemed to exist simultaneously, my mind constantly shifting between the two.

With a sense of urgency, I tried to warn the villagers of the impending destruction. I spoke of the visions, of the flames and the shadowed behemoth, of the devastation that could befall their peaceful village. But my warnings fell on deaf ears. They all stared right through me, walking past me as if I wasn't even there. After trying in vain to warn the villagers, I came across a large wooden stake in the ground. Attached to it was a chain, its vorgrund links glinting ominously in the sunlight. At the other end of the chain was a vorgrund collar, holding a frail, weak man. He was foaming at the mouth, his eyes vacant as he muttered to himself.

His words were the ramblings of a madman. He spoke of flames, of demons, of destruction. His voice was a haunting echo of my own warnings, his words a chilling reminder of the visions that plagued me. He seemed to be the only one of the villagers who could see me. As I approached, he looked up into my eyes and his ramblings ceased.

"You... You've seen it too... I can *feel* it." he rasped.

"Seen... *what?*" I asked in response, my voice trembling.

"The flames... the destruction... the *suffering*... Are you the one to save us from the abomination? Will you redeem us from Mor'Kathra's grasp?"

As I watched the man, a horrifying thought crossed my mind. Could it be that I was devolving into this? Were my visions not prophecies of impending destruction, but rather the delusions of a disturbed mind? The thought was terrifying, a definite chasm in the belief that had guided my journey these last three cycles.

I stood there, the villagers' state of obliviousness, the madman's ramblings a haunting reminder of my own visions. I was left with a sense of uncertainty, my faith in my visions shaken by the villagers' obliviousness to my presence and the madman's disturbing similarity to my own predicament. With a heavy heart, I left the village behind, their inability to see or hear me and the madman's ramblings still haunting my mind. I ran, my feet carrying me further and further away from the village and the disturbing reality it had presented.

After what felt like hours, I found myself standing at the mouth of a remote cave nestled in the heart of a dense forest. The cave offered seclusion, a refuge from the world and the disturbing visions that plagued me. I stepped inside, the cool darkness a welcome respite from the bright world outside. As I settled into the cave, where I would spend the following four weeks, I could feel the wind outside, its gentle whispers beckoning me onward. It was the same wind that had guided my journey so far, its guidance leading me across the vast expanse of Alara. But for the first time, I ignored her call. I needed time. Time to process the disturbing reality of the village and the madman, time to understand the nature of my visions. The cave offered me that time, its seclusion a welcome respite from the chaos of the world outside. As I sat there, the wind whispering outside and the darkness enveloping me, I found myself questioning everything I had believed so far.

XXVII

Halindelar

As I sat in the darkness of the cave one evening during my fourth week within, my mind drifted back to Tornu, my mentor and uncle. I remembered his wise words and, for the first time, felt contempt for his constant encouragement to explore the world. His teachings had been the guiding force behind my journey, his belief in me a source of strength. But as I sat there, alone and confused, I couldn't help but question the path I had chosen. Look where exploration had gotten me. I had experienced wonderful things, met incredible beings. I had spent time with the elves, the dwarves, the goblins, the centaurs, the orcs, the gnomes. I had shared a special bond with Ilyafae. But what was it all for? Was I on a grand quest to protect the world? Or was I simply chasing after daydreams, my visions nothing more than the delusions of a disturbed mind? The thought was deeply unsettling. As I sat there, the wind whispering outside and the darkness enveloping me, I found myself questioning everything. My journey, my visions, my purpose - everything seemed uncertain. The world I had known, the beliefs I had held, everything was being challenged.

In the solitude of the cave, I was startled by a figure appearing at the entrance. My heart leapt as I recognized the silhouette. "Tornu?" I whispered, my voice echoing in the silence of the cave. But as my eyes adjusted to the dim light, I realized it was not my long-dead mentor but... *Xolesh*! His presence was unexpected, but not unwelcome. He stepped into the cave, his gaze meeting mine. "I didn't know what I would find here - but I certainly did not expect it to be *you*," he said, his voice echoing in the silence of the cave.

I managed a weak smile, "It's been a long time, Xolesh. The world of Alara is vast and unpredictable. What brings you to this remote cave?"

Xolesh sighed, "Much like you, I assume, I've been on a journey, seeking answers, understanding. The world is changing, and I feel a pull, a guidance, but I'm not always sure where it's leading me."

I nodded, understanding his sentiment all too well. "It's strange, isn't it? Feeling like you're being led by something, but not knowing its intentions. Honestly, Xolesh, these days, I don't know if I can trust my visions..."

Xolesh looked at me, his gaze steady. "Yoran," he said, his voice filled with a surprising amount of empathy. "You have to trust your instincts. If you believe it to be right, follow the path that you feel led down." His words were simple, but they carried a weight that resonated with me. In the midst of my confusion, his reassurance was a sip of fresh water to a parched soul. We sat in silence for a while, the weight of our shared journey distributing between us. The cave's stillness was only broken by the occasional, increasingly urgent, gust of wind outside.

Time seemed to stretch on, and the weight of our shared experiences hung in the air. After what felt like hours, Xolesh finally broke the silence.

"Yoran, have you ever felt... compelled? As if a force outside of yourself is pulling your strings, guiding you on this journey?"

Pausing, I replied, "Yes, I believe I have felt that. It's like a whisper, a gentle nudge, always guiding, always beckoning."

With a hint of distress in his eyes, Xolesh asked, "But how do you know it's right to follow? How do you know that this force isn't leading us astray, into the jaws of some grander scheme we can't yet fathom?"

"I've asked myself that same question many times now. But every time I feel its touch, there's a purity to it. A connection. It feels as if Alara itself is speaking to me. I suppose we just have to trust, Xolesh.

Trust that the force guiding us is doing so with a purpose that aligns with the heart of Alara."

Xolesh's voice trembled slightly, "I want to believe, Yoran. But the force that tugs at me... How can I be sure it's not leading me to my own destruction?"

"All we can do is trust in our connection to Alara. If you feel that connection, deep down, then let it guide you. And if you ever doubt, remember this moment, and know that you're not alone on this journey."

After several days of shared stories, journey-wearied laughter, and contemplation, the time had come for Xolesh and me to part ways. The cave that had been our refuge now echoed with the weight of our shared experiences. The wind, my forsaken companion, whispered its secrets, hinting at the paths I was to take. As we stood at the entrance of the cave, Xolesh turned to me, his eyes reflecting the vastness of Alara.

"Yoran," he began, his voice heavy with emotion, "our paths may diverge, but remember that we are both guided by forces greater than ourselves. Trust in your journey, and in the wind that guides you."

I nodded, feeling a lump in my throat. "Xolesh, our time together has been a beacon in the darkness. I hope our paths cross again, and until then, may the wind guide you true." We shared a final, lingering look, understanding the weight of our separate journeys. Then, with a nod, Xolesh turned and began his trek, his silhouette gradually fading into the vast landscape.

I took a deep breath, feeling the wind's gentle caress. As I began my own journey, flashes of visions continued to dance before my eyes. Flames, consuming everything in their path, the world around me burning. The intensity of the visions was jarring, intermingling with the reality of the serene landscape before me. I shook my head, trying to dispel the images, but they persisted, a distinct separation from the peaceful world I was walking through. With every step, I tried to focus on the present, on the wind guiding me, and, for the first time, on the hope that these visions were a foretelling of things to come, and not a telling of my descent into madness. As I moved forward, the weight of uncertainty pressed down on me, and I couldn't help but wonder what the future held for Alara, for Xolesh, and for me.

Eventually, after a week of following the wind's beckoning, I found myself at the edge of a village, its small, cozy houses nestled amidst rolling hills, two months after leaving Vindelkor. The inhabitants of the village were unlike any I had seen - save for once before - the funny little man with curly red hair and beard, who had once forgotten his hook-stick near a stream I had been struggling to catch fish in, long ago and far, far from here. They were small in stature, just as he had been, their faces kind and welcoming. I ended up staying with these creatures for nearly three months. Seventy-nine days, to be exact.

One of them, a kind-hearted healer named Paemia, took me in. She was small, like the rest of her kin, but her presence was comforting, her gentle demeanor a balm to my troubled mind. Aside from the one instance, I had never seen creatures like them before, their small stature and kind hearts a blatant distinction from the other races I had encountered. When I asked Paemia about her kin, she told me they called themselves '*halindelar*', which translated to "Hearth-keepers of the Rolling Hills." The name was fitting, a linguistic mural of their warm hearts and the rolling hills that were their home. But for simplicity's sake, I took to calling them halflings, a name that captured their small stature and the rolling hills they called home.

As I settled into the halindelar village, under the care of Paemia, I found a sense of peace that had eluded me since my days with Tornu. The halindelar, with their kind hearts and welcoming homes, offered a refuge from the doubts and suspicions that had plagued me, their presence a reminder of the goodness that still existed in the world. On the second day in the halindelar village, I found myself again in the care of Paemia, the halindelar healer. Her small cottage was a sanctuary, filled with the scent of herbs and the soft glow of candlelight. The walls were lined with shelves filled with jars of herbs and potions, their contents an announcement of her knowledge and skill. Paemia was a constant presence by my side, her small hands deft as she administered potions and applied poultices. Her touch was gentle, her movements precise.

She worked in silence, her focus entirely on her task. But despite her silence, her care spoke volumes, her actions an acknowledgement of her kind heart. I spent most of my time resting, the comfort of the bed and the warmth of the cottage a welcome respite from my journey. The soft rustle of the wind outside and the gentle hum of Paemia's activities were a soothing backdrop, their rhythm lulling me into a state of relaxation. Despite the confusion and fear that had brought me to the halindelar village, I found a sense of peace under Paemia's care. Her kindness and the tranquility of the village were a balm to my troubled mind.

By the third day in the halindelar village, I could feel my strength returning. The weakness and disorientation that had plagued me were fading, replaced by a renewed sense of vitality. Paemia's care had worked wonders, her healing skills evident in my swift recovery. With my strength returning, I found myself with time to observe the halindelar and their way of life. Their village was a paragon of love for nature and simplicity. The houses were small and cozy, their structures blending seamlessly with the rolling hills. Gardens filled with vibrant flowers and lush vegetables surrounded each house, their colors a vibrant splash against the green of the hills. The halindelar themselves were a joy to watch. They moved with a grace and ease that spoke of a deep connection with the world around them. Their faces were always lit up with smiles, their laughter a constant melody in the air. They worked together, their actions a harmonious dance of cooperation and mutual respect. I watched as they tended to their gardens, their small hands deft as they cared for each plant. I saw them cooking, their kitchens filled with the mouthwatering aroma of hearty stews and freshly baked bread. I observed their gatherings, their voices raised in song as they celebrated the simple joys of life.

By the fourth day, I began to notice something amiss in the halindelar village. Despite their smiles and laughter, there was a subtle undercurrent of worry among the halflings. Their gardens, usually vibrant and lush, were beginning to wilt. The hearty stews and freshly baked bread were less abundant, their portions smaller. It didn't take long for me to realize what was happening. The halfling village was on the brink of a famine. The signs were subtle, but they were there. The wilting gardens, the smaller portions, the subtle worry in the halflings' eyes - they all pointed to the same conclusion. Despite my own troubles, I found myself wanting to help. The halindelar had taken me in, cared for me when I was weak and disoriented. They had shown me kindness and warmth, their simple way of life a beacon of hope in my confusion. I couldn't stand by and watch as they faced a famine. But how could I help? I was a wanderer, a seeker of knowledge. I had no experience with farming or dealing with a famine. But as I watched the halindelar, their faces filled with worry and uncertainty, I knew I had to try.

On the fifth day, I was introduced to the leader of the halindelar village, a stern-looking halfling named Belwan. Despite his small stature, he carried an air of authority, his gaze sharp and assessing as he looked me over. Belwan was skeptical of me, his eyes filled with doubt as he listened to my offer to help.

"You're a stranger, big-one," he said, his voice firm. "Why should we trust you?" His words stung, but I understood his skepticism. I was an outsider, a wanderer with no ties to their village. But I had seen their struggle, their worry. I wanted to help, to repay their kindness and care.

"I understand your skepticism, Belwan," I replied with the assistance of my Saela-Hathir, meeting his gaze. "But I want to help. I may not have the solutions now, but I'm willing to learn, to work with you and your people.

Belwan looked at me, his gaze thoughtful. "We'll see, Yoran," he said finally. "We'll see." As I left the meeting, I felt a renewed sense of determination. I needed to prove myself, to show Belwan and the halindelar that I was sincere in my offer to help.

By the sixth day, I had begun to formulate a plan. I spent hours in the quiet solitude of a nearby cave, my mind a whirl of ideas and possibilities. I knew I had to create something, a device that could help the halindelar combat the impending famine. I started to sketch out my ideas, the rough outlines of a device taking shape on a sheet of parchment I'd brought from Vindelkor. It was a simple design, a device that could harness the power of the wind to irrigate the fields. The halindelar village was nestled amidst rolling hills, the constant wind a potential source of power. As I sketched, I could see the device taking shape in my mind. A windmill, like the ones I'd seen between the tunnel entrance and the main square of Vindelkor, its blades turning in the wind, a system of gears and pulleys transferring the power to a pump. The pump would draw water from a nearby stream, the water then distributed to the fields through a network of channels. It was a simple design, but it had potential. The windmill could provide a constant source of water for the fields, helping to combat the effects of the famine. If I were to put an enchantment on the windmill, that would ensure the village would survive in perpetuity. I hadn't spent terribly long with the gnomarik people, but the time I had spent with them quickly became invaluable.

On the seventh day, I set out to gather the resources needed for my device. The halindelar village was small, its resources limited, but I was determined to make do with what was available. I started with the wood. The halindelar had a small grove of trees near the village, their trunks sturdy and strong. With Belwan's permission and a small axe I'd borrowed from Paemia, I began to cut down a few of the trees, their wood essential for the structure of the windmill. Next, I needed stone for the gears and pulleys. The halindelar didn't have a lot of stone for crafting, but I was able to use a simple spell, "*Oth-Zell*", or "Stone-Carve", to obtain stone from the cave I'd made my temporary abode. For the pump, I needed a flexible material, something that could create a seal and withstand the pressure of the water. I found my solution in the form of animal hides, their flexibility and durability perfect for the task. As the sun set on the seventh day, I looked at the resources I had gathered, my sketch of the device a constant companion. I knew I had a long way to go, a lot of work ahead of me.

On the eighth day, as I was working on the device, a young halindelar approached me. He was small, even for a halfling, with bright eyes and a mop of curly hair. His name was Loric, and he was fascinated by my tales of exploration. As I worked, Loric would sit nearby, his eyes wide as he listened to my stories. I told him about the elandari and their majestic forests, the dwarrin and their intricate craftsmanship, the kreegoblikar and their cunning jokes, the centarion and their vast plains, the orukuthûndar and their savage politics, and the gnomarik'n and their incredible inventions. Loric was captivated by my tales, his eyes sparkling with curiosity and wonder. He asked questions, his inquiries thoughtful and insightful. He was particularly interested in the gnomarik'n and their inventions, his fascination evident in his eager questions.

On the ninth day, Loric and I spent more time together. As I continued to work on the device, he would sit nearby, his eyes wide with curiosity as he listened to my stories. I found myself sharing more of my adventures, my tales of exploration painting a vivid picture of the world beyond the halindelar village. I told Loric about the time I spent with the elandari, the elves, and how they taught me to listen to Alara's voice. I shared my experiences with the dwarrin, the dwarves, and their profound yud, honor. I spoke of the centarion, the centaurs, and their deep connection with the wind and the earth. As I shared my stories, I could see the wonder in Loric's eyes. He was captivated by my tales, his curiosity a mirror of my own when I first started my journey. His questions were thoughtful, his interest genuine. It was a reminder of the joy of discovery, the thrill of exploring the unknown. As the days passed, Loric became a constant companion, his presence a welcome distraction from the challenges of building the device. His curiosity and enthusiasm were infectious, his questions sparking new ideas and solutions. Despite our differences, we found common ground in our curiosity and love for exploration.

On the tenth day, I continued to work on the device. The task was challenging, the lack of advanced gnomish tools a constant hurdle. The halindelar had simple tools, their design basic and their function limited. But I was determined to make do with what was available. I spent hours shaping the wood, the rough edges slowly taking the form of the windmill's structure.

On the eleventh day, I took a break from working on the device to spend time with Loric. The young halfling was eager to learn, his curiosity a constant source of joy. I decided to teach him some basic survival skills, lessons I had learned during my travels. We started with the basics of foraging. I showed Loric how to identify edible plants and berries, how to spot the signs of a nearby water source, and how to avoid the plants and creatures that could be dangerous. His eyes were wide with fascination as he listened, his hands carefully mimicking my actions as he learned to identify the different plants. Next, I taught him how to start a fire. I showed him how to gather dry wood and tinder, how to arrange them for maximum airflow, and how to use a flint to create a spark. Loric was a quick learner, his small hands deft as he practiced starting a fire. Finally, I taught him some basic navigation skills. I showed him how to use the position of the sun and stars to determine direction, and how to use landmarks to avoid getting lost. Loric listened attentively, his eyes focused as he absorbed the information. As the day came to an end, I looked at Loric with a sense of pride.

The twelfth and thirteenth days I remained hard at work on the device, noticing the signs of the famine increasing steadily. The rest of the first month was spent in a flurry of activity. Between working on the device and spending time with Loric, the days passed quickly. Loric was a quick learner, his curiosity and eagerness to learn an attestation of his character. I found myself teaching him a few basic spell words combinations, his fascination with magic evident in his eager questions. We started with simple combinations. '*Su-Nis*' for a warm breeze, '*Qar-Flec*' to bend a stream of water, '*Ra-Vin*' to move a small stone. Each combination was a lesson in control and focus, the power of the spell words evident in their effects.

Halflings could use magic, and regularly did. However, their magic was less focused and powerful than the magic practiced by the gnomes. They used single spell words, their gestures simple and their effects limited. But with the combination of spell words, their magic could be more powerful, more focused. I showed Loric how to combine the spell words, how to focus his energy and control the magic. His eyes were wide with fascination as he watched the effects of the combinations, his hands carefully mimicking my gestures as he practiced the spells. As the days passed, Loric's control over the spell words improved. He was able to combine the spell words with ease, his magic more focused and powerful.

The second month in the halindelar village was a whirlwind of activity. The device was entering its second phase, the structure of the windmill now standing tall against the backdrop of the rolling hills. The gears and pulleys were in place, their intricate design a revelation of the hours of work I had put into them. The pump was taking shape, the animal hides forming a flexible and durable seal. In my free time, I continued to mentor Loric. His control over the spell words was improving even further. We practiced new combinations, each one a lesson in control and focus. '*Su-Tha*' to create an embrace of wind, '*Qar-Vad*' to move water, '*Oth-Mut*' to change the shape of a stone. As the second month came to an end, I looked at the device with a sense of accomplishment. It was not yet complete, but it was closer to completion.

On the sixty-first day, I began the final phase of the device. The gears and pulleys were in place, their intricate design ready to harness the power of the wind. The pump was ready, the animal hides forming a flexible and durable seal. The final phase was the most crucial. It involved connecting the windmill to the pump, ensuring that the power generated by the windmill would be transferred to the pump. It was a delicate task, requiring precision and patience. As I worked, I felt a sense of anticipation. The device was nearing completion, each piece falling into place. I could almost see it working, the windmill turning in the wind, the pump drawing water from the stream, the water flowing through the channels to the fields. I continued to work on the device, the final phase requiring my full attention. In my spare time, I shared stories and lessons with Loric, his progress with the spell words a constant source of joy.

On the sixty-fifth day, the device was finally complete. The windmill stood tall, its blades ready to harness the power of the wind. The gears and pulleys were in place, their intricate design ready to transfer the power to the pump. I had been working on a combination of spell words over the last couple of months, refining them until they were perfect. I stood before the device, my heart pounding with anticipation. I took a deep breath, focusing my energy as I began to chant the spell words.

"*Bex... Flum-Fin-Kan... Zek-Ni-Wid...Cii*"

The words echoed in the air, their power resonating with the device. I could feel the magic taking hold, the device responding to the enchantment. 'Object-River-Enduring-Shield-Equalize-Harmony-Protect- Enchant.' The windmill began to turn, the gears and pulleys moving in harmony. The pump began to draw water from the stream, the water flowing through the channels to the fields, just as I had imagined.

The following day, the sun rose to a scene of hope and anticipation. The device was working, its structure standing tall against the backdrop of the rolling hills. The windmill turned in the gentle breeze, the gears and pulleys moving in harmony. As I watched the device work, I felt a sense of joy and accomplishment. The land was beginning to respond, the parched soil soaking up the water, the plants showing signs of life. The threat of the famine was receding, the device a beacon of hope in the face of adversity. I shared this joyous moment with Loric, the young halfling's eyes wide with wonder as he watched the device work. Over the next several days, I watched as the lands began to thrive. The device was working, its magic bringing life back to the parched soil. The plants were growing, their leaves a vibrant green, their blossoms a riot of colors. In the following days, I continued to share stories of my adventures and exploration with Loric. I found myself slipping into a mentor-like role, guiding Loric as he navigated the world of magic and exploration. As I shared my stories, I was reminded of my own experiences with my uncle and mentor, Tornu. His guidance had been instrumental in my journey, his wisdom a constant source of inspiration. I found myself echoing his teachings, passing on his wisdom to Loric.

On the seventieth day, a sense of celebration filled the air. The halindelar village was thriving, the device bringing life back to the evergreen hills. That day, the halindelar leader, Belwan, approached me. His eyes were filled with gratitude, his voice filled with respect.

"Yoran," he said, his voice echoing in the quiet morning. "Your contributions to our village have not gone unnoticed. You have brought hope to our people." His words filled me with a sense of acceptance and respect. I had been a stranger in their village, an outsider with strange ideas and unfamiliar magic. But they had accepted me, healed me, embraced my ideas, and trusted in my knowledge. And now, they were acknowledging my contributions.

"I am honored, Belwan," I replied, my voice filled with gratitude. "I am grateful for your acceptance and trust. I am glad that I could help."

The next eight days were filled with laughter, learning, and camaraderie. I continued to mentor Loric, his progress with the spell words a reflection of his determination and curiosity. Every evening, the villagers would gather around, their faces illuminated by the soft glow of lanterns, eager to hear my tales. With every story I recounted, their eyes sparkled with fascination, drawing them deeper into the world of my adventures. The feasts, though, were where the halflings truly showcased their culture. The *"Lundle Bun Dubbl"*, or "Sunlit Barrow Pie", was an edible masterpiece. Its flaky pastry exuded buttery aromas, and as I took my first bite, the rich creamy filling burst forth with flavors of honey-roasted root vegetables, complemented by the tender and succulent leaftail rabbit. The added sprinkle of *"Hundin Gilfri"*, *"Golden Rootspice"*, not only made the pie glow enchantingly but added a unique spicy-sweet undertone. Then there was the *"Gulderr Brellon"*, "Dewdrop Soup," a clear aromatic broth that was like sipping the essence of the earth itself. It had this fresh, rejuvenating quality, like morning air, with subtle notes of earthy mushrooms and the occasional delightful surprise of the twilight truffles' unique flavor profile. The tiny moon minnows within added a slightly briny contrast to the earthy flavors. Yet, it was the *"Denril Burtle"*, "Starberry Tartlets" that truly took me on a sensory journey. The fragrance of the tartlets was intoxicating, with hints of lavender wafting from the buttery pastry crust. Biting into one, the tangy-sweet jam made from starberries, 'denril', which I learned bloomed only under the crescent moon, tantalized my taste buds. The clotted cream on top, silky and rich, perfectly rounded off the flavor profile.

On the seventy-ninth day, it was time to say my farewells. I felt the call of Alara's wind beckoning me ever onward. I said my farewells to the villagers. But my final farewell was for Loric, the young halindelar who had become like a protégé to me.

"Loric," I said, my voice filled with emotion. "You have a spirit of exploration, a fierce curiosity that is an omen of your character. I know that you will explore the world one day, that you will face dangers and challenges. But remember my words, words that my mentor, Tornu, once told me."

I looked into his eyes, my voice steady as I echoed Tornu's words.

"Fear is a part of the journey, Loric. But do not let it become the journey itself."

XXVIII

The Sundering

As I journeyed away from the halindelar village that frigid day at the end of Ithendar, three cycles and eight months after I had initially committed myself to this journey, my heart, now having beat for 19 cycles, approaching my 20th with the upcoming Aravell, was filled with a sense of peace and contentment. The halflings had healed my spirit, their kindness and generosity a balm to my weary soul. Their village had become a sanctuary, a place of respite in the face of adversity.

Paemia, the kind-hearted halfling healer, had nursed me back to health, her gentle care an indicator of her kindness and compassion. She had healed my body. But more than that, the halindelar had healed my spirit. They had shown me the power of community, the strength of unity. They had reminded me of the joy of exploration, the thrill of discovery. They had reignited my passion for magic, their fascination with my spell words, a standard of their curiosity and eagerness to learn. And perhaps most importantly, I had not had a vision of destruction since my time with Paemia. The constant visions that had once plagued me, that had filled my mind with images of destruction and despair, had ceased. I was free from the visions, my mind clear and focused.

Of course, that couldn't last. Just as I was beginning to feel a sense of peace, a sense of belonging, I was struck by another vision. This time, it was different. It was more vivid, more real. This time, I saw the silhouette of a man standing in front of the abomination, his figure a notable departure from the backdrop of destruction. The sight filled me with a sense of dread, a sense of impending doom. The man was manipulating spell words with a darkness I had only seen once before. The words were heavy, their power resonating with a darkness that sent chills down my spine. The only one I knew who had the ability to manipulate spell words with that kind of darkness was Xolesh. The realization hit me like a punch to the gut. I couldn't ignore my destiny any longer. Somehow, I had to find Xolesh again, had to stop him before it was too late. The visions were not delusions, they were prophecies. Prophecies of a future that I had to prevent.

Once again, I surrendered myself to the whims of the wind, its invisible palms nudging me forward, its whispers echoing in my ears. It was Alara's voice, a siren's call that I could not resist, a melody that guided my steps and filled my heart with a sense of purpose. As I moved further from the halindelar village, the terrain became more treacherous. Mountains loomed in the distance, their peaks shrouded in mist, and the path became steeper and more winding. One evening, as the sun lowered, painting the horizon with golden strokes, I happened upon an ancient stone marker. Time had weathered its edges, but it still stood defiantly. Around its base, the very plants and grass that should've been lush and green bore the unmistakable signs of a mysterious affliction: discolored leaves, wilted stems, and a few patches already turned to ash. Carved into the stone with a precision that could only have been wrought by magic, were symbols that resonated with an eerie familiarity, reminiscent of the dark magic of Xolesh. A chilling wind swept through, carrying an odor of sulfur, murmurs of bygone eras, and ominous foretellings. Knowing I was on the right trajectory was of little comfort, for the afflicted vegetation served as a grim reminder of the lurking peril. With every step I took, I felt both the pull of my destiny and the oppressive weight of the looming confrontation.

For weeks, I journeyed, traversing through dense forests and crossing over babbling brooks, the wind my constant companion. It was a relentless pursuit, a dance with destiny that led me to the threshold of a new chapter in my journey. As I moved forward, memories of my journey flooded back. The elandari, with their grace and wisdom, who had stood by my side as we saved one of their own. The dwarrin, brave and resilient, who had fought fiercely for their mountain home with my aid. The centarion, who had shown me the vastness of the plains and the mysteries of the stars, gifting me the Saela-Hathir headdress, a symbol of unity and understanding. I chuckled as I remembered the kreegoblikar, their mischievous pranks lighting up the nights, Ilyafae and our magically entwining dance, and the trust she had placed in me as Eledhin's Protector; and the orukuthûndar, whose harsh ways had taught me resilience. The gnomarik'n and their Chrono-Core, a beacon of magic and technology, which I had helped save from the brink of darkness. And the halindelar, who had taken me in when I was on the edge of despair, restoring my sanity and hope. Each encounter, each race, had left an indelible mark on my soul, shaping me, preparing me for this very moment. The weight of their hopes, their dreams, and their trust rested on my shoulders. I wasn't just fighting for myself or against the darkness of Xolesh; I was fighting for all of them, for a world where every race could coexist in harmony. And there was still a part of me, after those four cycles of journeying, that was fighting to fulfill the promise I'd made to my uncle and mentor, Tornu.

 Finally, one afternoon in early Durathorn, I found myself standing at the edge of a vast expanse, a frozen expanse that stretched out as far as the eye could see. It was a sea of white, a tapestry woven from countless flakes of snow that lay piled silently atop the plains underneath. The expanse was open and unmarred by the touch of civilization. The sun hung low in the sky, casting long shadows that danced across the glistening landscape. The frosty light bathed the icy plains in a warm glow, contrasting with the frigid surface underfoot, transforming the ordinary into the extraordinary. It was a sight that took my breath away, a moment of tranquility amidst the chaos of my journey.

 As I traversed the frozen expanse, the tranquility of the field was abruptly shattered, like a sheet of ice struck by a stone. The serene landscape, once a sea of peaceful snow, was now marred by a scene of carnage that stood starkly in its center.

There, amidst a mass of slain orukuthûndar bodies, stood Xolesh. His form was a stark silhouette against the setting sun, a lone figure in a tableau of death. His clothes were drenched in blood, a grim specimen of the battle that had taken place. Among the fallen, I could discern the lifeless form of Kharok, the leader I had come to respect and with whom I'd shared moments of camaraderie during my time with the orukuthûndar. Xolesh's face was a mask of grim determination, his eyes burning with a fierce light. His hands were stained with the blood of his enemies, the slain orukuthûndar scattered around him like fallen snowflakes. It was a sight that spoke volumes of his might and resolve, a haunting display of his thirst for retribution. The wind, once a gentle whisper, now howled around us, carrying with it the scent of blood and the echoes of battle. The field, once emblematic of peace and tranquility, had been transformed into a battlefield, its white canvas painted red with the lifeblood of the fallen orukuthûndar.

I stood there, a silent observer to Xolesh's vengeance. His form was a stark reminder of the violence that had been wrought, a chilling disclosure of the price of vengeance. But amidst the carnage, I saw something else in Xolesh - a sense of resolution, a burden lifted. In that moment, as I stood on the edge of the blood-soaked, snow covered expanse, a chilling realization washed over me. The sight of Xolesh, standing amidst the carnage, his clothes stained with the blood of the slain orukuthûndar, was a stark revelation. It was as if a veil had been lifted, revealing a truth that had been lurking in the shadows of my doubts.

Xolesh, the man who had once been a brief companion in my journey, now seemed to be the embodiment of the evil I was destined to confront. The whispers of Alara, the wind that had guided me, seemed to confirm my fears. The wind howled around us, its mournful cry echoing my own sense of dread. His figure, once a symbol of camaraderie and shared purpose, was now a harbinger of destruction. The blood that stained his clothes, the bodies of the orukuthûndar that lay at his feet, they were all damning evidence of his capacity for violence and destruction. I felt a sense of betrayal, a sting of disappointment. But more than that, I felt a sense of resolve harden within me. This was the path that Alara had set me on, the destiny I was meant to fulfill. I felt in the core of my being that Xolesh had to be the darkness I was meant to confront, the evil I was destined to protect Alara from.

As the sun dipped below the horizon, casting long shadows across the field, I knew what I had to do. For Alara, for the world that I had come to love, I would face this evil. I would stand against Xolesh, no matter what it took. As I began my approach across the blood-stained ice, I reached for Faelthorn, the dagger I had forged during my time with the dwarrin thârûm. Under the watchful eye of Thrumir, I had shaped its blade, imbuing it with the strength of the dwarrin and the wisdom of the elandari. The moonstones embedded in its hilt, gifts from the elandari, glowed with a deep violet hue, a color I had never seen them emit before. It was as if they sensed something was amiss.

Drawing Faelthorn from its leather sheath, I held it in my right hand, its familiar weight a comforting presence. The moonstones pulsed with a soft light, their glow illuminating the path before me. It was a beacon in the growing darkness, a symbol of the hope and resolve that guided my steps. In my left hand, I drew my bûrz'kruk, the jagged black orukuthûndar stone blade. Its surface was as dark as the night sky, an unmasked contrast to the glowing moonstones of Faelthorn. The bûrz'kruk was a reminder of the battles I had fought, the challenges I had overcome. It was a memento of my strength, a symbol of my determination to protect Alara. With Faelthorn and bûrz'kruk in hand, I advanced towards Xolesh. Each step was a declaration of my intent, a promise of the battle to come. I was unsure of how to confront him, of how to combat the darkness that he represented. But I knew that I had to try, that I had to stand against the evil that threatened Alara.

As I moved closer, the wind picked up, its howls echoing my resolve. The field, once a peaceful expanse of pure white snow, was now a battlefield, the stage for a confrontation that would shape the fate of Alara. And I, with Faelthorn and bûrz'kruk in hand, was ready to play my part. Xolesh watched my approach, his eyes burning with a fierce intensity. As I closed the distance between us, he barked two sharp words in a language I did not recognize. It was the same dark spell language he had used when we first met, a language that seemed to echo with an ancient and malevolent power. From his hands shot tendrils of black energy, snaking through the air towards me. They moved with a life of their own, lashing out like serpents striking at their prey. In response, I called upon the Lunasil, the sacred faelari pendant that had been a shield and guide throughout my journey. Expecting it to shatter, being rendered useless, as Ilyafae had warned me it would be if it was ever used for or against an evil most pure, I felt its energy surge within me, a protective aura that enveloped me as I rushed forward. The Lunasil was my bulwark against the dark spells that Xolesh hurled in my direction, its light a transparent difference from the black tendrils of energy that sought to strike me down. Yet the Lunasil did not shatter.

As I ran, Xolesh continued to unleash his spells, each one more potent than the last. It was a barrage of darkness, a storm of malevolent energy that threatened to overwhelm me. But I held my ground, my focus unwavering as I countered his spells. Each step was a battle, each breath a vessel of my resolve. I could feel the strain of the confrontation, the toll it was taking on my body and spirit. But I did not falter. I could not afford to. The fate of Alara hung in the balance, and I was its last line of defense. With Faelthorn and bûrz'kruk in hand, and the protection of the Lunasil surrounding me, I pressed on. Despite the onslaught of Xolesh's spells, I continued my approach, my determination unwavering. With a final burst of speed, I reached Xolesh and launched myself at him, my body a missile aimed at his heart. The daggers in my hands, Faelthorn and bûrz'kruk, were extensions of my will, their blades gleaming in the dying light as I plunged them towards his chest. But Xolesh was not to be so easily defeated. His physical prowess was greater than mine, his strength honed by countless battles. He reacted with a speed that belied his size, his hands shooting out to grab my wrists in a vice-like grip. His fingers closed around my wrists, halting the descent of my daggers mere inches from his chest.

His grip was vorgrund, his strength formidable. I could feel the power coursing through his veins, a dark energy that seemed to pulse in time with his heartbeat. His eyes met mine, their depths filled with a fierce determination that mirrored my own. For a moment, we were locked in a stalemate, our bodies straining against each other, our wills clashing in a battle of resolve. I could feel the heat of his breath on my face, could see the beads of sweat trickling down his forehead. But despite his physical advantage, I did not relent. I could not afford to. With a roar of defiance, I redoubled my efforts, straining against his grip. The daggers in my hands, Faelthorn and bûrz'kruk, seemed to pulse with a life of their own, their blades yearning to find their mark. I was determined to break free, to deliver the blow that would end this confrontation and protect Alara from the threat that Xolesh posed.

With a sudden, brutal force, Xolesh wrenched the orukuthûndar blade from my grasp. The bûrz'kruk slipped from my fingers, leaving me with only Faelthorn in hand. For a few brief, heart-stopping moments, we dueled without the powerful primal forces of Alara, our battle reduced to a contest of physical strength and skill. But even in this, I was not without an advantage. Faelthorn, the blade I had forged under Thrumir's guidance, proved its worth. The dwarrin enchantments that had been woven into its creation and the elandari moonstones embedded in its hilt came alive in my hand. They pulsed with a power that seemed to resonate with my own resolve, their energy flowing into me and bolstering my strength. Despite my relative lack of combat prowess, Faelthorn made up for my shortcomings. It moved with a grace and precision that seemed to defy my limited skill, its blade dancing in the fading light as it parried and struck. Each clash of our blades was a herald of Faelthorn's might, a reminder of the strength that lay within its enchanted form.

Xolesh and I danced a deadly dance, our blades clashing in a symphony of steel and resolve. But even as we dueled, I could feel the tide of the battle turning in my favor. Faelthorn was the mightier blade, its enchantments and moonstones lending me the strength I needed to hold my own against Xolesh's superior skill. With each passing moment, I could feel my confidence growing. I was no longer just a wanderer, a seeker of knowledge. I was a protector, a guardian of Alara. Before long, Xolesh had cast aside the blackened blade, the orukuthûndar weapon discarded like a spent torch. The crunch of the blade hitting the ice echoed through the air, being absorbed by the falling snow, a clear signal of the shift in our battle. We were no longer warriors locked in physical combat, but mages engaged in a duel of magical prowess.

The air around us crackled with energy and the mixed aroma of petrichor and sulfur as we resumed our magical battle, our spell words echoing out across the plains. We cast spell after spell at each other, our hands weaving intricate patterns in the air as we summoned the forces of Alara to our aid. Each spell was a testament to our power, a display of our mastery over the primal forces that governed our world. But for every spell I cast, Xolesh had a counter. And for every spell he hurled at me, I had a parry. Our duel was a dance of magic and will, a contest of skill and resolve that saw neither of us gaining an advantage. We were evenly matched, our powers clashing in a dazzling display of magical prowess. The air around us was filled with the echoes of our spells, the ground beneath us trembling with the force of our magic. The field, once a peaceful expanse of white, was now a battlefield, its tranquility shattered by the clash of our powers. Until, in an instant, the tide of our battle shifted. Xolesh, with a cunning that belied his brute strength, found an opening in my defenses. With a swift, brutal punch, he struck me in the ribs, his fist a hammer that drove the breath from my lungs. But it was not the physical blow that took me by surprise. It was the surge of dark magic that followed. Xolesh called upon his malevolent powers, his hands weaving a spell that sent a chill down my spine. Before I could react, I felt an unseen force grip me, lifting me off the ground.

I was suspended in the air, my feet dangling above the blood-stained ground. The world around me seemed to tilt, the horizon spinning as I struggled to regain my bearings. The frigid wind howled around me, its mournful cry echoing my own sense of disorientation. Xolesh stood below me, his eyes gleaming with a triumphant light. His spell had caught me off guard, his attack a stark reminder of the power he wielded. In that suspended moment, a chilling realization washed over me. Xolesh had gained the upper hand. His dark magic held me aloft, his triumphant gaze bore into me, and I felt a sense of dread creep into my heart. The balance of our battle had tipped in his favor, and I knew, with a sinking feeling, that it would soon be over.

Everything around me seemed to still, as if time itself had paused to bear witness to our duel. The wind that had been howling around us fell silent, its whispers fading into nothingness. The open lands, a stark expanse of snow and ice, seemed to hold its breath, its tranquility shattered by the impending conclusion of our battle. The world around me was as silent as the falling snow, a highlighted variance from the chaos of our duel. It was a silence that echoed my own sense of despair, a silence that seemed to weigh heavily on my heart. I was suspended in a moment of stillness, caught in the eye of the storm that was our battle.

Then, breaking through the silence, a sound reached my ears. It was the whispers of Alara, her voice carried on the wind once more. It was a melody that seemed to echo in my heart, a song that filled me with a sense of hope and resolve. I found myself echoing the whispers, my voice joining Alara's in a chorus that resonated with the power of the primal forces.

"*Es... Tharn... Lae... Ruvan... Thar... Ardha... Nor... Vals... Su... Tha... Hal... Endil... Mor... Gareth... Kae... Lum... Dor... Zalah... Hir... An... Or... Kan... Fin... El...*"

As I weakly whispered the words, their meaning began to unfold within my heart. Each phrase was a key, unlocking a deeper understanding of the primal forces of Alara. And as I spoke them, I found myself agreeing with their essence, their truth resonating within me.

"Essense Sunder. Eternal Tides. Ire Heaven. Bind Root. Wind Embrace. Heart Shining. Break Shadow. Veil Pierce. Storm Herald. Sacrifice Soul. World Shield. Enduring Light."

Each spell word was a mirror reflecting my resolve, a declaration of my intent. They were more than just words, they were a manifestation of my will, a reflection of my determination to protect Alara. As the final word left my lips, a surge of energy coursed through me. It was as if a dam had burst, releasing a torrent of power that swept through the field. The darkness that had held Xolesh, the malevolent energy that had lifted me into the air, was shattered by the force of my words.

But with that release, my connection to Alara's primal forces was sundered. The whispers of Alara, the melody that had guided my steps, fell silent. The power that had surged within me, bolstering my strength and guiding my hand, was gone. I was left kneeling in the snow, the echoes of my chant still ringing in my ears. The darkness that had held Xolesh was broken, but so was my connection to Alara. The battle was over, but at a cost that was higher than I had imagined.

XXIX

The Pantheon

It was the final spell I ever cast. A spell of such magnitude, such power, that it had severed my connection to Alara's primal forces. As the echoes of my chant faded, I felt a sense of finality wash over me. It was an end, a conclusion to the magical journey I had embarked upon. And it seemed, it was the same for Xolesh. The darkness that had held him was gone, his form now just a man, stripped of the malevolent energy that had once surrounded him. But even in his diminished state, he was not defeated. He rushed towards me, my black orukuthûndar blade in his hand, his eyes burning with a fierce determination.

But before he could reach me, an arrow pierced his skull. It was a sudden, brutal end to his charge, his body falling to the snowy earth even as his momentum carried him forward. The sight of Xolesh, felled by an arrow, was the last thing I saw before my own consciousness slipped away. The world around me faded, the ice-covered expanse, Xolesh, the fallen orukuthûndar, all disappearing into a growing darkness. My strength was spent, my body and spirit exhausted from the battle. As my consciousness slipped away, I felt a sense of peace wash over me as my body sank into the blood soaked snow.

The next thing I knew, I found myself standing in the middle of a village. It was a human village, filled with tan-skinned people who towered over me. Their faces were unfamiliar, their forms larger than my own. I looked down at myself and realized with a start that I was just a child. Around me, the village was alive with activity. Children ran past me, their laughter filling the air. Adults moved with a purpose, their tasks carrying them through the village with a sense of rhythm and routine. The village was a tapestry of life, a vibrant community that buzzed with energy and warmth. I could feel the fast pace of my heart, a rhythm that echoed the excitement and joy that filled me. I was having fun, the simple pleasure of childhood filling me with a sense of delight.

Then, cutting through the noise of the village, I heard a voice. It was my mother's voice, a sound that was as familiar as my own heartbeat. Her voice was warm and inviting, a melody that filled me with a sense of love and comfort. At the sound of her voice, I felt a love like I had never felt before. It was a love that was pure and unconditional, a love that filled me with a sense of peace and contentment. As I stood there, in the middle of the village, I felt a sense of belonging. I was a child, surrounded by the warmth and love of a community.

Everything around me seemed to move in slow motion, as if I was caught in a dream. The world was distorted, the sounds and sights of the village stretching and warping, muted, as if I was moving through water. I turned to face my mother as she called out to me. But as I turned, the dreamlike quality of the world around me shattered. The dream turned into a nightmare, the tranquility replaced by a scene of horror.

Massively muscular orukuthûndar warriors held my mother and father in place, their bûrz'kruk blades gleaming at their throats. The sounds of joy and familiar labor that had filled the village were instantly replaced by sounds of terror and pain. A band of orukuthûndar warriors were making their way through my village, their path marked by destruction and death. They were burning, looting, killing, pillaging, their actions a marked opposition to the peaceful life of the village. Their skin, each a different shade of green, gray, or brown, haunted my vision everywhere I turned. The sight of them, their monstrous forms wreaking havoc on my village, chilled me to my core.

I couldn't move of my own accord, my body frozen, but my feet carried me forward, drawn towards my mother and father as if by an unseen force. I watched, helpless, as they fell, their bodies crumpling to the ground, their lives extinguished by the orukuthûndar warriors. The world around me was a nightmare, a scene of horror that seemed to defy the tranquility of the dream I had been caught in moments ago. And as I stood there, amidst the chaos and destruction, I felt a sense of despair wash over me, a sense of loss that threatened to consume me. I took a step forward, my body moving of its own accord. It was as if I was a passenger in my own body, watching the world unfold through someone else's eyes. Each movement, each breath, felt detached, as if I was caught in a dream within a dream.

As I stepped forward again, the world around me shifted. The village, the orukuthûndar warriors, my fallen parents, all faded away, replaced by a new scene. I was older now, no longer a child but a teenager. The world moved in slow motion around me, the sights and sounds distorted as if I was only getting bits and pieces of the reality around me. I was around the same age that I had been when I first began my journey after Tornu's death several cycles ago. The memories of that time, of the pain and loss, seemed to echo in the back of my mind, all but lost in the scene that was unfolding before me.

I was walking through a dimly lit forest, the trees towering above me like ancient guardians. The forest felt vaguely familiar, its sights and sounds a faint echo of a memory. The rustle of the leaves, the whisper of the wind, the scent of the earth, all seemed to stir a sense of déjà vu within me. As I moved through the forest, the world around me continued to move in slow motion. It was as if I was caught in a bubble of time, the world outside distorted and garbled. But even amidst the confusion, I felt a sense of purpose, a sense of direction. I was on a journey, a path that had been set before me.

As I continued my journey through the forest, a large dark monolith came into view. It stood tall and imposing amidst the trees, its surface smooth and unyielding. It was like nothing I had ever seen before, a stark contrast to the natural beauty of the forest. Yet, despite its unfamiliarity, something in the back of my mind stirred. It was as if a memory, hidden away in the recesses of my mind, was trying to surface. A memory that was not my own, but felt strangely familiar. I felt another sense of déjà vu, a feeling that I had seen this monolith before. As I approached the monolith, I felt a pull, a call that seemed to resonate within me. It was as if the monolith was calling out to me, its voice a whisper on the wind. "Xolesh," it whispered, its voice echoing my name in my mind. I stood before the monolith, its dark surface reflecting the dim light of the forest, and felt a sense of anticipation.

As I reached out to touch the monolith, a word echoed in my mind. It was a dark word, a word that seemed to resonate with the energy of the monolith. "Vol," I echoed, the word slipping from my lips like a whispered secret. As the word left my lips, the world around me changed. The forest, the monolith, the earth beneath my feet, all disappeared, replaced by the vast expanse of the cosmos. I was floating in the void, looking down on Alara from a vantage point I had never imagined. And there, on Alara, I saw myself. I was standing in front of the monolith, my hand pressed against its dark surface. It was a surreal sight, a moment of disorientation that left me reeling. I was here, in the cosmos, and there, on Alara, at the same time.

But just as quickly as the change had happened, I was back. I was standing in front of the monolith, my hand still pressed firmly against it. The cosmos, the view of Alara, my other self, all faded away, replaced by the familiar sights and sounds of the forest. As I turned away from the monolith, the world around me shifted once more. The seasons changed in an instant, the forest transforming before my eyes. The vibrant greens of Solara gave way to the fiery hues of Verindal, then to the stark whites of Isendur, and finally to the fresh blooms of Aravell. It was a cycle of life, an embodiment of the passage of time, all happening in the blink of an eye.

Once again, a dark word rose to my lips, unbidden yet not unwelcome. I spoke it, the word resonating in the air around me, its power echoing in the sudden change of seasons. As the word left my lips, I found myself back in the cosmos, looking down on Alara, looking down on myself. This time, however, a deep frustration welled up inside me. It was a desire for control, a yearning to shape the world around me, to bend the primal forces of Alara, and the creature I found myself staring at, to my will. But just as quickly as the feeling had come, it was gone. In another instant, I was no longer in the cosmos. I was back on Alara, the seasons stilled.

As I took a step forward, the world around me shifted once more. The seasons changed in an instant, the cycle of life spinning around me in a dizzying display of nature's power. It was a signal emphasizing the passage of time, a reminder of the constant change that governed the world around me. In the midst of this whirlwind of change, another dark word rose to my lips. It slipped from my mouth like a whispered secret, its power resonating with the changing seasons. As the word left my lips, I felt a shift within me, a sense of losing control. I began to fade in and out, my consciousness slipping away like sand through my fingers. I was losing autonomy over my own body and mind, my control slipping away to an unseen, almost all-powerful entity. It was a terrifying sensation, a feeling of helplessness that sent a chill down my spine.

My world became a blur, my senses overwhelmed by the rapid change of seasons and the loss of control. I was caught in a storm, my body and mind at the mercy of an unseen force. In an instant, the world around me shifted once more. I found myself looking up at the frame of a man, suspended in the air above me by a dark magic. He felt familiar, like a one-time companion, a figure from a past that seemed both distant and close at the same time.

He began to chant, his voice echoing in the air around us. The words were unfamiliar to me, their meaning lost in the echoes of the chant. But despite their unfamiliarity, they held an allure, a purity that seemed to resonate within me. As his incantation reached its climax, the world around me went dark. It was a sudden, disorienting shift, a plunge into darkness that left me reeling. But even in the darkness, I could see myself. I was charging forward, a dark blade like the one that had slain my parents gripped tightly in my hand. I was moving towards the man, my body propelled forward by a force I couldn't understand. The world around me was a blur, the darkness a backdrop to the scene unfolding before me. And then, an instant later, a whooshing sound filled the air, followed by an all-encompassing darkness. As the darkness closed in, I felt a sense of disorientation, a feeling of being caught in a moment that was both real and unreal. I was a spectator and a participant, a witness to a scene that seemed to defy the laws of time and space.

In an instant, it was all over. I found myself lying in a bed, the sounds of birds chirping filling the air around me. It took me a while to orient myself, to reconcile the peaceful surroundings with the chaos of the scenes that had just unfolded. I kept my eyes closed for a while, my mind replaying the events that had transpired. The battle with Xolesh, the dark words, the shifting seasons, the view of Alara from the cosmos, all seemed to play out in my mind like a dream.

After much thinking, a process that did not end there in the bed but continued for months after, I finally came to a conclusion. The spell that had sundered my connection to Alara had overexerted my magical energy reserves. It was a lesson I had been taught by the gnomarik Spellweaver, Felkur, a lesson about the dangers of overexertion. After exerting myself, I had lost consciousness. But in that state of unconsciousness, I had been connected to Xolesh. As he passed from this life into the next, I had been witness to glimpses of his life. It was a connection that had given me insight into his journey, his struggles, his losses.

I found myself gazing at the Lunasil pendant, a sense of wonder mingling with my confusion. It had remained unscathed in the clash with Xolesh, a fact that puzzled me. The pendant, a constant companion since my time with Ilyafae, had always been more than a mere trinket. It was a shield, a beacon, a friend. But its resilience in the face of such a battle was unexpected. The pendant lay cool against my skin, its familiar weight a comforting presence. The intricate faelari designs etched into its surface seemed to pulse with a quiet strength, a silent proclamation heralding the power it held.

A thought occurred to me, a whisper of an idea that seemed to echo in the silence. I found myself leaning towards the pendant, my breath hitching in my chest. "Ilÿsïl'æn," I murmured, the faelari verse slipping from my lips like a prayer. The word hung in the air, a spell woven from hope and curiosity. I watched, my heart pounding in my chest, as the pendant absorbed the verse, its glow brightening for a moment before settling back into its usual soft luminescence.

A moment later, a subtle shift occurred. The air around me seemed to thicken, the world around me fading as if a veil was being drawn over reality. The pendant, now glowing with a soft, ethereal light, felt warm against my skin, its energy pulsing in sync with my heartbeat. A tingling sensation started at the base of my neck, spreading outwards like ripples in a pond. It was as if a current was coursing through me, a wave of energy that was both invigorating and disorienting. My senses heightened, the sounds of the world around me fading into a distant hum, replaced by a silence that was heavy with anticipation.

Then, my vision blurred, the world around me dissolving into a whirl of colors and shapes. I felt a pull, a sensation akin to falling, yet not quite. It was as if I was being drawn into the sky itself, into the heart of the cosmos once more. The world around me vanished, replaced by a vast expanse of darkness. I was no longer in my world, but somewhere else entirely. Somewhere beyond the confines of time and space.

A figure, both majestic and ethereal, lingered at the periphery of my sight. It was like trying to grasp a dream, the details slipping away the harder I tried to focus. Recognition dawned on me like the first light of day and a sense of familiarity washed over me. It was a figure I had seen before, not in the ethereal plane, but etched into the wooden skin of the tribal totem pole back home. The Eternal Sentinel. The totem, a towering pillar of stories and legends, held the carved images of The Unseen - the Sentinel among them. It was a figure of reverence, its stoic features a signature exemplifying its eternal vigil.

I had heard whispers of such an entity in the hushed tones of my tribe's elders, but to see it was a revelation beyond words. The realization struck me like a bolt of lightning, connecting the threads of my past with the revelations of the present. The Sentinel was not just a figure of tribal lore, but a cosmic entity that watched over the realms, its gaze steady and unyielding. The vision, having shown me this connection, continued to unfold, pulling me deeper into the mysteries of the supernatural realm.

I watched, my breath caught in my throat, as a scene unfolded before me. It was me, a younger version of myself untouched by the harsh lessons of time, reaching out to touch a peculiar, yet familiar, arrangement of stones. The stones, ancient and weathered, seemed to hum with a power that was both inviting and terrifying. Placing my hand upon a strange configuration of stones, the Sentinel observed, its gaze as steady as the northern star. It was an entity of such magnitude that it seemed to dwarf the very cosmos, yet it focused its attention on the scene before it with an intensity that was almost palpable. Its gaze was fixed on my younger self, observing with an inscrutable calmness that sent a shiver down my spine. It was a moment frozen in time, a memory etched into the fabric of existence, observed by an entity that seemed as old as time itself. The vision held me captive, my breath trapped in my chest, as I watched the scene play out, a silent witness to my own past. A nod, a simple gesture, yet it held a world of meaning. A whisper of spell words left its lips, carried on the wind, reaching my younger self. '*Su-Tha*'. The words were a guide, a beacon in the darkness of ignorance, leading me on my path. The vision shifted, like sand slipping through my fingers, and I saw the Sentinel again and again, guiding me with the wind and whispering words of Alara's primal forces in moments of need.

The vision was a tapestry of moments woven together. Each piece was a part of a larger picture, a story that was still being written. The vision morphed once more, and from the swirling mists of the ethereal plane, a new entity began to coalesce from the swirling mists of the ethereal plane. A sense of recognition washed over me, a feeling akin to the shock of cold water. The Sifter. Another figure from the stories of my tribe, a being whispered about in hushed tones around the fire. The puppeteer of fate, the manipulator of destinies. Seeing it here, in this vision, was like watching a character from a story step off the page and into reality. The entity was as elusive as a fleeting shadow and as unpredictable as a tempest in full fury. It was a manipulator, a puppet master pulling unseen strings in this cosmic dance. Its tendrils of influence stretched out, reaching for a man. Xolesh. After several clumsy attempts, the strings attached themselves to him, unseen yet palpable, like the pull of the moon on the tides. The Sifter, a spectral puppeteer, began to weave its intricate dance, and Xolesh, caught in its web, was drawn into the rhythm of its cosmic ballet. Each attempt by the Sifter was like a gust of wind, sending Xolesh's consciousness spiraling into an expanse that was not an expanse. A place that is everywhere and nowhere - a paradox that defies understanding. A liminal space between realities. His echo was swallowed by a darkness that was not merely the absence of light, but the absence of everything. It was a void that was not empty, but full of nothingness - a contradiction that made my mind reel. The echo was alone. Utterly alone, in a way that went beyond physical isolation. It was as if he was the only being that had ever existed or would ever exist. The echo of Xolesh drifted in this place where there was no up or down, no warmth or cold. It was a place where silence was a tangible presence, a weight that pressed against the echo, threatening to snuff it out. The echo was adrift, lost in a timeless drift where moments and eternities are indistinguishable.

When he returned moments later, he was altered, transformed in a way that was both subtle and profound. He carried with him a new spell word, a dark echo of the ones I knew. It clung to him like a shadow, a weapon that seemed to have been shaped in the crucible of that unimaginable realm. This spell word was different, it pulsed with a power that was both mesmerizing and terrifying. It was as if he had reached into the heart of that abyss, that place of nothingness, and pulled from it a force that defied understanding. The spell word was a tangible manifestation of that place, a piece of the void made real. It was a weapon of incredible power, a tool forged in the fires of a realm where reality unravels and time loses its meaning. It was a stark reminder of the place he had been, a symbol of the darkness he had embraced.

The vision held me captive, a mute observer, as the Sifter's machinations mirrored my own trials. Each instance of its ethereal reach towards Xolesh synchronized with the moments I was seized by visions of ruin. Those haunting glimpses I'd had of the monstrous figure wielding a greatsword - a scene of devastation that left a sour residue in my consciousness. The Sifter's dance with Xolesh seemed to be a dark reflection of my own experiences, a shadow play that echoed the dread and despair of my visions. The tableau of destruction, the greatsword-wielding abomination, it all seemed to be tied to the Sifter's manipulation.

The vision transformed once more, the periphery of my sightline tinged with a darkness that set my heart hammering in my chest. A scene of unspeakable terror unfurled before me, a tableau daubed with the most chilling hues of dread. At the epicenter stood Xolesh, his eyes ablaze with a dark magic that seemed to devour the very light around him. He was a tempest of devastation, mercilessly annihilating an entire tribe of orukuthûndar with a brutality that turned my blood to ice. Among the fallen was Kharok - the chieftain of the blâdur, a figure I had come to respect and who had welcomed me into their fold. In my naivety, I had unwittingly provided Xolesh with their location when our paths had first crossed. He had found them and dragged them to this frozen wasteland, where the veil between worlds seemed thin. The vision seemed to waver, as though shying away from the atrocity it was forced to display. When it refocused, I found myself there in the snow, standing in defiance against Xolesh, his mind no longer his own, lost entirely now to the void. The recollection of the battle flooded back, a deluge of fear, resolve, and desperation. The clash was fierce, a dance of death between two forces. But as the dust settled, Xolesh lay lifeless, a puppet devoid of its strings. The once formidable figure was now nothing more than an empty shell, his reign of terror brought to an abrupt end. In the wake of the conflict, the Sifter receded, withdrawing into the obscure recesses of the cosmos. It was akin to a predator deprived of its quarry, biding its time for another chance to exert its dominion over Alara.

The Lunasil, the talisman that granted me this insight into the ethereal plane, remained intact. This faelari pendant, my magical shield and constant companion since my time with Ilyafae, did not fracture under the weight of these revelations. I had once believed Xolesh to be the herald of the impending doom that would befall Alara. But I was mistaken. Perhaps he might have become that harbinger one day. Or perhaps he might have broken free from the Sifter's influence. The possibilities were as numerous as the stars in the sky. But one thing was certain. The Sifter would attempt its manipulations again. And when that day arrives, we, the children of Alara, must stand prepared. We must be ready to face whatever darkness the Sifter might unleash upon our world.

The vision, having shown its tale, began to fade, leaving behind the echoes of a battle fought with everything at stake. The vision was a mirror, reflecting not just the past, but also the future. It was a glimpse into the machinations of beings beyond my comprehension, their actions rippling through the fabric of reality. As the vision faded, I was left with more questions than answers, the pieces of the puzzle still scattered before me.

As I opened my eyes, I found myself in a familiar setting. I was in the elandari forest, the very place where my journey had first begun several cycles ago. Illadrathil, the wise and powerful daughter of the leader of the elandari, had received a vision from Alara. Guided by this vision, she had come to my aid just in time. It was Talathion, one of her guardsmen, who had plunged an arrow through Xolesh's skull, a decisive act that had undoubtedly saved my life. Ilyafae, the faelari, had also played a crucial role in my rescue. She had returned to her fairy-kin people and informed them that she had found Eledhin's protector. The faelari Seer, in turn, had informed Ilyafae that the protector would be needing assistance in the frozen expanse in the north. Both the elandari and the faelari had set out to find me, their paths converging just as my battle with Xolesh had reached its climax. They had arrived in the nick of time, their presence turning the tide of the battle. Afterwards, they had brought me back to the elandari forest, the place where my journey had begun. Here, amidst the familiar sights and sounds of the forest, they had helped me to recover. They had nursed me back to health, their care and kindness a balm for the physical and emotional wounds I had sustained.

As I lay there, in the heart of the elandari forest, I felt a sense of gratitude. I was alive, thanks to the timely intervention of the elandari and the faelari. My journey had come full circle, bringing me back to the place where it all began. After a period of around three months of recovery with the elandari, in the month of Loriven, I made the journey back to my roots - to the tribal lands of my people. This was the place where I had grown up, the place that had shaped me into the person I had become. It was here, amidst the familiar sights and sounds of my tribe, that I chose to spend the majority of my remaining cycles.

Though my connection to Alara was sundered, I found a new purpose in teaching my fellow humans how to hear Alara's whispers. I shared with them the knowledge I had gained on my journey, the lessons I had learned from the other races. I taught them how to discover and combine spell words, sharing with them the power and mystery of magic. It was a gift, a legacy that I could pass on to the future generations. It was a way for me to give back to my tribe, to contribute to the growth and development of my people, and to hopefully prepare them for the day that the Sifter does attempt again to inflict his destruction on the lands of Alara.

I had never intended to remain settled in the same tribal lands that Takka, the first human, had lived out his days in, and where the last nearly 500 cycles of my tribe had followed suit. But there I found myself, settled and content, dedicating my life to teaching the generations to come.

I was no longer an explorer, venturing into the unknown and facing the challenges of the world. I had become a teacher, sharing my knowledge and wisdom with my tribe. I had become an elder, a respected figure in my community, a guide for the future generations. After nearly 40 cycles of imparting my wisdom to the younger generations of my tribe, I finally fulfilled a promise I had made long ago. A promise to Zanmin and Orrick, my gnomish companions. In my old age, I made my way back to the Vindelkor, the place where I had spent many memorable cycles. It is from here that I pen these words, in the city that I plan to call home for the rest of my days.

Upon my return, warm and familiar faces greeted me. Orrick, showing little signs of aging due to the gnomish longevity, was there with a hearty welcome. He had settled down, started a family, and carved out his own path, becoming the city's most skilled Master Inventor, embodying the legacy of Urigim. Felkur, having just completed his groundbreaking work on the Master Cube, was revered throughout the city. His innovations and the Cube's potential were recognized by all, earning him the title of Grand Arcanist. His wisdom and direction served as a beacon for the community. As for Zanmin, he had ventured out, starting the Brimildelv clan, dedicated to the exploration of advanced magical theories. Though not present, whispers of his accomplishments and the respect he commanded reached every corner. Quovyn, with his ever-present eccentricities, remained a highly regarded Spellweaver in the city. His unorthodox take on magic continued to inspire and intrigue many young aspirants. It was during this initial return to the gnomarik city that I truly came to appreciate one of the more, seemingly, insignificant gifts Orrick had gifted to me at my departure. Gnarvend Gnomarik. A children's gnardok. At first, we all thought of it as a humorous reminder of my confiding in them that I did not actually know their language, one night at the drink house, due to my Saela-Hathir headdress handling the translation during my first time spent with the gnomes, and their hurried nature not affording me time to learn before being thrust into becoming productive.

And so, my tale comes to a close. A tale of adventure and discovery, of battles fought and wisdom gained. A tale of the whispers of the wind, the guiding force that led me on my journey. A tale of all the children of Alara. As I sit here, in the heart of the gnomarik city of Vindelkor, I look back on my journey with a sense of contentment. I have lived a life full of adventure and purpose, and now, I am ready to embrace the peace and tranquility of my remaining cycles. This is the end of my tale, but the whispers of the wind will continue, carrying my story to future generations.

Epilogue

New Faelish Prophecy, in Original Faelish:
"*Tholari Beelelis Phostsaelin, Ginorin-Lyselis,*
Huraelin Fylwina Aelwenis, Godrien Chilnaelis Eledhin,
Hinthaelin Zektaeli, Worelin Lyselinar Eledhin.
Faitrin Heldonaeris, Filtecalis Forelin Fildis,
Ligaelis Viimaelin Vikaelis, Pruvaelin Ritilis Ciolin.
Thingaelin ne lilu Thosaelis,
lil Gliraelin Silfaelin en Yulaelis,
Ne noh Fiirelin liith Vudaelin, Enthaelis Heldonaeris il Sitaelis.
Tir Ginorin-Lyselis's Tilis firi Cillaelin,
Ri tir Pruvaelin firi Nae Filnaelin,
Lilu Tilis tan noh Ziphaelis,
Noh Crinael neh noh Remaeli Dirigaelin
Solnivaelis rin, viricraelin lir nae sulna, Priivaedry rinla rinla dorvaelis foraela finellin surdaelin. Rin firnaeli poldaeri ilnaelin, jintaelini rilgaelin,
Fhadaela dorvaelis sirmaelin progaeli.
Terilaes lilthaelis, pilaelin hali ithla rulaeli dinael, Zivilae girellin ortellis, il irieldra firaelin mofiel. Pruvaedry ritilis tilthil, erindryli niraelosil, Virovaelin ilsaelis vilora, lyn forelin Eledhin.
Tan viindry,
Lyselinar Eledhin,
Rin uli rulaeli viraelis tallis,
Centarion, Ginorin, lyn Elandari,
Woraedry Heldonaeris' delinaera.

Halindelar, Dwarrin, lyn Orukuthûndar klifaedra, Gnomarik, Kreegob-
likar, lyn faelari,
Ortellis van ulilaelu inhaelis.
Lethian folinaedris il firilaela,
Krinilaela, iltilaelin, Ligaelis ritilis pruvaelin,
Forulinaelin kiridaelis.
Findaedry li zintidaela,
Ridisaelis rulaeli foriidry
Siminilaelin rocoliidry inilaela rinla.
Fordaelin rin Tosdaelin gin Lyselis coraedra,
Ilthaelin Vondraelis,
Pruvaelin rulaeli undaelin.
Rin espraeli Eledhin lir nae oltaeli fircallis,
Tan indry Ridisaelis,
Forulinaelin illilifaendaedry.
Tel Zintidaela Riilae,
Torili rin faedra lyn faedra,
Daelaesi rin huraelin Uli,
Pilaelin vikaelis lir roesii.
Firnos ilkaefaylin tiris,
Firnos liistaedry Ginorin,
Rin Ridisaelis,
Lyselinar Lyselis,
Uli sinaelin Firnos."

Rough Translation Into Common (Literal Translation Excluded To Preserve the Intended Meaning and To Establish Rhyme Structure):
"In the shadowed ebb of history, a Man-child,
Guided by whispers of the wind, sought the corners of Alara,
Encountering in his quest, the myriad Children of Alara.
He bore the weight of destiny, the world's protection his due,

Against a looming darkness, an evil of purest hue.
Misguided in his pursuit, he crossed blades with kin,
In a duel of mystic power, neither destined to win.
The Man-child's foe was fallen, yet the evil was not gone,
His foe but a puppet, a pawn in a game foregone.
Grieve not, for his sacrifice was not in vain,
His wisdom through the ages would break the dread chain.
For as the wheel of time turns, and centuries take flight,
The seed of his knowledge will bloom in the night.
In the era forthcoming, yet afore iron and steel reign,
A sinister force will return, to spread terror and pain.
The evil of purest form, its roots deep and furled,
Will rise to claim dominion, over Alara's world.
But fear not, Children of Alara, for you shall stand tall,
Centaur, Human, and Elf, answering destiny's call.
Halfling, Dwarf, and Orc of the plains,
Gnome, Goblin, and Fairy, free of their chains.
Nine shall become one, in heart, in mind, in deed,
Against the purest evil, together they'll proceed.
Bound by a prophecy, in unity they shall engage,
Their harmony echoing in the annals of the age.
Aided by the wisdom of the Man-child long passed,
Through fierce combat, the evil shall be outcast.
For the spirit of Alara lies not in one race alone,
But in the unity of all, they shall atone.
This prophecy I weave, with thread of truth and lore,
In hope it shall guide you, when the darkness is at your door.
Trust in the legacy left, trust in the Man-child's sight,
For in unity, dear children, you will find your might."

Appendix

Yoran's Journey Timeline

3 months
Loriven - Orendar:
Spent with the Elandari

2 months
Maruvial - Thalindor:
Traveling

4 months
Valandar - Nolariel:
Spent with the Dwarrin

1 month
Nolariel:
Traveling

5 months
Duravorn - Sylthal:
Spent with the Centarion

3 days
Orendar:
Spent with the Goblikar

2 months
Orendar - Maruvial:
Traveling

4 months
Thalindor - Ithendar:
Spent with Ilyafae

12 months
Ithendar - Nolariel:
Spent with the Orukuthûndar

1 month
Duravorn:
Traveling

5 months
Elaris - Orendar:
Spent with the Gnomarik

2 months
Maruvial - Thalindor:
Traveling

3 months
Valandar - Ithendar:
Spent with the Halindelar

1 month
Nolariel:
Traveling

1 day
Duravorn:
Final Encounter

Alara History Timeline
0th Era (Age of Prehistory)
(PHY: Pre-Historic Year)

c. PHY 10,000
Dawn of Creation

c. PHY 9,500
Whispers of the Wind

1st Era (Age of Iron & Steel)
Coming Soon

2nd Era (Age of Piracy)
Coming Soon

3rd Era (Age of Industry)
Coming Soon

4th Era (Age of Civil Rights)
Coming Soon

5th Era (Age of Digital Revolution)
Coming Soon

6th Era (Age of Sustainability)
Coming Soon

7th Era (Age of Post-Scarcity)
Coming Soon

8th Era (Intergalactic Age)
(IGY: InterGalactic Year)
Coming Soon

Human Calendar

Seasons
Aravell (*Spring*)
Solara (*Summer*)
Verindal (*Autumn*)
Isendur (*Winter*)

Months
Elaris
Tavarin

Loriven
Sylthal
Orendar
Maruvial
Thalindor
Valandar
Esriven
Ithendar
Nolariel
Duravorn

Days
Saraday
Telenday
Orladay
Melladay
Isilday
Tharaday
Elenday

Printed in the USA
CPSIA information can be obtained
at www.ICGtesting.com
LVHW091516201223
766878LV00004B/38

9 798218 305130